# REVEALING HER BEST KEPT SECRET

## HEIDI RICE

# A VOW TO SET THE VIRGIN FREE

## MILLIE ADAMS

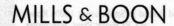

**MILLS & BOON**

First published in Great Britain 2023
by Mills & Boon, an imprint of HarperCollins*Publishers* Ltd,
1 London Bridge Street, London, SE1 9GF

www.harpercollins.co.uk

HarperCollins*Publishers*
Macken House, 39/40 Mayor Street Upper,
Dublin 1, D01 C9W8, Ireland

Revealing Her Best Kept Secret © 2023 Heidi Rice

A Vow to Set the Virgin Free © 2023 Millie Adams

ISBN: 978-0-263-30662-0

d FSC™ paper
ent.
co.uk/green.

ble Electricity

# REVEALING HER
# BEST KEPT SECRET

## HEIDI RICE

MILLS & BOON

To Rob, my hero.

# CHAPTER ONE

*DO NOT PANIC. There's no way on earth Brandon Cade will remember you.*

Lacey Carstairs recited the mantra for the fiftieth time. Unfortunately, it was doing nothing to steady her galloping heartbeat or reduce the boiling pain in her temples at the thought of the interview which loomed large in her future with the man who had ground her heart—and her career prospects—to dust beneath the heel of his handmade Italian leather loafers.

'Do you know how much longer Mr Cade is likely to be?' Lacey asked the receptionist in the stark and stylish penthouse offices of Cade Tower on London's South Bank.

'This interview is not his top priority today,' the woman replied, with enough haughty superiority to put Lacey firmly in her place. 'But he should be with you soon. He has a meeting scheduled in Paris in...' she clicked on her tablet '...two hours.'

'Two hours, but surely...?' Lacey trailed off, her anxiety catching up with her reporter's instincts. Cade's tight schedule could be a bonus. Surely he would have to reschedule? It took longer than two hours to get to Paris from here.

'We have a heliport on the roof,' the receptionist replied, crushing that hope like a bug. 'He won't have to leave till two.'

*Fabulous.* 'Right.'

So, no reprieve. But the good news was he had less than an hour now before he had to leave, so the interview would have to be brief—a reprieve of sorts.

Her gaze strayed to the glass wall behind the receptionist's desk, and the sky-high view of the Thames snaking lazily past the steel-and-glass blocks of London's Square Mile, the City's financial hotspot.

How fitting that the most powerful media mogul in Europe should conduct his empire from the top of the continent's tallest building. Unfortunately, the bubble of vertigo wasn't doing much for the nausea lying low in Lacey's stomach.

The thought of having to see Brandon Cade again had kept her up all night. So she now had the foggy feeling of exhaustion to add to the double whammy of terror and stress which had slammed into her yesterday evening, when her editor, Melody, had phoned with the 'stupendous news'—Lacey would be handling the Cade profile because Tiffany Bradford, the magazine's star feature writer, had flu.

Unless Lacey wanted to kill her career a second time—and/or come up with a viable explanation as to why she was the only female magazine journalist in the known universe who would rather shoot herself in the head than spend sixty minutes with the world's handsomest and most dynamic billionaire bachelor. Refusing simply hadn't been an option.

Not that Melody had given her an option.

This interview was a seriously big deal for *Splendour* magazine. It had been three months in the offing, the result of intense negotiations between the magazine's executive editor and the might of Cade Inc's PR department. Even so, Lacey had no doubt at all Brandon Cade would have refused, but for the media furore surrounding his ex-mistress's kiss-and-tell book, which was currently threatening to derail the company's acquisition plans in the US.

Misty Goodnight had painted an evocative portrait of an impossibly handsome, powerful, sexually dominant and yet wholly unknowable autocrat of thirty-one, who treated his women with the same cool, calm, ruthless detachment with which he ran the empire he had inherited from his father at seventeen.

Lacey happened to know Misty hadn't lied—or rather, her army of ghost writers hadn't lied. The tabloid press had taken the story and run with it, dubbing Cade 'the Great Gasp-by', thanks to Misty's lurid depictions of his sexual prowess.

Lacey's nipples drew into hard peaks at the visceral memory of her one time with Cade. She swallowed down the aching pain in her throat and crossed her arms over her swollen breasts.

*Don't go there. Do not go there. Ever.*

The evidence Cade still had a sexual hold on her body after one thirty-minute encounter five years ago was as mortifying as it was disturbing.

*He will not remember you.*

She repeated the mantra to quell the rising tide of hysteria.

He would never put the smart, sophisticated, perfectly styled magazine journalist together with the eager-to-please intern he had once seduced. She'd changed her name, cut her hair down from long chestnut waves to a curly bob, lost nearly ten pounds—thanks so much, Ruby and her terrible twos—and changed her wardrobe from the second-hand clothes she'd once kidded herself were vintage to the chic lines of the designer labels that were just within her reach now, if she budgeted accordingly.

But, most of all, she'd got a lot less stupid in the intervening years. He'd destroyed her, simply because he could.

He'd seduced her at the Carrell launch party and had then napalmed her career. She still hadn't quite figured out why he'd had her sacked. It wasn't as if she'd made any demands of him, or expected anything after that mind-blowing encounter. Perhaps she should add paranoid and vindictive to his list of character flaws.

*He doesn't need to know about Ruby.*

The familiar guilt pricked her conscience.

Maybe one day, if her daughter wanted to know who her biological father was, she could tell her. But, until that day came, Lacey refused to throw herself or her daughter on Brandon Cade's mercy. Given the ruthless way he'd treated her once, she didn't hold out much hope of his reaction to an illegitimate child being good, or even rational.

And she would never subject a child to a father like her own.

She bit into her lip. Tasted the tiny hint of metal to remind herself not to get carried away.

*You're not scared or heartbroken any more, like that starry-eyed nineteen-year-old. You're cool, aloof and indifferent now. Just like him.*

Brandon Cade was even on record as saying he didn't want children. So why would she tell him about Ruby?

Thank goodness Cade's PR team had insisted any discussion of his private life was out of bounds. Of course, Melody had implied a good feature writer ignored those kinds of rules. Well, not Lacey. Not this time.

The musical chime of the receptionist's smartphone startled her.

'Yes, I'll send her up, then.' The receptionist clicked off her phone. 'If you'd like to take the lift to the top floor, Mr Cade's EA will be waiting for you.'

Lacey crossed the lobby with as much purpose in her stride as she could muster to step into the scenic lift. The panoramic view of metal and glass across the water glittered like jewels in the noon sunshine. She pressed the top floor button. The buildings dropped away while the writhing snakes in the pit of her stomach plummeted to her toes.

*You have nothing whatsoever to worry about. No way on earth will Brandon Cade remember the likes of you.*

# CHAPTER TWO

BRANDON CADE STARED at the muddy brown line of the River Thames eighty-five floors below him. He drew in a tight breath, his nostrils flaring as he counted out on the exhale. He'd taught himself the breathing technique in childhood to stop himself from crying—and eventually from showing any emotion at all—at his first boarding school, age five. The technique had also come in useful to help him control his anxiety on the rare occasions when he'd come face to face with his father. But as he waited for his assistant to usher in the feature writer from *Splendour* magazine it was the first time he'd had to use it in years, to maintain the icy demeanour he was famous for.

He never talked to the damn press—ironic, when one considered Cade Inc owned ten global newspaper titles, a raft of cable and digital broadcasters in the UK and Europe and was currently in negotiations to acquire a media conglomerate in North America. But Cade Inc's brand was all about hard news. He didn't own any lifestyle magazines and had no social media interests for the simple reason he despised the kind of powder-puff journalism glossy magazines such as *Splendour* peddled to the masses.

And now, thanks to his affair with a woman who had bored him in bed after approximately ten minutes, he found himself in a straitjacket of his own making. The intrusion infuriated him.

He was suing Misty, of course, and given the expertise of his legal team, and the might of the media empire he controlled, he knew her memoir of their not-at-all memorable sexual exploits would never reach the shelves. But enough of it had been leaked online to make his negotiating team concerned about finalising the deal to acquire the very conservative Dixon Media Group in Atlanta. Hence the need for this damage limitation exercise.

*Next time, maybe don't date social media influencers who are as shrewd and ruthless as you are.*

'Mr Cade, Ms Carstairs from *Splendour* magazine is here, shall I show her in?' Daryl, his executive assistant, announced.

Brandon unclenched his jaw and took another careful breath. 'Sure.'

He turned from the window, thrusting clenched fists into the pockets of his suit trousers. But as the woman stepped into the office behind his EA, her slim figure accentuated by a demure power suit and her head bent, a bizarre thing happened. A ripple of reaction streaked down his spine, and his senses, which had been jaded ever since a torrid encounter with a very different woman during a company event five years ago roared back to life.

His gaze narrowed on the short cap of wavy curls, the lightning strike of awareness firing through his system as irritating as it was unexpected.

'Ms Carstairs, Mr Cade,' Daryl announced, showing Brandon's unwanted guest into the large airy office. 'You have exactly twenty minutes before Mr Cade has to depart for Paris, Ms Carstairs,' he added. 'Would you like anything to drink?'

'No, thank you,' the woman replied, her voice a smoky purr, which tugged at Brandon's memory and did not help one bit with the inexplicable reaction. The slight tremble in her tone and the way her fingers clutched her bag in a death grip suggested she was nervous.

*Good*—she ought to be. He didn't want her here. But then she crossed the room and he caught a lungful of her scent—citrus and spice, and as annoyingly intoxicating as the rest of her.

His jaw tensed as visceral heat pounded into his groin.

*Great*. Was he actually getting turned on?

As if it wasn't bad enough he was having to speak to this journalist, he noticed the tempting glimpse of cleavage peeking from the vee of her blue silk blouse, and the toned legs accentuated by her pencil skirt. He shook his head to dispel the vivid image of his tanned hand cupping the pale swell of her breast, the mouth-watering thought of her nipple elongating against his tongue…

'Take a seat, Ms Carstairs,' he said sharply as Daryl left the room. 'What is your first name?' he asked, surprised to realise he was curious. He wanted to see her face, to gauge her reaction to him—because he felt at a disadvantage, and he didn't like it.

The brusque enquiry did the trick. At last, her head rose and she looked directly at him. But only for a second. That single glimpse was enough for him to make several important observations, though.

Her eyes were a fathomless chocolate-brown with hints of amber, and had a similarly slanted cat-like shape as those of the girl he remembered. And had tried very hard to forget. He'd never seen the colour of that girl's eyes. It had been too dark in the club and the empty manager's office where they'd ended up making love—or rather having raw, frantic, sweaty sex over a desk. But he still remembered the shape of her cheek in the moonlight, the tilt of her eyelashes, and could still hear the sound of her broken sobs as she'd climaxed.

*Stop thinking about her, dammit.*

He forced his mind away from the unsettling memory. And concentrated on the other thing he'd seen in this woman's eyes.

*Awareness.* Wary and guarded, but there none the less. Apparently, she was attracted to him too…but was equally as unhappy about it.

*Unusual.* When was the last time a woman had desired him and not been eager to follow through on it? Her novel reaction made the need surge.

'Lacey,' she said, and he heard the tremble of nerves again. 'Lacey Carstairs.'

She took the seat he'd indicated, brushing her skirt over her lush backside to sit.

*Is she doing that deliberately?*

But then her knuckles whitened on her smartphone as she retrieved it from her purse. She wasn't just nervous, she looked scared, as if she would rather be anywhere else but in his office—with him—despite the mutual flare of attraction.

*Interesting.*

She had to know he was giving this interview under duress, and if she had done her research she would also know he wasn't a good man to cross. If someone displeased or threatened him, he acted swiftly and without mercy. Just ask that artless girl who had lured him in and sacrificed her virginity, believing their rare sexual chemistry could be bartered for something more.

He frowned, aware he was thinking of that girl again whom he'd exorcised from his consciousness five years ago.

'Do you mind if I record this, Mr Cade?' the journalist asked, engaging the voice app on her phone with shaking fingers.

'Go ahead, Lacey,' he said, pleased when the use of her given name made her stiffen.

Of course, he had no intention of allowing anything to go into print he hadn't agreed to. One of the stipulations his PR team had insisted on was that he would have final approval on the article before it went to press. And he would also demand any notes or tapes be destroyed as a matter of course. But, even so, he didn't usually allow his words to be recorded.

'And please call me Brandon,' he added.

As expected, the offer had her head jerking up. This time, their gazes locked and held. The surge of heat crackled in the air between them. But he was prepared for it now. Enough to find himself enjoying the flare of reaction lighting the gold shards in the rich brown of her irises and flushing her pale skin a vivid pink.

Yes, she could feel it too, this rare electric chemistry. But what had unnerved him five years ago with that girl excited him now. His sex life had been non-existent since the Misty debacle, and had lacked the visceral spark of attraction for years, which this woman had ignited without even trying.

Why not play with it, and her—see how far she wished to take it? It wasn't as if he would be risking anything. At thirty-one, he was even more cynical and ruthless than he had been five years ago. No way would she be able to get under his skin and fray the tight leash he kept around his emotions, the way that virginal girl had once done.

And who said she even wanted to? She was a journalist. She had to know how to use an attraction like this to her advantage—despite the pretence of nerves. The tremor in her voice, the wary tension in her gaze and the white knuckles were probably a carefully rehearsed act. But, even so, it was a good act. And an original approach, which he found surprisingly beguiling. After all, when was the last time he'd been treated to the thrill of the chase?

'Fire away, Lacey' he said, husky desire deepening his

voice as he said her name again, his gaze still locked on hers, daring her to look away.

She blinked, the flicker of panic unmistakeable, but then she took a deep breath and let it out again. The movement made her breasts lift against her blouse.

Lust gathered like a fireball in his groin. He crossed his arms and leant his butt against the desk, gratified when her gaze lingered for a second on the bulge of his biceps in the fitted shirt.

*Bingo.*

Her gaze rose, but alongside the turmoil he could now see a fierce determination not to be intimidated.

A slow smile spread across his lips.

*Good luck with that, Lacey.*

'Mr Cade, I'm sorry to disturb you, but the helicopter is ready to depart now for Paris.'

*Oh, thank You, God.*

The knots in Lacey's gut loosened as Brandon Cade's executive assistant interrupted them signalling the end of the longest twenty minutes of her life.

What had made her think seeing this man again would be doable? Every single thing about him still disturbed her. The intense focus in his dark, penetrating green gaze. The way his body had filled out in the last five years—his biceps bulging under the starched cotton of his tailored shirt every time he crossed his arms over his broad chest, his suit trousers stretching over his thighs as he leaned on the desk in front of her. The gruff murmur of his voice which prickled over her skin every time he spoke. The way he said her name with a deliberate intimacy, which was clearly meant to disarm any woman who came within a ten-mile radius. Sitting less than two feet from him, no wonder her pheromones were toast.

Everything about him was imposing, exciting, overwhelming, just as it had been five years ago. But then she'd been an untried girl. Now she was a mother, a career woman, a proper journalist—even though, from the hooded look in his eyes, she knew he didn't rate her as one.

How did he still have the power to unsettle her so completely? Maybe because he wasn't just physically imposing any more, though the chemistry between them was still disturbingly volatile. Now so many things about him reminded her of her little girl.

*Their* little girl.

Given the brevity of the encounter which had created Ruby, it had been easy to persuade herself Cade had contributed virtually nothing to her daughter's DNA, but seeing him up close and personal, in broad daylight for a full twenty minutes… Not so much.

Ruby had the same mossy-green eyes with hints of steel. When Lacey had first forced herself to look at him properly, she'd recognised the colour with startling clarity. But, whereas the colour of Ruby's irises was sweet and beguiling, and so innocent, on Brandon Cade it was completely the opposite. The look in his eyes was so harsh, and yet so sharply observant, she'd been struggling to breathe, scared he could read all her secrets.

Ruby also had the same dimple in her left cheek. But, whereas on Ruby that dimple looked endearing, appearing whenever she giggled, on Brandon Cade it signalled cynical amusement, not innocent joy… Unlike Ruby's, his smiles weren't cute, they were smug and predatory. When Brandon Cade's sensual lips curved and the playful dent in his cheek appeared, Lacey's heartbeat accelerated and her breathing clogged in her lungs, making her feel like a mouse being played with by a panther.

But what was far worse than that smug, cynical smile was the way it could beckon the thoughtless, foolish girl out of hiding again. The girl who had become completely enthralled by the endorphin rush of his attention, enough to do stupid things.

*Except you don't regret that stupid thing, because it gave you Ruby.*

'I guess that's my cue to leave, then. Thank you for your time, Mr Cade.' She swallowed down the lump of guilt, trying to keep her expression bland as she clicked off her phone and shoved it into her bag. 'I'll email over a copy of the piece for your final approval,' she began to babble, the relief making her light-headed. 'But, until then, I'll get out of your hair.'

The truth was she'd managed to prise absolutely nothing of any use for a decent profile piece. Cade had batted away any of the remotely probing questions she'd had the guts to ask with practised ease. But she really didn't care. For once, she wasn't going to stress about her by-line. She would wax lyrical about his imposing presence, his stunning good looks and the effect of being trapped in a room with him for twenty agonising minutes…with every one of her senses on high alert…and get the art department to source some photos of him looking devastating in a tuxedo to illustrate the piece and leave it at that.

Melody would be furious Lacey hadn't managed to get any exclusive titbits out of him, anything remotely personal, but had her editor really expected her to? Honestly, the real purpose of a piece like this was to make the readership jealous of her as a journalist getting to meet the man, and overawed by how glamourous the magazine was to get this kind of access, and she'd achieved that much.

If they only knew just how close she'd got to him. Once.

She stood, ignoring the wobble in her knees, the memory which she'd had locked in her solar plexus threatening to erupt again. But as she prepared to shoot out of the room, his voice—low and deep—stopped her in her tracks.

'Not so fast, Lacey.'

She swung back to find him watching her with the challenging glint in his eyes she'd noticed several times already. As if he were enjoying her discomfort, like the panther he was.

'Why don't you accompany me?' he said, his tone casual, that all-seeing gaze anything but. 'After all, you've hardly had a chance to ask me anything interesting.'

'Accompany you where?' she stuttered, confused now, as well as wary and impossibly turned on. His searing gaze swept over her before returning to her face. Could he see her pulse hammering her throat like a heavyweight champ? Or her nipples hardening painfully under her blouse?

His lips quirked in that almost-smile again, not just smug and cynical now, but challenging, provocative and loaded with innuendo.

She took an uneven breath, trying to ease the vice clamped around her ribcage.

*Breathe, Lacey, breathe. You've got this.*

'To Paris, of course,' he said, the loaded smile widening.

The devastating dimple appeared as if by magic—making him look like his daughter... And yet *so* not. The vice cinched tight.

'You're not serious?' she managed.

Why was he toying with her? And why was he looking at her like that? As if her answer mattered to him, when she knew it couldn't.

'Actually, I'm deadly serious,' he said, the smile sharpening, his gaze narrowing. 'As it happens, I need a plus one for the Durand Ball tonight.'

'But I'm a celebrity journalist,' she blurted out.

She'd sensed his hostility towards her profession as soon as she walked into his office. Weirdly, that had been easier to handle than the strange atmosphere which had built between them during the course of the interview... Watchful and wary at first, but eventually becoming provocative, charged with possibilities, none of which Lacey knew she should entertain.

At first she was sure she had imagined the abrupt change in his attitude—from hostile to fascinated. She had dismissed it as a throwback to that delusional girl who had been spellbound by his interest five years ago—until their chemistry had detonated and derailed her life.

But she could feel it in the air again now, rioting over her skin, awakening her already far too responsive body, pulsing at her core—and making her yearn to say yes to his proposal, even though she knew she shouldn't.

She couldn't fall under his spell again. Because, not only would she be the only one who would get burned, but this time it wouldn't just be her in the firing line. It would be her daughter. The little girl she'd kept a secret from this man for five years—for good reason.

One dark eyebrow arched, the smile twisting his lips, not just devastating now but also disturbingly intuitive. 'Precisely—isn't this just the sort of opportunity you want? To see me in my natural habitat?'

It was a fair question. And one she had no idea how to answer without revealing more than she should. He hadn't recognised her, and she had to be pathetically grateful for that. But he was a sharply intelligent and extremely cynical and intuitive man, and she really didn't want to give him any reason to be suspicious.

'Yes, but…do you really want to give me that kind of access?' she asked. They both knew she wouldn't be able to put anything into the article he didn't approve of, but giving a journalist access to his social life was unprecedented. 'Especially after what happened with Misty,' she added.

To her dismay, though, instead of looking offended or annoyed by the intrusive comment, he simply stared at her for a moment. Then the dimple in his cheek jumped and he let out a deep, rusty chuckle.

'*Touché,*' he murmured, then levelled that searing gaze on her again, setting off another series of bonfires. The twinkle in his green eyes was disturbingly captivating, though, because for the first time he looked genuinely amused. 'Are you planning to write a tell-all article about my sexual prowess, then, Lacey?'

Flaming colour exploded in her cheeks at the deliberately provocative statement. 'No, of course not! I'm a journalist, I'm not interested in your sexual prowess...' she protested, a bit too much.

He was still laughing at her. She could see it in his eyes and the twitching dimple.

'So there shouldn't be a problem, then, should there?' he said, as if it were a question when clearly it wasn't.

'I suppose not,' she said.

She only realised the concession she'd inadvertently made when he added, 'I assume you have your passport with you, to get past the security on your way in?'

'Yes, but...' she began, but before she could say more he glanced past her.

'Have Jennifer book a suite at the George V for Ms Carstairs tonight, Daryl,' he said.

Lacey's cheeks ignited all over again at the realisation Daryl had just witnessed their whole compromising conversation. But she didn't really have time to contemplate the true horror of that indignity before Cade spoke again.

'And tell the pilot she'll be accompanying us.'

'But wait,' she said as he cupped her elbow to lead her out of his office.

She stumbled to a stop. The brush of his fingers was electric—just as it had been five years ago.

He frowned as she tugged her arm free. Had he felt it too? He must have.

'I don't have anything to wear to a ball,' she managed,

clinging to the practical as she instinctively rubbed her elbow where his fingers had touched.

*And I have a four-year-old daughter who I'm supposed to be reading a bedtime story tonight.*

He nodded, still watching her, the amusement gone from his eyes. He *had* felt it… Why did that make the conflagration at her core so much worse? The guilt started to engulf her… Not just because she would have to leave the precious bedtime ritual she and Ruby enjoyed so much to her sister Milly tonight but because she had to deny her daughter's existence to the man in front of her. The man who was also responsible for Ruby, even though he didn't know it.

*You made that decision five years ago with no regrets. Ruby's yours, not his. You chose to have her. You chose not to involve him.*

He'd cut her out of his life that night, quickly and ruthlessly, wrenching her out of the cloud of afterglow and thrusting her into cold, hard reality as she'd lain on that desk, her heart hammering and her breasts still tender from his kisses.

*'That should not have happened, and it won't happen again. The condom appears to have split, so if there are any consequences contact my office and I will deal with it.'*

She tried to remember the cruelty of his dismissal that night, but the guilt and shame pressed against her throat as other even more disturbing sensations flooded her system. Sensations which had derailed her common sense once before.

His gaze lifted from her burning face back to his assistant. 'Have Jennifer arrange for a stylist to come to the hotel and dress Ms Carstairs.'

'Yes, Mr Cade.'

Cade lifted his arm as his assistant shot out of the room to do his bidding, but she noticed he was careful not to touch her again. Perhaps she had a mite more power here than she realised.

'After you, Lacey,' he said.

*But I haven't agreed to go.*

She should tell him where to stick his arrogant assumptions. But as she looked into his eyes, the deep jade so much like her daughter's, it occurred to her this might be the only chance she'd ever get to really get to know this man. Or at least, to get to know him enough to find out if she'd made the right decision five years ago never to tell him about his child.

Perhaps it was time she stopped running from that reckless girl and found out if Ruby's father deserved to know he had the sweetest, smartest, most engaging child in the known universe.

# CHAPTER THREE

'INCREDIBLE WORK, LACEY, you just got yourself a promotion. You're now our star writer. But how on earth did you manage to get Cade to invite you to Paris?'

*I have no idea.*

Lacey stood on the ornate balcony of the luxury Parisian hotel suite, gazing at the Eiffel Tower glittering in the distance, as she gripped her phone and struggled to come up with a coherent answer for her editor.

'Um, I think maybe he wants to set the record straight. About Misty,' she managed, although she didn't believe that for a second.

The truth was she had no clue what Cade's motives were any more. It had been four hours since he'd left her at the door to the suite, and she hadn't seen him since.

She'd tried to engage him in conversation during the helicopter ride to Paris, to keep up the pretence she was still on assignment. But with the noise in the chopper it had been impossible, and anyway, Cade had seemed keen to ignore her as soon as they'd strapped in.

*Thank God.*

After the intensity of the twenty minutes in his office, she'd been relieved at his taciturn behaviour. She'd needed time to gather her wits—not to mention fire off a quick text to her sister Milly, asking her to put Ruby to bed tonight and drop her off at her nursery tomorrow.

As usual, her younger sister—who had lived with her since before Ruby had been born—had been happy to step up. Milly had been more like a second mum than an aunt to Lacey's daughter and Ruby adored Milly right back. Lacey knew her daughter wouldn't question Mummy needing to work late too much…

But that hadn't stopped the guilt from strangling her once she'd found herself in the lavish three-room suite at the mercy of a scarily efficient French stylist, being fitted for a stunning jewelled evening gown and styled to within an inch of her life by a team of hairdressers and make-up artists.

*What am I actually doing here? I couldn't feel more out of my depth if I were trying to land a space shuttle on Mars.*

'By inviting a *Splendour* journalist to the Durand Ball?' Melody laughed. 'It's too delicious. We can totally play up the Cinderella angle. The readers will love it. A hard-working single mum who gets to go to the ball on the arm of—'

'Absolutely not, Melody.' Fear wrapped around Lacey's torso as she cut into her editor's excited pitch. 'I don't want Ruby mentioned in the piece. My daughter's not for public consumption.' And she sure as heck didn't want Brandon Cade reading about Ruby when he reviewed the piece. She'd kept her secret safe from Cade for this long. She certainly didn't want it revealed on a technicality before she was ready.

'But it's such a great angle.' Melody sighed, and Lacey could almost hear her editor pouting from two hundred miles away.

'Please, Melody, let me handle the story. He seems surprisingly cooperative. I can give you a great piece out of this, all the glitz and glamour of the Durand Ball and a night as Brandon Cade's date. We really don't need Ruby to go for the Cinderella angle,' she added, trying not to cringe so hard Melody could hear it.

She was hardly Cinderella. She had a good career, which she'd worked her socks off to create from the bonfire of being kicked to the kerb by Cade Inc five years ago. She had even earned enough to afford a mortgage on a small two-bedroom flat in Hackney last year. But she guessed it wouldn't be too much of a stretch to pitch herself as the starry-eyed, cash-strapped social outcast if Melody insisted on a Cinderella angle.

She didn't have any spare income once all the bills and Ruby's childcare were paid for. And she hadn't had a social life since Ruby had been born, keen to spend every waking minute she wasn't working with her little girl. And, even though she reported on the uber-rich and famous, she had no first-hand experience of the exclusive billionaire lifestyle Brandon Cade took for granted.

Except once, five years ago, when she'd ended up with a last-minute invite to the launch of Cade Inc's new cable channel at a Soho nightclub and had entered his rarefied world for one life-changing night.

She glanced at the sparkling jewelled fabric of the evening gown which draped luxuriously over her figure, making her slender curves look a lot less boyish than usual. The lingerie Madame Laurent had insisted she wear under the gown even made her breasts look like more than an A-cup.

She could feel the jewelled pins in her hair tugging at her scalp to anchor the hair extensions the hairstylist had spent hours arranging into a gravity-defying chignon. And imagined the smoky eyeliner, the glittery eyeshadow, the sculpted foundation and the glossy lipstick which had made her unrecognisable when the make-up artist had finally allowed her to look in the mirror.

She already felt so far outside her comfort zone, she was

practically on the Moon, and that was before she factored in Cade's effect on her pulse rate.

She needed to get that reaction under control ASAP, before Cade finally showed up to escort her downstairs.

'Fine,' Melody said flatly, going all business again. 'I guess you're in charge after getting this incredible opportunity for us. But, if you can weasel any details about his feelings on the Misty Goodnight situation when his guard's down, all the better.'

*But his guard is never down. And, anyway, he'll nix anything he doesn't like.*

She bit off the thought. 'Of course.'

She heard the sharp rap on the suite's exterior door, her heartbeat pummelling her throat with another one-two punch as she ended the call.

She jammed the phone into the exquisite clutch bag, also supplied by Madame Laurent.

Her thundering heartbeat began to deafen her as she walked through the dark, empty suite, her jewelled heels sinking into the thick silk carpeting, the lights from the city behind her reflecting off the polished antique furniture.

And gulped down the rising panic.

*This is a golden opportunity to get to know Ruby's father, and forgive that foolish girl from a lifetime ago. End of.*

'He can't intimidate you unless you let him,' she whispered to herself, then swung the door open with a bravado she didn't feel.

And almost choked. *Wow!*

Brandon Cade stood with his back to her—his broad shoulders blocking out the muted light from the hallway—in a black tuxedo perfectly tailored to spotlight his muscular torso, narrow hips and long legs. The dark hair, shaved close to his scalp, only accentuated the perfect shape of his skull.

He turned, and those moss-green eyes locked on her face, making her breath squeeze in her lungs. His gaze skimmed down—insolent, possessive—to take in the sleek, shimmering gown which suddenly felt completely transparent.

Her breathing stopped altogether, making her light-headed, and suddenly she was that artless, innocent girl again, trapped in the laser beam of Brandon Cade's attention, yearning for his approval, her heart thundering so hard against her ribcage she was surprised it didn't leap out of her chest.

His eyes narrowed as his gaze lifted to her chignon.

'What happened to your hair?' he asked. 'It looks as if it's grown several feet in a few hours.'

The offhand comment released the breath she'd been holding. She forced herself to drag in another.

'It's magic,' she said. 'Courtesy of Gigi, my new hair-stylist. And several feet of someone else's hair.'

He let out a gruff chuckle, then offered her his elbow. 'I guess we better get to the ball, then, before they ask for it back.'

She placed her fingertips on his forearm, her breathing accelerating all over again as a muscle tensed under the suit fabric and she captured his scent—clean soap and spicy cologne, an aroma she remembered far too vividly from five years ago.

He tugged her towards him until she could feel the hard line of his body against hers, then led her to the hotel lift as her heart attempted to punch its way out of her chest again.

*Fabulous.*

How had she ended up at the mercy of this hard, in-domitable man a second time? And how on earth was she

going to keep her secrets—and her unruly senses—safe
from him for an entire night?

*Cinderella, hold my beer.*

'Your date tonight is *très belle*, Cade, but also a surprise,'
Maxim Durand, the billionaire vintner hosting tonight's
ball to celebrate the spring bud-burst in his vineyards,
murmured in Brandon's ear.

Brandon let out a harsh laugh as he stared at Lacey, who
had been chatting with Durand's British wife Cara and
his four-year-old son Pascal ever since they had arrived.

Durand was so damn proud of his family, it seemed he
couldn't resist showing them off at every available opportunity. Brandon had to admit the guy's kids were pretty
cute, although the way the toddler in Maxim's arms had
been staring at him all night was starting to unnerve him.

He knew nothing about kids, except what he could remember about being a child himself—not a feeling he
wanted to revisit.

'Why a surprise?' he asked absently, although he knew
why—more than a few people had commented on his decision to invite a feature writer from a celebrity magazine
tonight. This was the sort of exclusive event where the
press stayed outside. But, then again, Lacey didn't seem
to be taking advantage of the opportunity he'd given her...
Which only made him more uneasy. Why hadn't she?

He'd heard her staggered gasp as he had guided her into
the palatial ballroom. Once attached to the private opera
house next door, the hotel's historic event space had been
built during the reign of Napoleon III, when pomp and circumstance had been a way of life in Paris. Gold chandeliers
hung from a ceiling decorated in artwork depicting a host
of Greek deities. Marble columns, sculpted statues—of yet
more naked Greeks!—and bronze busts adorned the ballroom's hidden alcoves and added to the gilded splendour.

The sound of a chamber orchestra echoed off polished marble but was drowned out by the chatter of conversation and the clink of glass wear and fine china from the lavish buffet of *cordon bleu* cuisine laid out in the adjacent banqueting hall. Once the reception was over, there would be a performance from Paris's premiere ballet and then dancing of a very different kind to an A-list band who usually filled stadiums.

Everyone who was anyone in business, politics and entertainment was here tonight, presenting a smorgasbord of the kind of celebrities who guarded their privacy almost as fiercely as he did.

He'd been waiting for Lacey to sneak off, so he would have an excuse to think the worst of her, but she'd seemed subdued and tense, unwilling or unable to make the most of this golden career opportunity.

'Don't I always date beautiful women?' he added. But, even as he said the words, he couldn't help being far too aware of the unfamiliar hitch in his heartbeat which he'd been struggling to control ever since he'd turned in the hallway upstairs to see his date in that damn evening gown.

The sight was still playing havoc with his control even now. Lacey Carstairs wasn't just beautiful, she was stunning—but in a wholly unconventional way. Those cat-like eyes had seemed even more sultry and alluring thanks to the glittery gunk on her lids. The shimmering fabric of the gown skimmed over her curves like a second skin, accentuating her coltish beauty and highlighting her pert breasts. When he added in the glossy sheen on her lips, which had made the desire to kiss her all but unbearable, was it any surprise he couldn't take his eyes off her? He even found himself mesmerised by that elaborate hairdo, his fingers itching to pluck out the pins and sink his fingers into the short cap of curls hiding beneath.

The need to touch, taste and torment every inch of her

until she begged had been driving him nuts all evening, even though he'd begun to question the decision to invite her tonight as soon as they'd boarded the helicopter in London.

'Yes, but you don't usually date celebrity journalists, *mon ami*,' Durand clarified, the wry amusement in his tone suggesting he wasn't so much irritated by Cade's choice of guest, more intrigued. 'I thought you had learned your lesson with the last one.'

Misty hadn't been a reporter, she'd been a self-publicist on social media, but he got Durand's point. He wasn't an impulsive guy, so where the hell had the decision to bring Lacey to this event even come from? And why had he only been more determined to get her here when she'd tried to put him off?

Had he fallen for the oldest trick in the book—a woman playing hard to get? And why couldn't he shake the feeling her reticence, her nerves, were one hundred percent genuine—and had nothing to do with the event and everything to do with him? He was used to women finding him intimidating, but he'd never been so aware of their feelings before now, so attuned to every tiny indrawn breath, every tensed muscle.

His awareness of her had only made him more determined to find out every damn thing he could as soon as he'd escorted her to her suite. So he'd spent an hour earlier checking her out on the Internet. Only to discover precisely nothing. How come a celebrity journalist didn't have any kind of Internet footprint—not one single social media account? Almost as if she'd appeared from nowhere two years ago when she'd got her first by-line at *Splendour*.

And how come her mysterious past hadn't done a damn thing to stem his desire? He didn't like secrets or surprises. And recklessness wasn't one of his go-to emotions either.

But the desire to take her to bed was becoming more intense, the more unsettled he became, rather than less so.

*Not good.*

'Although, I must say, Cara seems to like her very much, and she happens to be an excellent judge of character,' Durand added, the pride in his voice unmistakeable for his pretty blonde wife—whose staggeringly large baby bump made Brandon wonder if Durand kept the poor woman permanently pregnant. 'Also, your date has been here over an hour and no one has complained yet about her.'

'I guess she's on her best behaviour,' Brandon mused, not sure it mattered to him any more.

His reaction to Lacey Carstairs had been swifter and a lot more intense than usual. But surely all he needed to do was satisfy it? He certainly wasn't remotely scared of a sexual attraction which would be easily handled once they both indulged it. Her contrary behaviour, the nerves, the guilelessness, the secrecy, and that strange something which kept tugging at his subconscious, had intrigued him, that was all.

'This woman may be more of a keeper than you are used to,' the vintner said pensively as his young daughter tugged his hair—finally getting bored with unnerving Brandon.

'*A keeper?* Yeah, right.' Brandon's laugh released the tension in his gut. He didn't do permanent, not with women—not really with anyone—because he never let anyone get that close. 'I don't think so, pal. But what makes you say that?'

Lacey wasn't a keeper, not for him anyway. But he'd always respected Durand's opinion. The man had come from nothing and built a global empire, and he was surprisingly astute.

'Because my son likes her very much too. Your Ms Carstairs is a natural with children, warm and affectionate and honest—not qualities I have noted previously in British tabloid journalists.'

Brandon frowned, Durand's observation only increasing his confusion.

*Warmth? Affection? Honesty?*

Since when had he prized those qualities in a date? Precisely never. Shouldn't her abilities as a child whisperer make her exceedingly dull, instead of intoxicating?

Durand seemed amused by his confusion, but was forced to make his excuses as his daughter's giggles turned to tired tears.

'It is time we put our children to bed,' he said with remarkable patience as the little girl began to tug his hair again.

The three of them made their way across the ballroom. But, as Brandon approached, Lacey's eyes locked on him—and for one arresting moment she looked like a doe trapped in a hunter's rifle sites.

Heat pumped into his groin on cue.

Durand greeted his wife, pressing his hand to the small of her back and leaning down to kiss her cheek. Cara smiled at her husband and daughter, her eyes full of an unguarded affection Brandon found disconcerting. But then he noticed Lacey staring at the couple too, and an undisguised longing flashed across her face.

Something uncomfortable and wholly unfamiliar streaked through Brandon.

What was that about?

*You're not actually jealous, are you?*

He forced himself to relax as the Durands excused themselves to take their children to bed. As the couple left, Lacey's gaze was still fixed on Durand and his wife and children.

'What a wonderful family,' Lacey murmured, the wistful comment not helping untie the knot in Brandon's gut. 'They seem so happy together.'

He glanced after the Durands. 'I guess.'

She seemed lost in thought for a moment, but then she turned to him, the look in her eyes curious and strangely sad. 'You don't think so?'

Her tone was casual, and the question seemed innocuous, but her gaze was focussed on him as if his answer was important to her.

He'd been expecting her to attempt to pry details about his personal life out of him for her article. His opinion of the Durands' marriage hadn't been on his radar of questions to deflect, so he shrugged and gave her an honest answer.

'Maxim and Cara probably think they're happy now, but I doubt it will last.'

The curious expression died, but something leapt into her eyes that looked oddly like pity. *What the hell?*

'Why would you think that? When it's obvious they're devoted to each other?' Lacey asked, not quite able to hide her horror at Brandon Cade's cynical observation. Or the wave of sympathy engulfing her.

She knew she shouldn't be shocked and she certainly shouldn't feel sorry for him. The man was a powerful billionaire, not some lost boy. But, regardless, her skin chilled despite the warmth of the ballroom.

He shrugged, the movement deceptively casual. 'You didn't know Maxim before he met Cara,' he said. 'I did. No one could have been further from the family-man type. Except me.'

'You don't think a person can change?'

His gaze became flat and suspicious.

He probably thought she was asking about his views on the Durands' marriage to add to her piece. Nothing could be further from the truth—she might write celebrity features, but she had her principles.

She had promised Cara Durand any conversation they had would be off the record, but her job provided the cover she needed to probe Brandon's views on love and marriage.

He laughed, cynicism highlighting the gold shards in his irises. The dimple reappeared in his cheek, but his smile reminded her less and less of her baby girl. How could one man be so cynical, he would even doubt the sincerity of the Durands' affection for each other?

'Not really,' he said. 'Because whatever happened in Maxim's past to make him so ruthless can never be changed.'

*What happened to you, Brandon, to make you so ruthless and cynical too?*

The question echoed in her head. She had to bite her lip to stop herself from asking it. But it didn't stop the sympathy from pulsing in her chest.

'And why would he want to change it?' he added, his gaze searching her face, the heat as disturbing as the confidence in his own cynicism. 'When those parts of his past have to be the reason he had the drive and ambition to build so much from absolutely nothing?'

'But it's obvious Maxim Durand loves his wife *and* his children more than anything else,' she said. 'Which suggests he would happily give up all his success rather than risk losing them,' she finished, knowing she wasn't talking about Maxim Durand any more.

People's priorities changed when they had children. She could never have imagined loving anyone as much as she loved Ruby—from the minute she'd been born. She would always put Ruby's needs first now, above everything. But it made her unbearably sad to realise Ruby's father might well not have the capacity to do the same.

The truth was, as a nineteen-year-old, alone and pregnant, she hadn't told him of his child's existence because she'd been scared—not just of his power and what he might do, but also because of her own weakness. If he'd demanded she have an abortion, would she have been strong enough to insist on making her own choice?

Weirdly, though, his predictable responses to her questions weren't helping her with the guilt one bit. Because now she felt sad for him *and* Ruby. What if he *could* change, as Maxim Durand had done, but she had denied him the opportunity to find out?

'Spoken like a true romantic,' he said, the obvious distain in his tone cutting deep. She wasn't a romantic, she was a realist, because she'd had to be.

'I never figured you people actually believed all the sentimental hogwash you publish about guys like me,' he added.

He was laughing at her now, the harsh glint in his eyes as arrogant as it was cynical. The desire to wipe that smirk off his too-handsome face was irresistible.

'Sentimental hogwash, huh? I had no idea you were such an avid reader of *Splendour* magazine,' she managed, the tart reply going someway to cover the sympathy for him still pulsing in her chest.

He chuckled. 'Not so much, but I've got to say, you've made me wonder if I've been missing out.' His gaze intensified, but this time she didn't just see heat, she saw approval. 'You're not at all what I expected.'

The surprise that she'd impressed him was swiftly followed by concern as the green fire in his eyes made her thigh muscles loosen and the hot spot in her belly throb.

'And, while I don't do clichés as a rule, I've got to admit you're even hotter when you fight back, Lacey.'

His gaze locked on hers, the heat and purpose in it sizzling over her skin and making her nipples squeeze into aching peaks. But his approval was so much more intoxicating…and terrifying.

'Hot enough to make me break my golden rule,' he continued.

'Which is?' she asked, trying for indifference, but getting breathlessness instead.

'Never to sleep with a woman who thinks she can change me.'

He cupped her cheek. She jolted, the rough texture of his thumb trailing over her lips, and the fiercely possessive light in his eyes, making it impossible for her to look away. Or get her lungs to function.

The lights from the chandeliers dimmed as the guests were directed into the adjoining salon to enjoy the special performance of the Paris Opera Ballet. But the two of them remained in the ballroom, cocooned in the darkness, suddenly alone in the cavernous space but for the staff. Lacey's breathing accelerated, all the reasons why she shouldn't let him touch her queuing up in her head, but her body refused to listen as his fingers curved around her neck and drew her towards him.

'You really are exquisite,' he said, his mouth lowering to hers, his scent filling her senses, her heart beating double time.

Why had she never felt like this with any other man? Was it just that Brandon Cade was the father of her child, the only man she had ever made love to? Or was it even more specific than that?

She placed trembling palms on his waist, her hands reaching inside his tuxedo jacket. His stomach muscles tensed.

'Madame Laurent and Gigi will be pleased you think so,' she said.

He laughed, the husky sound strained, the rich approval in his gaze as heady now as it had been once before.

'I'm not talking about the gown.' His gaze flicked to her chignon. 'Or the hair.' Warm hands caught her waist and drew her close until she could feel exactly how much he desired her. 'It's what's underneath I want.'

She blinked, the arousal flowing through her body on a tidal wave of desperation. Now, as then, she couldn't seem to make her brain function because all she could feel was the need.

'That sounds like a very bad idea,' she whispered, trying to make herself mean it.

Fierce heat flared in his gaze, and suddenly his hands had moved to grasp her cheeks, to lift her face to his.

'I know,' he murmured against her lips, his voice hoarse as the heat pulsed and throbbed at her core. But then his lips captured hers in a forceful, demanding kiss. She gasped, shocked by the brutal yearning which surged from her core. His tongue delved into the recesses of her mouth, controlling her, possessing her, wanting her, needing her with a ferocity she remembered.

The part of her brain still clinging to sanity knew she should tell him to stop, but the heady joy of being wanted again—by him—was far too raw and all-consuming to allow her to do anything but surrender to the moment.

A moment she hadn't even realised she had been waiting to relive for five years.

She found herself kissing him back with the same fervour—no longer the young girl happy to absorb all the sensations battering her. Now she was a woman, with needs of her own. Her tongue tangled with his, her hands fisted in his starched shirt as she tugged him closer. Her body vibrated with yearning as she reached up on tiptoes and met his hunger with all the need and longing from so long ago.

The kiss became carnal, and devastating, a battle for supremacy. She ripped her mouth from his— trying to regain her sense of self, her equilibrium—but it remained out of reach, the harsh rasps of her breathing making her lightheaded.

His expression became fierce and determined as his hands skimmed down the gossamer silk of her gown, shattering her senses all over again. His hands landed on her bottom to press her into the thick ridge in his trousers and his mouth found the hammering pulse point in her neck.

She gasped, shuddered, as she lost herself again in his devastating caresses.

Her head fell back, her own fingers tensing and releasing, her mind drifting into the forbidden zone where nothing mattered except feeding this incessant hunger.

Suddenly he wrenched himself away.

His gaze focussed on her face, and his palms rose to cup her cheeks. Satisfaction roared through her as she noticed his hands trembled.

Yes, she wanted him, but he wanted her right back. She hadn't imagined that five years ago. All this time she had blamed that girl for allowing herself to be used, for not reading the signs. But she wasn't that needy girl any more who would be devastated when this night was over. She knew the score.

He swore softly, then growled. 'I want to take you to bed.'

She knew she should say no. But why did this have to be about Ruby? Why couldn't it just be about them? He didn't know who she was, didn't know he had once destroyed her.

She'd been careful, patient and pragmatic for so long, solely focussed on building a new life, a better life, for her and her little girl. But during the last five years she'd also hated the untried girl she had been that night, for giving herself to him so easily, for falling halfway in love with him after a few hours without ever really knowing him, and for allowing herself to be destroyed by his rejection.

Didn't that girl deserve the chance to enjoy this chemistry again, but on her terms now instead of his?

She let the heady excitement course through her veins. And nodded.

# CHAPTER FOUR

THE NEXT FEW MINUTES—as Brandon Cade dragged her out of the ballroom, through the heritage hotel's ornate lobby area and up the grand staircase to their suites—went by in a blur.

Lacey felt as if she were floating on a wave of euphoria…and dread.

The voice inside her head, demanding she stop this madness, was drowned out by the deafening thuds of her heartbeats and the brutal yearning burning like a hot brick at her core.

'Your suite or mine?' Brandon demanded, his voice raw, when they reached the first-floor hallway.

'I… I don't know,' she managed, her throat drying to parchment.

'Mine's bigger,' he supplied.

Seconds later, her mind still reeling, her body still yearning, still pliant, she found herself standing in the shadowy splendour of the hotel's Presidential Suite. He led her past upholstered sofas, ornate furniture, a spray of flowers in a priceless antique vase and out onto a large terrace, the full moon and the twinkling lights of the Eiffel Tower so close, it seemed as if she could reach out and touch them.

But then he swung her round. And all she could see was him. Tall, handsome, indomitable. He tugged off his jacket, dumped it on the marble tiles then grasped her hips in urgent hands and pulled her into his body.

His mouth fastened back on her neck, finding the pulse point, exploiting it ruthlessly and without mercy. She grasped his head, the short bristles of hair sending yet more sensation shimmering south as she held him to her, let him feast. Blood rushed to her breasts, trapped against his hard chest.

He lurched back. The harsh rasps of their breathing tore through the quiet night. He laughed, the sound husky, strained, and she wondered how she had amused him. But then he clasped her chin and lifted her face to his.

'Promise me this won't end up in your article.'

She blinked, the request disorientating and confusing at first—the intoxicating hunger rushing through her body so turbo-charged, she couldn't think.

But then it all came crashing back—who she was, why she was here, what she had worked so hard to achieve… She was a grown woman with a career, a life and a little girl who could be compromised, threatened, even destroyed by this man.

*You fool. The power you feel is an illusion, a trap. He holds all the power here. He always has.*

She staggered back, wrenching herself out of his embrace. She pressed a panicked hand to her head to discover the carefully styled chignon had been torn loose. The hair extension came away in her fingers—somehow a symbol of the shattered illusion.

Her breath heaved, and her heart pumped so fast, she was terrified he could hear it too.

'I… I have to leave,' she whispered.

But as she went to walk past him—to *run* past him—he snagged her wrist. 'Where are you going?'

'I can't… I can't do this. It…it would be totally unprofessional,' she said, clinging to any excuse, any way

to get away from the yearning she'd foolishly unleashed
downstairs—which was still charging through her body
and telling her to take the risk. To indulge the pleasure
without regrets.

'Are you joking?' he said. He didn't sound annoyed,
just surprised.

'No, I'm not.' She twisted her wrist out of his grasp,
rubbing the skin where his touch burned. 'And, FYI, I
don't write porn.'

She rushed back through the suite's lavish living area,
her body aching with unfed desire.

'Come back here!' he shouted.

This time, his hands captured her shoulders to drag her
round, and the tremble of reaction reached right down to
her soul.

'I didn't mean to insult you,' he said softly.

She clasped her arms around her waist. She had to get
out before the madness took her again. But somehow she
couldn't seem to move. She stood rooted to the spot as his
hands caressed the bare skin, his thumb skimming over
the pulse point in her neck he had devoured only moments before.

'Yes, you did,' she countered, knowing his intentions
hardly mattered now. All that mattered was that she didn't
give in to the sensations still pulsing at her core. He had
never treated her with gentleness before, only demand.
Why did the softness of his touch now, that strange feeling
of possession—as if both their bodies understood he had
a right to hold her—only make her heart pound harder?

He let out a gruff chuckle, self-deprecating and all the
more disarming for it.

'Yeah, I guess I did.' He lifted his hands from her shoulders, raising his palms in the universal sign of surrender.
'But, in my defence,' he added, his voice losing the lilt
of amusement. 'I'm a deeply cynical guy. And you're a

reporter who can make a fortune out of exposing all my secrets.'

She missed the warm weight on her bare shoulders instantly, but worse was the lurch in her chest at the candid direction of the conversation. And the thought of how he had been manipulated, his private life exposed by another woman.

She'd assumed he was a man who couldn't be hurt, but maybe he could.

She'd kidded herself she had accepted his invitation to Paris to find out more about him. She could see now that had never been the whole truth.

She'd also been compelled by the incendiary chemistry which had derailed her life once before…and made Ruby. But even so she was still desperately curious about him.

'Do you have a lot of secrets?' she asked, before she could stop herself.

'Are you asking as a reporter or a woman?' he replied.

It was a leading question. One she was wary of answering truthfully. But even so she said, 'As a woman.'

His lips curved in the half-smile. But this time, when the dimple appeared, it seemed genuine.

'Yeah, I've got a lot of secrets.' His thumb moved, brushing under her chin, then trailing down to trace the swell of her breast above the gown's bodice. His touch was subtle, alluring, devastating.

Her breathing accelerated, her heart pumping desire back.

'But then, doesn't everyone?' he added.

She jolted, her breath catching. Did he somehow know about Ruby? But, before the panic could take hold, he continued, 'It's what makes sex so exciting. Discovering a woman's secrets, figuring out all the ways to make her ache, make her moan, make her beg.'

Her breath gushed out on a staggered sigh, but with relief came the heady kick of desire as his devious thumb trailed down to circle the tight bud of her nipple, hardening beneath the silk.

*Sex.* This was all just about sex to him. Nothing more.

'Let me find out all your secrets, Lacey,' he whispered, his breath warm against her neck as his fingers found the tab under her arm and tugged it down. The sibilant hum of the zip releasing was deafening. But not as deafening as her racing pulse.

'I promise, not one of them will leave this suite,' he added, the seductive tone beckoning her back into madness. 'Just one night, that's all I ask.'

'Okay,' she said, on a gasp of pleasure.

'Good girl,' he said.

The bodice released, the jewelled straps of the gown falling from her shoulders as he brushed them aside.

The city lights glittered in his gaze as it roamed over her, making him look saturnine, fierce.

'Damn, you're beautiful,' he whispered.

His large hand covered the transparent lace of her bra, weighing her swollen breast in his palm. He bent his head to capture the stiff peak through the gossamer fabric.

She clasped his head, struggling to breathe now, struggling to stay upright, the warm, wet pressure so perfect, so right and yet not enough.

'I… Please… I want…' she stammered, holding his head, trying to drag him closer, to feel more, to feel it all.

'Yeah, I know,' he said, drawing back to scoop her off the floor with startling ease.

Her heart bounced in her chest as he strode into the next room with her cradled in his arms. The lavish bedroom had a large king-sized bed as its centrepiece. Through the patio doors, she could still see Paris's iconic tower, like a spear of light in the darkness, but all she could feel was the need streaking through her body as he placed her on her feet.

He turned her towards the glass. Her lacy push-up bra released, and suddenly his hands were on her naked breasts, caressing, stroking, plucking at the damp nipples. She bowed back against him, unable to protest as he lifted her arm and draped it around his neck, his hands sliding down her sides, making shocking sensation riot over her skin.

He worked the gown from her hips until it fell in a pool of glittery silk at her feet. His lips feasted on her neck, making her ache, making her beg, just as he had promised.

'Look at yourself, Lacey.'

Her eyelids fluttered open to see the decadent sight reflected in the glass. She stood naked—but for the swatch of transparent lace hiding the shadow of her sex. Her skin was so pale, her body somehow petite against the large, dark shape of him behind her.

His hands, captured, possessed, circling her breasts, making her buck and gasp.

'You're mine tonight, Lacey,' he said, the words strained and darkly compelling. His fingers slid down to glide under the lace covering her sex and locate the slick folds. She bucked against his hold as he circled the epicentre of her need. Teasing, tempting.

'Say it,' he demanded.

'Yes… I'm yours tonight,' she said, throwing caution away in the desperate pursuit of pleasure as his sure, steady fingers continued to stroke, to torment.

'Please, can you…?' The need clogged in her lungs as she offered her breasts to him, brazenly begging for his caresses.

'I want you to watch yourself, Lacey,' he said.

She forced her eyelids open again, saw her yearning body writhe against his hold in the glass.

His clever fingers found the very heart of her pleasure. At last.

'Come for me,' he commanded, beckoning forth the staggering orgasm on a brutal wave of release.

She cried out, bowed back, bucking against his perfect touch. And the pleasure soared through her as he stroked her through the shattering climax.

She collapsed against him at last. His touch was still firm, still there.

She grasped his wrist. 'Please, it's too much.'

He withdrew his hand, but then turned her to him, cradled her cheeks. His thumb trailed across her lips.

She could taste her own pleasure on his fingers. And something raw and erotic bumped and swelled at her core as he lifted her limp body into his arms and placed her on the bed.

She watched him strip off in the moonlight. Saw the sculpted muscles of his chest, the bold lines of his hip flexors, the dark line of hair that trailed through washboard abs and bloomed at his groin. Her gaze devoured the masculine beauty of his body, then settled on the column of erect flesh—so thick, so long—proving how much he wanted her.

She'd never seen him fully naked all those years ago. Why did this feel so much more intimate, so much more overwhelming?

But then her gaze rose to his as he crawled onto the bed, trapping her yearning body against his as he stripped off her thong.

He kissed her with feverish desire, fervent desperation. 'We're not through yet, Lacey,' he said with an urgent desire which held threat as well as promise. His lips traced down her torso to torment her too-sensitive nipples, first one, then the other, licking, nipping, sucking, until she was moaning again.

His lips trailed lower, kissing her quivering flesh, now aching with desperation once more. He spread her legs, opening her completely.

'We've only just started,' he said, his breath feathering her exposed sex.

Then he touched the molten heart of her. She jolted and cried out, the sensation too much and yet not enough. Licking and probing, his devious mouth drew her moans forth until his lips captured the swollen nub and suckled hard. Her sex pulsed and throbbed, another orgasm barrelling towards her with staggering speed. The shocking climax was brutal in its intensity.

She collapsed onto the bed, struggling to gather her breath when his big body loomed above her. She watched him, dazed, disorientated, her body still awash in brutal pleasure as he rolled on a condom with clumsy fingers.

At last, he grasped her hips, positioned the huge head of his erection at her sodden entrance then drove himself deep in one all-consuming thrust.

A guttural moan she didn't even recognise as her own echoed around the room. The slickness of her orgasms eased his entry. But, once he was lodged to the hilt, the stretched feeling she remembered was all but overwhelming.

She felt impaled, conquered, owned as the devastating waves began to build again, impossibly.

'Hold on to me…' He grunted.

She clasped his sweat-slicked shoulders and clung on as he began to move. Drawing out, pounding back, he forced her to new heights as the pleasure rolled back over her, even harder, faster and more furious than before.

This time, when release came, it slammed into her, sending her soaring into a delirious, welcome oblivion.

She heard him shout out from many miles away as he charged after her into the same stunning, scary, bottomless abyss.

Brandon pulled out of the woman beneath him, bracing his arms to stop from crushing her. He flopped back on the bed beside her, the last of the mind-blowing orgasm still rippling through him and turning his mind, and his senses, to mush.

*What the hell was that?*

His body felt altered somehow, the desire still pulsing through his system and making him feel more alive, more attuned to another human being than he ever had before... except maybe once.

He frowned and turned to see Lacey's bare shoulder. She'd rolled away from him and curled in on herself. The rise and fall of her breathing suggested she had dropped into a deep sleep.

*Who is she?*

Why had she responded to him with such unrestrained enthusiasm? And why had each soft moan, each sweet sob, each shudder of surrender, only made him more ravenous? More desperate to push her further, to take more?

Had it really all been an act?

But, even as he tried to convince himself, he couldn't. He was a good judge of people and he knew her reaction, when he'd insisted she keep any intimacy between them off the record, had been absolutely genuine. She'd been upset and determined to walk away.

He still wasn't entirely sure why he hadn't let her. Because, even before he'd got her naked and made her come apart in his arms—not once, not twice, but three times, with a wild abandon which had stunned him—he'd known this connection was too intense, too savage to be easily controlled.

He should wake her up, ask her to leave. He never slept with women through the night because he hated to encourage too much intimacy.

But, as he rolled towards her, his hand landing on her shoulder, he couldn't bring himself to shake her awake.

Instead, his palm skimmed down the curve of her body to rest on her hip.

She stirred but remained asleep, the murmur of her breathing—and the feel of her soft skin beneath his hand—making the incessant heat gather again in his groin.

*Seriously?*

He sighed and inhaled her scent.

The fresh, tempting perfume she must have dabbed on her neck had faded, to be replaced by the musty scent of sex and the rich, intoxicating scent of her skin.

Rich, intoxicating… And… He shifted closer to her to gather another greedy lungful. Disturbingly familiar.

His shaft swelled against her bottom as the memories the aroma invoked slammed into him.

Another woman. A girl. So eager and responsive, she had destroyed all his caution, all his control, in the space of a few heady hours.

*What the actual…?* He swore and jerked away from the woman in his bed now.

How could Lacey have exactly the same smell as that girl and affect him in the same incendiary way? The girl he'd banished from his life so long ago but had never been able to fully forget.

Could she be…?

*Dammit, Cade, get a grip.*

He forced himself to breathe through the wave of panic and stunned arousal and waited for his exhausted mind to engage.

How could she be the same woman? Wouldn't he have recognised her immediately? And wouldn't she have said something? But then he recalled everything about her—from the minute she had entered his office that afternoon—which had provoked and aroused memories of that night five years ago.

Hell, whether she was that girl or not, was that why

he had been so determined to bring her to Paris, to seduce her?

He dragged off the sheet, his skin tingling again, the
coil of desire in his gut tightening from the renewed overload of sensation which Lacey seemed to trigger without
even trying. Just like that girl.

How could those memories still be so vivid too?

He forced himself to get up, to get away from her. He
stalked into the bathroom, closed the door then turned on
one of the ambient lights. Bracing his hands on the marble
vanity, he stared at his face in the mirror as the sensory
overload continued to charge through his system like a
wild stallion—untamed, uncontrollable.

He breathed through it, waiting for the adrenaline rush
to subside. His pulse finally slowed and the strident erection subsided enough for him to think coherently.

He stripped off the condom, then washed his hands
and face. The splash of cold water brought him back to
his senses.

Surely Lacey couldn't be Lizzy Devlin?

But there was one easy way to find out. Because there
was another distinguishing mark on that girl he remembered far too vividly.

He walked back into the bedroom. Lacey hadn't moved,
her body still curled into a foetal position, her breathing
slow and even.

He switched on the bedside light, the soft glow add-
ing a lustre to her skin, but she still didn't stir. He tugged
the sheet down and watched it slide over the curve of her
backside to reveal the pale flesh of her buttocks in the
lamplight.

His breathing stopped and a wave of anger blindsided
him. A swear word hissed through clenched teeth.

Lacey Carstairs had a lot of explaining to do.

Starting with why the hell she hadn't mentioned he had devoured her in a similar frenzy five years ago.

But what infuriated him more was the blistering heat which followed as he examined the heart-shaped birthmark high on her right buttock—and the visceral memory of how he'd discovered it once before flowed through his system again like wildfire.

# CHAPTER FIVE

LACEY JERKED AWAKE, her body still humming, her mind a mess. She blinked, aware of all the places she ached. But then it all came rushing back—the ballroom kiss, the rush of panic on the balcony of Brandon's suite, the dark deeds which had followed as she'd succumbed to his seduction. Wildly, willingly. She shivered, aware of her nakedness, and the sensations still skittering across her skin.

She shifted in the bed, the glimmer of dawn seeping into the night sky illuminating the empty space beside her. A thin strip of light glowed under the bathroom door.

*Thank goodness.*

Cade had to be in there, even though she couldn't hear him.

Gathering the sheet, she tucked it around herself and scooted off the bed. She needed to get back to her own room before he reappeared. She must have been asleep for hours.

She found her discarded underwear and dropped the sheet to slip it on, wincing slightly as the lace brushed against the beard burn on her breasts, her thighs.

*Classy, much?*

The beautiful gown was hopelessly crushed, the creases in the jewelled silk a testament to her staggeringly ill-judged decision to revisit the catastrophic choices of her youth.

How on earth was she going to explain to Melody she'd missed most of the event? And how did she square the decision to sleep with Brandon Cade again with the knowledge she had given birth to his child and had never told him of Ruby's existence?

She tugged on the gown, scrabbling around until she found her heels.

The light from the bathroom was still on. Should she leave him a note? She dismissed the notion. Brandon Cade would be through with her now.

And, anyway, she was through with him too. So they were all good.

As long as she didn't factor in his four-year-old daughter.

*Don't think about that now. Once you're back in London, you can regroup, rethink, revisit all the things you learned about him tonight.*

Not that the new information she'd gathered amounted to very much. Other than the fact he still had the ability to make her lose her ever-loving mind, forget all her priorities and climax on demand.

She swallowed around the growing lump of guilt…and shame…and panic…and tiptoed out of the bedroom with her heels in her hand.

She shot through the dimly lit living area and grabbed her bag, which was sitting on a coffee table… Had she put it there? She couldn't even remember.

The staggering view of the Eiffel Tower was now lit by the red light of the approaching dawn. Gulping down an unsteady breath, she dived towards the door.

She was halfway there when a low voice—edged with fury—whispered through the darkness.

'Where are you off to, Lacey?'

She swung round, clutching her shoes and her bag, and

spotted Brandon sitting in the shadows of the room, watching her.

The lump rammed her throat and her heartbeat hit warp speed.

Had he been lying in wait for her?

She cleared her throat, trying to calm her frantic pulse and speak round the rapidly expanding lump. 'I'm going back to my room.'

*Then I'm getting dressed and heading for the Gare du Nord to take the first train back to London—and get the heck out of Dodge.*

He turned on a light on the table beside him. He wore sweat pants and a T-shirt, his feet bare. It was the most casual clothing she'd ever seen him wear. But, when he stood up and walked towards her, it didn't make an appreciable difference to her erratic heartrate. Or the power and purpose which emanated from him.

How could he still look so overwhelming?

He cupped her cheek, making her tense, drew his thumb across her lips—lips now red from his kisses. She let out a shuddering breath. She could still feel him inside her, taking her to places no other man had ever taken her.

*Focus, Lacey, for goodness' sake.*

She dragged herself away from his touch.

'Why are you in such a hurry, Lacey?' he asked as his hand dropped, but the harsh light in his eyes belied the conversational tone. 'Or should I call you Lizzy?'

She jolted. She could see the feral expression now and recognised it as anger.

Her stomach knotted, the lump of guilt and regret growing to impossible proportions.

'How long have you known?' she whispered.

And how *much* did he know?

Did he know about Ruby? About their child? The knots in her stomach became giant serpents.

But, as he continued to stare at her, her own anger surged, along with the devastating hurt she'd buried deep five years ago.

She let it burn under her breastbone now to protect herself from the shivers wracking her body, and the black hole of inadequacy threatening to open up in her chest.

So what if she'd lied to him about her identity? She refused to feel guilty about it. Refused to let him accuse her again, the way he'd once accused that foolish girl.

The girl he'd dismissed without a backward glance—and thrown away so casually.

What right did he have to be angry with her, when he had treated her so appallingly that night? And what exactly did she have to apologise for, when he had never apologised to her?

Brandon frowned, annoyed to see Lacey's initial shock turn to stubborn resistance, instead of the guilt and embarrassment he had been expecting.

That she only looked more stunning dressed in the creased gown, her short hair a mess of unruly curls, and the bold, belligerent light in her eyes turning them to a golden brown, was neither here nor there.

He wouldn't be fooled by her act a second time. Heat surged in his groin, calling him a liar.

Well, not until he'd got a few straight answers out of her—to the many, *many* questions which had been queuing up in his head while he'd been sitting in the dark for hours, waiting for her to put in an appearance. That she'd intended to run out on him, without even the courtesy of a goodbye, let alone an explanation, added to his sense of injustice.

'You may not know this, but you have a rather distinctive birthmark on your right cheek,' he said, his gaze drifting down to her bottom to make it abundantly clear exactly which cheek he was referring to. 'I noticed it the first time you tried to trick me into a commitment.'

'*Trick* you?' She sucked in a furious breath. 'I didn't try to *trick* you into anything five years ago,' she snapped, her exploding temper highlighting the gold sparks in her irises. 'You arrogant, insufferable, overbearing…' She sputtered to a stop, clearly struggling to locate an insult bad enough.

'Arrogant, insufferable, overbearing *what*, exactly, Lizzy?' he goaded, as his own fury pulsed like a ticking bomb. 'Halfwit, perhaps, given that is what you take me for?'

'Don't call me Lizzy,' she shot back. 'My name's not Lizzy any more, it's Lacey.'

'So I gather, which begs the question, why did you change it?' he sneered, letting his outrage at her deception show. 'Other than to deliberately deceive me, of course? And why did you choose not to inform me we had already met when you walked into my office this afternoon and proceeded to snare me again with your artless little act?'

'My artless little…?' Her cheeks exploded with outraged colour as her face turned a surprisingly beguiling shade of red. 'I did not *snare* you, you arrogant jerk. *You* snared *me*. *You* invited *me* to Paris, not the other way around. I tried as politely as I could to turn you down. And you refused to get the message, and refused to take no for an answer, like the overbearing halfwit you actually are.'

'Ah, yes, your not at all convincing attempt to turn down my invitation. Am I actually supposed to believe now that wasn't all part of your act too?' he sneered. 'To lure me back into your bed.'

'Oh, go to hell, I don't give a flying f—' She stopped dead, clearly making a titanic effort not to utter the swear word for no reason he could fathom. 'I don't give a flying feather duster what you do or do not believe!' she finally burst out.

He should have been even more angry, of course, but the ridiculous alternate swear word had his fury fading.

'A feather duster? *Really?*' he said, having to bite his tongue to stop from smiling.

This was not funny in the slightest. She'd tricked him, deceived him, and he still hadn't got a single straight answer out of her. But something about the way she was fighting back was making admiration for her—and her temper—build alongside the fury.

It occurred to him she was different from the girl he remembered. That girl had been quiet, subdued, deliberately close-mouthed when he'd confronted her that night about her virginity—making him sure he'd been right, that her 'sacrifice' had all been a deliberate ploy to trick him into a commitment. But this woman was a firebrand.

Her glare sharpened. 'Yes, really,' she declared. 'I try not to use profanity when I can help it,' she said with just enough strained patience to make his lips quirk again.

'Why?' he asked, because he was genuinely curious, the coy reply almost as beguiling as the rosy hue on her cheeks.

She looked away from him, but not before he caught the shadow of guilt.

What was that about? Why would she feel guilty about trying not to swear at him? It made no sense.

He tucked a knuckle under her chin. Her cheeks had reddened even more, but she stared back at him with a boldness which only made the hunger he thought he'd tamed flare anew.

'Why are you so worried about saying the F-word?' he asked again, even curiouser now as to why she wouldn't want to answer the question. 'Are you training to be a nun?'

She didn't reply, her lips flattening into a thin line.

'Because, I have to tell you, on last night's evidence

I fear you have chosen entirely the wrong vocation,' he mocked, still enjoying her temper too much.

He brushed his thumb across her lips again, unable to stop himself from touching her as she continued to glare at him defiantly. His thumb drifted down to caress the pulse fluttering in her collarbone like the wings of a trapped bird as he revelled in the awareness in her eyes, which she couldn't disguise.

'I have my reasons,' she said evasively, stepping away from his touch again. 'I need to leave.'

The fury surprised him as she turned to go, but not as much as the wrench in his chest.

'Oh, no you don't.' He grasped her wrist. 'You're not leaving until you give me a straight answer.'

What the hell was she hiding from him? And why? She wanted something from him—they all did. Eventually. So why wasn't she asking for it?

She tugged her hand free and rubbed her wrist. 'Fine, you want an answer. Here's one. You asked me why I changed my name. As if you didn't know!' She spat the words, her own temper rising.

He wasn't buying that diversionary tactic a second time, though.

'Obviously, I do not know, or I would not have asked.'

'Because you had me blacklisted,' she said, the pain that flashed across her face shocking him into silence, not least because it made the wrench in his chest throb. 'I couldn't get a job anywhere in journalism as Lizzy Devlin after that night.'

'What the hell are you talking about?' he said, genuinely perplexed, trying to remember what he'd actually said to his executive assistant the next day. He'd acted in haste, he remembered that, but he'd only asked Daryl to ensure their paths would never cross again. His kinetic, livewire response to her had rattled him. Her virginity and his complete loss of control in that damn office had rattled him even more. Not unlike his response to her tonight. But he would never have punished her in that way for something which he had eventually acknowledged was as much his fault as hers. In truth, *more* his fault than hers, given her lack of experience, whatever her intentions.

'I was summarily fired the next day,' she said, her anger now tempered by a sadness, a sense of injustice, which had the wrench in his chest widening. 'Without a reference and without any severance pay. And, when I tried to apply for other trainee jobs, I never even got a reply let alone an interview. I finally figured out why when a recruiter I applied to and who wouldn't take me on told me in confidence I should consider changing my name. That "powerful forces",' she continued, doing air quotes as the sheen of emotion glowed in her eyes, 'Had made Lizzy Devlin unemployable.'

He had never been one of those men who could be manipulated by a woman's tears—after all, he'd had no trouble at all withstanding Misty's big dramatic moment when he'd informed her their affair was over. But when Lacey blinked and the sheen disappeared from her eyes, it occurred to him there was something a lot more unsettling about a woman who refused to let the tears fall.

'I wanted to be a news reporter and you took that away from me.' Her tone lost the edge of temper, loaded now with accusation and injured pride. Something he could understand. After all, his father had once taken great delight in injuring his pride and making him aware he meant nothing to Alfred Cade other than being a means to an end. 'And I never understood why,' she said, the anger all but gone now, to reveal the hurt beneath. 'What did I do that was so terrible that made you want to punish me? That made you think I *deserved* to be punished?'

*You made me feel, too much.*

He locked the thought away. Because it was ludicrous. She hadn't made him feel, she'd made him want her too much—that was all. So much he hadn't stopped to think, hadn't used any of his usual finesse. She'd looked at him with that dewy approval in her gaze all evening, lapping up his conversation, being smart, cute and disarming... And all his smooth moves with women had deserted him until they'd ended up in a grubby little office with him pounding into her as if his life had depended on it. And, when he'd discovered she was a virgin, his incendiary reaction had only shocked him more.

'Does that answer your question?' she demanded, the harsh edge returning and yanking him back to the present.

Her face was lit now by the dawn. The artful make-up of last night, the elaborate hairstyle, were gone. But somehow it didn't make her any less beautiful, and suddenly he could see that girl again—in the tilt of her eyes, the naked emotion, the forthright expression.

But, when she turned to go this time, instead of anger all he felt was regret. So when he reached for her again, his touch was gentle, his voice even more so.

'Don't...' he murmured.

She stared at him, her expression carefully remote, but still he could see the hurt.

'Don't go,' he said, before she could tug herself free. He tightened his grip on her wrist. 'I want to apologise.'

Her brows shot up. He had stunned her.

The truth was, he'd stunned himself almost as much. Even when he was in the wrong, he never apologised. Because he refused to show a weakness. But this one time, he couldn't seem to stop himself.

He'd let her take the blame for everything that had happened five years ago. Because it had been easier than examining his own behaviour, his own shocking reaction.

But it was way past time he addressed that, or how was he going to handle the need now?

He still wanted her. One night had not been enough. And he intended to have her. Because he wasn't scared of his reaction any more. However volatile his response to her, it was purely physical. But, if the goal was to get her back into his bed, he needed to repair the damage he'd done. Luckily, he was an extremely goal-orientated guy.

'What for?' she said, the suspicion in her eyes crucifying him a little.

How typical of this woman not to take his unprecedented apology at face value. Was that another reason he found her so alluring—because she was proving to be a match for him in more than just the bedroom? How frustrating that he even found her contrary behaviour a turn-on.

'For what happened to your career,' he clarified. 'It was never my intention to have you blacklisted. I never even requested you be fired from Cade Inc.' Although he could see now why his ruthlessly efficient EA would have assumed as much from his remarks. No doubt Daryl had picked up on how rattled he had been by his close encounter with young Lizzy Devlin and had acted accordingly. 'I simply told my executive assistant to ensure our paths never crossed again. He clearly took that request and ran with it in a direction I had not intended.'

She stiffened slightly, and he could see he had hurt her again without meaning to. But instead of asking the obvious question…*why* had he been so determined to never to see her again?…she simply shrugged.

*Great*. Indifference. Just the effect he'd been aiming for.

'Right, well, thanks for clarifying that,' she said, the sarcasm not amusing him in the slightest. 'It makes me feel so much better to know my career got destroyed by accident.'

'What else do you expect me to say?' he said, becoming exasperated. 'I can't go back and change the past. That said, I will of course instruct my HR people to offer you a generous severance package for the way you were dismissed,' he finished, finally figuring out the best way to handle the situation. 'Whatever your annual salary was at the time, I'll have them double it as a one-off compensation payment.' Normally he would never admit liability but, given what had happened, and *how* it had happened, he could see she deserved restitution. And he could afford to be generous.

Last night had proved that, for whatever reason, this woman fired up his libido like no other. His sex life had been jaded for far too long. The thought of exploring this explosive chemistry in a great deal more depth excited him beyond reason. And he was more than happy to pay for the privilege.

But, instead of accepting his very generous offer, the glare reappeared. 'Is everything about money to you?'

It was his turn to flinch. 'What is the problem now?' he asked, because he genuinely didn't get it. He'd apologised, he'd offered her compensation. What the hell else did she want?

'Let me explain it in words of one syllable,' she said, the condescending tone starting to get on his nerves. 'I. Don't. Want. Your. Money,' she added, elucidating each word as if he were an imbecile. 'I never did. *You* were the one who accused me of trying to trap you into a commitment with sex. Not once, but twice. But I never asked you for one single thing. When we slept together five years ago…'

She huffed, the colour rising up her neck to suffuse her face. 'When we slept together tonight, it happened because I've never felt that kind of need before or since. It was a moment…well, more than a moment…of madness. And I revelled in it. Believe me, I did not have any ulterior motives. For goodness' sake, all I could do when you kissed me was react. I certainly wasn't thinking, because if I had been no way would I have put myself in a position to be insulted by you a second time.' She stopped abruptly, regret tightening her features, and he knew she knew she had said far too much.

Because the heat was charging through his veins all over again and pulsing in the air between them—like lightning ready to strike.

Her eyes widened, the lurid flush highlighting her cleavage. But the arousal had dilated her pupils to black, and he could see the fierce need she felt too in the tremor of her body.

She shot round, like a doe trying to escape the hunter, but this time he didn't hesitate. He grasped her upper arm and dragged her back. Until they were toe to toe, eye to eye, her breathing as ragged as his.

He wrapped his arms around her slender waist, notching the erection pulsing in his pants against the soft swell of her belly—and lowered his mouth to hers.

'You don't seriously think I'm going to let you leave now, do you?' he murmured, before capturing her sob of surrender, in a possessive kiss.

*Stop kissing him back!*

Lacey tried to prevent her tongue from duelling with his, tried to close her lips against the delicious invasion, tried to ignore the onslaught of sensation charging through her body. But as Brandon's hands cradled her head, angling her mouth for better access, the desperate objections were incinerated in a new tidal wave of need.

The madness returned, rippling through her body and making every pulse-point ache.

The buzz of something against her chest duelled with the hammering thud of her heartbeat. But then she recognised the intermittent vibrations, enough to drag her lips from his.

'My-my phone…?' she stammered, trying to get her mind to engage.

He released her abruptly.

Panic arrived hot on the heels of desire. How could she have succumbed to him again, been so willing to throw herself back into the inferno?

The frown on his face did nothing to cover the heat and purpose in his gaze.

'I need to answer it…' she said, finally gathering enough of her wits to welcome the interruption. She scrambled to open her purse and locate the buzzing phone. But, when she saw her sister Milly's number, panic turned to raw terror.

*Ruby?*

She turned away from Brandon to accept the call. 'Milly, what is it? Is everything okay?'

'Hey, sis.' Milly's voice came down the line, dousing Lacey's foolish hormones in a bucket of icy water. 'Don't panic. It's just Rubes has woken up with a slight temperature.'

'What?' Panic turned to guilt and remorse and every molecule of shame in between. 'How high is it?'

'Honestly, it's not that bad. I've called the NHS helpline and they're calling me back… Oh, I'm so sorry,' Milly added. 'It's only five o'clock. Did I wake you up? I should have just texted you.'

'No, it's fine, Milly, I'll get the next train home from Gare du Nord.'

It was what she'd intended to do anyway, before she'd been waylaid by Brandon Cade…and an apology she had never expected. Followed by a mind-blowing kiss she totally should have declined.

She gripped the phone, suddenly remembering the man was listening to every word. Had she mentioned Ruby's name?

'Honestly, sis, you don't have to come home. You should stay and enjoy yourself.' Milly's voice lifted with excitement. 'I saw the pics last night on the Internet. You looked fabulous, by the way. Where did you get that dress? And how the heck did you get an invite to the Durand Ball from Brandon Cade? I thought you were just interviewing him.'

'Um, I told you, it's a work assignment.' She interrupted Milly's stream of consciousness. Milly didn't know Cade was Ruby's father. No one knew. But Milly did know she had been dismissed from her job at Cade Inc when she'd got pregnant.

'Well, I hope you told him about the crappy way his HR department treated you?' Milly said, then chuckled. 'Although, to be fair, I don't think I'd have wanted to talk shop with him either. He is flipping gorgeous.'

'Right, Milly.' She sighed, her neck prickling at the thought Cade was listening to everything. 'I need to go, so I can pack and get to the station. And I should get off the phone in case the doctor is trying to call back.' She wanted to quiz Milly about her daughter's condition, but she didn't want to mention Ruby's name in front of Cade.

A sick feeling dropped into her stomach as she ended the call.

She'd created this situation with all her lies and evasions. Her decision not to tell Cade the truth five years ago. And all her bad choices in the last twelve hours.

She stuffed the phone into her bag with shaking fingers. He stood with his hands shoved into the pockets of his sweat pants, observing her with an intensity which only made the guilt and panic more acute.

'I really do have to go now,' she said.

He nodded. 'Who's Milly?'

'She's my sister, and she's not well,' she said, hating

herself even more for yet another lie. 'I need to get back to London.'

He didn't challenge the latest lie and her panic eased. She hadn't mentioned Ruby during the call, or he surely would have asked who she was too.

But, even as the relief washed over her, the nausea in her gut churned. She would have to tell Brandon Cade of his daughter's existence. Not today. Ruby's illness was a reprieve of sorts—not least from their latest insane kiss. But she would have to tell him soon.

She'd had no right to keep Ruby from him. All the reasons for her continued silence had collapsed in the last half hour like a pack of dominoes. Especially once she'd discovered he had never intentionally destroyed her career.

She hadn't wanted to accept his apology at first, hadn't even wanted to believe it was sincere. But she'd been hopelessly naïve to believe he'd even cared about her enough to go to the trouble of having her blacklisted.

What on earth had she been expecting from him all those years ago? A declaration of undying love after a half-hour hook-up in a nightclub office?

She could see now her decision never to tell him about his child had been cowardly, spiteful and wrong, on so many levels.

She still had no idea how he would react to the news. It was possible he would not want to acknowledge Ruby. He might also accuse her of using her child to extort money out of him... But telling Brandon Cade the truth wasn't really about how he would react, but what Ruby deserved.

Something she had never acknowledged.

Ruby deserved to have a father who knew about her existence. And a mother who didn't shy away from the tough choices because of her own cowardice.

Once she returned to London—and made sure her baby was okay—she was going to face up to all the consequences of that night, the way she should have faced up to them five years ago.

'You're close to your sister?' he asked with a curious expression on his face—not so much scepticism as confusion.

'Yes, very,' she said. At least that wasn't a lie.

She scooped her heels up off the carpet where she'd dropped them during their clinch. Humiliation washed over her again, as she slipped on the jewelled slippers, at the thought of how close she'd come to sleeping with him again. Of giving in to desire and letting his touch, his taste, his demands override all her priorities.

'I'll see myself out,' she said, and made a dash for the door.

He didn't try to stop her. Perhaps he had come to his senses about their latest moment of madness too.

She swallowed down the stupid lump of regret as she headed down the corridor to her own suite. The next time she saw Brandon, she needed to be in a lot better control of herself. So she could do the right thing at last for her little girl.

Twenty minutes later, though, as Lacey dashed into the hotel lobby, having showered and changed into the power suit she'd worn the day before, she discovered nothing was ever simple where Brandon Cade was concerned.

Because the man stood waiting for her.

'Brandon?' she said, her colour heightening. 'I... Hi.'

'Hello, Lacey.' Turning to the eager assistant standing behind him, he indicated the garment bag she carried. 'Take Ms Carstairs' bag to the heliport, and tell Jim we'll be ready to take off in ten minutes.'

'Wait? What?' Lacey stared, wide-eyed, as the garment bag—containing clothes which didn't even belong to her—was whisked out of her hand and the assistant headed for the lift, clearly all too eager to do his master's bidding.

Unlike Lacey.

'I have the helicopter waiting to take us back to Cade Tower in London,' he announced, cupping her elbow to direct her towards the lifts. 'My car can take you to your sister from there. Is she in hospital?'

*Us.*

The single word reverberated in Lacey's chest, disturbing her almost as much as the thought of spending several more hours in Brandon's company. Or the thought of the big reveal in their future which she was not remotely prepared for.

'No, Milly's at our flat, she's not that sick,' she sputtered as the lift shot towards the roof, and the feel of his fingers on her arm did all sorts of disturbing things to her equilibrium.

'You live with your sister?' he asked, then his lips quirked in that predatory smile which had disturbed her so much the day before. It wasn't doing much to calm her erratic heartbeat now either.

'Yes, we share a flat in Hackney,' she said, then realised she'd accidentally given him the location of her home. Her and Ruby's home, as well as Milly's. But, before she had a chance to kick herself, his smile widened.

'How gratifying,' he said.

She frowned, not sure what she was supposed to make of the smile now, because it almost looked possessive, as well as smug.

'Really, Milly's not that sick. I totally overreacted,' she added, determined to head him off at the pass—now that her worries about Ruby had been alleviated.

She had called Milly back after her shower to quiz her about Ruby's condition and her sister had confirmed the doctor had called and, after ruling out anything worrying, had told Milly to give Ruby a dose of children's painkiller.

Milly had re-checked Ruby's temperature at Lacey's request and it had already come down several degrees.

Unfortunately, her concerns about Brandon Cade were galloping off in the opposite direction with the speed of a runaway horse.

The guilt, which had been pushing at her chest ever since she'd left his suite, thundered under her breastbone as the lift glided to the hotel's rooftop heliport.

'Nevertheless, you are returning to London?' Brandon clarified.

'Yes, but…'

'Then it makes sense to take the chopper—it will be quicker.'

'But I really don't want to put you to all that trouble,' she said, getting a little frantic as all her lies threatened to choke her.

She didn't want him to meet Ruby. Not until she was ready. And she definitely was not ready now.

He let out an indulgent laugh which did not help with her growing anxiety at all.

'It's a little late for that, don't you think, Lacey?'

Ten minutes later, as the chopper lifted into the sky and Paris' Golden Triangle dropped away beneath them both, Lacey's stomach plummeted.

'I'm sorry, Mr Cade, the driver is on his way back from the Cade Estate, where you were due to arrive from Paris this afternoon.' The assistant at the London heliport glanced at his phone. 'We contacted him as soon as we heard about your change of plans, so he should arrive in approximately half an hour.'

Brandon frowned at the news.

'It's really okay, Brandon,' Lacey jumped in as they entered the lift together. 'I can catch a cab home. I really appreciate all you've done already,' she added, the relief on her face confusing him.

He wasn't buying the news her sister was okay, because he'd sensed her anxiety as she'd sat opposite him during the helicopter ride from Paris. He hadn't tried to engage her in too much conversation. Not only had it been difficult with the headsets on, but the only thing he really wanted to talk about was his plans for her... For *them*. And even he knew now wasn't the time.

He had planned to have his driver take her home to her sister, to give himself time to regroup and work out a strategy.

He wanted Lacey Carstairs to become his mistress. She was smart, engaging and prepared to stand up to him. And their sexual chemistry was off the charts. But he'd never dated anyone long term, just ask Misty. And he did not intend to embark on something he couldn't control. And at the moment his emotions where Lacey was concerned were a lot more volatile than he was accustomed to. She pushed buttons he had not even realised he had. And there was also the question of their past to handle—which was another novelty.

But, as he punched the button for the basement garage on the lift panel, he found he was reluctant to let her out of his sight.

'It's not a problem, I have several cars here,' he said, deciding not to second-guess his concern on this occasion. It made sense not to let her go until they had agreed a time to meet again. 'I'll drive you home myself.'

'Really, Brandon, there's no need,' she said again, becoming almost frantic.

The lift doors swished open on the parking garage. The garage concierge, who had been waiting for them, handed him a key fob.

'The Mercedes is fuelled and waiting in Bay Six, Mr Cade,' the man informed him.

'What's the address?' he asked Lacey, taking her elbow again to direct her to the hybrid sports car. Tension rippled through her as they reached the bay.

'Seriously, Brandon, I can catch a cab.'

The car doors unlocked automatically. He sighed as she stood stubbornly beside the vehicle.

Where was that mulish expression coming from? Because he was beginning to suspect her stubbornness was more to do with a desire to get away from him than anything to do with her sister's health issues.

She still wanted him, so why was she so determined to push him away?

'We can either have a stand-off, or you can give me the address. Your choice.'

Her brows lowered. 'Okay, fine. But I'm not going to invite you in,' she said.

He opened the passenger door and she climbed into the car. At last. 'I don't recall asking you to,' he said, strapping himself into the driver's seat.

He had no desire to meet her sister. He was not remotely interested in her domestic situation, other than the gratifying discovery she was not currently dating anyone. But then, he hadn't expected her to be. There was something strangely innocent about Lacey Carstairs even now—five years after he'd been her first lover—which convinced him she was not the kind of woman who would sleep with more than one man at a time.

And, although he did not like the thought she must have slept with several other men in the intervening years, the sweetness of the girl he'd once known which still clung to her was another big point in her favour. Why he should find it so, he had no idea, because innocence—or even the

suggestion of innocence—had never appealed to him before. But again, maybe it was simply Lacey's novelty value.

'Okay, as long as that's understood,' she said, finally
relaxing enough to reel off an address in East London. 'I
don't want Milly meeting you and putting two and two together to make five hundred,' she added, as he keyed her
address into the car's GPS.

The device estimated a drive time of thirty minutes—
past the Tower of London, through the City and then
along the leafy Georgian terraces of Islington before they
reached their destination in an up-and-coming neighbour-
hood he had never visited before. The car purred to life
and he headed out of the garage into the morning sunshine
and across London Bridge.

Thirty minutes was all the time he needed, he decided,
to steamroller over all her objections and get her back in
his bed, ASAP.

'What did you mean, your sister would put two and two
together and make five hundred?'

Lacey glanced over at the man she had been trying to
ignore ever since she had been forced to climb into his
luxury car twenty minutes ago. The question seemed innocuous. But there was nothing innocuous about Brandon
Cade. And she was just now beginning to come to terms
with that. Her abject panic, as his powerful muscle car
cruised through the empty streets of white stucco-fronted
Georgian terraces in Islington towards a date with des-
tiny, not so much.

If only she could have texted Milly, ensured she didn't
bring Ruby out of the flat to greet them when they arrived—however slight the chance—she might have been
able to stop freaking out. But how could she text her sister
when Brandon was sitting right beside her, his intense, all-
seeing gaze flicking between her and the road?

'I just meant, she'd totally assume we were dating,' she replied, knowing her sister's misconceptions about her love life were the least of her worries. 'Milly's a hopeless romantic and she saw the photos of us last night at the ball. You'd probably be subjected to a half-hour inquisition on your intentions,' she panic-babbled. 'And you've spent more than enough time and money dealing with my family issues already this morning...' The panic babble finally hit a dead end.

'Interesting. I never would have guessed you'd be quite so concerned about disrupting the schedule of an arrogant, overbearing half-wit like myself,' he mused, sending her a half-smile which made it clear he was teasing her.

She might have found his mockery disarming—might even have been able to see the funny side of the situation— if only she wasn't so hyper-aware of the height, breadth and precariousness of the house of cards she had constructed over five years...

Even though Brandon was unlikely to meet his daughter today—Ruby would surely still be sleeping?—sweat crawled down her back like the fingers of a corpse.

Brandon had been charming and thoughtful, as well as annoyingly forceful in his determination to take her home—which only made the lies she'd told him, and last night's booty call, all the more damning.

'I'm sorry I called you that,' she said, her contrition complete. Maybe he had deserved it once, but did he really deserve it now? Given all the things she'd kept from him? 'I apologise.'

'Don't apologise,' he said, surprising her again. 'I'm sure my business rivals will attest to the fact I'm not a halfwit, but overbearing and arrogant probably aren't far off the mark. I blame my over-privileged and entitled upbringing myself,' he said with a harsh laugh, which made her wonder exactly how privileged his upbringing had really been.

She knew, because she'd read everything she could about him once upon a time, that he had grown up in the sole care of his father after his parents' acrimonious divorce when he'd been only a few months old. He had never wanted for anything, materially speaking, his father having become a media baron long before Brandon—his only child—had been born. But she had often wondered what it must have been like growing up in the care of paid caregivers and in a string of exclusive boarding schools with no mother, no siblings and a father who must have been absent a lot of the time.

'That's very reasonable of you,' she managed, disturbed all over again by how accommodating he was being.

'I thought so,' he said. She huffed out a strained laugh, realising, however accommodating Brandon was, he would always want the last word.

The car drove past the park where she often took Ruby to play at the weekend. And the guilt came barrelling back.

Then he took another turn onto the street where she lived with their child.

'Which one is yours?' he asked as the GPS announced they had reached their destination.

She pointed at the Victorian terrace where her flat was situated, glad to see no small face at the window.

*Ruby is still in bed. Thank God.*

But as he braked and she unhooked her seatbelt, frantic to see her daughter and get away from the emotions threatening to overwhelm her, his warm hand landed on her knee.

'I want to see you again, Lacey. And soon,' he declared.

'What?' she yelped, the purpose in his gaze almost as terrifying as the blaze of heat at her core. And the elated leap in her heartrate.

'Come on, you can't be that surprised?' he said, the quirk of his lips suggesting he found her shock amusing. 'Given the intensity of our connection last night?' His land lifted off her knee to stroke her cheek, the rush of sensation as devastating as it was shocking. 'And the way we both went off like firecrackers five years ago?'

*Just get out of the car, Lace. You have to get out of the car.*

But somehow the instruction wouldn't compute. Her emotions were in turmoil again—her guilt and remorse as volatile as the need and the strange, idiotic joy. Because he wanted her.

'You excite me, Lacey, in a way no woman has for far too long,' he said, cupping her chin to lift her face. 'This kind of sexual chemistry is extremely rare.' She blinked, aware of the pheromones firing through her system alongside the panic. And that desperate, bone-sapping need to have him kiss her.

Almost as if he'd sensed her need, her yearning, his mouth took hers in a punishing, possessive kiss. She responded—because of course she did. She couldn't seem to resist him.

He tore his mouth free. 'Once you have satisfied yourself your sister is well, we should speak. Soon. How about I call you tonight?'

She couldn't think. Couldn't respond. Her lips were still buzzing from his kiss. Her brain whirring in about a thousand different directions. The yearning in his eyes was almost as devastating as the responding yearning in her heart.

But, before she could come up with a coherent answer, his gaze shifted to something behind her. 'Is that your sister?' he asked. 'You didn't tell me she had a child.'

She shifted round to see Milly walking down the steps

of the house towards them with Ruby in her arms, bouncing up and down.

Every molecule of blood drained from her head to slam into her heart as she scrambled out of the car.

*No. No. No. Please no. Not now. Not like this.*

As Milly and Ruby approached her, Milly's words seemed to come from a million miles away.

'Ruby wanted to come out and greet you. Her temp's back to normal and she's been waiting for you.' Her sister's gaze shifted to the muscle car parked at the kerb. 'Oh. My. God.' She whispered. 'That's him, isn't it? He brought you home. That's so romantic.' She grinned. Lacey heard a car door slam and footsteps—firm, inexorable—hitting the pavement behind her.

She stood frozen, her whole body going hot and cold and then hot again, the panic reaching fever pitch. The guilt choked her. Her daughter's arms lifted towards her, but it was as if Lacey were in the midst of a dream. A terrible anxiety dream, each awful aspect of which was unfolding in agonising slow motion.

Her daughter's smile spread over her face, her mouth forming the first word she had ever learned to say as Lacey was wrenched out of the dream and plunged into cold, hard reality.

'Mummy! Mummy! Mummy! You're home.'

# CHAPTER SIX

*THE CHILD IS LACEY'S?*

Brandon stared in disbelief as the woman he had just spent an incendiary night with, the woman he had been determined to make his mistress, scooped the round-faced little girl out of her sister's arms.

*Why didn't she tell me she has a child?*

Shock was swiftly followed by suspicion and a wary, strangely emotional, tension in his gut as he watched the child sling her arms around Lacey's neck… Her mother's neck… And begin to chatter as if her life depended on it.

Lacey, though, remained tense, her smile strained even as she greeted her daughter with effusive praise.

He couldn't move as he struggled to process this unprecedented new reality. But then all the opportunities she'd had over the last twenty-four hours to inform him she had a child occurred to him. Suspicion writhed in his gut. Something wasn't right here, he knew that much, but he could not seem to grasp what. And he hated that.

But then the little girl's babbling stopped and her bright gaze landed on him.

'Who is that man, Mummy? Is he your friend?' she asked.

Brandon tensed at the innocent question, feeling oddly exposed but not sure why. Lacey glanced over her shoulder again, her reluctance to introduce him to her daughter abundantly clear.

Confused and still stunned by this development, Brandon added irritation to the mix.

She should have told him she was a mother, but he didn't see how that changed anything. He still wanted her. Anything could be negotiated, if he was willing to be flexible, and it surprised him—and annoyed him a little—to realise that, to have her, he could be flexible even about this. If this responsibility was why she had been so surprised at his offer—perhaps believing he wouldn't have wanted her if he'd known—he could at least disabuse her of that fact.

So, as she hesitated, he stepped forward. 'Yes, I'm a friend of your mother's,' he said to the girl. 'My name is Brandon Cade,' he added, not really sure how one addressed a child.

The child giggled. 'Hello, my name's Ruby,' she said with a boldness which reminded him of her mother. As she grinned, the emerald green of her eyes sparkled with delight and a dimple appeared in her left cheek.

Something odd struck him right in the solar plexus. A strange sense of *déjà vu*. Of familiarity. Almost as if he'd seen this child before.

He shook his head slightly, trying to shake the disorientating feeling loose.

'Hi, I'm Milly Devlin, Lacey's sister. It's so nice to meet you at last,' the other woman said, holding out her hand.

Brandon shook it, noting the similarities between the two women. And the fact her sister looked perfectly okay. 'Hello, I'm glad to see you are fully recovered,' he said, the suspicion turning into a hole in his gut. A large black hole. Especially when the sister sent him a puzzled look.

'Oh, it wasn't me who was ill, it was Rubes,' she offered.

She stroked a hand down her niece's hair. 'But you're all better now, aren't you?'

'But I can't go to school today, can I, Mummy? Please, Mummy, I want to stay home with you and Milly,' the little girl said, the grin disappearing as she grasped Lacey's cheeks and sent her mother a winsome, pleading look that would have persuaded a stone.

'Yes, you can stay home today, Rubes.' She glanced at Brandon at last. And he spotted the shadow of guilt in her eyes. 'We should go inside. Thanks so much for driving me home, Brandon.'

She headed into the house with her daughter before he could reply. Her sister waved goodbye and followed.

But as he stood there on the pavement, watching the little girl and her mother disappear, he couldn't seem to move, couldn't seem to think.

The boa constrictor in his gut coiled and clenched into a tight knot. At last he forced himself to return to his car, but as he drove away from the house on the leafy lane the knot swelled and twisted.

Why had Lacey lied about her sister's health? About the existence of her daughter?

And then a new question struck him. And his breath seized.

Ruby went to school. Exactly how old was the little girl?

He stared blankly at the road ahead. After stopping at some traffic lights, he engaged the car's hands-free phone and tapped through to his executive assistant, his fingers trembling.

'Daryl, Lacey Carstairs has a daughter. I want you to find out when the child was born, and if there's a father listed on the birth certificate.'

But as he signed off, and continued to drive back towards the City, it felt as if he were driving into a fog. Because he could already feel the bomb, which Lacey had

armed with her silence, about to explode right in the middle of his carefully ordered life.

'What is going on between you and the extremely fit media
mogul?' Milly's gaze narrowed on Lacey's face.

'Nothing,' Lacey lied, busy filling a saucepan with
water so she could prepare lunch. She'd already had an
inquisition from her editor, who had allowed her to spend
the day at home to write the piece on the Durand Ball. But
what on earth could she write that was fit to print?

Not meeting Milly's gaze was a mistake. She'd never
been good at lying to her sister.

'She has his eyes, you know,' Milly said softly.

Lacey spun round, splashing water over her wrist.
'What?' she said, but she could already see the game was
up. Because Milly was looking at her with a devastating
mix of sympathy and concern.

'No wonder you were so nervous about going to interview him,' Milly mused. 'I thought it was because it
was such a big opportunity for you. And, well, he's him,'
she added as Lacey's anxiety shot back towards the danger zone—a level it had been hovering around ever since
Brandon Cade had introduced himself to his own daughter
half an hour ago, and that puzzled expression had crossed
his face as he'd got a good look at Ruby.

Lacey's stomach plummeted back to her toes and kept
on going.

Milly turned off the tap, the water having overflowed
the saucepan. She lifted the pan out of Lacey's numb fingers and placed it on the sideboard.

'He's Ruby's dad, isn't he?' she said.

The question reverberated in Lacey's soul.

And suddenly she couldn't hold the lie in any longer.
Not from her sister, not even from herself. And so she
nodded.

Milly swore softly. 'And I'm taking it he doesn't know?'

Lacey shook her head, the sting of tears hurting her eyes. Tears of self-pity which she had no right to shed. 'I think he probably does now. Or he will figure it out,' she said, then let the breath out which had been clogged in her lungs for hours.

She had absolutely no idea how long it would take Brandon to figure out the truth. Or what he was likely to do with the knowledge. But one thing she did know, he would not go easy on her.

She had blindsided him. Taken something from him she had no right to take. Whether he wanted to be a father or not, he was one. And he had been one for four years and three months.

She blinked, then scrubbed away the errant tear that trickled down her cheek. What was worse, she wasn't sure any more she deserved to have him go easy on her.

'Did something happen between you two last night too?' Milly asked.

Lacey's gaze darted to Milly's, her cheeks exploding with heat.

'I thought he looked rather possessive when he came striding out of that amazing car,' Milly murmured.

Lacey groaned. When exactly had she become so transparent?

'I'm so sorry I brought Ruby out with me,' Milly said, clearly picking up on Lacey's panic and distress.

'Don't be,' Lacey said, finally looking her sister square in the eye. 'You didn't do anything wrong.' And neither had Brandon Cade. Not yet, anyway. 'I should have told him about Ruby yesterday.' She swore under her breath, a word she hadn't used in years. 'The truth is, I should have told him about her when she was born.'

'Why should you have done that?' Milly said forcefully, always willing to offer support, even when Lacey knew she didn't deserve it. 'Ruby is happy and healthy. She has a good home and we love her. That's no small feat, considering how little support we got from Dad after Mum died.'

'Ruby also doesn't have a father,' Lacey said. 'And that's on me.'

'Well, maybe now she does,' Milly offered, always determined to look on the bright side. 'And the guy's a drop-dead gorgeous gazillionaire who appears to still be into you. So, that has to be good for something.'

'Except I don't think he's going to be into me any more,' Lacey said, fairly sure it would be better if he wasn't, because this situation was already catastrophic enough without factoring in the sexual chemistry, which made her do stupid things. 'And I have no idea how he's going to react.' Just thinking about all the things he might do was making her stomach hurt. 'What if he tries to take Ruby from me?'

'He won't,' Milly said with a cast-iron confidence Lacey knew was at best optimistic, and at worst totally misplaced.

Brandon Cade was a powerful man, and she knew he also had the ability to be incredibly ruthless.

If only she'd thought of that last night, when she had fallen to pieces in his arms for the second time in her life.

'But perhaps you should tell him the truth now, instead of waiting for him to find out,' Milly said.

Lacey nodded. Her sister was right. How could she fight for Ruby's best interests if she didn't even have the guts to face the man who had fathered her? She had to get out ahead of this situation now and stop hiding.

But as Milly took over lunch duties, and Lacey walked into the flat's small hallway to call Brandon's assistant—because she didn't even have his private number—her phone dinged.

She read the email from Daryl Wilson and the fear, which she had hoped finally to get a handle on, returned full-force.

Ms Carstairs, I have attached the solicitor's letter which I am sending via courier today to demand a DNA test of your minor child, Ruby Devlin Carstairs—who Mr Cade has reason to believe may be his biological daughter. Once the DNA test is completed, Mr Cade's legal team will arrange a meeting to discuss the results of the test and how their client intends to proceed in this matter. Feel free to contact me if you have any questions.

Lacey pressed a hand to her mouth, her fingers shaking as she scanned the contents of the letter Brandon's assistant had attached. Like the email, it was cold, clinical, demanding and totally devoid of feeling, almost as if each carefully chosen syllable had been steeped in Brandon's anger.

The musical jingle from Ruby's cartoon started to play in the next room, the notes light and airy and innocent, accompanied by the joyous, uncomplicated sound of her little girl's laughter... And in direct contrast to the suffocating feeling dragging at Lacey's insides.

She'd taken too long, been too much of a coward, and now her little girl could well be forced to pay the price.

# CHAPTER SEVEN

'MR CADE, MS CARSTAIRS has arrived, are you ready for her?' Daryl asked, peering around the office door as he addressed Brandon and the four solicitors who he had been discussing next steps with for two hours.

Brandon glared at his assistant.

*No, I'll never be ready for this.*

The words he wanted to speak echoed in his skull, alongside the anger that had been building steadily for the last three days, ever since he'd laid eyes on Ruby Devlin Carstairs. The anger that had surged yesterday when he had read the DNA test report he'd had commissioned once Daryl had got back to him with the details of the child's birth certificate.

Lacey's child had been born thirty-eight weeks and three days after he had made wild, passionate love to her in the manager's office of a Soho nightclub. When she had been a virgin, and the condom he had worn had split.

*Dammit. Not just Lacey's child. My child.*

The father had been unlisted on the birth certificate.

*Just one more injustice to add to all the others.*

He raked his fingers over his scalp. And took a deep breath, trying to steady the emotions which had been tying his guts into knots ever since discovering there was a ninety-nine-point-eight percent probability he was Ruby

Carstairs' biological father. Not that he'd really needed the confirmation.

Because he'd known somehow she was his as soon as he'd looked into her eyes and seen the same dark green as his own.

Lacey had lied to him for five years. And had made him a worse man than his father.

He had never planned to have children. Never even contemplated it. For the simple reason he was fairly sure he did not have the sensibilities to nurture or protect a child. But it was way too late to worry about that now.

He had to deal with what was, not what should have been.

Ruby Devlin Carstairs was a part of him. And, however angry he was with her mother for keeping her existence from him—however angry he was with himself, for not checking on Lacey after that long-ago encounter—he could not abandon the child…the way his own mother had abandoned him.

How the hell he formed a relationship with this child, he had no idea. He knew absolutely nothing about children. But one thing was certain, her mother would no longer be calling the shots.

'Sure, show her in,' he said, then stalked round to stand behind his desk and stare out at the morning skyline.

He forced himself to keep breathing, to stop his temper from exploding. The prickle of awareness—dammit, of arousal—rushing over his skin only made his control shakier as he turned to watch her enter the room.

She wore a similar outfit to the one she'd worn less than a week ago. In his office. When he hadn't known who she was. And she *had* known he was the father of her child. Demure, tempting, tormenting. But now the glimpse of cleavage, the heightened colour on her face and the shadows in her eyes only made the fury worse—because arousal exploded too.

He still wanted her. Even though she had deceived him for five years.

John Marrow, the head of his legal team, got the meeting started then launched into the first order of business.

'As you know, Ms Carstairs, the DNA test results we received yesterday afternoon confirm Mr Cade, our client, is the biological father of your daughter Ruby Devlin Carstairs.'

'Yes.' Her soft acknowledgement made his shoulders tighten, the anger gripping his insides. 'I know.'

The fury exploded, but right beneath it were so many other emotions he couldn't control and didn't want to name.

He braced himself against the wave of fury and glared at her.

'How long?' he snarled, the other people in the room fading from his consciousness, because all he could see was her.

'Mr Cade, I'm not sure that…' Marrow began.

'How long have you known she was mine?' he demanded, ignoring the solicitor's interruption, focussed only on Lacey.

She flinched, but her gaze remained direct, her tone flat. 'As soon as I discovered I was pregnant.'

'You bitch,' he snapped.

Marrow and his team stiffened in unison, but Lacey didn't flinch again, she simply stared back, as if she was absorbing his anger, his anguish. Which only made the emotions harder to control, the temper searing his insides now like a wildfire threatening to burn through the last of his composure.

'What gave you the right to keep my child's existence from me?'

'Mr Cade, I really don't think…' Marrow began again.

'Shut up and leave,' Brandon said, casting a searing glance at the man and his team. 'I want to speak to her alone.'

The rest of the legal team immediately packed up their briefcases, but Marrow hesitated. 'Mr Cade, you're not yourself. I don't think…'

'It's okay, Mr Marrow,' Lacey said, her gaze still locked on his, still calm, still stoic, but for the quivers running through her body. 'He won't hurt me.'

'If you're sure, Ms Carstairs?' Marrow said, but as soon as Lacey nodded the solicitor was out the door in ten seconds flat.

Brandon might have admired her courage, except he was still so angry with her, he could hardly see straight.

He stalked around the desk, bearing down on her, wanting to see her flinch, wanting her to see how angry he was. 'How do you know I won't hurt you?'

'Because you already did, and I survived,' she said, standing up, refusing to be cowed, the storm in her eyes matching the storm raging in his heart.

He had vowed, a long time ago, he would never give another woman the power to hurt him the way the mother he'd only met once had hurt him. But somehow this woman had slipped under his radar.

Right from the first moment he'd met her, she'd made him feel more, want more. And now here he was, being forced to pay the price for those moments of weakness. The fact he still wanted her only added insult to that madness.

'How did *I* hurt *you*?' He spat the question at her. But, instead of getting the litany of pathetic excuses for her deception he'd been expecting, she drew in a heavy breath. And broke eye contact.

'It doesn't matter,' she said. 'I'm not here to make excuses for what I did. I'm here to apologise and to make amends. If that's possible.' He didn't believe the contrite act—why the hell should he?—but, before he could formulate a suitably scathing response, her gaze returned to his. 'You can punish me all you want, but one thing I won't let you do is punish Ruby. None of this is her fault.'

'True, I think we can both agree it's your fault,' he shot back. But, instead of arguing and giving him the satisfaction of slapping her down *again*, the shadows in her eyes intensified.

She nodded. But her easy acceptance only annoyed him more. Where did she get off, playing the martyr?

He grasped her arm, tugged her towards him, the sizzle of heat electrifying. And not in a good way.

'So you admit, you deserve to be punished?' he said, just to be clear. He was not sure where the hell he was going with this, but knew he needed to establish control.

She tugged her arm free and rubbed her bicep, her eyes flaring with the fierce passion he had always found so irresistible.

By now he ought to find it repellent. Unfortunately, nothing could be further from the truth.

'I didn't say that,' she said. 'But, if retribution is what you require, I can live with it. Just please don't hurt my daughter.'

He blinked and stepped back, the look of genuine fear on her face like a bucket of ice thrown over the wildfire burning in his stomach.

He swore under his breath, then marched back towards the window to stare out at the host of London landmarks looking proud and indomitable in the sunshine. The Victorian majesty of Tower Bridge in the distance, the Baroque splendour of St Paul's Cathedral's dome nestled among the harsh modern geometric shapes of newer developments on the opposite bank of the river... Several agonising seconds passed as he struggled to regain the cast-iron control—which he'd just lost so comprehensively.

What was happening to him? He had intended to be ruthless, determined and, most of all, composed. Instead of which he'd behaved like a petulant bully. He was angry with her, and he had every right to be, but he had never intended to make her fear for the child.

'I think you mean *our* child, don't you?' he managed at last. Resentment still edged his tone, but underneath he sensed the reason for his spectacular loss of control.

*Panic.*

For the first time in his life, he had no strategy, no plan. He had no idea how to be a father, or if he even wanted to be one. And whatever he decided he knew he would need her help—which only made this situation more untenable.

He had never relied on anyone, had never trusted anyone since he'd been a little boy, and he'd learned not to trust.

And now he would have to rely on a woman who had lied to him for five years—whose effect on him he still had no damn control over—to show him how to be a parent to a child he did not know. And did not know how to get to know.

*Terrific.*

Lacey breathed through the anxiety as the hard line of Brandon's shoulders softened just a little.

She drew in a careful breath, easing the painful vice around her ribs which had been tightening ever since she'd received the text from his assistant three days ago.

She'd been scared of what would happen at this meeting, what he might demand, and the team of lawyers hadn't exactly put her at ease. She'd assumed he would be cold, clinical, frighteningly controlled. His visible fury, his loss of control, had shocked her to her core.

'Yes, our child,' she said, trying desperately to form some kind of connection with him. To reach out and soothe.

Stupid, really, that she should feel any sympathy for

him. He was her enemy now in a lot of ways, and an extremely formidable enemy at that. It was obvious he was furious with her, and she'd been going over and over in her head all the possible ways he could make her pay for her five years of silence.

But, despite her fear, there was something about his volatile response which felt familiar, almost reassuring in a weird way. Because it reminded her of her own panic—at the enormity of the task now facing her—when the two clear red lines had appeared on the pregnancy test kit.

Somehow Brandon's temper—his tenuous hold on his emotions—felt better than the clinical indifference of his solicitor's letter and the communications she'd had since about Ruby, all filtered through his assistant. She'd been terrified Ruby's existence would mean nothing to him—other than a means to punish her for defying him—but that, at least, did not seem to be the case.

He huffed and shoved his hands into his trouser pockets, still staring at the staggering view of the London skyline, his back turned to her.

'It's not my intention to hurt her,' he said, his tone clipped and still edged with bitterness, but she could hear the weariness too.

Was it possible he had struggled as much as she once had with the thought of becoming a parent?

*Of course it is.*

The guilt she'd tried to ignore dropped back into her stomach like a stone.

*And he hasn't had eight months to prepare, the way you did. Because you denied him that chance.*

'It was wrong of me to keep her a secret from you,' she said again. Seeing his back muscles tense, she had to force herself to continue. 'I persuaded myself it was in her best interests. Once I'd decided to have her, I convinced myself you wouldn't want her, wouldn't even want me to have her, that you'd put pressure on me not to.'

He swung round, his brows flattening. 'You thought I'd force you to have an abortion?' he said. 'On what evidence, for God's sake?'

'From what you said *that* night… After…after we made her…' She stuttered to a stop, the fierce expression making her feel like that naïve intern again.

'What did I say?' he asked.

'You said it shouldn't have happened. That the condom had split, and if there were consequences to contact your office so you could deal with it.' She repeated his words almost verbatim, because she'd never forgotten them. They had been etched on her memory like a wound.

He pressed his lips together—as if he doubted her recollection. It seemed what he'd said to her that night had not been etched on *his* memory. But then he leaned back against his desk, crossed his arms over his chest and dropped his searing gaze from her face. He swore softly. Uncrossing his arms, he shoved his hands back into his pockets, his gaze locking on hers again.

'I don't remember saying that, but I wouldn't be surprised if I did. I was still reeling from the shock of discovery you were a virgin and that I had taken you with such…urgency.'

She nodded, the grudging concession making her eyes sting—because it gave her some validation, for the girl she'd been. She had been young and foolish that night, but she hadn't been wrong about the intensity of their connection.

The steely light in his eyes hardened. 'Although, none of that explains why you didn't tell me about the child when you came to interview me, or while we were at the ball or…' His gaze drifted down, making her aware of all the erogenous zones he had exploited a week ago. 'Before we slept together a second time. You had a ton of opportunities, and you didn't take them. Why?'

The vice around her ribs winched tight again. And it was her turn to fold her arms around her waist, trying to protect herself once again from that searing gaze.

'I should have said something. You're right,' she said, hoping he wouldn't take it any further.

'You'll have to do better than that, Lacey.'

Heat exploded in her cheeks, matched by the fierce heat lighting his gaze as he stepped closer. She inched back a step, only to have her legs hit the chair. She couldn't retreat any further.

'I guess I got distracted,' she managed.

'Still not good enough,' he said, pulling his hand out of his pocket. The purpose in his gaze became all-consuming as his thumb skimmed down her burning cheek.

Her breath hitched painfully, her senses going haywire as the light touch inched down to sweep across her collarbone and glide over the upper swell of her breast. But, unlike four nights ago, this time she found the strength to brush his hand away, no matter how much she still yearned for his touch. 'Don't touch me, Brandon, it doesn't help.'

But he only laughed, the gruff chuckle as bitter as it was commanding. 'Really?' he murmured. 'Your body says otherwise.'

'So what?' she said, determined to be the woman she'd become over the last five years—strong, smart, brave—instead of that foolish girl again.

This situation was more than complicated, and combustible enough without them stoking the madness. And succumbing to it again would only leave her more vulnerable. More at his mercy.

The sharp knock at the door had him finally breaking eye contact.

He swore and raked his fingers through his hair as

Lacey wrapped her arms tightly around her midriff to hold in the throbbing ache, the devastating yearning.

*Don't let him intimidate you or bring that girl out of hiding. Not again.*

She sat, her knees turning to water as he stalked back behind his desk to sit down too.

'Mr Cade, there's been a development,' his assistant said as he rushed into the room.

'What development?' Brandon asked, and Daryl—usually so composed and professional—flushed, then handed him a smartphone.

'I just got this message from a reliable source at Drystar Media Group,' he said, mentioning a publishing company that Lacey knew owned a host of tabloid titles globally.

Brandon's expression tensed, his jaw hardening as Daryl continued. 'Apparently, they're going to run the story tomorrow across all their US titles.'

'How the hell did they get this information?' The suppressed rage in Brandon's voice made Lacey stiffen.

'I should go,' Lacey said, standing up, suddenly desperate to escape.

But, before she could move, Brandon's gaze flicked to her. 'Stay put,' he commanded in a strident tone which instantly put her back up. But then his gaze softened slightly. 'This concerns you too.'

*What? How?*

'We don't know. It may have been a leak at the DNA test facility,' Daryl supplied.

She collapsed back into the chair.

Drystar knew about Ruby? And they were going to publish a story about her child? The horrifying implications hit her.

She'd been concerned about how their lives would change now Brandon knew of his daughter's existence, but this...*this* could be so much worse. To have the details of her life, the circumstances of her child's birth, splashed all over the celebrity press, dissected and pawed over by every media outlet from here to Timbuktu...

'The angle they are going with is you as a deadbeat billionaire dad,' Daryl continued in a pragmatic tone. 'Who got a nineteen-year-old employee pregnant then fired her and refused to acknowledge her, let alone support his child.'

'But that's not true!' Lacey gasped.

Neither Brandon nor Daryl seemed to hear her.

'What else?' Brandon said, not even glancing her way.

'I spoke to Fiona in PR and Dan on the NA acquisitions team,' Daryl added. 'They both say it will sink the Atlanta deal, unless we get out ahead of it with an alternative narrative.'

Brandon nodded.

She could see his mind working, but had no idea what he was thinking as his gaze fixed back on her burning face.

'Why don't we just tell them the truth?' she offered. 'I can tell them you didn't know Ruby existed until three days ago.'

But he barely acknowledged her suggestion, instead turning to Daryl again. 'Get Marrow and the rest of the legal team back in here. And tell them we're going with Plan B.'

Lacey shifted in her chair, to give herself time to get her rampaging heartbeat under control as Daryl left the room. But, when she looked at Brandon, his expression had the panic clawing at her chest again like a wild dog. Because the volatile emotions on his face when she had first arrived, even the passion of moments ago, had disappeared, to be replaced with the same distant, determined and utterly ruthless expression which had devastated her five years ago.

'What's Plan B?' she managed, even though she suddenly felt as insecure and powerless as she had in that nightclub office.

The emerald fire in his eyes was shockingly explicit, but his tone was laced with ice. 'We get married.'

# CHAPTER EIGHT

'YOU'RE NOT... YOU'RE not serious?' Lacey stammered, not sure she'd heard Brandon correctly as Daryl trooped back into the room with the legal team.

But, as the group took their seats, the only person she could focus on was Brandon, his calm expression suggesting he had just supplied a perfectly reasonable solution to their problem instead of something completely insane.

Her breathing accelerated, alongside her panicked heartbeat, though the meeting proceeded as if she were a ghost, invisible to everyone but herself.

Brandon's gaze raked over her, then landed on the head of his legal team. He began firing out orders as if he were the captain of a ship about to go to war.

Marrow, his team and Daryl jotted down the directives—everything from drafting a prenup to how to divide his property portfolio—on their phones and laptops.

'But I haven't agreed to marry you...!' Lacey at last managed to butt into the conversation.

What was going on? Because she felt as if she were on a rollercoaster which was careering out of control, a rollercoaster she'd never even agreed to ride...

But Brandon and the rest of the room ignored her. *Again*.

'Daryl, talk to Claire in finance.' Brandon turned to his assistant. 'Tell her to arrange a monthly allowance of five times Ms Carstairs' current salary. She can't work as a celebrity journalist for the foreseeable future. And tell her to arrange child support payments to cover all my daughter's expenses. We can set up trusts, college funds, et cetera at a later date. And I want her officially named as my heir. Ms Carstairs and my child can relocate to the Cade estate in Wiltshire until the wedding.'

Lacey's mind was reeling, her panic so huge now it was beginning to choke her, when Brandon added, 'I want to announce the engagement in a press release by 8:00 a.m. tomorrow morning UK time—so we can pre-empt the headlines in the US. Everyone got that?'

They all nodded, except Lacey, who had rollercoastered her way into an alternative universe. Was she imagining this?

She had no intention of marrying Brandon Cade, or giving up her job, or relocating to Wiltshire, for that matter. But then, he still hadn't actually asked her to do any of those things.

'Okay, thanks, now get moving—we have a lot to do,' he announced.

With that, they all filed back out of the room.

The door closed behind them, the muted thud drowned out by the frantic beat of Lacey's pulse as she stared, incredulously, at Brandon.

He rose and walked round the desk to stand in front of her.

She forced herself to stand too, despite the liquid in her knees. She pressed her arms to her sides and squeezed trembling fingers into tight fists until her knuckles whitened.

'Aren't you forgetting something fairly important?' she said at last, feeling utterly overwhelmed but determined not to show it.

One thing she had always known—if you let Brandon Cade see a weakness, he would exploit it.

He leaned against his desk and folded his arms across his chest. The arrogant half-smile she was starting to hate played on his lips—but there was no amusement in his eyes. 'And what would that be?'

'I haven't agreed to marry you. In fact, you haven't even asked me,' she said, finally grabbing hold of the righteous indignation which was her only defence against his unbelievable arrogance.

'I haven't asked you because this isn't a choice, for either one of us,' he said, the dimple disappearing as well as the half-smile—somehow the sober, serious expression was even more arrogant. 'Marriage is our only option.'

'For you, maybe,' she shot back, her temper finally arriving full force. 'I realise the angle Drystar are planning to run with on this is not going to be good for your image or your US deal. And I will do everything I can to mitigate that, by stating clearly and unequivocally you didn't know of Ruby's existence until three days ago.'

It would be a public humiliation, and she had no doubt at all there would be little or no sympathy for her behaviour from the keyboard warriors on social media. But maybe that was the punishment she deserved for allowing her own hurt and cowardice to get in the way of doing the right thing, not just five years ago but a week ago too.

'I realise this is my fault,' she continued. 'But I'm not about to give up a job I love, or uproot me and Ruby and Milly to move to Wiltshire, and become your convenient bride just so you can—'

'You little fool.' He straightened as the mask of arrogance dropped to be replaced by barely contained fury. 'Do you really think this is about saving the Atlanta deal?'

'Yes, I do,' she said boldly.

'Do you have any idea what your life and our daughter's life—even your sister's life, for that matter—is going to be like when this story breaks tomorrow?'

She stared at him. 'I'm sure it will be a little fraught for a while but—'

'*Fraught?*' he shouted, his tone laced with bitterness as well as fury. 'All three of you will become the epicentre of a media storm. A storm I've been in the eye of my entire life. And my child will be in the eye of that storm too. You think the fact she's still a toddler will make any difference? It won't. And I refuse to let that happen. She needs and deserves my protection. And that is exactly what she will get.'

'I see…' She tried to get her mind into gear. To take on board what he was saying, and to deal with the sudden leap in her heart rate at the evidence he cared about their daughter enough to protect her.

Why had she doubted that so readily?

'I can arrange for me and Ruby and Milly to stay with friends if we need to, but I can't marry you.'

She didn't want to be dependent on Brandon. But there were so many other reasons why marriage would be a bad idea. They didn't know each other… She wasn't even sure they liked each other that much. And what about Ruby? Yes, she deserved to know her father, and vice versa. But they didn't need to get married for that to happen. And, anyway, how would a marriage between them even work? Was he talking about a marriage of convenience? To stem the media coverage? Or something more *involved*…?

She swallowed heavily, her cheeks igniting again.

Because underneath all her other misgivings was the biggest one of all. What if that lonely, anxious, naïve girl came out of hiding again? The one who had been so desperate for his approval she had convinced herself she loved him after only one night, and been so devastated by his rejection? She couldn't be that girl again, not even a little bit. But she wasn't sure she could be entirely rational where Brandon Cade was concerned…

'The story will surely die down in a few weeks,' she tried again, suddenly desperate to avert the marriage. Because it felt like too much. Just like Brandon Cade had always been too much.

'If you absolutely insist, we could announce our engagement,' she added, trying to find some middle ground—after all, this situation was not Brandon's fault, and she wanted to be fair to him, or as fair as she could be. But she refused to be railroaded. 'To deflect attention and supply a new narrative for the press until it all blows over? And then we can quietly announce the engagement's off six months from now.'

'That's not going to work for me,' Brandon replied, knowing it was God's honest truth. He *wanted* this marriage, and not just for all the perfectly valid reasons he had stated.

The desire to have Lacey where he wanted her—in his home, as his wife—was about more than just payback. It was also about more than his ferocious determination to protect his daughter from the things he had suffered when his mother had abandoned him to a man who had paraded him in front of the world's media as his heir...

And it didn't have much at all to do with his desire to safeguard the Atlanta deal. It wasn't even solely down to the fierce need which pulsed through his veins every time he got within ten feet of this woman. A need he had never experienced with any other woman. But he'd be damned if he'd acknowledge any of those wayward emotions in front of Lacey. Because it would give her too much power, and she already had more power over him than he had ever allowed any woman.

'Why not?' Lacey asked, her eyes wide with confusion now.

His temper snapped. 'Because she is my child and I want full parental rights,' he said. Marrow had outlined earlier that marriage, as well as establishing paternity, would be the best way for him to gain full parental rights for his child. Surely that fact was more than enough to explain his sudden fierce determination to marry Lacey Carstairs…? 'So you'll never be able to stop me from having a relationship with her again.'

She flinched. 'But you can still have a relationship with Ruby—'

'Not good enough,' he cut her off. 'Why should I trust you to keep up your end of that bargain?'

'Because I'm her mother…' she began. 'And I want what's best for her. I know I made a mistake not telling you about her, but—'

'So what if you're her mother? That guarantees nothing,' he cut in again, the bitter laugh disguising the hollow pain in his chest. He hated her in that moment, for bringing that old vulnerability back. The flash of anger—and agony—was so intense, he blurted out the truth. 'My own mother sold me to my father when I was three months old as part of her ten-million-pound divorce settlement. And then she turned up again when I was seventeen, after he died, to ask for more money. Because apparently she'd spent it all,' he snarled. 'A mother's desire to do the right thing for her child can be bartered to the highest bidder, just like everything else.'

'But that's…hideous.' The utter shock on Lacey's face had him realising he'd said too much.

Far too much.

What the hell was wrong with him? He'd exposed himself. Had told her something he'd never revealed to anyone, other than a few of his employees—who were legally bound to keep his secrets. Unlike Lacey.

'I'm…so sorry,' she continued, the compassion darkening her eyes only making him feel more exposed, and more angry—with himself now, as much as her. 'Your mother sounds like no kind of mother at all.'

He sucked in a staggered breath and yanked himself viciously back from the edge.

Damn it, he didn't need or want her sympathy. Nor did he need her understanding. Why had he even bothered to explain himself? He didn't even owe her that much.

'Don't worry, I got over it a long time ago,' he said, burying the old trauma deep again so he could forget about it. His mother had no power to hurt him any more and she hadn't for a long time.

He had exorcised Elise Cade from his life when she had turned up unexpectedly at the reading of his father's will. He'd seen through her simpering regrets and her desire to 'form a relationship' with him almost instantly... But he was still furious that, for one giddy, idiotic moment, he had believed she might genuinely care for him. He could still feel that sudden leap in his heartrate when she'd introduced herself—and thrown her arms around his neck—the resentment he should have felt momentarily blindsided by that idiotic spurt of hope, of emotion.

Of course, she'd jettisoned her maternal act as soon as he'd tested her, and had been all too eager to grasp the large sum of money he'd offered her to leave him alone and never contact him again. But it had taken considerably longer to destroy that hollow pain all over again—that feeling of inadequacy, of desperation, which had haunted him as a child. And made him want things he shouldn't need.

He stared at Lacey now, wishing he could take the stupid revelation back, especially when she spoke again.

'I can't marry you, Brandon, just because you don't trust me. I understand why you don't trust me. But you have to believe me when I tell you I'm willing to do everything in my power to help you form a relationship with your daughter, and make up for the terrible mistake I made not telling you about her existence much, much sooner.'

*Yeah, right.*

He could hear the regret in her voice, and the guilt. But he could also hear that damn compassion. Maybe she really believed what she was telling him. But it wasn't enough. He refused to be at her mercy, or anyone else's, when it came to claiming his child. Marriage was the only thing that would give him the power he needed, not just as Ruby's father, but also to explore whatever the heck it was about this woman that he couldn't seem to exorcise no matter how hard he tried. But he could see from the intransigent look on her face she was determined not to budge. And he'd be damned if he'd risk exposing any more of his past to persuade her otherwise.

'I'll have my driver take you home,' he said, vindicated by the stunned surprise which suffused her features. 'I'll contact you to arrange a meeting with my daughter.'

'Okay,' she said, her relief palpable.

But, as she rushed out of the office, his gaze tracked her the whole way.

She'd expected him to put up more of a fight. But there was really no need, he thought, as the turmoil of emotions finally released their stranglehold on him enough to allow him to think coherently.

The story would break tomorrow, forcing Lacey to realise exactly how untenable her position—and the position she was putting their child in—really was.

And, when she finally came to her senses and accepted the inevitable—that she needed this marriage—he would be waiting.

# CHAPTER NINE

'I CAN'T EVEN contact Ruby's nursery to say she can't come in today,' Lacey murmured as she peeked through the blind to stare at the press horde which had been massing outside their front door since before dawn. The crowd of photographers and reporters was now four rows deep, covering the pavement and most of the road.

She dropped the blind as one of the photographers spotted her and the barrage of shouted questions—which they had been attempting to ignore for two hours now—began again.

*'Lacey, tell us about you and Cade.'*

*'Where's your daughter, Lacey, is she okay?'*

*'Are you going to sue him?'*

Her stomach twisted, but the anxious knots in her gut were nothing compared to the guilt as she turned to see Milly, a concerned expression on her face, holding a sleepy Ruby—who had been woken by all the commotion.

'Mummy, why are they shouting?' Ruby said, rubbing her eyes.

Lacey crossed the room to lift her daughter into her arms. 'It's okay, baby. They'll get bored soon and go away.'

Although she didn't hold out much hope of that happening. They couldn't leave the flat, couldn't even turn on their phones, because both she and Milly had been inundated with calls and texts. How had they got her number and her address so easily?

She'd called the police an hour ago, but they'd said there was nothing they could do as long as the photographers and reporters remained off the premises.

And she was pretty sure she was now effectively out of a job. Melody had rung ten minutes ago—ostensibly to ask what was happening with the piece on Brandon. But she'd heard the wheedling tone in Melody's voice. Her editor knew about Ruby's relationship to him now, just like the rest of the world—and she was hoping for an exclusive. When Lacey had told her she couldn't write the piece, Melody had not been happy. Lacey had no doubt at all she would sack her eventually, when she refused to budge—and she was probably already bad-mouthing her all over the industry.

She'd thought she'd be prepared for this, thought she could weather the media storm, but Brandon had been right—they couldn't weather this. Protecting Ruby was her main concern now. Why had she lost sight of that so easily yesterday, when Brandon had demanded marriage? She'd thought she had a choice, but how long could she subject her child to this?

'Perhaps we should call Brandon Cade?' Milly supplied, having to raise her voice to be heard above the commotion outside. 'He's responsible for this disaster, after all,' she added.

Except he wasn't, Lacey thought, remembering the stark emotion on his face yesterday when he'd revealed the grim truth about his parents' divorce and his mother's mercenary behaviour.

She'd realised almost instantly he hadn't intended to tell her so much. Certainly, he hadn't wanted to elicit any sympathy. But it was there none the less, pounding under her breastbone, right alongside the panic and anxiety about

Ruby's welfare—and the choices she might be forced to make now to keep her child safe.

Brandon had offered her a way out. And she hadn't taken it. She'd refused to even consider it. She hadn't even questioned him about the sort of marriage he was suggesting. Because, when he had offered marriage, a foolish part of her heart had wanted to read much more into the offer than had actually been there. And that had scared the hell out of her.

If she called him now, she would at least have to consider his solution. But how could she ensure she remained pragmatic about such an arrangement? Because she didn't feel pragmatic about anything any more, not after getting that crucial insight into the boy he'd once been, the lonely, manipulated child behind the man. His mask of power and entitlement had slipped, and as a result the girl she'd been—that fanciful, romantic, needy girl—had come back out of hiding.

And that was before she even factored in his clear commitment to becoming a father to Ruby. He wanted full parental rights, and how could she argue against that when she had kept his daughter's existence a secret from him for so long?

'Do you think he'd be willing to help us?' Milly asked, getting a little frantic.

Lacey nodded. 'Yes,' she said, knowing the answer to that much at least was fairly easy. He had told her he was determined to protect Ruby and she believed him.

She handed Ruby back to Milly and tugged her phone out of her pocket. But, before she had the chance to switch it back on, the commotion from outside became deafening.

She rushed to the window. 'What the…?'

A long black limousine had pulled up at the kerb, followed by two more cars. The army of press rushed the vehicles, the camera flashes and shouts reaching a cre-

scendo of sound and fury. Several burly security guards
leapt out of the cars behind the limo and proceeded to push
the tidal wave back.

Then Brandon stepped out of the limousine, spoke to
the driver, who also appeared, then took the steps to Lacey's front door in quick strides. He ignored the shouts and
long lenses with a steely determination borne of familiarity, she suspected. Her own heart galloped into her throat,
though. Relief was followed by a stupid feeling of euphoria.

He had come to rescue them, to rescue his daughter.

His gaze locked on her face—implacable, determined,
but strangely devoid of judgment. She stared back at him,
frozen for a moment in the tractor beam of those cool green
eyes. Then he nodded at the front door.

She scrambled off the sofa and rushed out of the flat to
open the front door.

He stepped inside, then slammed the door, shutting out
the paparazzi and the barrage of noise behind him.

'Thank you for coming,' she said, feeling giddy with
relief and something that felt disturbingly like exhilaration. Why should she be so happy to see him? When everything about this situation was a disaster?

The anxious knots in her stomach tightened. He had
made what he wanted clear yesterday, and he would not
give up on his goal.

Reaction streaked through her—visceral and volatile
and yet somehow helping to stop her knees from dissolv-
ing—when he cupped her elbow and led her back down
the corridor.

'You have five minutes to pack what you need. You
and Ruby are relocating to the Cade estate in Wiltshire.
You'll be safe there until this dies down. I have a secure
apartment Milly can stay in near here if she doesn't wish
to join you there.'

She could have objected. He wasn't giving her a choice.

And it would mean resigning her job. But, given her editor was likely to fire her soon anyway, and with the feeding frenzy outside still audible, did she really *have* a choice? As they re-entered the living room, and she saw Ruby's head cradled on Milly's shoulder—her little girl trying to hide from the scary noise—the decision was made for her.

She would accept Brandon's offer of a safe place to stay, and deal with any strings he might attach to it later.

'About time you showed up,' Milly said, rushing towards them both. 'I'll take the flat, thanks. I've got to get to work.' she added, clearly having heard the conversation in the hallway. 'Here.' Lifting Ruby, she handed her towards Brandon. 'Ruby, Mummy's friend Brandon is going to hold you while Mummy and me pack some stuff to take with us. Then we can get away from the annoying people outside, okay baby?' Milly coaxed when Ruby continued to cling to her.

Lacey felt Brandon tense beside her. Her heart bounced painfully in her chest, knowing how big a deal this was for him. From the frown creasing his forehead, she suspected he had never held a child before now. But when Lacey stepped forward, intending to defuse the moment and take Ruby instead, her little girl lifted her arms towards Brandon—trusting him instinctively.

A sharp frown furrowed his brow, but he hesitated for less than a second before scooping Ruby into his arms.

'I don't like the shouting, Mr Brandon,' Ruby said, before shoving her thumb into her mouth and wrapping her other arm around his neck. She buried her head against his broad chest as Milly raced out of the room.

Lacey's heart swelled painfully as Brandon placed a comforting hand on his child's back and murmured, 'Don't worry. I'm going to take you away from the shouting.'

His gaze lifted to Lacey, who still stood rooted to the spot, trapped by the emotions charging through her body at the devastating sight of her daughter, *their* daughter, held so securely in his arms.

What she saw in his face—guarded tension, but also grim determination and fierce protectiveness—had the guilt all but crippling her. She had denied them both so much. How could she ever make amends?

But then she was jolted out of her revelry by his husky command. 'Stop standing there and start packing, Lacey. You have exactly four minutes left now.'

Thirteen hours later, Lacey stood on the steps of the lavish sixty-room Palladian mansion she had arrived at that morning, the manicured gardens now dark as night fell. A sense of unreality settled over her—which had been chasing her all day—as she watched the Cade Inc helicopter appear and settle on the side lawn, not far from the covered swimming pool where she and Ruby had been swimming that afternoon.

Nerves tangled and tightened in her stomach.

They hadn't spoken since Brandon's driver had dropped Brandon at Cade Tower that morning, before the limousine had headed towards Wiltshire and the Cade estate. And, during the brief time they had been together, she had spent most of it calming Ruby down after their scary dash through the herd of photographers and reporters—only barely held back by Brandon's security guards.

The chopper's noise wasn't muffled much by the nearby forest but she doubted even an earthquake would have woken Ruby, who had gone to sleep hours ago in the suite which had been prepared for them—complete with a slew of new toys for Ruby—in the house's east wing.

It had been an exhausting day—not least because Lacey's mind had replayed the parting words Brandon had whispered to her as Ruby slept in her car seat for the last thirteen hours straight.

*'Marriage is the only way to solve this situation, Lacey. Next time I see you, we are going to have that conversation again.'*

Lacey clasped her arms around her waist to control the speedy thumps of her heartbeat as Brandon emerged from the chopper flanked by Daryl and another assistant she didn't recognise. He strode towards her, his dark suit pressed against his tall physique in the downdraft from the blades.

She'd received a text from Daryl two hours ago, informing her Brandon would be arriving late and that he would speak to her in the morning. But she had decided not to wait. Sleep would be impossible with 'that conversation' hanging over her head. Plus, she needed to thank him properly for coming to her family's rescue that morning—and for letting her sister stay rent-free in a lavish gated condo in Islington which Milly had rung her to rave about that afternoon.

The anxiety that had been kept ruthlessly at bay all day squeezed Lacey's ribs as he approached.

What exactly was she going to do about his offer of marriage? Because yesterday's certainty that a marriage between them would be a disaster felt a lot less certain now.

He reached her at last, his eyes dark in the twilight. 'Hello, Lacey,' he said, his voice gruff. 'I told Daryl to tell you I would be late,' he added, the frown suggesting he wasn't *that* pleased to see her.

She tried not to take his abrupt manner personally. He had to be tired too. She knew he had been dealing with the fallout from the Drystar headlines all day. He'd even been forced to hold an impromptu press conference which she knew he must have hated. He was a man who guarded his privacy, and now she knew why. This morning had been a terrifying wake-up call. But, while she and Ruby had been whisked away to safety, Brandon had stayed to face the fallout alone.

'I know,' she said, and shivered, the nerves doing strange things to her insides. 'I wanted to stay up to thank you. And to…to discuss what you said earlier.'

Daryl and the other assistant bade them both goodbye and headed towards the staff cottages on the other side of the gardens. Brandon nodded at the doorman, who was waiting to lock the main door behind them.

'Let's get a drink,' he said abruptly, and touched her elbow to lead her into an imposing library situated off the main entrance hall.

The graze of his fingertips was electrifying in the quiet country night as the sound of the chopper blades outside finally died.

He crossed the silk rug to a drinks cabinet in the far wall. The scent of old leather and lemon polish filled the musty air. He switched on a small light that cast a soft glow over his harsh features.

He wasn't just tired, she realised. He was exhausted. The bruised smudges under his eyes made him look more unsettled—and somehow more vulnerable—than she had ever seen him.

Without asking, he poured them both a whisky and handed her a glass. 'Here.'

She took the crystal tumbler, shivering again when his fingers brushed hers.

He stepped back, watching her intently over the rim of the glass as he knocked the whisky back in one gulp.

'So, what exactly did you wish to thank me for?' he asked, breaking eye contact at last to pour himself another glass.

'For arriving this morning, and then protecting me and Ruby and Milly from what you had to go through today,' she said simply.

'She's my daughter. What did you think I would do?' he replied sharply. 'Leave the three of you to be picked apart by those vultures?'

She heard the bitterness in his tone, and the accusation, and the guilt she had been determined to suppress leapt from the shadows to torment her again. 'I'm sorry, I underestimated you.'

'Yes, you did,' he said, still studying her. Her heart started to make her gag, and she realised how close she was to tears.

Clearly, she was tired and emotional too, because maintaining the fragile truce between them suddenly seemed so important. It probably wouldn't last. But, now more than ever, she was determined to figure out a solution that they could both live with.

'I still want marriage, Lacey,' he said before she had the chance to say more.

Her breath hitched in her lungs at the determination in his voice. She thought she'd been prepared to deal with this conversation now... Apparently not.

She took a sip of the peaty whisky, the burn of the liquor as she swallowed masking the painful burn already there before she replied. 'I know you don't trust me to let you form a relationship without...'

He held up his hand and she stuttered to a halt.

'It's not just that,' he said, the strain lines around his mouth relaxing a little. 'You need my protection, Lacey. Both you and Ruby. Surely today's experience proved that conclusively? I can't give you that protection unless I claim her unequivocally as mine. And that means marriage.'

She stared down at the amber liquid in her glass. She could argue that they didn't have to be wed for him to claim Ruby. Or that Ruby was a child, not a piece of property who he needed to own. But the protests dried up inside her at the visceral memory of the way he'd held his child for the first time, and the sight of him charging through the crowd of reporters while Ruby had clung to him, trusting him completely, as they made their way to the car.

Ruby needed her father. How could she continue to deny that after this morning?

But, as she tried to figure out how best to proceed, he continued, his tone brittle but no less forceful.

'This isn't just about Ruby, though. It's also about us,' he said.

*Us.*

The word seemed to reverberate in her chest—part promise, part threat—as her head jerked up.

'What about us?' she managed, forcing herself not to relinquish eye contact. Whatever happened now, she would not let the fanciful girl she'd once been misconstrue his intentions again.

'I'm going to need your help getting to know Ruby,' he said. 'A *lot* of your help. Because, believe me, fatherhood is not something that is likely to come naturally to me,' he added.

The dark tide of sympathy pulsed in her chest. His uncertainty was surprising but also deeply touching...and illuminating.

He was struggling as well with the enormity of this situation—why hadn't she considered he might not be as confident as he appeared? It also seemed important that he'd let her glimpse his vulnerability. Because she suspected showing a weakness was something he despised.

'Marriage is the best way for us to get to know each other properly,' he added. 'I want Ruby to trust me. And, for her to trust me, I need to trust you. We need to spend time together for that to happen.'

She took another sip of the whisky. 'Okay,' she said.

Something fierce and visceral flared in his gaze. 'Okay, you'll marry me?'

'Okay, I'll consider it,' she replied.

Brandon let out a strained laugh. He'd been considering this conversation all day. He'd been prepared to bully and cajole her if necessary into doing what he thought was best. But, as usual, Lacey had blindsided him. Almost as much as the experience of holding his daughter in his arms for the first time had blindsided him that morning.

Seeing his child and Lacey and her sister trapped in their home by those bastards, feeling his little girl cling to him and rely on him for her safety, had changed something fundamental inside him. Until that moment, the concept of becoming a father had seemed purely academic in a lot of ways.

Now it felt very real.

'What exactly is there to consider?' he said, deciding to humour her. After all, they'd both had a long, tiring day. And she seemed a lot more malleable than she had yesterday in his office. Perhaps it was time to employ the carrot instead of the stick—something he should have considered sooner. He prided himself on being a master of negotiation, but for some damn reason as soon as he got a lungful of Lacey's scent, and saw the bold pride in her eyes, he found it impossible to back off with her.

Perhaps because he wanted this marriage, so much.

Eventually he would get bored with her. He had no track record when it came to long-term commitment, nor did he desire one. At which point they could consider a divorce. Somehow he doubted his fascination with Lacey would wear off any time soon—after all, it had lasted five years already—but when it did, if he had established a workable relationship with his daughter, then it would be all good.

'Exactly what kind of marriage are you expecting?' she asked, her cheeks mottling with colour.

He frowned. 'The usual kind.' Why was she talking in riddles?

'So you don't plan for this to be a marriage in name only?'

He choked out an astonished laugh at her naivety—breaking the tension in his gut for the first time in close to a week. 'Of course not. Why would either one of us want a sexless marriage?'

He cupped her cheek, no longer able to resist the powerful urge to touch her. Did a little of that girl still remain? And why did the thought of discovering the answer to that question feel as hot as it was beguiling?

'Sex happens to be the only thing we do well together,' he said. 'Why deny ourselves that pleasure when we're probably going to be fighting fires on every other front in this marriage?'

Funny to think, though, that fighting those fires with her appealed to him almost as much as the thought of taking her in every possible way he could imagine. And he'd imagined a lot.

She turned away, but he saw her throat contract as she swallowed.

*That's right, Lacey, why deny it when you know it's true?*

He let his hand drop, remembering that in any negotiation it was sometimes better to stake your claim then wait for your opponent to come to you.

'Of course, it will be your choice. I'm not going to force the issue,' he added.

*Not when seducing you will be so much more rewarding.*

At last she nodded, but something flickered in her eyes that he couldn't read.

'I see,' she said. He had to bite his lip to stop himself

from smiling again. She'd learn soon enough that resistance was futile when it came to denying their chemistry.

He tensed as her breath gushed out.

'Let me demonstrate,' he said, sliding a knuckle under her chin.

What the hell was he waiting for? He wanted this marriage, and he wanted her. But, more to the point, she wanted him with the same intensity. It was high time she admitted that.

Lifting her face to his, he slanted his lips across hers.

She opened for him instinctively, proving his point perfectly, but then the need and hunger overwhelmed him with startling speed.

She tasted of whisky and sweetness as his tongue tangled with hers—demanding, dominant, all-consuming. She kissed him back with passion and purpose, all the stress, the volatile emotions of the last few days, swept away on a furious wave of desire.

Her hands flattened on his stomach as he gripped her head, angling her mouth to take more. To take all. His abs trembled as her fingers fisted in the starched cotton to draw him closer.

He broke the kiss reluctantly, but he could see she had got the point when he searched her face—flushed and glowing in the muted light—and saw his own need reflected back at him.

'Marry me, Lacey,' he said, his voice husky.

She stepped back, her teeth chewing on her bottom lip. He waited, her answer suddenly meaning much more than he wanted it to.

She nodded, even as the wary tension remained.

'All right, I'll marry you,' she said. The spurt of triumph was swiftly quashed, though, when she added, 'But I would like separate bedrooms.'

*No way.*

He pursed his lips to stop the swift, knee-jerk response from shooting out of his mouth.

What was the matter with him? He never shared a bedroom—why would he wish to share one with her?

'If that's what you want.' He pushed the irrational anger down and forced an assured smile to his lips. 'I don't see that being a deal-breaker. But I want to arrange the wedding as soon as possible.' He wasn't going to allow her time to change her mind.

'Okay,' she said. As she turned and walked away from him, the triumph surged back.

After all, her request did not preclude him from exploiting their volatile chemistry as soon as they were wed.

# CHAPTER TEN

THE NEXT MORNING, Brandon strode towards the mansion's east wing, feeling drained and out of sorts—emotions he did not want to feel already playing havoc with his usual purpose.

Predictably, he'd had a virtually sleepless night—*again*—thanks mostly to their drive-by kiss last night in the library. And the realisation that, while Lacey had agreed to marriage, she still had the power to unsettle him far too much.

But then, he had been exhausted yesterday. It had been a horrendous day. He hated talking to the press at the best of times. And having to return to a house that held so many bad memories hadn't improved his disposition either.

He passed the door to his father's study and kept walking. But, even so, the familiar chill slithered down his spine, much as it had when he'd been a boy.

The news had never been good when he had been called to the austere room. His father had always had complaints, demands, criticisms and a host of other ways to show him how he was falling short as the heir to the Cade empire. Even now he couldn't remember a single word of praise or affection.

He rarely stayed at the estate unless he had to, because being here reminded him of that insecure, far too obedient child who had taken all the constant criticism and internalised them far too readily.

His footsteps echoed on the polished parquet flooring as he forced himself to forget that boy. At last, he reached the far end of the corridor that led to the rooms Lacey and Ruby had moved into the previous day.

He stopped outside the door to their suite and detected the muffled sounds of a child's laughter. His heartbeat accelerated, the familiar anxiety from so long ago clawing at his throat.

*Don't be an idiot, Cade. She's a four-year-old child. And you couldn't possibly be as much of a bastard as he was—even if you wanted to be, which you don't.*

The marriage Lacey had agreed to last night would smooth the way to forming a relationship with his child. Plus, the head groundskeeper had given him an idea about what to do with his daughter today. Even so, his arm felt as if it weighed several tons as he lifted it and rapped three times on the door.

The laughter cut off and the door swung open.

Lacey stood in front of him wearing a pair of yoga pants which accentuated her slender curves and a flimsy camisole top which clung to her breasts. With her feet bare, her face devoid of make-up and her short cap of curls rioting around her face, she looked as if she'd only just got out of bed.

Heat shot straight into his groin on cue. Heat and something far more volatile—which felt annoyingly like yearning.

*Damn.*

Why couldn't his feelings be as simple and straightforward as they should be where this woman was concerned?

'Brandon?' she whispered. 'Hi. We weren't expecting you.'

He frowned, realising maybe he should have mentioned

his planned visit to prepare the child for his arrival. Then he inwardly cursed himself. This was precisely why he was nervous. He had no clue what he was doing.

But, before he could figure out what to say, she swung the door wider to welcome him into the room.

'Why don't you join Ruby and I for breakfast?' she said, the smile on her lips somewhat contradicted by the mottled flush on her collar bone, visible where the worn camisole drooped.

'Okay, sure,' he said, but then wondered how Lacey would introduce him. He didn't want her to break the news to Ruby that he was her father yet. It was too soon—she needed to get to know him first. The last thing he wished to do was frighten her, the way his own father had so often frightened him.

*Perhaps you should have mentioned all that to her last night, before kissing her senseless.*

But, as he stepped into the room, Lacey solved the problem. 'Ruby, you remember Brandon?' she said. 'He carried you to the car yesterday. He's going to have breakfast with us.'

A little of his panic retreated until he spotted the child—his daughter—dressed in pyjamas decorated with multi-coloured dinosaurs, sitting at the breakfast table in the far corner of the room. And the same thought he had had yesterday when she'd clung to him so readily blindsided him again.

*She's so small. How can she be so perfect and yet so tiny?*

He cleared his throat as he stood suspended in the room. 'Hello, Ruby,' he managed.

She looked at him inquisitively. 'Hello, Mr Brandon,' she said.

The 'Mr' made him wince, reminding him of his father, who had always insisted he call him 'sir'. 'You can call me Brandon,' he said. 'If you prefer.'

'Okay,' she said, looking nonplussed. He knew how she felt. Could this get any more awkward? How on earth did you talk to a four-year-old?

But then he recalled what his groundskeeper had mentioned that morning when he'd gone for his morning run. He knew nothing about children, but he remembered what it was like to be a child himself. And he wasn't above bribing his way into his daughter's affection if need be.

'I thought we could go to the groundskeeper's cottage this morning. His dog, Maisey, had some puppies two months ago and they are looking for homes for them.' He glanced at Lacey, who was watching him with a soft light in her eyes, which would have been unsettling if he hadn't already gone right past awkward to extremely uncomfortable. 'If your mother agrees, I thought perhaps you might like one,' he added.

'A puppy!' The little girl gasped, her whole face lighting up as if stars had exploded behind her eyes. 'Really? Can I have a puppy, Mummy? Can I?' she asked Lacey, her small voice rising and her whole body bouncing with so much excitement, Brandon became momentarily concerned she might actually burst.

'Yes, of course, I think that would be a wonderful idea,' Lacey said.

Before she finished talking, the little girl leapt off her chair and shot towards Brandon as if she had been fired from a gun.

He barely had a chance to brace before she barrelled into him and wrapped chubby arms around his knees.

She tipped her head back to beam at him. 'Thank you, thank you, thank you, Mr Brandon,' she said, having forgotten his suggestion about dropping the Mr already. But somehow it didn't seem to matter, as her green eyes sparkled with happiness, the dimple in her cheek winking at him in delight.

He stared down at her, with absolutely no idea what to say or do, his heart hitting his chest wall in painful thuds, the protective instinct wrapping round his heart like a lasso at the thought of how vulnerable she was, how innocent and guileless.

Could it really be this easy to win her trust?

'Can we go now? Can we, please?' she asked.

It occurred to him how much he had to learn as he opened his mouth to say yes—ready to give her whatever she wanted—but Lacey interrupted them gently.

'We need to finish our breakfast first, Rubes. And then you need to get dressed. You can't pick a puppy in your pyjamas, now, can you?'

The child giggled, still delighted. 'No, I can't. I don't want my puppy to think I'm silly.'

Instead of being intimidated, or even phased by his obvious inexperience with children, she let go of his legs and held her small hand up to him. He took it instinctively. As her soft fingers tightened on his, miraculously the clawing panic began to loosen its grip on his throat.

'If it's a girl puppy, I'm going to call her Tinkerbell,' she said as she tugged him towards the breakfast table.

She continued to chatter at a staggering rate as Lacey served him breakfast. Luckily, his daughter didn't seem to require any input from him—which was good, because he was actually speechless.

For the first time ever, though, he found himself more than happy simply to go with the flow.

Lacey eased the door shut to Ruby's room, where her daughter had finally collapsed for a well-earned nap—after spending the morning with her father and her new Jack Russell puppy, Tinkerbell—and sent a careful smile to the man beside her…who was frowning as he stared at the door.

'She's exhausting,' he murmured.

Brandon Cade looked shell-shocked—but somehow the perplexed expression as he turned that fierce green gaze on her only made her heart swell more.

He'd been so patient with Ruby today—thoughtful, attentive and utterly fascinated by everything Ruby did or said. He'd also seemed more than a little nervous, which was a new look for him. Lacey had sensed as soon as he had walked into their room four hours ago—and Ruby had treated him to one of her 'special hugs'—he was completely and utterly out of his depth.

The puppy suggestion, though, had been nothing short of inspired. And she couldn't help wondering where it had come from… Because, for a man who had told her he didn't think he would be a natural at fatherhood, he had already found a direct route into his little girl's heart.

'She's excited,' Lacey clarified.

He nodded. 'She really adores that puppy,' he said. 'I never knew someone could be so erudite and articulate on a single topic for four solid hours.'

Lacey chuckled, the warmth in her chest glowing. It felt good to be able to talk about her child with him. *Their* child. Who knew?

'Yes, she already loves Tinkerbell,' she replied. 'She also likes you rather a lot.'

A flicker of surprise crossed his features. 'I'm glad,' he said, sinking a hand into his pocket. 'I just…' He hesitated. 'I don't want her to be frightened of me.'

'She isn't,' Lacey replied, puzzled.

Why would Ruby be frightened of him when he had been so careful with her today? He'd answered all of her questions and listened intently to the endless stream of information on her new puppy. He'd even carried her back from the groundsman's cottage after she'd begun to tire, holding Ruby securely as she dropped off to sleep with surprising confidence, given Lacey was sure it was only the second time he had held a child in his life.

'I'm sure the puppy didn't hurt,' he added wryly.

'Tinkerbell's not the only reason,' she said, determined to reassure him and knowing it was true. 'What made you suggest the puppy?' she asked, intrigued.

'I've never been above using bribery when it comes to getting what I want,' he said, his voice deepening as his gaze met hers. Even as a familiar reaction pulsed in her abdomen, she could hear the evasive tone. Was he trying to distract her?

'True,' she said, the provocative comment reminding her of last night's kiss, as she was sure it had been intended to do. 'But a puppy was a brilliant idea. I just wondered if there was a reason you thought of it,' she probed again, determined not to be distracted.

He shrugged, but the movement was tense. He didn't answer straight away. Instead, his gaze slid away from hers to contemplate the view, from the room's huge paned window, of the mansion's manicured lawns now drenched in sunshine.

Instinctively she knew there'd been more to the idea now. And that he was trying to decide whether to confide in her or not.

Her chest tightened as she realised how much she wanted to know the truth, because it might give her another crucial insight into his childhood.

At last, his gaze met hers, direct, unflinching, but filled with a depth of emotion she suspected he had not intended her to see.

'Tinkerbell is the descendant of a puppy I once owned when I was a child here,' he said. Something flashed in his gaze that looked bitter and angry, but beneath it she could see the shadow of hurt.

His voice, though, remained flat and hollow when he continued. 'I adored that little Jack Russell. He was my best friend. My *only* friend, really,' he said, then let out a humourless laugh. 'I was brought up alone by the staff here ever since I was a baby. I didn't see my father often, but on one of his rare visits he must have spotted me playing with my puppy. The head groundsman—John's father,' he added, mentioning the man they had met that day. 'Had given him to me for my fifth birthday two months before. When I was called into my father's study, I was excited. I had some childish notion he was going to give me a birthday present, even though he'd never given me one before. Instead, he told me it was high time I went to boarding school and that the puppy would be taken from me and rehoused—because the staff couldn't look after it while I was gone.'

Lacey gasped. 'But…how could he do something so cruel?' she said, shocked not just by his father's cruelty, and the decision to send his son away to boarding school at such a young age, but also by the lack of emotion in Brandon's voice.

He shrugged, as if the incident was of no importance, the expression on his face blank. 'He wanted to toughen me up, he said.'

'Your father sounds like an ass,' she said forcefully, suddenly furious with the man. Was this why Brandon controlled his emotions so carefully?

'He was.' He stared at her, a muscle twitching in his jaw. 'But, to be fair to him, it worked.'

'Did it?' she asked, the compassion welling in her chest.

Unlike when her father had rejected her and Milly, Brandon had had no one, and that sickened her.

She cradled his cheek, felt it harden beneath her palm.

'Don't…' He tugged away from her touch. 'Don't mistake me for that lonely boy, Lacey.'

She lowered her hand, seeing the shutters she had managed to pry open—at least a little bit—slam back down.

'I'm not that pathetic, defenceless child any more,' he added. 'These days, I consider solitude my strength.'

It was a warning. She got that. A warning not to assume that any kindness, any affection he showed towards his daughter, would be extended to her.

But, even so, she couldn't help imagining that small boy, treated with such callous indifference by the man who should have nurtured him.

And the man that boy had become, who had worked so hard today to form a bond with his own child, a child he hadn't even known existed a week ago.

Maybe he didn't want Lacey's compassion. But he had it regardless—along with her admiration.

Plus, she had never considered solitude a strength, and she was damned if she was going to start now.

'Have you spoken to Ruby yet about the wedding?' he asked.

'Um…no, not yet,' she said, disconcerted by the change of subject, but willing to go with it. She needed time to get all the emotions making her chest ache under control so she could face him again tomorrow with her armour intact.

'I thought…' She paused. 'I thought maybe we could tell her together?'

His brow furrowed. 'I'm afraid that won't be possible, not unless you want to wait for at least a fortnight. I'm heading to the States this afternoon—the Atlanta deal fell through, so I'm going to scope out alternative options. I probably won't be back until the wedding.'

'Oh.' Lacey's heart sank. Despite the constant tension between them, she realised she would miss him.

Seeing him with his daughter, finding out more about

his childhood, had given her a compelling insight into the man behind the mask of power and control he wore for the world.

He didn't want her to know that man—he had made that clear. But she had agreed to marry him in three weeks' time—which meant she needed to find out much more about him, whether he wanted her to or not.

'By the way, the PR team have suggested we consider a honeymoon after the wedding. A week at Cade Island in Bermuda should be enough to convince the media this is a real marriage.' His gaze focussed on her face, making the skin on her neck and chin, sensitive from last night's voracious kiss, prickle. 'We can take Ruby with us, if you would like?'

He was offering her a way out, a chance to use their child as a go-between. And, while on one level she suspected the offer was a genuine one, the look in his eyes suggested this was also a challenge, to see if she would take the coward's way out.

If they went on this honeymoon alone, there would be no avoiding the chemistry that had exploded last night without warning. But why should that be a bad thing? Surely a week in paradise would give her the opportunity she needed to find out if this could really be a real marriage?

She took a deep breath, let it out slowly.

*Go for it, Lacey. It's worth the risk.*

She shook her head. 'Ruby's had too much disruption to her routine already. Plus, she'd never want to leave Tinkerbell for that length of time. And Milly will be here to look after her.'

Her sister was arriving at the end of the week, as the school where she worked had been besieged by the press too, and the decision had been made for her to join them in Wiltshire for a week or so.

Heat flared in his eyes. 'Okay, I'll make the travel arrangements for the two of us.' He checked his watch. 'I need to leave.' He glanced back towards the bedroom where Ruby slept. 'Say goodbye to Ruby for me. I guess we can tell her about the wedding arrangements together on a video link?' he offered.

The intuitive suggestion made her realise that, while Brandon had been out of his depth first thing that morning, he was growing in confidence as Ruby's father.

Why did that not surprise her?

'Okay, I think that would work,' she said.

As he turned to go, an empty space opened up in her stomach at the thought of not seeing him again, in person, for weeks. But then he stopped and turned back.

'FYI, Lacey,' he said, his gaze blazing with that devastating combination of heat and purpose. 'You should organise a more reliable form of birth control than condoms before the honeymoon.'

Without another word, he walked out—leaving her hormones *and* her emotions in tatters.

*Blast the man.*

# CHAPTER ELEVEN

*Three weeks later*

'RUBY, IT'S TIME to sleep now,' Lacey said as she eased her daughter's arms from around her neck.

'But I'm too happy, Mummy.' Ruby gave a huge yawn and settled back into her bed. 'Tinkerbell was such a good bridesmaid. She didn't even pee on your dress,' she added with a tired giggle. 'Isn't that true, Mr Brandon?' She sent Brandon, who stood behind Lacey, a sleepy grin.

They'd barely had a chance to talk since exchanging their vows five hours ago. Lacey in the designer concoction of lace and silk, with Brandon and her young daughter and the mischievous puppy—who Ruby had insisted on including in the ceremony—sandwiched between them as five hundred carefully selected guests had laughed and then applauded.

The lavish event seemed to have gone by in a blur of nerves and adrenaline, but Lacey's first sight of Brandon—in the perfectly tailored wedding suit, his green eyes gleaming—had sent her senses into overdrive, and they hadn't really touched the ground since.

She was exhausted now. And saying goodbye to her daughter was only making her more emotional. What had she done, marrying this man she barely knew? Every aspect of her life in Brandon's world seemed overwhelming, except the one thing that drew them together... Ruby.

So why had she agreed to leave her little girl behind tonight?

'Tinkerbell was a good bridesmaid,' Brandon said, resting a heavy hand on Lacey's shoulder, no doubt to present a loving front to their daughter. 'But not as good as you were, Ruby. I was so proud of you today.'

It was of course exactly the right thing to say, making Ruby's eyes brighten and her tired smile beam.

But then Ruby's smile faltered and her eyes filled with a longing Lacey didn't understand.

'Are you my daddy now?' she asked.

Brandon's hand tensed on her shoulder as Lacey's heart leapt into her throat at Ruby's innocent question. Brandon had video-called Ruby and her a number of times in the past three weeks while he'd been in the US—but, once they'd spoken to their daughter about the wedding, he had chosen not to broach the subject of his true identity.

Lacey had decided not to push. It was Brandon's decision when he told his daughter he was her father and she needed to respect that. But, even so, she could hear the thickening in his voice he couldn't disguise as he spoke.

'Yes, Ruby, I am your daddy,' he said. 'If you would like, you can call me Daddy instead of Mr Brandon.'

'Can I really?' Ruby asked, the innocent request made Lacey's heart break a little.

'Yes, I'd like you to,' he replied. 'Very much.'

A sleepy grin spread across Ruby's features. 'Latisha said it's sad I don't have a daddy,' she said, mentioning one of her little friends whose family they had invited to the event. 'But now I do.'

Guilt tightened Lacey's throat. Ruby had never mentioned not having a father to her before.

Leaning past her, Brandon planted a kiss on Ruby's

forehead then pulled back, his expression for once un-guarded, his eyes warm with affection. 'Your daddy says it's time to go to sleep.'

Ruby nodded. 'Okay, Daddy,' she said, clearly wanting to use the word as often as possible.

Lacey smiled, forcing the guilt back down as she tucked Ruby into the bed and kissed her too. 'Daddy and I will video-call you from the island every day over the next week. And Milly will be here to look after you, okay, Rubes?'

Ruby nodded again and did another jaw-breaking yawn. 'Milly says we can play with Tinkerbell tomorrow,' she said, sounding excited about the prospect. 'Night-night, Mummy and Daddy,' she added, then promptly turned over and dropped into a deep sleep, no doubt full of dreams of mischievous puppies and new daddies.

Lacey's heartbeat hammered in her throat as she stood, to find Brandon staring at her.

With his tie and jacket gone, the first few buttons of his white dress shirt undone and the shadow of new stubble covering his jaw, he looked rugged, relaxed and impos-sibly handsome. The fierce glow in his eyes didn't look remotely relaxed, though.

There were so many things she wanted to say to him—starting with apologising again for robbing him of the first four years of his child's life—but before she could unstick a single word he cut through the silence.

'You have twenty minutes to get changed and say your goodbyes, then I'll meet you at the heliport,' he said, his tone forceful and oddly detached, even as his gaze raked over her with deliberate intent.

As the heated look burned through the layers of silk and lace, and her nerves began to jump and jive, Lacey could sense the barriers he had let down during the day for the sake of the press, their friends and their child being put firmly back in place. Again.

She forced herself not to let her usual fear of rejection overwhelm her, though. Brandon Cade wasn't like her father. Maybe he didn't trust her yet. But, after seeing him with Ruby today, after feeling his eyes on her throughout the ceremony and reception, she was not about to give up hope.

She'd made a mistake five years ago. But she couldn't keep apologising for it for ever. This honeymoon would give them a chance to move past it. And she was determined not to squander the opportunity.

Brandon stood at the steps of the helicopter twenty minutes later and watched his new wife walk across the dark lawn towards him—the emotions he'd kept on a tight leash for five unending hours beginning to break their bounds. Wearing jeans, a T-shirt and a long jacket to guard against the evening's spring chill, she looked no less stunning than she had that morning when he'd turned to see her heading down the aisle of the small chapel on the mansion's grounds. Her sister and his daughter had been following behind her in matching gowns, the crowd enchanted by the antics of the little girl and the puppy she was trying to control on its leash, while his heart had jumped into his throat and remained there most of the day.

But all his attention was now focussed on the woman. She had her sister Milly by her side again, still dressed in her maid-of-honour gown.

The two women embraced and Milly sent him a wave.

He waved back before Milly turned to go back into the house, where the reception banquet had given way to a dance set by a famous DJ several hours ago.

Putting her head down, Lacey picked her way across the grass towards him, gripping the small backpack she had slung over her shoulder. The rest of her honeymoon luggage had been loaded on the chopper ten minutes ago.

He'd felt her nerves all through the day—from the moment he'd lifted her veil and seen the sheen of emotion and determination in her eyes.

However much of a formality this marriage was supposed to be, to give Ruby the full protection of his name and his wealth, however much of a damage limitation exercise it was to shore up his reputation after the media furore of the past three weeks around the disclosure of his 'secret child', it now felt startlingly real.

He couldn't give her his heart and, more to the point, he didn't want to give her his heart, because the need for love had once made him weak.

But as she made her way towards him, her steps slowing, the wary tension in her body building, he recalled the stunned emotion piercing his chest when his daughter had called him Daddy for the first time.

Okay, maybe he did have a heart. The fierce pride and protectiveness he felt for Ruby was surely something close to love—or as close to love as he was ever likely to get?

But loving his child was very different from loving her mother. And he needed to remember that. Because loving his child did not hold the risks that came with loving Lacey. He steeled himself against the emotion squeezing his ribs as Lacey reached him and he welcomed the swift spurt of arousal.

This wasn't love, it was simply lust.

The chopper's blades accelerated as the pilot prepared for take-off, the engine noise whipping away any possibility of conversation.

But, as she stopped in front of him, he lifted her chin to take her lips in a harsh kiss, his tongue plundering her mouth. So what if this wasn't a love match? He wanted her to know she was his now, in every way that mattered.

Her palms flattened against his abdomen.

He tore his lips away, refusing to take the kiss deeper, determined to maintain control.

He'd waited for three weeks, the hunger building each time he'd seen her on the video link, going a little nuts when she had been beside him while they'd exchanged their vows and later as she'd sat next to him during the never-ending wedding banquet.

But there was something about seeing her with Ruby… with *his* child…that only made him want her more… And he wanted her too damn much already.

She'd played the part of the eager bride well during the day. But he knew the stunned desire in her gaze was entirely genuine. Good, because he planned to make her wait now, even if it killed him.

He refused to allow this fierce desire to put him at a disadvantage again.

Leading her into the chopper without a word, he watched her strap herself in with trembling fingers.

He was glad she had agreed to honeymoon with him alone. As much as he adored Ruby's company, adored getting to know all the fascinating facets of his child, he also needed to ensure he took the edge off his desire for her mother. He didn't want his physical needs to detract from what this marriage was meant to achieve.

His feelings for Lacey were far more complex than they should be. He'd already told her much more than he'd ever told any woman about his past, his miserable childhood. He couldn't afford to let Lacey get any closer or he could fall into the trap of wanting more from her. And that would give her a power over him he had never allowed any woman to have.

As the helicopter lifted into the night, he caught a whiff of her scent—that tantalising mix of citrus soap and rose perfume which had beguiled him in the past.

Fierce need dug into his guts as he forced himself to look out into the night. The lights of the mansion glittered as guests milled around the gardens and the terrace and waved at the retreating chopper.

He wouldn't consummate their marriage tonight. They had an eight-hour plane journey on the Cade jet once they got to Heathrow, then a two-hour boat transfer to the island.

He'd arranged for them to have separate bungalows, as per his original promise—which would give him as much time as he needed to get this incessant hunger under control while ensuring that any wayward emotions remained on a tight leash at all times too. So, when he finally took his new bride, he intended it to be on his terms—and at a time of his choosing.

# CHAPTER TWELVE

LACEY YAWNED, WOKEN by the bright mid-morning light coming through the luxury beach bungalow's shutters.

She sat up, feeling disorientated, and strangely bereft as the memory of last night's trip to Bermuda came back to her. The short helicopter ride to the airport and the overnight plane journey in Brandon's deluxe private jet. The transfer to a motor yacht on Ireland Island—and the rows of colourful cookie-cutter houses brightened by torch light as they drove from the airport to the port several hours before dawn. The glorious sunrise over the iridescent sea as the launch had skimmed towards the horizon and finally arrived at a wooden dock on a stunning white sand beach. The lavish facilities of the main house—complete with gym, restaurant and large oval swimming pool—and the expertly designed and beautifully appointed bungalows dotted along the beach which had literally taken her breath away.

But, most of all, she remembered Brandon's silence.

He'd barely spoken to her and hadn't touched her once since their mind-blowing kiss on the steps of the helicopter before they'd left Wiltshire.

She'd felt branded, owned, after that kiss. But, in the exhausting hours since, she'd been left to feel almost like a discarded toy, a play thing, which Brandon possessed but didn't wish to play with... Yet...

She frowned, her skin prickling alarmingly with that feeling of over-sensitivity. Of hyper-awareness, which he could trigger just by looking at her.

Had he ignored her on purpose? To make her even more aware there was only one thing he wanted from her?

Was this supposed to be another punishment of some sort? Did he expect her to spend the rest of her life atoning for the bad decisions she'd made as a nineteen-year-old? Yes, she'd misjudged Brandon—and his capacity, so far at least, to be a much better father than her own—but she'd been young and scared and she had, in her own misguided way, thought she was protecting her child.

Even if Brandon couldn't forgive her, she had to forgive herself. Or she would turn into that defensive girl again, who had blamed herself because her father couldn't love her.

Brandon was going to have to get past his anger—and learn to trust her. He couldn't blame her for ever. That wasn't healthy for her, or Ruby, or ultimately even for him. And it certainly wasn't a good way to start a life together.

Her pulse jumped. Assuming they had a life together… She swallowed heavily and forced down the ripple of insecurity.

She knew Brandon didn't see this marriage as a lifetime commitment, but as a means to an end. He'd made that abundantly clear more than once. But she'd made the decision to come here, to be with him here alone for the week so she could explore the possibilities, to see if there could be more. And she refused to be put off…or put in her place…

She'd allowed him to have the lavish wedding he'd wanted and had been overwhelmed by the whole process— the highly sought-after wedding planner and her team of designers, florists, caterers et cetera had made her feel as if she'd been playing a role in an elaborate spectacle, rather than being a woman on her wedding day.

Had that been Brandon's intention? To make her aware she had no real place in his life other than the one he had designated for her?

*Think again, Cade.*

Flinging off the covers, Lacey jumped out of the king-sized bed with a new sense of purpose.

She had no idea where Brandon was. But she had no intention of going in search of him like a lost puppy looking for attention.

The concierge who had showed her round the bungalow early that morning had mentioned a number of the island's natural attractions, including a waterfall only a two-mile walk from the beach.

She began to hunt through the drawers of designer clothes that had been selected for her by a stylist. Because, apparently, she couldn't even be trusted to dress herself appropriately as Brandon Cade's trophy wife.

After dressing in a ludicrously tiny bikini, a linen beach tunic and some sturdy sandals, and packing a small rucksack with water, sunscreen and mosquito repellent, she set out along the white sand beach.

Her breath caught as sunshine glinted off the turquoise water—a coral reef visible under the translucent sea. A breeze fluttered through the palm trees that edged the sand, refreshing her skin—and reminding her of what it felt like to have Brandon's eyes on her.

A cold swim in a waterfall was just what she needed to take back control of the devil's bargain she'd made with her domineering, overbearing new husband.

Perhaps he didn't plan this to be a real marriage, but she'd be damned if she'd simply fall into step with those plans.

If he thought he'd got himself a convenient wife, this

honeymoon would show him that Lacey Carstairs—she caught her breath as she took the path into the island's interior: make that Lacey Cade—was nobody's pushover.

'Where the hell is my wife?' Brandon demanded as he waylaid the concierge at the resort reception.

'I'm sorry, Mr Cade, is she not in her villa?'

'No, she's not,' he said, getting increasingly annoyed. He'd decided to pay a call on her. He'd waited long enough.

Unlike her, he'd chosen not to take a nap to sleep off the jet lag, but had instead gone for a long run on the beach and then spent an hour lifting weights in the on-site gym to take his mind off the sexual frustration—which, instead of being controlled, had only become more explosive during the long journey to the island.

After a shower, he'd headed to her villa. Because she was his wife, and she wanted him just as much as he wanted her. And he was through playing games.

And now this. Where was she?

'The housekeeping staff did mention she wasn't in the villa when they went to clean it an hour ago, sir,' the concierge said.

'An hour ago?' Frustration turned to something that felt disturbingly like panic.

'She seemed interested in Jewel Falls when I mentioned it,' the concierge offered. 'I told her how to get there. Perhaps—'

'Have the boat crew check the coastline,' Brandon interrupted him, the panic scaling down a little. She had probably gone into the interior. But there were a number of coves carved into the rocky headland on the south of the island which could trap the unwary tourist at high tide. The cliffs were a good five miles away—surely Lacey couldn't have got that far? But he wasn't taking any chances.

'Yes, sir,' the concierge said, all but saluting him. 'Would you like me to send a search party to the falls too?'

'No, thanks. I'll head there myself.'

If Lacey was at the falls, he couldn't think of a better place to confront her about her failure to inform him or the staff of her whereabouts, and then give her a hands-on demonstration of her new role as his wife.

And for that he did not want an audience.

Lacey sighed with pleasure, the cold water pounding down from the fissure in the rock wall reinvigorating her hot, sweaty skin. She'd taken her time during the walk, admiring the island's spectacular flora and fauna. But once she'd found the falls she'd been awestruck. Crystal-clear water cascaded from the mossy limestone rocks formed from a volcano—which had built the island's reef millions of years ago, according to the guide book—while its sandy pool nestled in a fragrant grove of hibiscus and oleander.

But she wasn't as interested in the geology now, or the spectacular beauty of her surroundings, as she was in enjoying the tranquil setting and indulging the refreshing feel of the cool water against her skin.

Tipping her head back, she let out one last guttural moan of pleasure before stepping out of the stream. But, as she opened her eyes, she jolted—visceral sensation slamming into her.

The tall, dark figure of her husband stood five feet away, ankle-deep in the water, wearing loose cotton trousers, an open shirt to reveal the tanned contours of his chest and a frown.

Vibrant sensation sank deep into her abdomen under his focussed gaze. Her already pebbled nipples hardened to poke against the skimpy bikini, not from the cold this time, but from the warmth spearing through her body like wildfire. But with the familiar arousal came the swell of emotion.

How long had he been standing there? Watching her?

Tugging a hand out of his pocket, he crooked his finger at her without speaking, directing her to come to him. His movements seemed casual, but the fierce demand in his face was anything but.

She shivered, not from the cold, but from the sharp yank of desire and the tug of annoyance. She slicked the hair back from her face, trying to decide how best to react.

She could refuse to do as he asked. Refuse to allow him to use her as his toy, one he was finally prepared to play with. But that vicious yank—compelling her to do anything and everything he wanted—also made her feel alive…and seen. And she knew denying him would also be to deny herself.

The need twisted into a knot in her abdomen.

He had all the experience here, and she knew how much he liked to dominate and control their sexual encounters— she suspected so he could keep a tight rein on his emotions. But surely, if she was bold, brave and unafraid, she could wrestle some of that power out of his hands?

She walked through the pool towards him, refusing to break eye contact, and stopped a few feet from him.

Exhilaration flowed through her as she noticed the thick ridge of an erection under his trousers. She resisted the urge to cross her arms over her chest.

His dark-green gaze dipped, burning the chill from her wet skin, then fixed back on her face.

'Take it off,' he said, indicating her bikini top.

She sucked in a breath, shocked by the arrogant demand. But, as she steadied her staggered breathing, she acknowledged the delicious thrill charging through her body.

However volatile, however overwhelming, this insistent desire was as much a part of this marriage as the feelings she had begun to nurture and protect. The feelings she hoped one day he might return.

So she looked him in the eye, then forced a smile to her lips—which she hoped looked confident and defiant—and lifted her arms to tug on the string holding the bikini's halter-neck in place.

The bow gave way, releasing the top. She wasn't particularly busty, but her breasts felt heavy, the nipples painfully swollen as she exposed herself to his gaze.

It was his turn to suck in a breath. He looked his fill, the flare of approval, of yearning, in his face like a physical caress leaving a trail of fire in its wake.

When his gaze met hers again, his expression had tightened, tensed, the fierce desire something he was no longer able to control.

'Now take off the rest of it. I want to see all of my wife.'

She shuddered. The emphasis on *my* was deliberately provocative…and possessive.

But still she refused to be cowed, to be intimidated by his need. Or her own. She wanted this, she wanted him. He was the only man she had ever made love to, the only man ever to see her naked. Why should she be embarrassed or ashamed of the silvery marks on her belly left by her pregnancy? Maybe her breasts weren't as pert as they had once been, maybe her hips weren't as narrow, but she was proud of what her body had become to nurture their baby.

Unfortunately, she had never stripped for a man before, and certainly not in the open air, so she completed the striptease with more tenacity than skill. Clumsy fingers released the back hook on the bikini top to let it fall, then she eased off the panties and flung the swatch of fabric onto the bank.

He didn't say anything, didn't speak, as his gaze roamed over her skin. She folded her arms around her waist, lifted her head and stared into his eyes—bold and defiant.

'Now it's your turn,' she managed round the lump of need and terrifying emotion growing in her throat as the wildfire sizzled over her exposed skin. 'I want to see all of my husband too.'

*She's magnificent.*

Brandon let out a gruff chuckle through dry lips, tantalised by the glorious sight of his wife's naked body—and painfully aroused by her bold request. Need throbbed in his groin, the desire to touch, to taste, all but unbearable ever since he had spotted her standing under the waterfall, her curves glistening and wet, her body barely covered by the strategically placed straps of red fabric.

Ordering her to take off the bikini had been a double-edged sword, because instead of resisting she had met his demands with defiance.

Added to that, the sight of her erect nipples, ruched and reddened by the cold water, the tremble of her breasts as she stripped with unpretentious allure and the trimmed curls covering her sex—where he planned to feast very soon—left him struggling not to explode.

*'Touché,'* he murmured, stripping off his shirt and chucking it on the sand. He unbuttoned the loose cotton trousers, kicking them off to reveal the swimming trunks which could barely contain his painful erection.

Her gaze drifted down and the explosive need pooled in his groin. Reaching out, he tugged her closer.

He couldn't wait any longer.

She gasped as he devoured her neck and licked off the fresh water. Her curves were strong and supple under his hands and he felt her instant response, the moist heat between her thighs, as he explored the swollen folds, torturous and tormenting.

He lifted her easily into his arms and carried her out of the pool, the urgency to bury his length in her tight warmth—to finally claim his wife—something he could no longer control. But, as he placed her on her feet on the bank, she covered the hard ridge in his trunks with her palm, testing the shape and length of him beneath the swimwear.

'You're not naked,' she said, her accusation contradicted somewhat by the vibrant flush on her cheeks—and the devastating desire in her eyes.

'Because I'm about to lose it.' He grasped her wrist, amused by the flare of triumph in her eyes as he brought her marauding fingers to his lips before she won this battle outright.

'Are you on the pill?' he managed.

She nodded.

*Thank God.*

But, as his lips found the taut nipple and she moaned, her body bowing back, his relief evaporated. He wanted to make another baby with her. Because the thought of seeing for himself the changes to her body as his child grew inside her was even more erotic than watching her strip in front of him, seeing the subtle signs of her previous pregnancy and the uninhibited desire in her eyes.

He recoiled at the vicious wave of arousal that followed.

*You need to get inside her before you lose what's left of your sanity.*

He turned her to face one of the palm trees that edged the lagoon. Clasping her hips, stroking the silvery scars where his child had marked her, he positioned her and released the massive erection from his trunks.

'Brace yourself,' he murmured against her neck.

She obeyed instinctively, pressing her hands against the trunk as he dragged his fingers through the drenched folds of her sex.

She bucked and sobbed as he circled her swollen clitoris, testing her readiness.

'I need you inside me,' she said. The staggered pants of her breathing, the unequivocal demand, was a siren call to his already fractured senses.

He cupped her breasts to anchor her in place, found the tight entrance to her sex and thrust into her from behind.

She took him to the hilt, her body clamping down hard as she cried out and soared straight to peak.

He held still, the clasp and release of her orgasm, the depth of his penetration in this position, almost more than he could bear.

But, as she began to come down, he started to move, desperate to force her to peak again, stroking a place deep inside he knew would intensify her orgasm.

He kept moving, rolling his hips, gritting his teeth to hold back his own orgasm, determined to claim her, to brand her, to show her she was his. Now and always. But as he struggled to cling on to control the pulse of desperation became overwhelming…and he wasn't sure who was in charge any more. But, what was even much more disturbing, he wasn't sure he cared.

The brutal pleasure kept intensifying, battering Lacey, driving her to new heights. Each time she got close, he forced her further, turning her into a throbbing mass of sensation.

A sob escaped, but she refused to beg, digging her fingers into the rough tree bark to hold herself steady, to hold herself upright for the deep internal stroking.

He dragged her hair aside to kiss her nape. His hands caressed her heavy breasts, trapping her for the relentless thrusts. So deep, so overwhelming, but never quite enough to take her over again.

But then one hand glided down, stroking over taut sinews, quivering muscles, and located the pulsing centre of her need at last.

'Come for me, Lacey,' he commanded, just as he stroked where their bodies joined.

The wave barrelled through her, splintering pleasure like a tornado, making her shudder and sob.

She heard his grunt of release, the massive erection getting bigger still as he pumped himself into her at last. She was shaking, trembling, as he dragged himself out of her then scooped her shattered body into his arms. But, even as she understood he had destroyed her, she knew she had destroyed him too, his gait uneven, his arms shaking as he carried her into the pool.

They sank together into the cool water to wash off the evidence of their love-making. She flinched, too sore and tender to take the brutal intimacy as he cleaned her.

But she could hear the strain in his voice when he spoke. 'Look at me, Lacey.'

She opened her eyes to focus on him.

'Don't ever go off without telling me where you are again,' he said.

She could see the grooves of strain around his mouth and the muscle flexing in his jaw, as well as the concern in his eyes.

A part of her understood his command was the only way he could articulate to her that he had been worried about her. But, even as her heart opened on the tidal wave of hope, of possibility, another part of her could hear the subtle hint of ownership in his tone and she knew she couldn't let him get away with it.

She drew away from him. 'I'm not a child, Brandon.'

He frowned. 'Yes, but you are my wife.'

She nodded. 'But that doesn't mean I'm obliged to tell you where I am every minute of the day.' Especially as he had tried to treat her on the journey here as little more than a play thing that he could ignore at will.

'Aren't you?' he asked, clasping her wrist to drag her

closer and band his arm around her bottom. 'Well, you damn well ought to be.'

Emotion pulsed deep in her chest. Did he feel it too, this brutal connection, the yearning for more?

'This may not be a conventional marriage,' she said, suddenly knowing she had to stand up for herself now, for what this marriage could be, or he would never open himself to her. 'But it is a marriage of equals.'

Maybe it was still the afterglow—the intensity of their lovemaking—which had left her dazzled and disorientated. But even so she cupped his cheek and let the last of her own defences down as she stared into his eyes—and allowed him to see the hope she was trying to keep in perspective. 'If you were worried about me, Brandon, you're allowed to say so. And I'd be happy to put your mind at rest.'

The muscle jumped beneath her palm, but the wary expression on his face only made the emotion pound harder in her chest.

He didn't love her, not yet. It was far too soon for that. For either one of them. They both had insecurities when it came to making themselves vulnerable. She understood that. But, if they were going to have any kind of a marriage, they needed to be honest about their feelings.

His frown deepened, but then he let out a heavy breath and turned his head to press a kiss into her palm. 'Fine,' he said. 'I was worried about you. I didn't know where the hell you were. Is that good enough, Mrs Cade?'

A chuckle popped out of her mouth at his annoyed expression. 'Absolutely, Mr Cade,' she said lightly, euphoria gripping her insides. Then, grasping his broad shoulders, she leapt into his arms.

He swore as they both tumbled backwards into the water together. But when they came up for air, both choking and spluttering, a playful smile danced over his sensual lips.

'You little witch, you nearly drowned us both,' he said. 'I should punish you…'

'You can only punish me if you catch me first!' She yelped, pushing a wave of water into his face.

She danced away from him, shrieking and laughing as he chased her out of the pond. But, when he finally did catch her, the buzz cut glistening with water, the dimple in his cheek winking at her from the stubble on his jaw and his eyes glittering with amused approval, he looked so damn handsome it made her chest ache.

# CHAPTER THIRTEEN

'BRANDON, WE NEED to talk about what's going to happen when we return to the UK.' Lacey sliced into the juicy char-grilled tuna steak and tried to keep her voice nonchalant.

But, as her husband lifted his head across the table, the green of his irises flickering with jade fire in the glow of torchlight, and the waves lapping lazily against the nearby shore the only sound, it wasn't easy to ignore the heady pulsing of her heartbeat.

Their honeymoon would be over tomorrow—and it had been nothing short of idyllic. She'd indulged in every pleasure—they'd made love all over the island, as she discovered things about her body she had never known. And she'd thrown herself into every new adventure Brandon had suggested—from snorkelling on the reef, to abseiling into a private cove, to an exhilarating jet-ski safari out to a sand bar where the staff had been waiting to serve them a three-course lunch.

It had bothered her that Brandon had refused to spend the night with her in her bungalow. He'd given her some excuse about not being a good sleeper the night of their mind-blowing tryst at Jewel Falls. But she had been determined not to panic. Patience was the answer. Getting to know her new husband would be a long-term project, because she knew from the little Brandon had confided in her about his past he had been alone for a very long time. He wasn't used to sharing… Not a bed, not a life and certainly not his secrets.

But she knew they had also both been avoiding any difficult conversations about their life together going forward. She'd been okay with that up to now. This week had been a chance to enjoy themselves, to let their guards down, at least a little bit. But when they returned to the UK they'd have some important decisions to make about how their family life would be organised—as she began the mammoth task of reinventing her stalled career.

She couldn't stay in Wiltshire indefinitely. The kind of work she was looking for was mostly based in London. And Ruby had mentioned her old nursery friends that morning during their last video chat—she missed them, and it made sense for her to return to the nursery she loved.

He swallowed, his gaze narrowing. 'What do you wish to discuss?' he said, but he didn't sound pleased at the prospect.

She ignored the foolish blip in her heart rate. This was the kind of conversations a wife had with a husband, and a mother had with the father of her child, something they both needed to learn how to do.

'I got a text from an old colleague at *Splendour* today. Apparently *Buzz* online magazine are looking for a feature writer, and I'm going to apply for it next week.'

He put down his knife and fork, his jaw clenching and his brows flattening into a sharp from. '*Buzz*? Isn't that owned by Roman Garner?'

'He has some shares in it, yes,' she said, not sure why that should be a problem. Garner Media was a rival of Cade Inc, but the small online publication could hardly be seen as a competitor to any of Cade Inc's huge portfolio of news titles.

'Then the answer's no.'

'I'm sorry, what?' Lacey stiffened, shocked, not just by the outrageous statement but the brittle, uncompromising tone.

'You heard me,' he replied. 'I don't want you working for that bastard.' He picked up his cutlery again and sliced neatly into his steak as if the conversation was over.

'I wasn't asking your permission, Brandon,' she said flatly, trying to contain her anger at the dictatorial way he was behaving. 'I was simply letting you know what I plan to do.' Had she been kidding herself about the progress she thought they'd made this week?

It seemed as if she had. When his gaze rose back to her face, the look in his eyes was intractable. Did he really not understand?

'If you want a job, I can find you one at Cade Inc,' he said.

'I can't work at Cade, Brandon. I'm your wife,' she said, her voice rising as she tried to control her indignation.

'So what?' he replied, not budging an inch.

'So everyone would know I got the job because I was married to you. It would make my working relationship with my colleagues untenable, surely you can see that?' she finished, her anger downgrading a notch when he gave her a curt nod.

At last, a concession.

But then he ruined it.

'Fine, how about I buy *Buzz* for you? If you own the title, you being my wife shouldn't be an issue. And you'll be able to decide how much or how little you do.'

'Don't be daft, Brandon.' Was he actually serious right now? 'I appreciate your willingness to do something so...' *Overwhelming, OTT, insane...* 'So generous,' she settled on. Maybe in his own dogmatic, dictatorial way, he was trying to be helpful. 'But I haven't got the experience to own and operate a title like that.'

Nor did she particularly want to. Writing was what she enjoyed. 'And, anyway, you hate celebrity media,' she added, beginning to wonder if she had completely misconstrued his objections to her taking the job with *Buzz*. Was this really just about his dislike of Roman Garner? A need to dictate her role in their marriage? Or something much more fundamental? Because his solution was out of all proportion to a problem that didn't really exist. 'I don't want you to buy me a magazine,' she said. 'I just want to work. My career is important to me.'

'Why?' he said. 'Why isn't being Ruby's mother enough?' he added.

It was her turn to frown at the harsh question, the accusatory tone.

But suddenly she remembered what he had told her about his own mother. Was it possible his objections had nothing to do with Garner, or her need to work, and everything to do with the way his mother had once abandoned him for money?

She heaved a sigh.

'Are you finished eating?' she asked as she stood up. 'Because I'd like to continue this conversation in private.'

The waiting staff was at a discreet distance, but even so she didn't want to have this conversation with them in earshot.

'I'm not going to change my mind,' he said, but followed her and stepped away from the table.

'Let's walk,' she murmured.

She strolled past the torches flickering in the warm island breeze and onto the soft, sandy beach. The sound of the waves lapping lazily against the shore and the soft green glow of phosphorescence shimmering on the surface of the sea seemed impossibly romantic, almost as romantic as the feel of him, tall and indomitable, and so guarded beside her.

The silence stretched out between them as she tried to figure out how best to approach the conversation.

He hated talking about his emotional needs. She got that. She suspected it was because he had spent so much of his life denying he even had any. She'd learnt enough about his dysfunctional relationship with his father, and his lack of a relationship with his mother, to understand why that might be. But she needed him to trust her—as a mother as well as a wife. And to do that he had to forgive her, all the way, for the mistake she'd made in not telling him about Ruby.

And to do *that* he had to understand a lot more about why she'd made that decision. He hadn't asked her for an explanation and she was beginning to realise he probably never would. Because it would mean straying into an emotional landscape he had no experience—and no desire—to navigate. So she would have to make this move, for both of them.

'Can we talk openly?' she said at last.

'I suppose so,' he said, but she could hear the edge in his voice.

She had to let her own guard down, to let him see she had scars too. It was way past time she told him the truth she had recently discovered, about why she hadn't told him about Ruby much sooner. That her silence hadn't just been a result of that naive girl's insecurity, but also her broken relationship with her own father.

'I just want you to know that I know exactly what it feels like to have a father who's an absolute jerk...' she began.

Brandon saw the familiar compassion darken Lacey's eyes. And he recoiled against it instinctively. How had they ended up talking about his father?

'Mine walked out when Milly and I were still too young to remember him,' she added gently, the quiet, pragmatic tone somehow all the more powerful because it was so carefully devoid of sentiment. 'And he never returned,' she continued. 'We discovered after Mum died that he had another family. Sons he was proud of, a wife he loved when we contacted him after my mother's funeral. He didn't want to know us—which I guess was why my mum avoided conversations about him when we were kids. But she had always made it clear to us his failings were not ours. That just because he couldn't love us it didn't make us less than. Something I realised recently, I had always struggled to accept.'

She sighed. 'I'm just incredibly sad you never had that from your own mum. Having two selfish bastards for parents was really bad luck.'

He stared at her, the strange pulsing in his chest turning into something disturbing. He hadn't asked about her past for two specific reasons—it would increase the intimacy between them, and he had no desire to reveal more of his own. But something about the way she spoke of her father, without bitterness, without regret, seemed incredibly brave.

'How old were you both, when your mother died?' he asked, curious about something he had tried hard not to care about.

'Milly was fifteen, I had just turned eighteen.'

'That must have been tough,' he said, remembering her as she had been at nineteen—eager and erudite, ambitious and smart, and already on a fast track within Cade Inc's internship programme. Of course, he hadn't realised at the time she was still a teenager, and had assumed she was several years older because of her confidence when she'd flirted with him.

But why hadn't he ever confronted his own culpability that night? Why hadn't he ever considered how vulnerable she had been?

She shrugged. 'Luckily, social services were happy to declare me as Milly's guardian. And I already had the internship at Cade Inc lined up.'

'Which I destroyed for you,' he said abruptly.

He had tried to get over his resentment about her refusal to tell him about Ruby when she became pregnant. But the truth was, he'd been happy to dismiss his own actions. And he had never once asked about her circumstances. Had never considered she was the sole breadwinner for her and her sister. Had never felt any guilt about the fact he'd left her pregnant and jobless as a direct result of his own carelessness.

Why had he never checked up on her to make absolutely sure there had been no consequences?

'That was a mistake,' she said, giving him leeway he now knew he didn't deserve. 'You didn't destroy my career on purpose.'

'Dammit, Lacey, you were a virgin and only nineteen. I knew the condom had failed and yet I never contacted you to be sure you were okay.'

She blinked, clearly taken aback by his outburst, which only made him feel like more of a bastard.

'If it hadn't split, we wouldn't have Ruby, so I'd say it's a moot point.'

'Even so, I owe you an apology,' he said tightly, finally saying what he should have said when he'd first discovered Ruby's existence.

'Okay.' She nodded slowly, her eyes glowing with an emotion he didn't really understand…and wasn't sure he wanted to understand. 'Apology accepted, but it doesn't mean much if you can't forgive me.' She turned towards him in the moonlight, the breeze blowing in her hair and making it dance around her face. She looked so young and earnest…and brave in that moment, he felt something shift and break open inside him.

'What for?' he asked, hopelessly confused now.

'I made a terrible mistake not telling you about Ruby. I didn't trust you, but I can see now a lot of the way I reacted was all wrapped up in the way my father had rejected me and Milly. I blamed you for what he did. I didn't even know you. And yet I judged you. I assumed you would be a terrible father. And that wasn't fair.'

He frowned, feeling strangely threatened by the forthright apology, her easy acceptance of the way he had behaved. 'I was an arrogant, entitled bastard that night, let's be honest, which might also have had something to do with why you kept Ruby from me.'

Why was she letting him off the hook so easily?

She squeezed his hand, a smile spreading across her face. 'True,' she said, with a complete lack of anger. 'But I was a clueless idiot, so I would say we're even. And, if you can forgive me, I can certainly forgive you.'

He turned his hand over to link his fingers with hers, the need to touch her suddenly about more than just sex, more than just the intense physical connection which he had exploited so vociferously in the last seven days.

She'd met every one of his demands with demands of her own. And he'd enjoyed the time he spent with her—not just in bed, but out of it too. Lacey had a playful, adventurous nature which intrigued and excited him. And in the last seven days, as she had spoken at length about their daughter, he had come to realise what a good mother she was too. Patient, supportive but also fascinated and amused by Ruby, despite the circumstances of her birth.

'I know you don't trust people easily, Brandon,' she said as she held onto his hand. 'And I think now I know why—because the people you should have been able to trust as a little boy both let you down horribly. You asked me why being Ruby's mum isn't enough for me, and I want you to know that it absolutely is. I love her with everything I am, and everything I'm ever going to be, but I don't see being a mother and a career woman being mutually exclusive,' she continued. 'I know I can do both. And I want you to trust me on that, if you can.'

He tensed, drawing his fingers out of hers as the crack in his chest threatened to become a chasm.

'Okay,' he said, his voice thick with an emotion he did not want to feel, was determined not to feel ever again. He did trust her, he realised, perhaps much more than he should. How had that happened without him even realising it?

Because it made him think of that young boy who had begged his father for affection—for so long—and had never received it.

He wasn't that kid any more. But the thought of her being able to see that boy scared him. Because that boy could be hurt.

Placing his free hand on her waist, he tugged her into the lee of his body, letting her feel the erection which was never far away. 'Although I'm not sure what any of this has to do with you working for Roman Garner,' he said gruffly.

He didn't want her working for Garner, for the simple reason she was his. Eventually she would figure out there was a limit to what he could offer her. But he intended to ensure she was bound to him by then, in every way that mattered.

She smiled, then rubbed against him, making the erection harden. 'I just wanted to establish that this is a partnership, Brandon. One in which we can both get what we want. If we're open with each other.' She grinned, the sparkle of affection in her eyes as spellbinding as it was disturbing.

Grasping his hand, she drew him towards her cabin, making his heart beat a hasty tattoo against his ribs. She was taking the initiative, and for once he felt no need to fight it as arousal roared in his gut.

*This is about sex, and making a home together for the child you share. Nothing more. Nothing less.*

He climbed the wooden steps in silence, clasping her hips as she threw her arms around his neck and stretched up on tiptoes to capture his lips. He drove his tongue into her mouth on her sob of need, but let her lead the dance of temptation and retreat. Let her feast as the hunger raced through his blood. He needed to have her, to keep her, by whatever means necessary.

But as they made love, first fast and furious on her bed, then slow and easy in the rainfall shower—and she gave him everything, while holding nothing back—he kept that hidden, vulnerable part of himself ruthlessly in check.

Because he was never going to give anyone the power to hurt him again.

But, as he lay in her bed hours later, he listened to the low hum of the cicadas outside and the soft murmurer of her breathing and struggled to close the chasm in his chest the only way he knew how.

Lacey felt Brandon shift in the bed beside her and forced her eyelids to open, her exhausted body still humming from the intensity of their love-making. But, as Brandon eased her out of his arms and threw off the sheet, she reached out to grasp his arm.

'Brandon, where are you going?' she murmured, hating the neediness in her voice, but hating the hollow ache under her ribs more.

Was he leaving her bed *again*? *Tonight*? Why? When she had been sure they had made so much progress?

He glanced down at her, his hand covering hers, before his thumb skimmed down her arm. 'You're still awake?' he said, his voice gruff. Her heartbeat accelerated, the warm, seductive touch triggering an instant response in her abdomen. 'I thought I had exhausted you.'

It wasn't an answer, but she forced herself to let go of him.

'You did,' she said, flopping back onto the bed. 'Were you going to your own cabin?' she asked. 'You don't need to,' she added. Did he still think she would hold him to that asinine promise about separate bedrooms after everything they'd shared this week? 'I'd like to wake up with you in the morning.'

He chuckled, but the laugh sounded strained somehow. Evasive…? Or was this her insecurity talking again?

'You're insatiable,' he said.

This wasn't about sex, or not just about sex, not to her. She wasn't even sure she could have sex again, after all the times he'd had her that night already.

But, when he relaxed back onto the pillows and pulled her into his embrace, she let herself sink into his arms. The moment seemed fragile somehow and, while she didn't want to push, she also didn't want to let him go, not tonight. Because she was desperately afraid she was falling in love with him.

His fingers threaded through her hair, hooking the unruly curls behind her ear. He pressed his lips to her temple.

'I've been thinking,' he said, his voice a soft rumble in the still night. 'Why don't you stop taking the contraceptive pills when we get back to the UK?'

*'W-what?'* She jolted upright, wide awake now, so shocked by the suggestion, she wasn't even sure she'd heard it correctly.

His palm covered her belly over the sheet, rubbing seductively. His gaze when it met hers again was dark with arousal, but also full of possessiveness. And her heart jumped into her throat.

'Ruby will be five in a few months, and I don't want her

to be an only child,' he said, his voice forceful now, and thick with purpose. 'I've been one my whole life, and believe me, it sucks,' he added. But then his hand settled on her belly, making the skin prickle and throb. 'Plus I want the chance to see you pregnant with my child,' he said, the passion in his tone as disturbing as the intensity. The leap in her pulse, and the blast of hope, was as terrifying as it was exciting. Surely he wouldn't suggest such a thing if he didn't think their marriage had a future?

His thumb cruised up to circle her nipple and make it ache.

'I can't think of anything more erotic,' he said.

For a moment she was speechless, sucked under the tidal wave of longing he could exploit so easily. But this wasn't just a longing for physical pleasure any more, not for her—it was so much more than that. It was a longing for his approval, his love.

She trapped his hand against her breast. She mustn't get ahead of herself, not again, not the way she had as a girl of nineteen before she'd been dumped so cruelly. Not least because there was so much more at stake now.

He wanted her. He might even need her. She got that. She was beyond flattered, and stupidly touched that he would want to have more children with her. But she couldn't let herself get carried away by the giddy hope making her heart pulse and pound in her chest.

'Can I think about it?' she asked, knowing she already wanted to have more children with him, but knowing neither of them were ready to have them yet. 'We've only been married for a week,' she added, to cover the brutal swelling in her chest.

She wanted this to work. She wanted to have a future with him. But was that really what he was offering?

He let out a rueful laugh. 'Sure,' he said. He tucked her back against his side. 'Now, go to sleep, we have to leave early in the morning. And we need to find a place for us to live back in London. If that's what you want?'

She nodded and yawned, settling back into bed, loving the feel of him beside her. And beyond happy that he seemed willing for them to live in the city. Together.

When she awoke the next morning, she found him gone again. But this time she convinced herself it had to be the flight that had torn him from her side in the early hours.

And when they returned to the UK, and he told her he had arranged to buy a gated mansion in Islington so Ruby could return to her old nursery—and he could spend more time with his daughter—she convinced herself it didn't matter if he still couldn't stay the night in her bed. Or that they never seemed to get much quality time alone together—unless they were busy tearing each other's clothes off.

Surely greater intimacy, more trust, would grow in time? She just needed to be patient.

And why did it have to be a bad thing she was falling in love with this hard, indomitable man when he was also her husband? And the father of her child?

# CHAPTER FOURTEEN

*One month later*

'BRANDON, DO YOU have a minute?' Lacey asked breathlessly, overjoyed to find her husband in his study for once, having rushed back after dropping Ruby at nursery to catch him before he left for the day. She had exciting news she could not wait to share.

'Actually, yes, I wanted to talk to you too,' Brandon said, closing his laptop. Lacey's excitement downgraded a little as she spotted the rigid expression on his face. Was something wrong?

After all, it was unusual to find him still at home when she got back in the mornings.

She dismissed the blip of panic.

*For goodness' sake, stop freaking out. That's old, insecure Lizzy Devlin talking, not new, loved-up Lacey Cade who now has a brand-new dream job to go with her new improved marriage.*

She had been forced to put her job hunt on the back burner ever since they had returned from Bermuda, while she'd concentrated on the move and getting her daughter back into some semblance of a routine. But she'd interviewed for the position at *Buzz* over a video link yesterday afternoon and had received a call ten minutes ago, while she'd been walking back from the nursery, to say she'd got the job.

She was hoping Brandon would be excited too, despite his earlier misgivings. After all, she'd come to terms with the fact she'd fallen hopelessly in love with him in the last four weeks. And watching him fall in love with his daughter—and Ruby fall in love with him—and seeing them begin to form a strong, sweet bond together had only made her love him more.

Having Brandon fall in love with her too was always going to be a long-term project. But he was already an integral part of both her and Ruby's lives. And the sex was amazing. Brandon was a dominant but generous lover who liked to push her boundaries, while also being supremely sensitive to her needs. And she'd adored every second of exploring and exploiting their kinetic physical connection.

It still bothered her that each night, after she fell asleep in his arms, exhausted, he would slip away from her to sleep in his own room. And each morning she would wake up alone again. But she was determined not to freak out about that either. She knew he had trust issues. And, even if they hadn't discussed it again since that magical night on their honeymoon, she felt sure it was only a matter of time before he opened up the rest of the way.

'Fab, me first, because I have some wonderful news,' she said.

At exactly the same time, Brandon said, 'I understand you've been offered the job at *Buzz*.'

'Um…y-yes,' she stammered, more than a little deflated he'd stolen her surprise. 'How did you find out? They only told me ten minutes ago.'

'That's beside the point,' he said, but something sparked in his eyes which she couldn't read—because it looked weirdly like irritation. 'I thought we agreed you weren't going to work there,' he said. It wasn't a question.

'When did we agree to that?' she replied carefully. Why was he looking at her like that? As if she'd done something wrong? This wasn't just annoyance, it was disapproval.

'I thought we were having another child,' he said, his gaze becoming flat and remote, his tone accusatory. 'You said you would think about it. But I found out this morning you just got prescribed another six months' supply of contraceptive pills.'

Shock came first, swiftly followed by anger, but right beneath it was that dropping sensation in her stomach. That brutal, unrelenting feeling of inadequacy she remembered so well from the last time she had seen her father the day after their mother's funeral, when he had told Milly and her ever so politely that, while he was sorry for their loss, he had another family now and he simply did not have time to deal with their problems.

'How do you know about my prescription?' she demanded, wanting to be angry but unable to muster anything past the ball of misery in her stomach.

'I found the pills in your bathroom cabinet,' he said, striding round his desk, the look on his face making it clear he believed he was the injured party. 'After I heard about your job offer.'

The hope she had been nurturing for over a month—ever since that beautiful night in his arms in Bermuda—died slowly inside her as he continued.

'We had a deal, Lacey. You asked me to trust you, and I did. Then you applied for that damn job behind my back.' Something flickered in his eyes that looked almost like hurt. But how could she even think that, when she had been wrong about so much else?

She'd thought they were building something important here, that he was starting to fall in love with her. But his approval had always been conditional, she suddenly realised, on never crossing that line in the sand he had drawn between them.

'You had no right to check up on my prescription,' she managed. 'And there's no reason I can't have a job *and* a baby.' She shook her head, the brutal yearning in her chest mocking her. 'But that's not even the point. I said I would think about it, but it's clear now I'd be a fool to consider having another child with you.'

'Why the hell not?' he said, the temper in his voice upsetting her even more.

He hadn't opened himself to her, opened himself to the possibility of love. Not really. She'd hardly seen him in the last four weeks, except when he'd wanted to sleep with her, and even then he refused to spend the night with her. Why had she been so ready to accept that? To accept the crumbs of his affection, rather than demanding more?

'Because I'm not ready to bring another child into a marriage that obviously isn't working,' she said, the words hurting her throat.

His expression went from sharp to fierce. 'Of course it's working,' he said. 'We're making a good home here for our child. *Together.* I want you. I can't stop wanting you. And you want me. What the heck else is there?'

'Love.' She blurted the word out, hating how needy it sounded.

*'Love?'* The astonished expression only crucified her more.

She hugged herself, her heart splintering in her chest. 'I've fallen in love with you, Brandon,' she murmured, finally telling him the truth she should have told him weeks ago. But she had never imagined telling him like this. She had thought it would be a declaration full of promise, possibility and excitement. Instead it felt cloying and pathetic, when he simply stared at her, his expression blank.

He looked genuinely stunned, but then his gaze intensified, holding something she didn't understand. 'If you love me,' he said slowly, his voice rough with an emotion she didn't understand, because it sounded almost like regret, 'Why won't you have another child with me?'

She stared at him, her whole body beginning to shake—sadness and longing making the boulder in her stomach grow. 'Because you don't love me back, Brandon. And I'm not even sure you're capable of loving me back any more.'

Brandon swallowed down the panic threatening to consume him.

He couldn't lose her. Not now, not after discovering what a life with her and Ruby…and hopefully more children…would be like.

Each night he made love to her with a fury, a desperation, he hoped would bind her to him for ever. But, as soon as he watched her go over, his desperation only got worse.

He understood why she wanted to work. But he didn't want her working for that libidinous bastard Roman Garner.

He'd been thinking about Lacey having another baby ever since the night he had suggested it in Bermuda, the erotic thought morphing into something so much more compelling.

It was the perfect solution.

Sex would never be enough to bind a woman like her—full of fire, passion and honesty—to a man like him, but he had hoped that a baby…a new life they could share in this time…would be enough.

And now he'd blown it.

She wanted love. But he could never give her that. Because he simply didn't know how to love. Even the thought of letting his guard down to that extent made the anxiety build like a tsunami—and took him back to all those times in his father's study when he had yearned for one single sign of affection or approval, only to have his child-ish hopes destroyed.

Sure, he could fake it, tell her what she wanted to hear. But he knew she was far too emotionally intelligent not to see through it.

'I don't want you working for Roman Garner,' he man-aged, trying to keep the panic out of his voice. If she knew how much he needed her to be here every time he came home in the evening, and when he left in the morning, she would use it against him.

She stared at him, her eyes sheened with an emotion that reached into his chest and gave a hard yank.

*Disappointment.*

The feeling of inadequacy, of confusion, churned in his gut—reminding him far too forcefully of that lost, needy kid.

'You're my wife and he's a rival,' he added stiffly, to try and distance himself from that boy and turn himself back into the man he had become... A man who never let the fear and insecurity which had dogged him throughout his childhood show.

'We can revisit the question of another baby when you're more amenable.' He let his gaze sweep over her figure to settle on her belly in the jeans she wore, the fierce desire to see their child grow there all but overwhelming.

She blinked slowly, the sadness in her eyes only mak-ing the storm in his gut pitch and roll.

*Ignore it. You can't give her what she wants. You know it. And eventually she will realise it too, and will hopefully be prepared to live within those parameters.*

'This isn't about the job, Brandon, or another baby. This is about what you're prepared to give to this marriage. To give to me.'

It was hardly the concession he'd been looking for.

'I want you here with me, in my life, as my wife and the mother of my children. Why isn't that enough?'

If she wasn't ready to have another child...*yet*...he'd have to compromise and find her a job at Cade Inc, he thought frantically.

'And yet you still can't spend the night in my bed,' she said, her eyes sheened with unshed tears.

'I told you, I'm not a good sleeper, I'd wake you up.' The anxiety he remembered so well from his childhood—coupled with the cruel realisation he could never do enough, never *be* enough, to make anyone truly care for him—gripped his throat. He couldn't give her that, couldn't let her see him at his most vulnerable.

'And I've told you I don't care,' she replied. 'You have to let your barriers down, to let me in. To let me know you. Why does that terrify you so much?'

'I'm not good with that much intimacy...' he said, but even he could hear the cowardice in his words, the note of panic and desperation, and realised how pathetic he sounded.

Could she hear it too? She must be able to. But, instead of calling him out on it, she brushed away the single tear that flowed down her cheek. 'Then we don't have a real marriage, Brandon. And a real marriage is what I want.'

And then she turned and left him standing alone in the study. He stood there for what felt like an eternity, the walls closing in around him, trying to shore up all the defences he'd worked so hard to build over so many years.

At last, anger flowed over the panic, inadequacy and fear. She would come around. This was what they'd agreed to—she couldn't change the terms of their agreement after only one month. And what about Ruby? What about the daughter she'd denied him? She owed him this marriage.

But, as he strode out of the study and out of the house, he could already feel his mind working, desperately trying to come up with a plan to fill up the huge, empty hole opening up all over again in his gut. And threatening to swallow him whole.

# CHAPTER FIFTEEN

'WHY DIDN'T DADDY come home tonight?' Ruby yawned, the sleepy question making Lacey's heart hurt.

'I told you, baby, he had to work late, but he'll make it up to you tomorrow. Daryl says Daddy has bought tickets to take you to the zoo, just the two of you.'

The text from Daryl had arrived twenty minutes ago, saying he had purchased the tickets at Brandon's request and informing her of her husband's plans.

As soon as Lacey had read the text, though, it had reminded her of the curt demands she had received from Daryl when Brandon had first found out about his daughter.

And she had known the decision to contact her through his assistant, not to return home tonight, was deliberate. Brandon was avoiding her and the messy emotional demands she'd made that morning.

She'd been drained and on edge all day. The last of the hope she had relied on for four weeks dying as she went through every aspect of their conversation that morning over and over again. And she knew she hadn't read any of it wrong.

She'd asked him to love her, at least to try to love her, and he'd refused.

Where did they go from here?

'*Really*, Mummy?' Ruby said, her eyes brightening with

excitement. 'Can Daddy and me spend the whole day there? I love the zoo.'

A day spent with her father all to herself was Ruby's ultimate gift and Lacey refused to spoil it. But as she tucked her daughter into bed, and finally got her to go to sleep, she knew she had some tough decisions to make.

She couldn't stay in a marriage with a man who refused to open himself to at least the possibility of love. Because it would destroy her in the end, and bring back that girl who had once believed she was the problem, the reason her father couldn't love her.

The staff had the night off on Friday—which was usually an excuse for Brandon and her to make love on the living room rug. But tonight she made herself a simple dinner alone in the kitchen.

She glanced at her phone to check the time.

Where was he? Wasn't he going to come home at all tonight?

After finishing the food and loading the dishwasher, she poured herself a glass of wine and waited in the sitting room. As the hours ticked by, her hopelessness and confusion increased, but with it came determination.

Brandon was a man who she suspected had never had his defences tested. Had never had to bend since his father's death. But he would have to bend now or she would be forced to give him an ultimatum.

She couldn't live without love. She understood if he couldn't love her yet. But she had to know if he intended them to be bound by nothing more than their daughter… and their sexual connection…always. Because that wasn't enough, not for her.

She'd begun to doze off when she jerked awake to find his dark shape filling the doorway.

'Lacey?' he murmured. 'You're still up?'

He sounded surprised, which made the hurt pulse in her chest.

'Of course. I wanted to speak to you about our conversation this morning,' she said.

He strode across the room to grasp her hands and pull her out of the chair. But then his lips descended on hers to devour her mouth like a starving man.

The kiss was dark, demanding, possessive—triggering the instant wave of arousal she couldn't stop. But she stumbled back, out of his grasp, folding her arms around her waist to stop the shivers of response.

'It's no good, Brandon, it won't work any more. We can't fill the holes in our marriage with sex.'

She had expected him to seduce her, had expected him to argue, demand, coerce, coax so that he could get what he wanted. But instead he jerked backwards, then sat down heavily on the couch and sunk his fingers into his hair.

'I know,' he murmured.

It was the very last thing she had expected him to say. But suddenly she noticed the stoop of his shoulders, the grooves in his short hair, as if he'd run his fingers through it many times.

He looked up at her then and she saw the turmoil in his eyes he could no longer disguise.

'If you want to take the job with Garner, you can,' he said, his voice hoarse. 'I won't object. And we can wait as long as you need to talk about having another child.' He sounded broken and desperately unhappy.

She sat next to him, lost for words. This wasn't about the job, or the possibility of more children. But she could see how hard these concessions had been for him to make, and finally she began to understand why. This wasn't about controlling her. It was about controlling his own need.

'Just…' He cleared his throat. 'Just please don't leave me.'

She heard it then, the echo of pain and fear, of insecurity, and suddenly she understood what he was doing. He was bargaining with her for her affection, the way she suspected he must have once bargained with his father and his mother.

She placed a hand on his thigh and felt the muscle tense beneath her palm. And let her heart melt. 'I'm not like them, Brandon.'

His head jerked round. 'What do you mean?'

'I won't leave you if we have a disagreement. Or if I don't get what I want. Marriage is a negotiation, and I'm sure we'll have lots more disagreements in our future. But it's also about love. About the freedom to make your own choices.' She took in a deep breath.

He'd come to her—he'd tried to fix this and that meant a lot. Maybe she hadn't been wrong after all. Maybe he could love her, but he just didn't know how to show it.

'I know it's scary,' she said. 'I was scared to love you too. But what I'm giving you is a gift, with no strings attached. I won't take it away, use it against you, the way they did. Because I love you, and they never did. All I'm asking is that you open yourself to the possibility of love in return.'

She breathed the words, her heart shattering when he stiffened and stood up. He swore under his breath and marched across to the room's fireplace to stare into the empty hearth.

She sat still, but her heart broke for him when his reply sliced through the silence. Because what she heard in his voice wasn't anger, or even demand, it was despair.

'You don't know what you're asking of me,' Brandon said, his jaw tight, his whole body rigid with the need to hold firm against the emotion in her voice.

He'd agreed to her terms. Why couldn't that be enough to make her stay?

'What are you so scared of, Brandon?' The quiver of vulnerability in her tone, the emotion, sank its claws into his resolve, tearing through the last of his reserves, the last of his control.

He shook his head, his whole body trembling now as the emotion he didn't know how to stop battered him.

He sunk his hands into his pockets and tried to brace himself against the swell of panic, of fear. But it did no good, because he was back in his father's study again. He was that forlorn, desperate child, terrified to be alone, but even more terrified to let himself ask for more when he knew it would never be given to him.

A hand settled on his back, spreading warmth through his system and burning through the chill.

'What is it, Brandon? If you told me, maybe we could fix it.'

*We.*

Could it really be that easy? The cynic in him said no way, but there was enough of that lonely child inside him to turn and look at her. To gauge her reaction.

She gazed at him, those chestnut eyes rich with an emotion he had been determined to dismiss that morning but wanted so badly to believe now.

'How can you love me?' he said, the broken child talking now inside the man. The child he had silenced for so long, it hurt to know he had always been there, lurking, waiting, needing.

A lone tear ran down her cheek. 'Oh, Brandon,' she said as she brushed it away with her fist.

She reached up and clasped his cheeks to drag his mouth down to hers.

But as he gripped her waist, desperate to kiss her, she whispered against his lips, 'I love you because you forgave me for the terrible mistake I made in not telling you about your child.' She searched his face and he realised she could see him as no one else ever had. Could see his flaws and his weaknesses, as well as his strengths, and it didn't disgust her.

'I love you because you were determined to be Ruby's father even though you didn't know how.' Her eyes glowed, full of compassion and affection, resolve and tenacity, but most of all full of love.

'I love you for all the things you are—a father, a lover, a husband—and all the things you can be, if you'll just open your heart again.' She smiled, the rich dark amber full of new hope. 'And let me in too, as well as Ruby.'

He felt the answering glow in his heart melting the block of ice which had been there for so long, stopping him from feeling.

It hurt to be this vulnerable. To be this unsure.

But she was right. He loved his child. Why should loving Lacey be so difficult when everything about her fascinated and excited him, captivated and beguiled him? Her strength, her intelligence, her bravery and even her total refusal to let him hide from his own feelings, or hers.

He touched his forehead to hers and let out an unsteady breath, his hands sliding under her T-shirt to caress the warm skin beneath.

She was really here, and she would stay. No matter what. But…

'I want to love you,' he managed, the words rough, rusty, the commitment terrifying even now. 'But I can't…' He wrapped his arms around her, crushing her to him. 'I can't bear to lose you. And I'm bound to screw this up from time to time,' he whispered against her neck, burying his face into the soft spray of curls, breathing in the sweet, erotic scent of roses. 'So you have to promise me…'

He huffed out a breath and drew back, feeling foolish, needy, even a bit pathetic, but knowing he had to ask, to be sure. 'You'll let me know if I mess up. That you won't walk away without giving me a chance to fix it.'

Lacey stared at this big, bold, indomitable man, heard the vulnerability in his voice and knew he loved her. Maybe he couldn't say it yet. Maybe he didn't really even know it yet. But he would, eventually.

She had hope now and security. But most of all she understood why he had tried so hard to hold himself back. Because he was even more terrified than she was.

'I'm not like him, Brandon,' she said again, letting him see everything inside her—all the love, the fear, the hope and the longing. Letting him know that they were equals. Always.

'He didn't deserve you. But Ruby and I...' She grinned as she took his hand and pressed it against her belly. 'And any other babies we have...eventually,' she added because, as much as she wanted to have more children with this man, children they could watch grow together, she also wanted more time with just the three of them. 'We *do* deserve you.'

'I hope you know I consider that a binding agreement—which I will require in writing, Mrs Cade,' he murmured, only half-joking.

She laughed, the joy in her heart creating a heady ache that was still scary but so right. 'I'll sign anything you want, Mr Cade,' she replied. 'But only if you sign it too.'

He lifted her up and held her aloft, his gruff chuckle joining her laughter, then let her body slide down against his, making her tantalisingly aware of the hard ridge thrusting against her belly through their clothing.

'Count on it,' he murmured, then proceeded to strip her naked and seal the deal with the ruthless efficiency she adored.

# EPILOGUE

*One year later*

'DADDY, IS THE baby all cooked now, then?' Ruby bounced on Brandon's hip as he strode down the hospital corridor. His daughter looked as if she were ready to explode with excitement.

He knew the feeling. After leaving Lacey and his brand-new baby son in the exclusive private maternity hospital in Mayfair at 3:00 a.m. that morning, his heart had been ticking over so fast he'd been sure he might never sleep again this decade.

As it happened, he'd crashed out as soon as his head had dropped onto the bed he now shared with Lacey all night, every night—thanks to her unstinting love and support, and the hours of therapy he had finally admitted he needed to get over the fear of intimacy he had developed in childhood...

The same bed which had felt so empty over the past two days since Lacey had gone into hospital for observation. And their son had decided to put in a scarily hasty appearance three weeks ahead of schedule.

The glorious dreams of his son's tiny mouth latching onto his wife's breast for the first time had swirled in and out of his exhausted brain, chased by the terrifying nightmares of six far too fast, but also never-ending, hours of pain and fear as Lacey had laboured like a pro and he'd completely fallen to pieces inside while trying not to show it.

'Yes, he's all cooked and ready to meet you now, Rubes,' he said, suddenly grateful he had not had to go through the labour experience twice.

His daughter meant so much to him—and he would always regret the four years he'd missed watching her grown into the bright, brilliant nearly six-year-old she was now— but her actual birth, not so much.

One thing was for sure—no way on earth was he touching her mother again until they had had a serious conversation about effective methods of contraception. He couldn't get the picture out of his head of her in agonising pain as the contractions had hit in waves. Which should take at least a decade.

Funny to think he'd been desperate to get her pregnant when they'd first been married. But he had been totally okay with waiting, once their marriage had morphed into something real, beautiful and so full of promise and possibilities, it made him ache.

He told her he loved her now every chance he got but, much more importantly, he knew she believed him.

Lacey challenged him and provoked him, excited and fascinated him, always. But, as well as being a wife and a lover, she was also his best friend and the woman he couldn't wait to share every new adventure with. She—and Ruby— filled up all the holes in his life he'd thought could never be filled for so long, and he couldn't wait for the new baby to add another layer of joy and insanity to that glorious chaos.

He'd taken a back seat in his business for the last year— finally forced to acknowledge that so much of his relentless drive and ambition had been linked to the subconscious need to impress a dead man. He still loved his work, and he hadn't entirely given up on expanding Cade Inc into the US market, but he didn't work seven days a week any more. He took school holidays off now, and weekends, and happily played hooky from work to hang out with Ruby if Lacey had a feature to finish or an interview to do. He had even got into the habit of showing off his wife at the sort of media parties and society events he had once despised.

His life had become rich and full, something he would never have envisaged it being. Because for the first time ever he'd discovered what true happiness actually felt like. Not sealing a deal with a media conglomerate in Spain, or launching a new cable news channel in Kenya—but spending a sun-kissed day mucking about with his daughter on a beach in Bermuda, or snatching a make-out session with his heavily pregnant wife in the shower before his chatterbox daughter and her nutty dog bounded into his bedroom to turn the chaos right back up to eleven.

When Lacey had fallen pregnant by accident eight months ago—a result of a stomach bug messing with her contraceptives—he'd actually been more shocked than overjoyed. Had they really been ready to take this step now?

But, as he'd watched Lacey's slim figure ripen with their child, he'd discovered the process was at least every bit as erotic as he'd thought it would be.

As he shoved open the door to Lacey's hospital room, and Ruby wriggled out of his arms to dash across to her mother, he stopped in the doorway to take in the scene—and stamp it on his memory for ever. His wife cradled their new-born in a chair by the bed, the light from the window gilding her soft curls and the tiny bundle in her arms as she lowered them to introduce Ruby to her brother.

His heart took another direct hit—one of so many over the last year—and felt as if it had stopped beating for several seconds as he absorbed the tableau they made.

*Doesn't matter if you're ready, Cade. This is it. This is everything. Scary, yeah—terrifying, even. But also the only thing that will ever really matter.*

Then Lacey's gaze connected with his as Ruby began

chattering a mile a minute to her brother. Poor kid—he was unlikely to get a word in edgeways for the foreseeable future. Good thing he couldn't talk.

His wife smiled, her expression tired but so happy. And his heart kicked back into gear and began to beat double time.

'Hello, Mr Cade,' Lacey said. 'I hope you guys have come to bust us out of here, because Junior and I are ready to go home.'

*Home.* A word which had meant nothing to him for so long and now meant everything.

His heart expanded as he strolled to his wife and lifted the now fussy baby out of her arms—his son looked somewhat indignant at being so rudely awakened by his inquisitive big sister.

*Welcome to my world, kid.*

He leant down to whisper to Lacey, 'Why do you think I brought my accomplice with me?' Then—because how could he resist kissing that gorgeous mouth?—he touched his lips to hers.

She opened for him as she always did, tempting him deeper and taking the kiss to a sweet, sultry place. It occurred to him, as the familiar heat settled in his groin, that not making love to his wife again for a decade might be a bit too much of a punishment for both of them. Perhaps a year of abstinence would have to do.

They were forced to break the kiss when Ruby started making 'yuck, yuck' noises, and the baby in his arms began crying and fretting in earnest.

He chuckled as his wife's smile turned into a knowing grin and the steady beat of joy, happiness and fulfilment—which he'd become so comfortable with over the last year—settled back into his heart.

'Time to get our kids home, Mrs Cade,' he murmured.

*And let the chaos continue.*

\* \* \* \* \*

# A VOW TO SET
# THE VIRGIN FREE

MILLIE ADAMS

**MILLS & BOON**

To Jackie Ashenden,
who is such a legend that her book inspired me,
and is why this book happened at all.

# CHAPTER ONE

ATHENA COULDN'T REMEMBER life before the compound.

On the Black Sea, in Russia, with high walls and heavy security, it was nearly a fortress. It dominated her memories.

She knew she must have had a life before the compound, she just didn't remember. She had been eight years old and she had been brought there. That's what she remembered. Being eight and standing before a sad, beautiful woman. She'd had tears on her cheeks and she had smiled when she had looked down at Athena. "My daughter," she'd said.

And that was who she had become that day. Their daughter.

A doll for her mother to play with, and never let out. The outlet for so many of her fears…

Her disappointments.

Athena knew enough to know her life was not terribly normal. She was never allowed out of the compound for a start.

And her only friend was a girl named Rose, who served as a maid.

Athena often wondered why Rose was a maid, and Athena was treated as their daughter. She couldn't fathom it.

She had far too much time to wonder about things.

Especially after her friend Rose left. After that, she was alone. Lonely.

And then her father—the man who had always acted as her father. The man she *remembered* as her father, had told her that she would be leaving too. That it was high time she got married.

Athena was twenty-eight, though in many ways, younger. She had no practical life experience, so she knew enough to know that she couldn't compare herself to a twenty-eight-year-old woman who hadn't just taken her first plane ride.

She had been surprised when her father had told her of the marriage bargain, because she hadn't truly thought that her mother would ever let her go. For as long as she could remember, she'd known the name Naya. Naya had been her mother's first daughter. Her perfect, treasured daughter. Athena had been adopted to replace her.

She could only assume that she had been an orphan. That her being taken in was an act of charity. She was grateful. She had never truly thought that she would have a life outside the compound. Marriage. She had wondered at first if that might be exciting. No, she did not know the man that her father was giving her to, but… She did not know anyone. So what did it matter. Perhaps it would be wonderful. Perhaps it would be exciting. A chance to live a different life.

To see something. To be someone new.

Romance had always been a distant fantasy for her. She had not ever truly thought that she could have it.

And so, she had decided to see what might happen. And then she had met him. An older man, with a deadly energy. Her mother had wept. *"Don't give her to him."*

But he was intent.

"You indulge her," her father said, as though Athena wasn't in the room. "You have indulged yourself most of all. She has been your doll to dress up and play pretend with, but now she will be of use to me. She will marry Mattias, there is no other option. We had debts and they must be paid."

"Surely when Ares bought Rose, we were able to settle those debts."

"I will not go to Ares again. And it was not enough."

A doll.

The words had jarred her, and yet she'd known they were true. She had been a stand-in for her mother's beautiful only child who had died as a young woman after she'd left the compound and gotten married. Athena had been her replacement and her mother had both depended on her, and resented her.

Athena understood. She'd always been aware of Naya's place in her mother's heart. And the ways in which she'd been different.

But she'd been loved, she'd thought, even if it wasn't always easy, it was the only love she'd known. She'd been a daughter, or she'd thought she had been.

Rose had been the maid, Athena the daughter.

In the end, both would be sold to pay her father's debts.

She must not have been a good enough daughter in the end. For what good daughter would be sent to such a fate?

Mattias scared her. He looked at her as though he had plans for her. She did not wish to know what those plans were. She could see it in his eyes. He was a man who enjoyed hurting others.

Even Athena, for all that she had never left the compound before, understood that.

She was now being delivered to him, to be married. Mattias made his home in the Northern Highlands of Scotland, which is where they were driving now, after a long flight from Russia. The scenery couldn't have been more different here.

She was in the back of a shiny black SUV. A convoy of them.

For safety.

Her father had said.

No one could know which of them was in which vehicle.

The spread would be advantageous to her.

She would've loved to have been excited by the view.

The mountains were craggy and awe-inspiring, the sky gray, the clouds heavy with rain. It was so very different than the stern view of the Black Sea she was accustomed to.

She had spent her life in a beautifully gilded cage. The compound was styled as a luxury villa. It was the heavy security, the isolation from the outside world that gave it its name. Her rooms were soft and safe.

She was under surveillance at all times.

Never alone, yet somehow lonely. It had been part of her life from the time she could remember, and it had only been as she grew older that it had become notable.

It had begun to feel oppressive just a few years ago. It was like something in her had clicked.

Naya, her predecessor, had gone off to have a life. Athena had no life at all. She'd asked her mother once, when she could be free to go live her life.

*"Naya died living outside these walls. I will not lose you, Athena."*

It was not a proclamation of tenderness, but of desperation, and Athena could see she had no choice.

The compound was too secure. Too isolated.

Perhaps that was when she had become aware that she was a prisoner.

Such a prisoner that for a moment, marriage to a stranger had seemed an adventure.

She was wide awake now, and she could never go back to before she'd realized how astonishingly wrong that was.

She knew now. She was not their daughter, she was a prisoner. She was being used as a bargaining chip.

She would not go quietly.

She had no choice now. She had to do this. Or she would spend the rest of her life as this. This creature who had been fashioned to be pliable and dependent. To exist for others only, and never herself.

A doll, the man who had called himself her father, had said.

He was not wrong. A thing to be dressed up, looked at, played with.

She was nervous. But she was resolved. Her decision was made, she would not waiver from it now.

She had pretended to be excited for the wedding. She had peppered the man she'd come to think of as her father with questions, and because he underestimated her, he had answered them all. He'd told her how they would travel, when, where. She'd told him she was just so excited to travel. She'd pretended to be starry-eyed about the marriage.

She had not known she was duplicitous, but it had turned out she was when need be.

He had given her every detail she needed. Then she'd used the limited access to maps and the internet that she had to study the area.

There was a forest they would drive by in two miles, she could see it in her mind's eye. It would be her chance. Her one and only chance. And she would take it. She would get caught, very likely. She could not imagine a scenario wherein she was not captured and restored immediately by one of her father's men. She was fast, but they would overtake her. They had guns.

She had to.

She had to try.

Athena had spent her life shut away, and every decision

in her life had been made by others. It had been the only reality she remembered, so she accepted it. That reality had broken when she had seen the true nature of her father. First when she had discovered that he had sold Rose to Ares, as though she were an *object*, and then with his willingness to marry Athena off, completely disregarding her feelings.

And more than her feelings, her safety.

She no longer accepted what she was given.

She would escape, she would find out the truth of who she had been the first eight years of her life. Perhaps the truth was not a good truth. But what did it matter? Her present truth was not especially good either. So she would run. In futility, but with bravery.

She only had to wait for the moment.

And then it happened. They rounded the corner just next to the woods, right at the very edge. If she could make her way through them, then she could run out the other side and there she would find a village. She would be able to get refuge. Help.

Eventually, to find herself.

She needed that to be true.

She was wearing a cloak, which was very dramatic but her parents—she hesitated now to call them her parents but didn't know what else to call them—hadn't commented, it wasn't unusual for her to be dramatic. She'd hidden a small bag in the folds of it and had been quite warm on the plane, but it was worth it. And she had a small amount of food and water to carry her through, plus something to offer protection from the elements.

She needed to try, she quickly unbuckled her seatbelt, opened the door and held her cloak tightly around her and flung herself out of the moving vehicle.

She guided herself toward the forest, tucking and rolling as she did, landing sprawled out on the grass before scrambling, not bothering to look at what was behind her, and if the limo had managed to stop. She ran. She ran as if the hounds of hell were on her, because they were. She ran with all her might. She ran for all she was worth. The forest was dark, the trees dense. She knew that. Because she had done her research.

She hopped a short left, just as she had planned, because she knew that was the direction that would take her to the village. She wove under trees, and around them. Taking the thickest and most impassable way, one that they would never guess she had taken, because it would be so difficult to traverse.

Everybody simply thought her a cosseted girl.

Nobody knew the fire that was inside of her. The fire that had been ignited by all of this betrayal. The determination that she carried with her.

They underestimated her, and they would lose her for it. She ran until trees started to thin out, and she felt nothing but confusion. She could not recall this on any map. But then, this was an extremely remote forest, and it was possible that there were pieces of it that remained unknown.

She walked until her legs ached. Until she was freezing. It had started to rain, and as the foliage grew wet, it became a liability. Everything she touched left water droplets on her, which bled into the fabric of her billowing cloak—protective, she had hoped—rendering it a sodden mess.

She was lost, and she could hear twigs snapping in the distance. She didn't know what sort of creatures were in these woods. She had missed a very important piece of research.

Exhaustion and hypothermia were becoming a fear for her.

And then, there in the dimness, she saw it.

A small heap of stones with a straw roof. It was in disrepair, but she imagined the inside would be dry.

She scrambled forward and pushed the wooden door open.

It was silent inside. All thick stone walls and a stone floor. It was dry. Surprisingly warm, and she imagined the lack of moisture and the efficiency of blocking any wind contributed to that.

If they were to find this place, surely they would look inside for her.

But what other option did she have?

Curling up outside under a fern wasn't going to work, and she was about to collapse.

She sat down on the floor. It was hard, but she felt safer in here. She would actually be able to rest for a while. She curled up into a ball of soggy misery and tried to stop herself from shaking.

Eventually she fell into a fitful sleep, consciousness hovering about the edges, tinged by fear. Dreams mixed in with a strange sense of wakefulness, and she could feel herself suddenly floating above the earth. Warm. Held tightly. She clung to that, tried to savor the feeling. She felt secure then when she'd otherwise felt alone.

But then everything went to blackness, and she lost her hold on the brilliant dream that had made her feel so safe.

She awoke with a start.

She was sitting in a plush chair, her feet up on an ottoman. To her right was a table, and on it was a steaming mug of some sort of hot liquid, and beside that was a pastry.

She was starving, and still so cold.

She looked around the space, her eyes still bleary. It was all gray stone and gothic details. It looked like an old castle. She wasn't in the little hovel she'd fallen asleep in earlier.

She thought back to the dream…

Of being lifted. Of being held.

That hadn't been a dream. Someone had found her there and brought her...here.

She looked around the room, and then suddenly, the large fireplace against the back wall ignited.

It was a rush of flame and sound, and she recoiled in shock.

"Who's there?" she asked, her voice trembling.

She did not believe in magic.

She had never seen it. Not living as she had in the compound.

This... This did seem like an enchantment. The entire thing. Or a dream. That this place could be here, in the forest. That someone had found her, sleeping, hidden away in that shack and brought her here...

She reached her hands out, and realized that they were still quite cold.

Then, shaking all over she reached out and picked up the mug. She knew she perhaps shouldn't trust the substance in it, but she also knew she was thirsty and hungry and freezing. She had to let her more immediate needs take precedence.

And once she was warm, and full, she found herself drifting off to sleep again.

Something woke her. She could not pinpoint it. A strange sensation that filled her and made her chest feel like it was expanding until she was jolted from her sleep.

"What do we have here?"

The voice was rough, with a heavy Scottish accent, deep and frightening, and she found herself gripping the arms of the chair hard.

She was trying to shake off her sleep.

"Speak, lass."

She tried to find the source of the voice, looking to her

left and right, but she couldn't find it. She felt the voice, as much as she heard it. A rumble through her body.

"I… My name is Athena."

"Athena. Goddess of war. Tell me, Athena." The voice became lower, rougher, close to a growl. "Have you come to make war with me?"

She looked all around, and she could not see where the voice was coming from.

"No. I've run away. From my…from my captors. And someone brought me…here."

"Captors?" He said the word hard and harsh.

"Yes. Well… My father. My adoptive father. I came to live with him when I was eight years old. He's selling me into marriage now."

"I see. And you are running away from your arranged marriage?"

"Yes. Wouldn't you?"

He laughed. Hard and harsh. "No. I've no need to run from anyone."

It was nearly a growl, that voice, and she tried to imagine what sort of man would accompany such a voice, and failed.

"Who are you?"

"An interesting question. And not one that I am obligated to answer. You are the intruder in my house. Keep talking."

She had nothing to say except…except…

"Will you protect me? If my father's men come for me, will you protect me?"

"That all depends, wee Athena. In what manner will they be armed?"

"They have guns."

"Guns. Barbaric, don't you think? There were days when men engaged in hand-to-hand combat. Broad swords. And they were called barbarians. At least then you could look your foe in the eye. At least then, you had to be aware of what it was you were doing when you struck him down."

"Philosophy on the ways in which people wage war does not help me."

"Does it not?"

"Goddess of war I may be, but no one has bothered to fight one on my behalf."

"I think that perhaps Athena fights for her own self."

"This is me fighting. I need someone to fight with me."

"A sad thing for you that I do not work for free."

"What is it that you want?"

Fear streaked through her. But for all that she could not see the man who spoke, for all that she knew nothing about him, she did not hear the cruelty in his voice that she heard in Mattias's. Perhaps that was crazy, but she trusted her instincts. Her father did business with a variety of people. Many of them were dangerous. Many of them were very bad men. She could sense that. It was a matter of survival.

"It is no matter to you what I want. You are now my part of my collection."

*Collection?*

She stood, panic rioting through her. "No! I'm not… I need your help. I need my freedom."

"Lass," he said, his voice becoming hard. "No one lives free."

She turned and she ran. She flung herself against the door and it didn't give.

"It won't open," the voice said.

"But…"

"You are mine now."

"Let me go. You don't have to do anything for me."

"I already have. My fire. My food. You have stolen from me. And I need be repaid."

And then suddenly, there was a figure who swept into the room. Concealed by a cloak, his body huge and hulking.

He moved to her, and he swept her up into his arms. It was too dark for her to see his face.

Terror rolled through her as she found herself being carried away further and further from the door.

She struggled, but he was too strong.

He carried her up a curved staircase and kicked open the third door on the left. "Here. You will stay here until I decide what it is I want to do with you."

His voice boomed less so close, but was no less impacting. He was strong and hot and smelled of sandalwood.

She was suddenly unbearably conscious of the fact this was the closest she'd ever been to a man.

He set her down slowly, and she felt…cold. Bereft of his touch. She tried to move to get a better look at him but the room was too dim.

The room was also not quite what she'd expected.

"A…a bedroom?"

"Would you prefer the dungeon?"

"No."

"Then do not complain to me, lass."

And then he stepped out of the room and slammed the door shut. She tried it, but it was locked tight.

Somehow she had leapt from a moving vehicle, right into the enchanted fire.

# CHAPTER TWO

"THERE ISN'T ANY time left, Cameron. The launch of the product is next month, and if you can't put on a good showing we're going to lose every investor who backed us through all of this. I am planning something extravagant. It is not just a dry event where investors and buyers will sit in chairs and watch tech wizards speak. There will be food, and dancing. It will be the biggest event in the history of the company."

Cameron looked at the screen and growled. "Why can't *you* put on a good show?"

His business partner, Apollo Agassi, looked at him with dark, deeply concerned eyes.

"Because it's *you* people want to hear from when it comes to technology, Cameron."

"You said it would not be speeches."

"I said it will not be all speeches. This is going to be a hub of all that is to come in smart home technology, self-driving cars... Gunnar and Olive Magnusson will be there and you know she is one of the most captivating people in the tech industry right now. I want them there, they will raise the cachet of the event. I do not want them to outshine us. I cannot accomplish what you can. I can raise money, but you need to cement the goodwill of those who are counting on the smart home system to be as comprehensive as you said it would."

His friend's doubt was an affront. Cameron's face might have been ruined, but his mind was as sharp as ever.

"It is. Believe me. I have a medieval castle wired to do whatever I ask it to do. Fire in the fireplace? Done. Meals of all kinds cooked to perfection? Done. Laundry, comprehensive lighting systems. Every door armed. Security. All managed through either voice, but only the user's voice, or in some cases nonverbal commands accomplished by a device that fits in your pocket."

"A very good sales pitch."

"It hardly needs a sales pitch. It is leagues ahead of all other smart home technology in terms of seamlessness and versatility."

"You say that, but most people—myself included—don't know what that means in a practical sense. Compared to you, we might as well be children when it comes to the depth of our understanding, and that is why you need to explain it."

"Flattery will not move me."

"I will find something that will, by God." Apollo was quiet for a moment. "This is your triumph, Cam. Get out there, and do what I know you can."

"What I *could*," he pointed out.

Apollo suddenly looked weary. "The Cameron I knew would never have sat at home for all these years. The Cameron I knew was a fighter. Against all odds, against ever terrible thing that ever happened. He never took no for an answer, and when he was knocked down, he never stayed down."

Cameron laughed. He had to. Because Apollo's take was so wildly simplistic. So firmly spoken as a man who had no concept of what the accident had meant for him. "The Cameron you knew could dazzle the world with his looks *and* his wits. And that man is dead. There is nothing of him left."

"I don't believe that," said Apollo. "I think it's a neat story that you tell yourself."

"It does not matter whether it is a story I tell myself or the reality. Short of dragging me out of the castle yourself…"

Apollo's face went hard. He knew that look. "Don't think I won't do it, Cameron. I have so much money tied up in this…"

"And it is everything I have, so don't you think I care even more?"

"You don't need anything. You sit in that moldering wreck day in and day out. You have no need of money. You might as well redistribute your wealth."

"Careful," Cameron said, his tone dry. "You're beginning to sound like a radical."

Apollo laughed. "Once upon a time we were both quite radical."

"No," Cameron growled. "Once upon a time we were a pair of selfish assholes. Once upon a time we left a swath of destruction so great that it was bound to turn into a reckoning. And it did. Perhaps not for you. Your jaw is as sharp as ever, your smile as winning. So perhaps, you should do as I say and spearhead this endeavor."

"You are grim, Cameron, and I find I have no stomach for it."

"Tired of looking at my face?"

"You never even show me the whole of it. You sit there, shrouded in darkness."

So he did. Cameron had gotten used to moving about in darkness. There was not a single mirror in the castle. It was by design. He did not need the reminder. Not ever.

And now… She was here.

She was so beautiful. It was nearly painful to look directly at her.

*Athena.*

Goddess of war.

And he had felt that war ignite inside of him from the moment that he had set eyes on her. Liquid dark eyes, hair black and shiny. Her lips were full, her curves generous.

He could remember what he might've done, Once upon a time. How quickly he could've seduced a woman so clearly and thoroughly built for sin.

He could have had her underneath him in minutes, crying out for release.

And so what had he done? Kept her captive. For now he had to do it with locked doors, so terrifying was his visage.

Not that she had seen him.

Had she seen him, she would have fought much harder.

Since moving onto these grounds he'd started a collection of beautiful things. What came to him here, remained.

She had come to him, and she was beautiful, so he had taken her.

There was a part of him, somewhere, in the back of his mind that recognized that as…insane.

There was also a part of him that wasn't entirely sure he wasn't insane, so why fight it?

Either way, she was here with him now.

He'd always felt that when he found something, it was fate in some small way. And he had not thought it wise to deny fate, so he kept the thing to see if he ever needed use of it.

Athena was no different.

"The truth is," he said, "Apollo, you do not know the extent of my life. What I choose to share or not share with you is my concern."

"Well, you could make it my concern, considering I'm bound to you professionally."

"That is exactly why you don't know."

"Cameron," Apollo said, sounding weary. "At one time you considered me a friend."

"And I still do. As much as I have friends."

"I have not seen you face-to-face in nearly ten years."

"No one *needs* to see anyone face-to face, not these days."

"Sadly for you, they do. They need to see you." Apollo sighed heavily. As if he was resigned, when he made every rule that he lived by and had no reason to be resigned to anything. "I'm giving you an ultimatum. Either you do this, or I will engage in a hostile takeover of the company."

Cameron's lip curled. "You bastard. You just said that the company would be worthless if I didn't engage in this launch, then what good will it be to you?"

"I will have to galvanize you, perhaps. And don't think I won't do it. Do not think I won't cut off my nose to spite your face, Cameron McKenzie, because we have known each other too long for you to think that I will swerve when I have given my word."

He growled. He knew that Apollo wasn't lying. He knew that he would do exactly as he said.

"I will not be forced."

"You will be whatever you need to be. The time for licking your wounds has ended. They are scars. They will not heal, deal with it."

"You say that now, but when I stand before a room and investors looking as I do, you will perhaps change your tune. Lights."

He treated his friend to the full effect of his face, for the first time in a decade.

And he was satisfied to see Apollo react.

Satisfied enough to smile. Which he knew only made him look all the more fearsome.

"Don't tell me it isn't that bad," he said. "We both know that for a lie."

"Cameron…"

"What?"

Apollo looked…thoughtful rather than horrified. "I think it will be effective. To have you show your face."

"Why?" His smile became a sneer. "Do you suppose we might engender the pity of the investors?"

"I do not think that. I think perhaps they will appreciate your strength." Did his friend pity him too? That was unbearable.

"My *strength*," he bit out. "My strength in overcoming an accident that I caused? An accident that killed an innocent woman?"

"The facts are the facts. We cannot change them. But we can spin them. You're supposed to be a genius. In technology, in business. In people, once upon a time. Create a story for yourself. Or I will make the company mine."

And with that, Apollo ended the call. Cameron dimmed the lights. He did not like sitting in full brightness. It made him feel exposed.

He thought of Athena yet again.

His prisoner. His beautiful jewel.

It was not even unprecedented for him to take living things from the grounds.

He had tamed a stag who now visited him in the gardens and took apples from him.

There was a horse who had wandered onto the property, looking emaciated and dull, and he had claimed him. The only time he went out was to ride Aslan across the moors. The black stallion was now beautiful and glossy and foul of temper.

He was the only thing Cameron loved.

His life was very different now than it had been a decade ago. It was easy for Apollo to talk as if there was a life he could step back into. Apollo did not understand.

He and Apollo had been given to the same excesses, and they had experienced the same ease in their lives once they had become rich and successful. Because they were handsome. He had taken his looks for granted, as he knew his friend did as well. He had not been a vain man, rather they had simply been another tool with which he could accomplish what he set out to accomplish.

And he had used them. Shamelessly. And well.

It shamed him to realize just how much he had depended on his looks. For it was no small thing. That had become apparent after the accident. He could not stand to look at himself.

It was deeper than that, though, the reasons he needed to stay away from people.

It was the pity he could not stand. And he had seen much of it when he had been in the hospital. Doctors and nurses had looked at him as though he was a monstrous thing, and they ought to be used to seeing people altered by accidents.

To realize that you had the look of a man who should not have survived... To realize that you, a man who had been successful, who had been envied by all, was now pitied was...

He could not stomach it.

But he worked in technology, so he had fashioned for himself an aura of mystery, and had made his reclusiveness part of the mystique.

If he were truly honest with himself, he could see why Apollo thought it was time for him to reappear. It would create waves. It would say volumes about the smart home system.

He sat there in the dark, and asked himself truly if he cared at all.

If he did not do this, if he let the company die, what did it matter to him? That he could live out his days here, alone, did he truly care if everything else crumbled?

He thought of Apollo.

Apollo was the only person who cared for him. His

lifelong friend, who he had met at fifteen when they had both been school dropouts living on the streets in London, because it had been an easier place for them to scrape by then their home countries.

Never mind the ways they had gotten there. They had shown each other their internal scars back then.

And they had found their strength together.

But even now, Apollo was willing to hurt him for the sake of his own survival.

Of course he was. Survival was what they knew.

Apollo still had his looks. Apollo still had a legion of sycophants.

Without him, Apollo's life would still be full.

But his life? Without Apollo his life would be completely desolate.

Apollo was the only person he spoke to with any sort of regularity. Everyone else he spoke to through messages. He did not speak to them.

His house was stopped by people he never saw. Cleaned by people he never saw.

His whole life was orchestrated from behind a shroud.

And Apollo was his only connection in the world.

The truth was, had his friend given him time to think about it, he wouldn't have even needed to blackmail him.

Because very few things scared Cameron. But falling all the way into the blackness of his own soul was one of them. And his only link to the light was Apollo.

He would do this. He would find a way.

He paused for a moment. Athena.

Athena was the key. The stag had taught him that he did not frighten everyone.

Aslan taught him that he could still have connection.

And Athena? Like the other two, she had been brought here for a reason. If there was one thing he had begun to believe in these years of isolation, it was that there were forces in the world that would give you what you needed when you were connected.

He had become disconnected in his years of access. All he had cared about was money. Drugs. Sex. When he had lived on the streets he had to be rooted in the signs of the universe. For he had needed them to survive.

He had gotten back to that here. Athena was a sign. Something that had been brought to him for his use.

It was why it seemed logical to keep her.

Now he only had to decide what to do with her.

# CHAPTER THREE

ATHENA LAY SPRAWLED out on the beautiful bed, unable to sleep. There was a glorious bathroom adjoined to the bedroom, and she could only admire the way technology blended seamlessly with the ancient architecture of the place. She was quite accustomed to luxury. Her father's home had been filled with the finest of things. But there was something different about this place.

And then she thought of the man who occupied it, and she shivered.

*You are part of my collection.*

She had no idea how she was going to get out of this.

Collection, what a strange word.

It meant prisoner, though. Just as daughter had really meant prisoner for all of her life.

But she would think of something. She had not spent all of her life a prisoner only to become one yet again.

She would think of something. She was resourceful, if nothing else. She was not stupid. She was not weak.

That was what everyone thought of her. A doll. A toy for her mother. Not a woman of any sort of substance. That was what her father had thought. As for her mother? Athena had never been able to quite measure up to Naya.

No one really saw her.

They looked at her and they saw what they wished to see.

Now, that would benefit her.

She kept telling herself that. Over and over again.

"You may go down to the kitchen for dinner."

She scrambled off the bed. "*Who is this*?"

She knew it was him. But his voice wasn't coming from outside the door. Rather it felt all around her.

"You know who I am, Athena."

She didn't know why his voice made her stomach go tight. Only she remembered his strength. The smell of sandalwood.

She had never been as dainty as Naya—one of the things her mother had often told her.

She had felt tiny held in this man's arms.

*What a silly thing to think of.*

"The voice of God?"

"Or the devil, more likely." When he said devil, he practically purred.

"I am not afraid of devils," she said. "I grew up surrounded by them. It took me years to figure that out. That my father was not a good man. But... I know now. And I know the men that came and sat at his dining table were monsters. I have sat at dinner with the devil and smiled. Why should I fear you?"

"I did not ask for your fear. You offered freely. You can try to pretend that you do not but..."

"Do you have cameras in here?"

She was actually used to being under surveillance. It was something that she accepted as part of her life, but she did not know him, and she did not have to accept it here.

"No," he said. "It is simply an intercom system with which I can speak to you. The common areas of the home have cameras, but not the private spaces."

"But you can hear me at all times."

"No. Only when I have the conversation opened up. I have no desire to hear you at all times. If I wanted that kind of distraction I wouldn't live here."

"Perhaps, if you are so attached to your solitude, you should set me free."

"Back into the woods?" He paused for a moment. "You must have been hiding from someone who truly frightened you, my goddess, to have scrambled out into the forest and curled up in a shack such as that."

He wasn't wrong. And it alarmed her how that insight curled its way through her stomach, and felt warm. Nearly felt like care.

"You asked for my protection," he continued. "I can offer it to you."

She looked around, as if she could see him when she knew she couldn't. "How?"

"Go have some dinner first."

"Will you be joining me?"

He laughed. The unkind, hard-edged sound filled the room. And cut her like a knife. What had been warm and sensual a moment before now felt frightening.

"No. And you will not thank me if I do."

"H-how do you know I won't thank you? You cannot simply make assumptions about me. You don't know me at all." And she was tired of people assuming they could speak to what she wanted or needed.

"And *you* do not know *me*."

"You say that you don't wish me to be scared of you, and yet you do seem to go out of your way to engage in intimidation tactics. To make yourself as mysterious as possible. You call yourself the devil, and yet you have not hurt me. I know more about you than you might think."

"So you think. Go and have your dinner. We can speak like this."

She huffed, but found the door to the room unlocked.

"The castle is still locked," he said, his voice following her. It was disconcerting. She had wondered if he could read her mind, but realized that it was a natural thought process to have, when she had been previously kept in the room. So it wasn't as if it was a reach for him to guess that she was wondering about her range.

"You're headed the right way," he said.

"This is really annoying," she responded.

"I'm sorry that your prison isn't to your liking."

"You say that as if I should expect to be in a prison. I believe this is quite a high price to pay for a croissant and a cup of tea."

"So you say."

She didn't know why the conversation verged on enjoyable, he was being ridiculous.

"So would say *most* people."

"And what do you know about the world?"

He had a point, she couldn't deny that. "Very little. I have been kept in my father's compound for all this time. But… I have had the chance to observe the way people behave when they are jockeying for power. And so, I think in some ways I know quite a bit. I know that you can be surrounded by luxury, and yet, the people around you can be craven. I know far too much about things like that."

"And what else do you know?"

The question, so simple, made her breath catch. Perhaps it was because she had never really conversed with a stranger—not freely anyway—or perhaps it was simply him, but speaking to him without having him in the room didn't seem as strange as it should.

And even more strange it felt…good to have him ask. About her. About her life.

He wasn't really asking. She knew that.

But she felt connected to him all of a sudden in the strangest way.

"I know how to smile prettily through all of it." She grinned then, looking up, though she had no idea where his cameras were.

"An interesting skill, I should think."

"No one has ever found it particularly interesting before."

"No?"

"Someone would have had to realize it was a skill. My mother never much considered me, not as myself. It was always…me as compared to someone else. My father barely ever looked at me at all."

"Many people grow up in isolation," he said.

"Yes," she agreed. "I assume so."

"Your father was having you marry a business associate of his?"

"A kind way to describe him. He's a man my father owed money to. And he was selling me."

"I see. Not an ideal situation."

"No."

She walked into the dining room, and saw that there was a meal set out for her. "Did you do this?"

"Just enjoy the magic," he responded.

She looked around the cavernous room, candles in gold candelabras all lit, the chandelier above the expansive table glittering. The place setting was fine china and silver, the chair elegant and finely carved. It made a mockery of this idea that she was a prisoner. Or it tried.

She was well familiar already with gilded cages.

"This is very strange," she said.

"It's normal to me."

"I'm not sure that that means anything. But then, I'm not sure that strange to me means anything either."

"Perhaps it doesn't."

She stared out at the spread before her. "Why don't you join me?"

"I do not join people. In anything."

He was hiding himself, and yet it was hard to imagine such an authoritative-sounding man would hide.

"Why?"

"You are not in a position to ask questions."

"I never am." She sighed. "Is this because if I see your face, you'll have to kill me?"

This time when he laughed, it wasn't cold.

This time, it was booming, and it made her feel…electrified.

"No, little goddess. No. Just accept that I…keep my own ways, however strange you might find them. And this line of conversation is done."

Dinner, however, was not strange, but it was very delicious.

Lobster and mashed potatoes, and steamed vegetables. She could not complain.

There was also a glass of wine. She looked at it, but was afraid to touch it.

"Do you not like wine?" It was the first time he'd spoken in a moment and she found it a bit jarring.

"I'm not allowed to drink it," she said, a bit disquieted by how easy it was to transition into speaking to this disembodied voice.

"That is not a condition of your imprisonment. I have offered you wine, and therefore you can have it."

"Imprisonment?"

"Go on," he said, his voice taking on a quality she had not yet heard. It was different. Silken.

It did not possess the growl she had become accustomed to in only these short hours of conversation.

She had never had to pay such close attention to how someone spoke.

"All right," she said slowly. "But only because I want to."

She had the opportunity to try something new, and so she would, though she didn't want him to think it was because she had his *permission*.

"I would not dream of having you try it under any other circumstance."

She took a sip, and blinked.

"And what do you think of it?"

She wrinkled her nose. "I don't know."

"Tell me," he urged. "Tell me what you taste."

There was something about the edge in his voice that made her feel…excited. Determined.

"Grapes, I suppose. But something more. There is a tartness to it, like citrus. A sense of something smooth. It's rich. Buttery. Yes. That's it. Sharp, and very crisp."

"You are very attentive to detail," he said.

"My life, for all these many years has been quite small. Relishing the small details is what makes it interesting. The taste of food, the feeling of the fabrics that I wear. The way the sun feels against my skin, and the smell of the sea air."

He made a strange sound, humming perhaps in the deep part of his throat. "I have not seen the sea for many years."

"But it isn't far from here."

"No indeed it is not."

She wondered at that. Marveled at it in fact.

"But you could go and see it. You're free. No one is keeping you here."

"No, it is true. My exile is self-imposed. But that does not make it less real."

"I do not understand why you won't take dinner with me." She thought she'd push there at least once more.

"Because this is not a dinner party, lass," he said, firm, uncompromising. "And I am not… I am not your host."

"No indeed. You are my captor."

She only drank a bit more of the wine, because it began to make her feel fuzzy, and she did not wish to be fuzzy in the surroundings.

"There was dessert," he said. "In the kitchen. A tart."

"Well, I shall have that."

She got up from the table and walked into the kitchen, where she saw many modern conveniences, and a glorious-looking fruit tart sitting in the center of a stone countertop.

The pieces were already sliced, and she took one and put it on a crystal plate that was sitting there beside the serving dish.

"This looks wonderful."

"Yes. All the food here is."

"Do you make it?"

"Yes. I do."

She hadn't expected that.

"I…"

"I also have a garden on the grounds, which I tend myself. That which I do not grow is brought in for me once every few months by helicopter. But there is a joy to self-sufficiency. Or if not joy, perhaps a deep practicality to it that I appreciate."

"Oh."

"This castle is run entirely on a combination of wind and solar panels."

It was so cloudy here she couldn't fathom that. "How can it possibly run on solar?"

"The panels are not here. But they are directed here by a grid."

"Oh. That is… Interesting."

"Like I said, I do strive to self-sufficiency. Now, I have enough money to have made it so. Though I envision a future where it will not take access to the resources that I have to live the sort of simple life."

"You consider this simple."

She picked up her fork and took a bite of the tart. "Oh. This is delicious."

"Thank you."

In spite of herself, she smiled. He had thanked her.

"I have never shared this with another person."

There was something raw in his voice then. Just a hint of something less…controlled, and she felt it resonate in her like a low note vibrating through a song.

"You've never cooked for anyone?" she asked.

There was a pause.

"No. Never."

He was a strange man. But then, she could only assume that a man who lived out of the woods like this, had no one else in an entire castle with him, and communicated by intercom, could be nothing other than strange.

She began to move around the kitchen while she ate, poking around the fridge, a bread cabinet. And there were many baked goods in it.

It was clear that food was important to him.

There were gourmet cheeses, and an abundance of fruits and vegetables.

He enjoyed the simple pleasures in life. She could see that. Because she understood. She herself had lived a cloistered existence, and knew that it was details such as the food you ate that made it all worthwhile.

"And what else do you do with your time?"

"Everything in this house is my invention. The intercom system, the different automated features."

"Oh. That is… It's what you do."

"You have not an inkling who I am, do you?"

"No," she said. "I don't. Why would I?"

"I had thought that you might have a guess by now. I'm Cameron McKenzie."

He waited for her to respond to that. To respond to his name.

She did not. Rather she simply sat there, a considering look on her face as she chewed another bite of his tart.

"I'm sorry, if that's supposed to mean anything to me, I am hopelessly ignorant. I have never been one to follow the outside news, because I can only follow what my father allows. He does not approve of pop culture or concept."

"So you know nothing of me?"

"Nothing."

What a rare creature she was. She would have no concept of who he had been before. No preconceived idea of how he would be or how he should look.

The more he thought about it, the more the plan he was forming began to make sense.

He would never touch her, of course. She was… She made him think of a rare gemstone. Something spectacular.

Singular.

The more he had watched her, the more he had been transfixed.

She was a sensual beauty. And yet he could see that she was innocent.

The way that she had tasted the wine and carefully considered the complexities of the flavor had been fascinating.

The way she spoke of things…

He wished to listen to her speak for hours.

A novelty. But then, he had been alone here all this time. His only real contact in the outside world was Apollo. And that was different.

She didn't know him. She was a true stranger.

"Tell me, Athena. What do you want to do with your life?"

She tilted her head to the side. "Do you care?"

"I am interested. Whether or not I care remains to be seen."

"I don't understand."

"You were running. From your father. From an arranged marriage. Were you simply running *from* him? Or were you running *to* something."

She considered it for a moment. "No. I was running

toward whatever life I could grasp. Whatever life might be of my own choosing. My own making. You see, I have never had the luxury of choosing anything. Even though I might choose what I wear on a given day, the clothes were all chosen for me. Choice is an illusion."

"One might argue that it always is."

"Perhaps. But for me, even more so. For they are all set out before me. It is not for me to decide who I am, not truly. And so I was willing to go toward an unknown life. I was willing to run into the unknown. Perhaps I would wait tables. Perhaps I would be desperately poor. But I would be free."

He laughed. He could not help it. "That is spoken like a person who has never experienced poverty."

The corners of her lips pulled down. "I haven't. But isn't making your own choice higher existence?"

"When you must fight for every meal you seek out, you do not feel as if you are living a high existence. I personally have experienced this. I feel you have no concept of what you will sacrifice to survive. You break off pieces of yourself in order to live. There is not a part of yourself you will not sell if you do not know how you will make it through the day otherwise. There is no dignity in that sort of poverty."

"I see. I feel... Even now, I feel that at least this is a prison cell I walked into on my own two feet. I'm certain that you might find that hard to understand. But I would prefer the cell to the one my father chose."

"And why is that?"

"Mattias Hamilton is a cruel man. You can see it in every line of his face. He looked at me, and I know that what he saw was something that he could easily break. I have been so protected all my life, all anyone thinks is how soft I am."

They were wrong, he could see that. She was soft. But

there was a strength to her, a steel, that was surprising. Anyone who underestimated her would be doing so at their peril.

She was also intelligent, and stunning. She would make a glorious accessory to his triumphant return.

He was beginning to think that there was only one way that he could reenter the world and not garner pity. There had to be another story. A story so compelling that no one thought to pity him.

Athena was that sort of story.

"Tell me more of your past."

"I don't… I don't know much more of my past. I came to live at my father's compound when I was eight. I have no memory of what happened before then. There is a sense of fear. Of sadness. Loss. I can only assume that I was an orphan. But I do believe that the trauma of it… I did do some reading on this from some psychology books that were in my father's library. I believe the trauma of whatever happened to me before I came to live at the compound was overwritten by better memories. By easier things. It is blank and dark and I think it might be for a reason."

"You think it is to blot out a loss?"

She nodded. "That is my theory. It seems to make the most sense."

He wondered.

"And this man, this father of yours, he was going to marry you off to a man who you believe to be cruel. Does he believe this man to be cruel?"

She tilted her head to the side, her jet-black hair sliding over her shoulder like a shimmering waterfall. "I don't believe he thought of it at all. I believe that he saw it as a means to an end, and did not consider even the slightest bit what would befall me after he sent me to Mattias. He knew only that it would solve his problem. He thought nothing of whether or not it would create problems for me. I do not believe he has the capacity to care deeply. I was…" She cleared her throat. "My mother had a daughter. A daughter who died. She was an adult then, she died in a fire. Her husband… Everyone was grief-stricken, is my understanding. But especially my mother, and her husband, Ares. My father gave me to my mother. And only recently he gave Rose to Ares."

"Who is Rose?"

"She was another girl who was brought to the compound, around the same time that I was. That was the beginning of the end. The beginning of me truly seeing what was around me. My father was going to sell Rose to settle his debts, and then Ares demanded her. He could not deny Ares. He was his former son-in-law, after all. And he's very rich and very powerful. He sold her. Like she was a commodity. I am… I could not be unmoved by that. And then it became my turn. And I realized that no matter that I was treated as a daughter, and she as a servant, we were the same. A commodity. Now I do question my past. With all of these revelations."

"Do you exist in the outside world?"

She shook her head. "I don't. I am not real. If I am married off to a man who is cruel to me, if he crushes me, if he takes what he believes to be a doll and plays with me to his own ends and leaves none of me behind, who would ever know? And no one would seek justice for me. Do you see? Do you see why I had to escape, no matter what?"

If he were a different man, he might feel some measure of guilt for his treatment of her. But he did not feel guilt. He only felt fascination at the evidence of her strength.

"So now I know where you came from. I know you had no plans for your future. But what are your dreams?"

Her expression softened. "I would see the world. Everything that was kept from me all this time. I would watch whatever I wanted to on TV. And read whatever books I chose. I would use the internet. Without anyone watching me. And I would… I would have romance. And I'll find Rose. She is my friend. My real friend. I would choose what I wore, and I would probably try different kinds of wine. And perhaps a drink with an umbrella in it."

It was such a charmingly innocent list. There were some things on it he could not give her, but many that he could. And what he could not himself offer… He could set her up for a life where it would be possible after. Not because he was a good man. Because he was a fair man. And because there would be no more women who were used as his victims.

Yes, he had decided to keep her. And yes, he was going to leave her no choice when it came to going through with his plan.

But she would be less a prisoner, and more an employee. For he would offer payment.

"What if I told you I could give you that life?"

"I would be very skeptical of that. For I have never seen charity on that scale being handed out freely."

"And I already told you I didn't engage in charity."

"Yes. You did. And here I am, having eaten a lovely meal, eating a glorious dessert, and all I have done in exchange for it is remain trapped in a bedroom. And so I do deeply question what the cost of this offer will be. I had a very expensive cup of tea earlier, surely this has cost much more."

"Yes. Because, Athena, I need you to marry me."

# CHAPTER FOUR

ATHENA WAS STUNNED. She dropped her fork down onto the counter. It clattered loudly. "What?"

"I need you to become my wife. And when our marriage is over, I will set you up with enough money to live whatever life you choose."

"But…"

"Freedom, Athena. I offer you freedom after a time. Real freedom. The kind that comes with having the financial assets that you require."

"Marriage…"

"Is likely the only thing that will keep you safe from Hamilton. If you are married to another man, particularly one of my status, then you will exist. And you will exist out of his reach."

"Are you a man of status?"

"Yes. Or at least I was, once upon a time, and with you on my arm, I will return to that place."

"You need my help," she said, because she knew he was not asking out of a sense of altruism, this man who had called her part of his collection.

"Less than you need mine. But yes. But as my wife, you will see the world. You will choose your own clothes. You may eat whatever you like. You may watch whatever you want. You can read whatever you want. I will not give you romance, lass, but I can give you many of the other things on your list. And when I am done with you, you will be free to go out and seek whatever you wish."

"That sounds…" She stopped. She had never even seen this man. "I need to see you."

"You will. In good time."

There was a reason he would not let her, and it…it was disquieting to say the least.

"But before I agree…"

"There is no agreement or disagreement, Athena. The question, my goddess, is whether you agree happily, or angrily."

"I could cause a scene, and let everybody know that you've forced me into marriage."

"You could. And give your current fiancé opportunity to play the part of rescuer. It would end up being the perfect sort of void for him to step in. However, if you step out with me for all the world to see as though you are dazzlingly in love with me, we will both benefit. It will be a story that the media will adore, and it will leave no space for Hamilton to step back in to claim you for his own."

"You make it sound as if it's so easy."

"I know how the media works. I know how public opinion works. There was a time when I knew how to spin these things better than you can possibly imagine. I may not have been outside these castle walls in ten years, but I still understand the way of the world. I have been watching. Believe me when I tell you, this is the best way to ensure your safety. Your freedom."

"And what do you get from it? Because there must be something. More than something."

"I need this for my reentry into the world. This is for the launch of the very system I use here in the castle. It will be available to the whole world soon. But my business partner has decided to make a whole spectacle of it. A gala, dinner, dancing, speeches. As I said, I know how public opinion works. Better for me to come back into this world with someone on my arm."

"Because you have been here. Not out in the world?"

"Clearly."

"Why?"

"Something happened. Something…terrible, and I had to go away for a while, and now I must go back. All will become clear."

"I would like it to be clearer now."

"Do shiny rocks and old coins talk back?"

She blinked. "What?"

"The rest of my collection does not cause me such problems."

"Uh… The rest of your collection hasn't been asked to marry you."

"I do not recall asking."

He was so arrogant. How could a man who never showed his face be so arrogant?

"How long will we…?"

"It depends. On how long you are required for my purposes, and how long it takes for you to feel safe that your father will no longer come for you. Again, it is your legal marriage to me which will make you impervious to another man's reach."

"But we…"

"I will not give you romance, Athena. That will come later. With someone else. Ours will be a marriage in name only."

"Oh."

Of course it would be. Anything else would be absurd. She had never even set eyes on the man. It was only that… Truly, she had not imagined he would offer her marriage without also wanting to lay claim on her body. He was a mystery, Cameron McKenzie. And not simply because she had never seen his face.

She knew that he was tall.

She knew that he was heavily muscled. And smelled of sandalwood and made her feel safe and small. That his voice could be fire or ice. It could cut, or it could warm.

She knew that he had not left these walls in ten years. What she knew made him even more confusing than what she didn't know.

What she did know, was this mess, this…business of being part of his collection, was related to choices she'd made. She had made no choices at eight, when she'd come to live with the people she thought of as her family. She'd made a choice when she'd jumped out of that car.

She had suddenly been more than that doll. She'd been Athena, and this was where that choice had led her.

So she would see where this led her too.

"Yes. I will marry you."

The next day, breakfast was waiting for Athena when she got up. And still, there was no sign of Cameron. It wasn't until she was having her second cup of coffee, that he spoke to her. Still through his intercom, and not face-to-face.

"In one month, we will make our debut as husband and wife."

"Oh!" She jumped, sloshing coffee over the edge of the cup.

There was a long pause. "My apologies. I have forgotten certain things about interacting with people."

"Yes. *Why* is it that you don't interact with people?"

Something had happened. He'd come here.

But why cut everyone off? Why see no one?

"That is a story for another time. Until then, I wish to tell you the rules of the house. You may go anywhere you wish. The library, the gardens, the stables. You may eat whatever food you wish. If you need something, you simply need tell me over the intercom system, and I will procure it for you. Anything can be brought here by helicopter from the outside. You can have whatever your heart desires in less than an hour."

She was overwhelmed by that. "Oh. Well, that's…"

"You are never to go to the north tower. It is my domain. And you are not allowed. Am I clear?"

There was the ice again. It should repel her, and yet it only made her more and more curious about him. Who he was. Why he hid. Why he collected things.

And why should she care?

Was it only that he was the first person she'd been able to truly get to know in years?

"I… Yes. You made yourself clear."

"It does not give me anything to be cruel to you, lass. It would bring me no joy. I do not make rules for my own amusement. But you will remember who is in charge."

"Yes. How can I forget."

"You will be given whatever you need to be comfortable. All I ask is that you respect the boundaries that I have given you." He made an attempt to warm his voice, and she was disappointed with herself for caring he had done so.

"Yes," she said, feeling frustrated. "I wish that you would…"

"It is not up to you to decide how this arrangement will play out. Tell me. What is it you want? What is it you *need*."

She felt increasingly frustrated by the distance between them, and she knew she shouldn't think about him at all. He was offering her protection so she could get out into the world safely. So she could be free. So she could find out who she was. If she had a family.

She should care about that.

Not that she had grown attached to the man's voice, and

yet somehow felt lonely for having not been in his physical presence since the day he'd picked her up and…

"Nothing," she said. "Nothing now."

"Good. I will be making arrangements behind the scenes as needed to. Until then, make yourself comfortable. Neither of us is familiar with what waits for us outside. It has been too many years for me, and a lifetime for you. We must be ready."

"In that case, I need something to watch TV on. I must familiarize myself with the culture."

"Whatever you wish, as I said."

She decided to test him. "I should like an assortment of chocolates. To choose from whenever I wish. And I would also like a horse. I am an accomplished rider, you know. It was a skill…it was a skill that my mother prized."

Naya had been excellent with horses, and so should Athena be.

"It will be given to you." He paused for a moment. "You test me. You think I am not as good as my word."

He knew exactly what she was doing. The bastard.

"I shall also need a trousseau," she sniffed. "Fit for your bride. I shall put in my order when I have the chance to gain access to the internet and look at what I wish."

"That you cannot have."

She spread her hands wide. "Why not?"

"Because you can't."

"You're maddening." She had to stop herself from stamping her foot. "You said that I could. You said that I'd…"

"And I have changed my mind. You do not make the rules. I do."

"You are a petty tyrant," she said.

And what she resented most of all was how conflicted she felt. Angry with him one moment, intrigued the next.

Missing him, of all the strange things, and then ready to find him and attack him with her bare hands.

"I," he said, "have been called much worse."

"And yet you have no desire to reform?"

He laughed then, a dark, unsettling sound. "Oh, I have been reformed, little goddess. On that you will have to trust me."

Cameron sat down at his desk and called Apollo. "I have a plan."

"Why do I not like the sound of your tone?"

"These days it seems that you don't like anything about me, Apollo. It seems strange that we still consider ourselves friends."

"Don't take it personally. Or do. It is of no concern to me."

"In one month I will be in London for the launch of the new product. I promise you that. But I will not be alone."

"You won't be?"

"No. I will be bringing with me a wife."

# CHAPTER FIVE

HE GOT HER a horse, as promised. Over the intercom he told her to go outside one afternoon, where he had the animal waiting for her.

He watched from the shadows as she lit up with glory, pleased over the appearance of the creature.

Then he slipped back into the passages that he used in the house. The ones that carried him through secret halls so that he could move around as needed and remain unseen.

He had historically used them when the staff had come to clean the house, but now he used them to navigate around Athena.

He would face her. When he was ready.

Or rather, when she was.

He wondered what the girl would think of him. She was cosseted.

She would never have seen anyone who looked as he did.

He told himself that this was not about his vanity. He also told himself it had nothing to do with the fact that this was the closest he had been to another person in a decade.

There was no room left for tenderness inside of him. Had it ever existed?

He and Apollo had always been jaded playboys. He felt in many ways that he had been born one.

Growing up on the streets both he and Apollo had sold

their morality and their bodies and had thought little of it. If you were closed off completely inside then nothing could touch you.

It was easy to sell yourself. It was a renewable resource, after all.

But there was more money in being brilliant, and thankfully, he and Apollo were that as well.

Finding an old computer had changed their lives. It had just made sense to Cameron. And his natural ability with programming had sparked something else in Apollo.

*"You know, we use what we were born with to make money. We should use this. Your skills. You're a genius."*

*"I don't know about that."*

*"No doubt you can change the world with this, most people would need the most cutting-edge technology and a college education."*

*"Instinct. Just like sex, I suppose."*

*"For you, maybe. This is our change. You don't want to earn money like we do now for the rest of your life. What's sadder than a whore, Cam? An old whore."*

He'd laughed at that because it was true enough.

Apollo had always been the marketer. The master at getting them the meetings. Getting them into the rooms they needed to be in. He was also the one who knew how to dress. A wealthy lover of Apollo's had provided them with custom suits back in the day. They had been nineteen, maybe, ready for their first product pitch. Apollo had been the one that said they must dress at the level with which they wished to achieve someday.

Thankfully, Apollo's lover had agreed.

It was Cameron who had been the inventor. Always. Had he not looked as he did, he might have been called the computer geek. But no one could ever accuse him of such standing as he did at six foot five and with the face of a fallen angel.

Of course, his face had been a casualty of his excess.

He was still a hulking brute. In fact, only more so now. He had nothing to do beyond care for his fitness. His body was no longer decorative in any regard. All that mattered was that it was able to accomplish exactly what he wanted. His mind had to function more sharply than it ever had, and he prized his physical strength and agility. His endurance. Because those things he could control.

And that, he felt was the real issue with this present moment.

He could not control the way that Athena reacted to seeing him. There had been a time when he had known precisely how his every social interaction would go.

His masculine beauty had been an asset that he had not appreciated at the time.

And now…

Likely, he would frighten her.

He did not mind being frightening, but he preferred it to be because of something he had done, and not simply because he had walked into a room.

One of his security cameras flagged that Athena had come back into the castle. She was wearing the cloak that she had arrived in, her cheeks flushed, stained a glorious rose. She had been riding, he could tell. She had that look of joy that she had when she was out galloping on the back of the horse, and he recognized it, for it was the same sensation that he felt when he did the same.

"Did you have a good afternoon?" he asked.

She did not even react to the sound of his voice. Hearing from him in this way did not seem to shock her anymore. "Yes. Thank you."

"There are scones. In the kitchen."

A smile tugged at the corner of her lips. "Have you been baking in the middle of the night?"

"Perhaps."

"Well, I thank you. Your hobby has benefited me greatly."

"Is this the sort of thing you expected living in your father's house?"

She had a thoughtful look on her face as she moved from the entry down the hall into the kitchen. He followed her every movement on the cameras. "It sounds strange to hear him called that. Though I don't know what else to call him."

"My apologies."

"None necessary. But he did not care for me. And I do not think he ever saw me as a daughter. My mother did." Though there was something hollow in her voice then, as if even that had not been simple. "I will continue to think of her that way." She sounded resolved then, determined. "I believe that she loves me, in a fashion. I also believe that she is firmly underneath the thumb of my father, and she does not possess the wherewithal to seek her freedom." She shook her head. "That isn't fair. As you pointed out, poverty is not something a person should readily race toward. She would have no way to take care of herself."

"Have you learned so much lounging about my castle?"

"I have been *thinking*. And while this is not a wholly different existence than the one I had before, it is also entirely separate in many ways. I do not feel so much a decoration around here. And it is… Wild. Gloriously so. It makes me feel the same."

"Good."

He found that he meant that.

He was fascinated by her. By his opportunity to observe such a beautiful creature without inserting himself in her path directly. Without his face impacting their interaction.

"The scones look lovely," she said, taking one off the plate. He had left jam and cream out for her as well, which she spread on with much relish. He enjoyed watching her eat the food that he provided her. He had not realized that he was... Hungry for such things. For this matter of interaction. For the ability to share something with another person.

It made him appreciate, truly, the connection he had to Apollo for most of his life. Without each other, they would have been truly alone. And he had never fully considered what that would be like. Even in his concealment in the castle, he'd still had access to Apollo.

There was something about Athena that made him extremely conscious of what he'd not had all this time, and what he had.

His desire for her was...

He shut it down ruthlessly.

He had gone a decade without sex.

It was an appetite. Like any other. Not special or unique in that regard. Except, unlike sleep, or hydration or nutrition, you did not need it to survive. It could be denied. He'd had enough sex in the first twenty-eight years of his life to last him.

First he had sold it as a commodity, and then, the ultimate excess had been the ability to give it away for free. To anyone he chose.

And he had.

The drive could be denied easily enough now, and when it could not, he handled it dispassionately and alone.

But she was... She was glorious. And even just gazing upon her over the cameras was intoxicating.

"I do feel that it is a bit of an unfair advantage," she said softly. "That you can see me, and I have not seen you."

"And yet it is not a new development."

She must've been able to feel his gaze on her. So bright that his desire for her burned.

He wondered...

Did he truly fear her response to him... Or his own to her?

He had no idea what thwarted desire was.

If he wanted a woman, she had always wanted him in return.

The power of being desired had always flowed his direction.

When his focus had been for sale, he had taken satisfaction in the fact that people were willing to pay handsomely for a chance to have him. If he could not find desire for the person buying his services, he could at least manufacture arousal from the rush of power he felt at their desperation.

But to want someone who looked at him and recoiled...

He never wanted to be one of those people. The one so desperate for the touch of the person they desired that they would beg. They would pay.

It could never be him. Never.

He would live a life alone. He would live a life of celibacy before he debased himself.

And perhaps that's what all this was. A fortress to avoid that level of debasement.

His refusal to leave until he had secured himself a bride whose beauty far outstripped his own was certainly evidence of that.

"There are things about me that are far more interesting than how I look," he said.

She seemed to consider this. And then she looked up, her eyes unerringly finding a camera he knew she couldn't actually see. And yet...

She was looking at him.

Like she could see him.

It sent a shock down his spine to have those large, dark eyes staring right into him.

"Is that so?" she whispered. "Tell me one of those things."

He shook off the feeling that had overtaken him, that had left him frozen.

"Your father wished to sell you to pay off his debts," he said, the words more caustic than he intended. "Mine never knew me."

"Never?"

He did not know why he was compelled to answer that challenge, to share himself. Why should he? She was merely a shiny rock. A new trinket.

*And yet a rock does not have eyes, no matter how shiny. She is one who will see you.*

Soon, all the world would see him, so what did it matter?

Yet he found it did.

And he found himself replying to her.

"No," he answered. "I was with my mother, off and on until I was fourteen. We lived in Edinburgh. Times were very hard. Sometimes, my mother was bright and happy and looking forward to a clean future. In other times, she was mired in her addictions. I loved her very much. She died of a drug overdose when I was sixteen, but I had not been living in her house for two years at that point. I met another teenager named Apollo. Two years younger than myself, he had been out on his own since he was ten. After my mother died we managed to get ourselves to London, we made money however we could. Eventually, we were able to take our ill-gotten funds and transform them into something legitimate. The foundation will always be made of those hardscrabble years. And I do not regret them."

"Oh. I don't know why, but I always imagined you in this castle."

"No. I bought the castle ten years ago. As a refuge."

He waited for her to ask why he needed a refuge. But at this point, she seemed well versed in what he refused to answer.

"How did you make money?"

"Do you really wish to know the answer?"

"Yes."

"Petty theft at first. We were very good pickpockets, and Apollo has always been a great distraction. He was small for his age for a time." It was hilarious now to think of his friend who was well over six feet as the small, scrawny boy he'd been with wide dark eyes, but he had been the sort of creature to ignite the pity in every passing woman on the street, and while he had sold a hard-luck story... Cameron had been ripping them off.

"Of course, that only got us a pittance. And we quickly realize there were other ways to make money. Elaborate scams take a long time to set up. The easiest thing to sell is sex."

He watched her closely, to see if she was disgusted at the revelation.

"You... You sold yourself?"

She said it gravely, and yet he heard no judgment there.

"Yes. Easily. At that point we were hardened. It was of no cost to us. We were able to make quite a bit of money that way. Especially if you added a bit of blackmail on top of it. There are very few people who want to expose that they are paying for sex with teenage boys. Trust me on that."

"That's awful."

She did pity him. But not his looks. His past.

What a strange creature. Where had she learned feelings such as this in the life she had lived?

Perhaps it was a testament to what he already suspected to be true. Life had to steal the softness from you. As it had done to him.

He had disconnected himself from his feelings to the point he could not find them if he tried.

When he'd found that guilt over Irina...

He added that to his collection. Like a dragon might hoard gold.

He was a monster, it was true.

But he felt that guilt. And that seemed significant.

And now he felt the echo of her pity across the space.

"It is utterly no consequence to me," he said. "I felt nothing about it then, and I feel nothing about it now. It was just another con. We never felt anything beyond disdain for them. We walked away with their money. We always had the power. And that is the important thing, Athena. You can sell anything but your power."

"That is terribly cynical."

He leaned back in his chair, all of his focus on the screen. On her. "*I* am terribly cynical. Life has given me no reason to be an optimist. I have had successes, and I have had failures. For all that life gives you, it will be standing in the wings waiting to take something away. There is no use getting attached to anything. And I have found these years spent here have at least been… Mine. I am in control of all around me. The first and only thing to ever defy that control was… You."

"But you didn't have to come get me from the hovel. Why did you?"

He looked down at his hand. At the thick scar tissue there. "I wanted you."

She looked up, her face in full view of the camera. "For what?"

"I didn't know. When I find something beautiful here on the grounds… I often take it back with me. I am isolated here and… I look for things to pass the time."

He had some ideas of what to do with her. Certainly. But he had known, even then, that he would never seek his body's ultimate desire with her. But he had gotten a great deal of pleasure from simply having her near.

"I need to know more about what's to happen next."

"All in good time. When I decide."

# CHAPTER SIX

ATHENA RODE LIKE she was being chased. By her father. By his men.

She rode until the breath left her lungs.

Until the green around her blurred together into a rush of velvet.

She had no idea what she was doing here. No idea what would happen next. And it was beginning to feel… Unbearable.

One thing she had taken for granted living with her father was that at least she understood what her day-to-day routine would be.

At least, prior to his determination to marry her off.

There had been a sameness. A deeply expected ebb and flow.

She had risen from bed, she was prepared for the day. Her mother provided her with an excess of beautiful clothes and each day she would be outfitted several times. Her hair combed until it was glossy. If her mother wished to have spa treatments, they would have spa treatments. If she was in the mood to read by the pool. They would read by the pool.

Her doll…

Not a daughter, perhaps.

Just a hollow thing to fashion as she chose. No choice, no mind of her own.

Not here.

Perhaps here she was breaking out of that plastic mold. Perhaps here she was finding who she was.

And though it was not answers about her past, she felt that it brought her closer.

Cameron spoke to her often. Throughout the day. There was always a different sort of treat setting out for her on a plate.

She could not decide if it was a gesture of care or not.

She was somewhat ashamed to admit that she was beginning to have… A strange sort of attachment to this man that she had only ever spoken to remotely.

His story about his childhood had left her feeling raw. Sad.

He was… An extremely tragic figure, that much she knew. She couldn't remain unaffected by his story, though why it should feel like grief she had no idea.

Why she should feel compelled by his dark voice and tragic circumstances when he had told her she was an object, she could not say.

Any more than she could understand why he wouldn't face her, when it was inevitable.

If they were to be married…

The word made her take a swift, indrawn breath.

She also realized that he moved around the grounds much more often than it seemed.

He had to. He had arranged for her to get the horse. He seemed to observe things that would be outside the purview of his tower.

He went to the kitchen, obviously, though she could not figure out the pattern of his movements.

And whatever his voice came over the intercom, her heart gave a little jump.

The sound of his voice was soothing. It made something warm expand in her chest.

*My goddess.*

She should not like him calling her that, and yet she did. She rode harder, faster, to get away from herself. To find the edge of this cage.

It was only another cage.

She should not allow herself to have grown so content here.

She should not let herself feel anything for him.

This was not the world. It was just more walls.

On and on she rode. Until she saw the edge. Until she came to the wall.

At the far end of the grounds. Kilometers away from the house.

It was vast, and tall.

And yet… She took the horse down to the other side of the perimeter, and saw that there were loose rocks.

She would be able to climb over that. It would take hours for her to get here without her horse but…

It would be possible. For some reason, her own line of thinking frightened her, and she turned the horse and raced back to the castle.

She was surprised when she came back in and Cameron didn't speak to her.

"Cameron?"

She said his name, and received no answer.

Was he gone?

It seemed nearly impossible.

He didn't leave. He'd said so himself, and yet…

Hours went by, and he did not greet her. He did not contact her.

A strange sense of disquiet started to fill her, and for the first time, she felt as though she might actually be alone.

The feeling of abandonment, stark and upsetting, shocked her. To her core.

He could not be gone. The very idea was a loss, deep and aching.

It went beyond her need for him to protect her. It went beyond anything rational. It had nothing to do with what he might do for her when they left here, or how her marriage to him would insulate her.

The idea of not seeing him, not ever, made her feel devastated. The idea of not hearing his voice...

Of Cameron McKenzie remaining a mystery she could never truly unravel.

That all but destroyed her.

And something called her. Beckoned her. Toward the north tower. The place that she wasn't allowed to go. She was curious. But more than that, she was compelled, as if by his very voice. Why did he not wish for her to go there?

*Because it's where he is.*

And she was propelled by that.

She began to walk toward that tower. Cautiously taking the winding stairs that would carry her up, up to the very top.

A strange sense of unease filled her as she moved slowly up the staircase.

Surely he had cameras. He would see her if she was approaching.

He would stop her. Call out if he needed to.

But he didn't. So she kept on going.

At the very top of the stairs was a door. She pushed it open slowly. And she sighed... Everything.

Cameras. Video screens filled with different views of the property. Everything that she already knew he could see. And, true to his word, her bedroom was not present.

"At least there's that. At least he's... Well he's not a pervert."

She turned around the space, trying to find some identifying feature. But the place was Spartan. There was nothing to be gleaned from it. There was technology, but she already knew that. About this place, and about him. It was other things, about him as a human being, those were things that she didn't know.

And she could not find...

She turned in a circle, and then she saw a huge piece of metal, twisted and set up on a shelf, underneath a glass case. And then, on the other shelves...

Rocks. Coins. Gems.

His collection.

The thing he said she was part of.

She reached out, curiosity directing her movements before she could think it through.

"What are you doing?"

She turned around and jumped back. Because there he was, standing in the doorway, his hood over his head, casting a shadow over his features.

Her heart contracted, then leapt into her throat.

"I told you never to come here." That familiar voice was so close now, and it was all ice.

"Cameron... I..."

She was stunned at the sight of him. He was so much taller than her. So much larger than she remembered or realized that moment he'd carried her to her room. She was frozen. And he was thunderous.

"Leave," he said, his voice a low growl.

A shaft of light fell across his eyes. Only his eyes. They were bright, electric blue.

Beautiful.

Terrifying.

"I..."

*"Get out!"*

His voice vibrated through her, not low now but thunderous.

"I... I'm sorry... I didn't know..."

"You knew *exactly* what you did," he said. "I told you never to come into the north tower, and here you are."

She took a step back, fear and something…else, spreading through her.

He was so large, so imposing and terrifying. The threat felt…she did not think he'd hurt her. She felt almost drawn to him, even in his fury. Like a magnet.

He was here. He was outraged.

But…

He was in front of her.

"I was looking for you," she whispered, taking half a step toward him.

"Enough," he said, halting her movements. "Do not blame me for your deception."

"It was not a deception, I…"

He took a step forward, and the cloak fell away from his head, as he reached out and took hold of her wrist. He drew her toward him, and she was frozen completely in shock.

The first thing was the scent of him. Sandalwood. His skin.

Then his strength. His heat.

It stole her breath, made her feel bound up in him. In his intensity. He was more than a man, he was something altogether much more dangerous.

Much more compelling.

And then…

He had long dark hair and a heavy beard. And his skin was…

*Ruined.*

Twisted from scarring. His forehead was rough, a gash causing a dent on his right cheek where it looked as if he had not only been cut, but broken. His nose was crooked, like a prize fighter who had taken too many blows. Three bare slashes crossed his left eyebrow.

Whatever other damage was on his face was covered by

the beard, save one spot, another slash of bare skin, where hair did not grow, down one side of his face. And the hand that held her wrist had more thick, heavy scar tissue.

Whatever had happened to him… It had been horrific.

It was the reason he didn't leave this place. It was the reason he only spoke to her over the intercom.

"I…" she tried again.

"Leave," he said, flinging her back, releasing his hold on her.

"Cameron, please…"

"I said, get out!" And he turned over the table with the video screens on it, they went crashing to the ground. "Do you think I'm serious yet?"

Fear overtook her then. Because he was a beastly sight. Hardly a man. But it wasn't the scarring.

It was the rage. Red and violent, terrifying.

"Out!"

She fled down the stairs. And out the door.

She ran. Ran to the fields, ran through the grass until she couldn't breathe. She knew exactly where she was going.

To the wall. To the weakness in the wall.

She couldn't stay. Not with him. Not like this.

That man couldn't be reasoned with. And she would not ever put herself in danger. She was not a prisoner.

She told herself that. Repeated it over and over again as she scrambled over the fields, making herself breathless, fear and desperation dogging her every step.

When she came to that spot in the wall, she scrambled up, climbing over the top and flinging herself down to the ground below. She kept on running. Running and running.

Only to come to the edge of a cliff. Overlooking the sea. The sea was this close? And he said he hadn't seen the sea in years…

And then she heard a sound.

A growling.

She looked up, to the left and saw a dog. Feral and skinny, his lip curled. He was a huge, rangy hound, and fear shivered through her as she stood and faced him down.

"Don't… I'm not going to hurt you. I'm not…" She took a step back, the water behind her, the animal in front.

And then she heard a sound. The pounding of hoof-beats, and the dog heard it too. He paused and looked up, behind them, his muzzle still a snarl, his body still oriented toward her, ready to pounce.

But it was Cameron. On the back of a black horse. Riding with his cloak billowing behind him. "Athena!"

The dog turned away from her, looking at him.

He jumped off the horse and ran toward her, but the dog leapt at him, clamping its jaws around his forearm. Cameron growled, and shook his arm violently, the beast flying away from him. But crimson red bled through the fabric of Cameron's shirt.

She gasped in horror. "Cameron…"

He was not a monster.

He bled.

He was bleeding now because of her.

She felt slapped, confronted with the consequences of her actions.

And overcome by his presence. So grateful she wanted to weep.

So overwhelmed by the sight of him she could hardly sort through what the feelings meant.

Fear? Certainly.

But something else.

He picked her up off the ground, his grip firm and strong. "You little idiot." And then just as he had done two times before, he carried her as if she weighed nothing. But this time, he put her up on the back of his horse. And then he got up behind her, one strong arm clamped around her waist as he began to guide the horse at a flat-out run toward the castle.

The heat pouring from him was something like rage and another thing altogether, and she was locked against it by the strength of his forearm, trapped between that arm and his solid chest.

"You're mine," he said, that familiar voice in her ear, along with the heat of his breath on her neck, she shivered helplessly with it, unable to understand what was happening to her. "We have a deal."

"You're bleeding," she said, looking down at his arm.

"I've bled far worse than this. Or have you not yet come to understand that?"

"Cameron..."

"I know that you needed to flee my hideous visage, but this is why you were told not to go poking your nose in places where you're not allowed. This is why I told you we would wait to see one another, but you didn't listen."

"You *frightened* me," she said.

"You did not do as you were told."

Neither of them spoke for the rest of the ride back to the castle. They did not go back in the way she came out, but rather rode through a gate that opened automatically for them.

She wanted to lean against him and struggle against him at the same time. She knew that the stirrings in her stomach, and lower, were related to desire. She was not stupid. She might be innocent in some ways, but she had explored her own body. She'd had spare little else to do in the compound.

She understood sexual desire.

She simply didn't understand it here.

Now.

"Does it recognize you?" she asked, desperate to think

of something other than the strange ache between her thighs.

"Yes, it does."

"Facial recognition?"

He laughed. "Yes. I get a great deal of pleasure from that. From the fact that I have forced it to learn to recognize this face."

"Your face is not why I ran." He didn't say anything, rather he growled. And she could feel it vibrate against the back of her shoulder blades. She was so distressingly conscious of how large he was. How broad. And hard.

"Go inside," he said.

"No," she said, getting off the horse along with him.

He began to lead the steed toward the stall.

"Do not argue with me."

"You are hurt," she said, taking the lead rope from the stallion. "I can take care of the horse."

"He answers only to me," said Cameron, refusing to let go of the lead.

"Perhaps he will do just fine with me," she said, maintaining her grip on it as well.

"Why must you test me so."

"You're bleeding," she said.

Finally, he dropped the lead rope, and she knew that it was not a gift, but rather he was trying to teach her a lesson. She snarled to match the growl he had given her earlier and went toward the stables. She took the horse's saddle and blanket off him. His bridle. She checked his hooves for stones, then patted his flank as she set him back into the stall.

"You see," she said. "He tolerates me just fine."

"A very brave lass."

"Perhaps he likes everyone, Cameron, it is only that no one else has ever been here."

And much to her surprise, his ruined mouth twisted

upward into a smile. "I cannot argue with that, though I might try."

"I have a feeling you might try to argue with anything. You are extraordinarily hardheaded. I asked to see you two weeks ago. Another two weeks until you claim we are to be presented as husband and wife."

"We will not just be presented as husband and wife. We will marry."

"You thought that hiding your face from me was the only way to do that?"

"I had thought…" He cut himself off, and then his voice went hard. "I thought it best you know me first."

"I do know you now. Except, I don't, do I? Because the moment that I saw you face-to-face, you showed me an entirely different side of yourself. Your anger. You ruined all the monitors in your office. And to what end? To frighten me? That was a silly thing to do."

"It is not for you to decide whether or not my actions are silly," he said.

"And yet I have. I refuse to be a prisoner. Not anymore. We are partners in this endeavor. In your protection of me, and in my aid of you. But I am not your prisoner."

He gripped her wrist again, moving closer.

He smelled of sandalwood. Of the moss here in the Highlands. Of clean skin.

He was incredibly tall. Powerfully built.

There was a strange hint of something… Power? It reminded her of someone, from long ago, but she couldn't quite say who. Or how or why.

It made her mouth dry and her heart pound heavily.

"I am angry. That is why you saw my anger. That's why I'm here. That's why I keep myself away from the world. I do not know how to have a partner."

"You said you had a friend… Apollo."

"Yes. But if Apollo had met me now, we would not be friends."

"Apollo could not have met you now. Unless he fell asleep in a hobble in the woods and you carried him to your castle."

He growled. Releasing his hold on her.

"You still cannot have access to the internet."

She was right back to being frustrated with him. But the awareness of his presence didn't ease.

"Why?"

"You will… You will find things about me."

"Things that you don't want me to find?"

"I simply wanted us to find one another first. Our own rhythm. I wanted you to know me without knowing who I was before."

"How can I know you when I had never seen your face?"

And she meant more than just the way he looked. She meant so much more.

She looked down at his arm. "You're going to need to see a doctor…"

"We will call one in," he said. "And get the necessary shots."

He looked pained, but resigned.

"Come inside," she said, finding it her turn to take hold of his wrist.

He looked bemused as she tugged him toward the castle.

"Go on," she said. "Call a doctor."

"I do not see people."

"You just agreed. You need vaccinations, among other things. You've been bitten."

"Fine. I do have a doctor I use."

"You're a liar then!" she said.

"No," Cameron growled. "He does not count."

"Why not?"

"Because I decided he did not."

"Well call him now," she insisted.

She pushed him down into the armchair by the fireplace.

"Magic some fire," she commanded.

"Fire," he said.

The flames erupted, and she looked critically at his wounded arm. The shirt was stained, and there was a hole in it where the beast's tooth had punctured the fabric. So she decided rather than pushing the sleeve up to go ahead and simply tear it. She rent it wide, exposing the deep wound there.

"Oh," she said. "I'm sorry."

"You should not have run away."

"You shouldn't have *chased me*. You shouldn't have…" He leaned in closer to her and her breath caught and released tremulously. "Frightened me."

Yet it was not fear that made her voice shake as she looked into his blue eyes.

"You should have stayed where you were told you could be. I gave you the entire run of the property, the one place I told you not to go…"

"And why not?"

"Because it is mine."

She looked at him, at the ferocity in his gaze. "I'm not afraid of your face," she said again. "What happened?"

"And this is why I delayed our face-to-face meeting, little goddess. It is the only conversation to have when one beholds this."

"Call the doctor."

What he did was send a message to his chief of staff to have his trusted physician sent to the castle.

He would be brought by helicopter quickly, Cameron assured her.

"I do not count Dr. McCall as a person. He is a tool for my use," he said.

"Like part of your collection?"

"I was badly injured after the accident and even after the initial recovery there were complications to watch for and the man saw to them when I had a need."

"Practical. You know, Cameron, I am realizing I was merely an object to my mother. Something to represent what she lost, not really who I was. It is painful, to treat a human being that way."

"Many things in life are painful, lass."

They lapsed into silence for a moment.

"Tell me," she said. "While we wait."

"It was a car accident," he said.

"I'm very sorry," she said. "It must've been a terrible one."

"You have no idea. It was… A horror."

"It looks as if it was a miracle you survived."

"It was. My passenger was not so fortunate."

"Oh… I'm sorry."

"There is no need for you to be sorry. I am. I will be. Forever. Irina's life is over. And mine was spared. There is no justice in that. I was driving at a high rate of speed. It is my fault."

"Was she… Was she your girlfriend?"

He laughed. A cold, hollow sound. "She was my lover."

"Oh, I'm so sorry. It must've broken your heart."

He looked blank then. "No. It didn't. And that, little goddess, is the very worst thing. I was not in love with her. She was merely an amusement. It might've been any woman in the car with me. But it was Irina. Beautiful, vivacious, with all that life ahead of her. With parents who loved her very much. She was a model, she was about to be in her first movie. She had everything in her life to look forward to. She would have eventually married, she would've had children. I was simply a detour along the way for her. She should have had that life. She had sisters.

She had a family. I do not have that. So many people are alive who miss her."

"And so you have to live as if you died?"

"Is that not justice?"

"No. It is not justice. It is just… I don't even know what it is. Needless punishment."

"And what would you know of it, Athena?"

"I…"

He moved all of a sudden. "He's here."

"I'll get the door."

She jumped up and went to the doors, which Cameron opened by voice. The physician was an elderly man, who took one look at Cameron's arm and began to work without saying a word. He got out his medical bag and vigorously scrubbed at the wound before stitching it dispassionately. And then he took out two very large needles and gave Cameron shots. He did not explain what they were.

She had to wonder if that was the bargain Cameron had made with the man. Care for him, but never speak. As if they really weren't sharing the same space.

The doctor left quickly after that, with Cameron sewn back together and a bottle of pain pills left on the table. Cameron took the pain pills and threw them in the trash.

"You can grow dependent too easily when you're in constant pain," he said, his voice rough, speaking of hard-learned experiences. "I have trained myself, all my life, to not feel pain. I learned to extend it to the physical so that… I did not live a half-life on these pills."

All of the things that had happened since he had found her, his anger had ebbed.

And she was beginning to grow accustomed to him. More than that, even.

She reached toward him, and he jerked back. "I'm fine," he said.

"Oh. You seem… I…"

"Do not worry about me. I'm not worth your concern."

"You're not ready for this," she said.

"Who are you to tell me what I'm ready for?"

"The woman who has been living in your home these past two weeks. Do you remember how to dance? There will be dancing, you mentioned that."

"Do you know how to dance?" he asked.

"I do," she said. "My father made certain that I was apprised of all the necessary social graces for... Well I suppose it was for me to become somebody's wife when the time came. It was just beneficial to me to ignore it."

None of that life had been for her.

She had felt privileged. To not be like Rose. To not be a maid.

She had not been occupied with doing work, her life had seemed easy, and it had seemed indulgent. But it was never for *her*.

Much like now.

She had been collected, and she might have been anyone.

For some reason that hurt. Sharp and painful in her chest.

"I'm certain that I remember how," he said.

"And will there be a dinner? You will be expected to sit and make conversation."

"That's why I have you."

"I cannot make all the conversation for you. How will you tell people we met?"

"That I found you in a hut on my property."

"You can't do that," she said. "I have only ever been one place in my entire life, and even I know that you can't do that."

"You make too many demands," he said.

"I have been made your prisoner. How is it that I'm

too demanding? You're the one who decided everything needed to be difficult."

"Fine. Then we will prepare. Your way."

"One thing you prove to me for certain today is that you need more practice dealing with people. Turning tables is not going to help win you any favors whether you show up with a wife or not." She frowned. "Why do you need a wife?"

"Look at me," he said.

She tilted her chin up and looked him full in the face. "I am."

"Be honest with me. Do you think anyone would look at me and see anything but an object of pity?"

"Perhaps it's because you were yelling at me, but I do not pity you."

"Perhaps it is that you need to see me before."

"Show me."

He took his phone out of his pocket, and very quickly pulled up the photograph. The man in the picture was unrecognizable. His brown hair was short and pushed off of his forehead, he had no beard, and he was... He was so handsome he verged on being beautiful. His blue eyes bright as gemstones, his jaw so sharp it could cut glass. His features were perfectly symmetrical.

She looked at him. His eyes.

To recognize those eyes.

"That's you."

"It's me. So you can see... You can see."

"You..."

"Be honest with me, little goddess. Do not lie."

"You were very...beautiful."

"I was. Understand, I was not a vain man, but I used my looks to my advantage. And when people hear my name, that is what they see. I have not shown my face to the public."

"But they know."

"Of course they know. They just do not know the extent of it."

"And you thought…"

"By showing up with a wife, I am showing up at the suggestion that I have done more than simply sit in this castle for the last decade. I will have proven that I am not simply an object of pity."

"Then we will make sure they know that. We will make a story, one that convinces everyone. One that sweeps them away. If you're going to take control of it, then take full control. It will be a story unmatched. And there will be no way for my father to come for me, because we will be so well regarded as a couple, that my disappearance would create alarm across the world."

"There you have it, Athena. You are indeed the goddess of war. This is what you look like riding into battle."

She felt… Strong. Resolved. Like he had seen her. Like maybe…it did matter that she was Athena. Not a rock or a coin or a doll.

Not Naya.

She had started the day by running away. But she wasn't running. Not now.

"And a war we shall have. But first, we will dance."

# CHAPTER SEVEN

HE DID NOT know how she had so effortlessly upended his control. It did not seem rational or reasonable. It did not seem *possible*. He had pursued her today out on the moors, and he would have said he would never pursue another person.

Already, she had forced him to contend with a lack of control that he found unacceptable.

The dog bite on his arm was… It was inconsequential. But that she had seen him face-to-face; that she had made demands of him…

He called Apollo.

"Things did not go as planned today."

He relayed everything about Athena to his friend.

From the moment that he had carried her out of the hovel, and to being viciously attacked by the dog, to her demanding that they dance.

And of course, along with that, her seeing him.

"It sounds as if you have met your match."

He laughed. "Apollo. There is no match for me. No match for *this*."

"Not in your looks, friend. In your spirit."

"In what sense?"

"You are a stubborn asshole. This Athena sounds like she has a backbone made of steel. And how? Do you not marvel?"

"Marvel at what?"

"If everything that you've told me about her is true, her father spearheading her off to be married to a stranger. The fact that she has never left her family compound before these past couple of weeks... She is extraordinarily self-possessed."

"Yes. She is that. But it is only irritating. For she does not do that which I asked."

"Good. You deserve that."

"She is beautiful," he said. "And I am pleased with that. Because when I present her to the public, it is all the better that she is stunning. She will make a triumphant prize. A tale as old as time, don't you think?"

"Obviously. And yet you do not sound pleased with her beauty."

A smile curved his lips. "Look at me."

"I am. I have. These past ten years. But you don't trust me to see you face-to-face. I have seen you."

And yet he could not shake the fact that it felt as if Apollo had not seen him. They had the ability to have a screen between them. He could control the setting, the lighting. How long he was comfortable with the interaction.

It was different, to be seen. Really seen.

To have Athena look at him, fully look at him, with those dark, liquid eyes was almost more than he could bear. He felt as if his skin was being flayed away from his bones. And he knew what that felt like. He had actually experienced it.

It was a strange thing. The bite from the dog had felt like nothing. But Athena's gaze? That had been nearly unbearable.

"I want her."

The words nearly cut his throat.

"Unsurprisingly," Apollo said, the word brushing Cameron's statement away. "Have you been with a woman these past ten years?"

Cameron laughed. *Laughed* at his friend.

With all the rage and bitterness in his soul.

What did Apollo think he had been doing here?

"*Of course* I haven't been. I've seen no one."

"Truly no one?"

"What did you think, Apollo? That I was playing games with you?"

"No. I didn't. And yet I could not quite believe that you had actually concealed yourself to that degree. I had thought that at least you would…"

"That I would pay for sex?" he said, flatly. "That I would become one of those sad men or women that we mocked mercilessly as we took their money, as we took their desire? No. I would die celibate before I debase myself in such a fashion."

"I did not mean to suggest…"

"But you did," he said, hard. Ruthless.

"I meant that you might see it as a practicality. If you order food, you might as well order sex."

"I learned to cook. Apply that how you will."

Apollo laughed. "All right. Point taken. But your right hand can hardly be a true substitute for physical passion."

"I've had enough to last a lifetime."

"Obviously not, if you have a desire for her."

"It is inconvenient. And I've no wish to act on it. I just do not wish to feel it either."

"It must be galling for you. To want something you cannot have."

"I am very familiar with the feeling."

"Not in this context," said Apollo.

"You certainly know nothing of it."

Apollo laughed. Bitter. Hard. "Oh, you think you know everything about my life? About what I feel. About what

I can have. When you have not been a part of my life, not really in all these years." His friend shook his head. "You have no idea what I want."

"No," he said, feeling somewhat shamed. "I don't suppose I do."

"She wishes to dance with you?"

"Yes," he said through gritted teeth. "And I have no wish to put my hands on her."

"Your mistake is believing that the only thing anyone ever wanted from you was your face, Cameron. You have other attributes. Focus on those and find her charm."

"My money?"

"I believe the gentler ladies would call it your manhood, Cam."

He gritted his teeth. "Thank you."

"Of course, I'm assuming that everything is fine there... I feel as if you would've told me."

"Enough," he said, waving his hand. "Everything is fine there, thank you."

"Charm her. Anyway, you need to figure out how to look as if you are doing so when we are at the product launch. And by the way, I have begun marketing it as an event not to miss. One with a very special guest."

"You are very good at what you do."

"As were you. So figure out how to become good at it again."

"I don't know how to be who I was. It feels... Wrong somehow."

He sighed heavily. "Irina is dead. Whether or not you get on with things."

Then Apollo hung up, and left Cameron to contemplate that. He dug into his closet, and took out a suit. It had been a long time since he'd worn one.

Then he went downstairs, where he knew Athena would

be waiting in the old ballroom. He had not—for the first time—looked ahead at her.

And the moment he walked into the room, he regretted that choice. For he was not prepared. Not for the devastation of her beauty. Not for the way the yellow gown she was wearing conformed to her curves. Soft and draping around her breasts, highlighting the subtle golden glow of the supple mounds. The waist was corseted, the skirt flaring out in a soft chiffon followed her hips.

Her black hair was swept up into a bun, curls trailing down and framing her face. She had no makeup—he'd provided none, it had not occurred to him—but she glowed all the same.

She was like a sunrise.

And he had been in the darkness for far too long. She stepped forward, her eyes grave. And then she extended her hand.

He could only look at it. Soft and perfect. Like the rest of her.

It felt as if there was a barrier to touching her. As if doing so might break this. Might break her.

The last time he had held a woman, her body had been broken.

The last time he had held a woman, there had not been enough regret or anguish in all the world, in all his soul, to make the moment endurable. He felt… As if touching Athena now would be compounding his sins, and that was something he would've thought was impossible. How could his sins possibly be more than they already were. When they were so… Unforgivable.

Perhaps that was the real justice in the world. That he wore the truth of who he was outside now. Before it had been concealed.

His brokenness. His ugliness. And now… All the world could see that he was a monster.

"Is there something wrong?" she asked.

"No," he said, his voice hard.

He reached his hand out, and pulled her to him.

And they were more than face-to-face. They were so close they could share the same breath.

Today he had seen her, and a doctor. Ten years of not sharing space with anyone, and in the weeks since she had appeared, there had been two.

And then there would be countless more. Because he was resolved. He would go forward, and he would do as Apollo asked. He would see his friend.

But all of that was drowned out by the feel of her hand against his. That soft, enticing skin, the soft press of warmth that bled into his body. Into his soul.

And then he pressed her body against his, held her close as he had done long ago, and yet it was not an echo of things familiar. It was like something else entirely. Something new and sharp. Something enchanted.

He had never believed in such things. Not in the past. But things had changed in these last ten years.

He had learned to watch the grass grow. To marvel at the simple magic involved in rising bread dough.

He had changed.

Even if he had changed far too late to prevent the greatest tragedy he had ever been a part of.

That was the real trick of it.

His ego, his selfishness, his insides had shifted. But it was too late now, for he had earned a visage that matched who he was.

But for now, he would focus on the magic inherent in holding Athena in his arms.

"Do you remember how to do this?" she asked, her eyes downcast.

He reached down, placed his forefinger beneath her chin

and tilted her face up. "You never forget such things. The simple pleasure of holding a woman in your arms, carrying her over the dance floor."

Although, it was not the pleasure he was thinking of now. And he did not deserve to have that thought. He did not deserve to allow that desire to take root in his soul, for even the need of it was more pleasure than he had experienced in all these long years.

Even the ache of desire felt better than the decade of cold that he had lived in. For him, desire had been nothing more than an inconvenience to satisfy. Something that he resented, and certainly not anything he reveled in.

If he had to, he would ruthlessly dispense with the need in a matter of minutes. He did not allow himself the chance to luxuriate in fantasy. And he did not allow himself to think of it as pleasure, rather a simple release.

But this… This promise of something. The suggestion contained in the brush of her fingertips against his shoulders, that hint of questioning in her dark eyes, the curve of her lips.

*No. You are misinterpreting.*

There was no desire there.

He was acting as if he was the Cameron that he had been.

A man who easily called up the desires of women the moment that he entered the room.

A man who was sought after by all.

No, he was the man who had lived alone in a castle for ten years with not but his right hand to keep him company.

He was a man who had only hours ago chased this woman from the room with nothing but his face and a shout.

He was maimed.

Ruined beyond measure.

But it had been true always. It had been true before.

It was just now he could not fool anyone.

"One, two, three," she said, urging him on. And then he instinctively began to lead as Athena counted.

"Thank you," he said, "but I do know how to count."

"You weren't moving. I thought you might have needed some help."

"How nice for you, to have found a husband the world will think a brute."

"Better a husband who appears to be one than a husband who does not, but will create devastation in private, don't you think?"

"I am capable of devastation."

"You speak of the loss of Irina."

"I was carefree then. I thought that I had beaten the game. I was born into nothing, and I had become something. And I made the mistake of believing that I might very well be everything. I thought that I might be God. I had created a world from nothing. And who else does that? I fancied myself all-powerful. Not subject to the rules of anything. There was nothing but what I wanted in the moment. I loved fast cars and fast women. I loved being able to choose where I went and what I did, what I ate, what I wore. Who I took to bed. It was all intoxicating. I had, up until that point lived a life where everything was dictated by need. Need in the most basic, survivalist sense of the word. And then it became about want. And I got lost in that."

"An accident is an accident."

"Yes. Of course it is. But when you drive at a high rate of speed, and you are both distracted…"

"It sounds as if you were both along for the ride."

"But I was not God, was I?" He smiled, and he knew it was a bad imitation of the expression. "Yet I could not bring her back to life. That's a lesson for you. Creating things is not the ability to create life, Athena."

She moved her hand up his arm, where he gripped her at the waist, past his bicep, to his shoulder. The touch was so unexpected, so sensual, and he had to grit his teeth against the effect of it.

"Men can create life. I don't even think creating life is what makes you particularly special."

"And what is then?"

Her eyes met his, luminous and unafraid. And he wanted to draw closer to that light. "What you *do* with that life."

He ached to draw closer to her and yet he knew...

The accident with Irina had been his reckoning. His curse. The moment his outsides had transformed to match his insides, so he could no longer snare anyone into his toxic circle by convincing them he was an angel, when he was instead, a devil.

He did not draw closer to her.

"I suppose you don't consider sitting in a castle for a decade to be a worthy use of life," he said.

She shook her head. "I have been forced to hide. Forced to stay put. To stay concealed. You can leave whenever you want to, and yet you don't. I have a hard time understanding that."

"Even with what you have now seen?"

"Yes. Even with that."

She didn't say it wasn't that bad. She didn't say no one would notice.

He appreciated the honesty.

"You are beautiful. What would you know of it?"

She lifted a shoulder. "I don't know what good my beauty does. I can't say that I've never thought much about it. I was protected, all that time, from the gazes of men, and when my father saw fit, he decided to use my beauty as a commodity. I have no idea what my beauty might do or work against out in the real world."

"You will know soon enough. The headlines will scream of it. Especially when you're on my arm."

"Will it hurt you?"

"No." And without thinking, he lifted her hand and put it to his neck. "Many places on my body feel nothing." He dragged her fingertips down to his collarbone, just to the very edge, where he began to feel touch. Where all the nerves had not been severed. But by God he would swear he felt it anyway. Burning him down to his soul. He had not expected to be so undone by her touch, least of all when he'd been dictating her movements. "It is a metaphor," he gritted out. "For what you will find inside."

She looked up at him, and the confusion and questioning he saw in her eyes, made him step back.

Hunger.

This touch that had transcended medical science and made him *feel* had created a reaction in her. And God above it was unbearable.

"Don't look at me like that."

"Like what?" she whispered.

"Like you want answers to primal questions. Because you do not want me to be the one to teach you. You don't even know what you're asking for, do you?"

She shook her head.

Because she was reacting to him only because he was a man she was in close proximity with. Judging by what she had said about her life, about her childhood, it was a rarity.

It had nothing to do with him.

"Tomorrow we will be married." She swayed slightly in his arms when he said that. "And we leave for Europe in two days. The event is in London. We will go first to Paris."

"Why?"

And he decided on honesty. Because what else was there?

"Because I have always loved Paris."

# CHAPTER EIGHT

THE WEDDING WAS arranged quickly after that. She still felt terrible about his arm. About the fact that he had been bitten coming after her. She didn't know why she should feel terrible. He had taken her captive. And then he had frightened her.

*Because in actuality what he's offering you is protection. And you know it. Because in actuality, without him, you would be in trouble.*

That was true enough. Without him, she would be on her way to marry a madman.

He had taken her prisoner, initially, it was true.

But still, the wedding, the thought of it made her tremble. He had made it very clear that he wanted nothing physical from her. She saw a flash of his face in her mind's eye again.

He was... He was terrifying.

Would he kiss her?

The thought made her stop and press her fingers to her lips.

A kiss...

She knew what it was like to be held in his arms. She knew what it was like to feel all that power clinging to her...

What would a kiss be like?

It made her shiver, but not from cold.

She put on her cloak and wrapped it tightly around her as she went outside, the early morning air heavy with the scent of dew.

She looked around, and found flowers. She wanted flowers for her bouquet. This was her wedding, after all.

What was it about him that compelled her so?

He wasn't beautiful. But then…

Weren't the mountains here in the Highlands beautiful without being soft or symmetrical? They were wild, craggy and dangerous and lifted her soul and filled her lungs all the more for it.

She thought back to the girl that she'd been, just a couple of months ago. The girl that she had been who had wanted a wedding. Who had almost been willing to be okay with being sold into marriage for the adventure that might come along with it. This would not be romance. But it would be her wedding. Surely that had to mean something. She would not let it go by without there being something real to mark it.

So she clipped flowers, and a matching one to put in his suit jacket.

The thought made her smile. Because she knew he would scowl.

How did she know that? She had only just seen his face for the first time. How did she know that he would scowl at her.

She just did. She could hear scowls in his voice often when they spoke. Just like she could hear amusement, though she could not imagine him smiling.

She had gotten to know him these past weeks.

And even though he had frightened her, he had also come for her.

He had rescued her.

She had gone off into an unfamiliar place and gotten herself into trouble. He might have been angry, but he had kept her from coming into harm of any kind. Her dress and cloak were wet from the dew on the ground by the time she made it back to the palace. Breakfast was waiting for her.

A smile touched her lips.

Of course, the man himself was nowhere to be seen. He had simply made her a gorgeous stack of waffles with fresh fruit, and vanished.

She wasn't really hungry. Not with anticipation of the day. But when he made her food, she always ate it.

She frowned. She didn't know why. Perhaps because he was a hard man, and this was something of a gift.

She knew that it was. The way that he could show feelings of some kind.

Or maybe she was attaching too much meaning to something that was quite basic.

She went up the stairs to her bedroom, and stopped.

There was a white lace dress hanging from the top of the wardrobe, the train fanned out across the floor.

Had he brought this? Had he brought it and set it out for her?

With shaking hands, she undressed.

There was a necklace with the dress. A beautiful necklace, with what looked like a large gold coin. She looked at it more closely. It was Athena.

The goddess of war.

She had her sword brandished, her hair flying wild in the wind. Around the perimeter of the coin in flowing script it said: *Have courage. Take heart.*

She smiled, rubbing her thumb over the gold pendant, it was perfect.

He did see her.

She was not just any woman.

She was Athena.

She slipped the dress on, and was surprised how well

it fit. It had long sleeves, and conformed to her body perfectly. She looked like a bride. She took some of the flowers that she had picked and braided them into her hair, and then she used some of the makeup that had been provided for her recently to put gold on her eyes, and red on her lips. She found a ribbon amid some of her things and tied the rest of the flowers into a bouquet. Except for his.

She nestled his into the center of the bouquet to make it easier to carry, and then she put on the necklace.

*Have courage. Take heart.*

She took a breath and headed down the long spiral staircase. And there he was. Waiting. Looking imposing in his dark suit.

Imposing, but stunning.

He was not a man who could be accused of being handsome. And yet there was something about him that drew her. Would it have been so if they had not spent those weeks talking? If he had not saved her from the dog? Would it have been so if she had not seen him bleed for her. If she hadn't been eating his cooking, if she hadn't felt his care in that way?

There was no way to know.

But he was incredibly tall. Six foot five at least, with broad shoulders and a broad chest. He was like a warrior of old. A man who was scarred by battle.

A man who would go to war with her. *For* her.

"It suits you," he said, looking at her with dispassionate blue eyes.

Except there was something there. A banked ember she sensed had the potential to become a whole wildfire.

She swallowed hard.

"Thank you," she said.

"Let's go."

"Wait," she said.

She moved toward him, and plucked the flower out of

the center of her bouquet. She looped it through the buttonhole on his lapel.

She patted his chest. "There."

He frowned. "What are you doing?"

"I thought that it was right. For a wedding."

"I see."

He did not thank her. He turned and began to walk away, and she caught up to him, and draped her arm over his, almost without thinking.

But it *did* just seem right. It was their wedding, and she was to be his bride. Shouldn't they walk together? Shouldn't he hold on to her?

He looked at her, a question in his eyes.

"It also seemed right. For a wedding."

"Come on, lass."

They walked out of the doors of the castle, and down a quiet path. The birds were singing and she felt something lift inside of her soul. She hadn't expected that. She expected none of this.

She gasped when they came around the corner and there was a little stone chapel.

"Oh," she said. "How lovely."

"There was a whole village here once. And it had everything that people might need."

"Is that why there was that little place that I stayed in?"

"Yes. Very standard hut that the villagers would've lived in back then."

"And this was the church."

"For all the good it did them. They clung to life here for as long as possible, but... Well, that's a history lesson for another time."

"It must have done their souls good," she said. "A church like this. I've never been in a church."

"Really?"

"No. As I said. I've never left the compound until recently. I have always thought they looked beautiful. Serene."

"My mother took me to church on Christmas. For all the good that it did *her*. She was no better than those doomed villagers, was she? And she certainly didn't manage to do any work saving *my* soul. Much less her own."

"Perhaps you have to meet God halfway." He stopped walking, and she kept on. "Come on."

He shook his head, but said nothing, and they continued on into the chapel. There was a priest standing there, collar and all, waiting for them.

"Mr. McKenzie," the man said. "Very good to meet you. And this must be your lovely bride."

"Yes," said Cameron, his voice hard. "Let's make this quick."

"Of course," said the older man, slightly taken aback, clearly, but his gentle demeanor was not disrupted.

They approached the altar, and the priest opened his Bible.

He read a Scripture, and then from the Book of Common Prayer.

The vows were very traditional, the kind of thing she had seen in movies and read in books. But it felt utterly unique. Utterly special and wonderful, as they spoke the words. As if no one had ever spoken them before. And she knew that it wasn't real. He was not genuinely pledging to love her. They were not going to stay together.

But with the stained-glass window casting fractals of color around them, she truly felt like she might be experiencing romance.

That this might be what they wrote songs about. That this might be what people started wars over.

She was not immune to getting swept up in it.

Though Cameron look swept up in nothing. He was stoic, that ruined face of his completely flat and unreadable.

"I now pronounce you husband and wife. You may kiss your bride."

Her stomach dropped, her heart giving a great thud against her breastbone. They would kiss. He would take hold of her and lower his head and…

"No kissing, thank you," said Cameron.

And she felt the sting of that. Of the rejection. Why does it feel like a rejection?

None of this mattered. It wasn't real. They would never see the priest again after today. There was no one else here to act as a witness.

And when it was all over, they stood there with legal documents in front of them, and Athena only looked at them.

"I don't know my last name," she said.

"Yes, you do," Cameron said. "You're Athena McKenzie."

And it took her breath away. Because he had not only given her this. He was not only protecting her. He was showing her to the world, making her real. And he had given her a name. She knew, right in that moment, that whatever happened between the two of them, whether they parted ways after this, and she never saw him again, she would keep that name. She would.

And she signed the paper.

*Athena McKenzie.*

"We will have documents made for you eventually, in that name. It will make things easier for you."

"Thank you. How…"

He shrugged a shoulder. "Money accomplishes many things. And it most certainly buys an identity if you've need of it."

"Thank you, Cameron."

When they finished, they walked back down the path

together. There was no wedding party. There was nothing. Just the two of them.

And they were married now. Husband and wife. She felt it. Felt connected to him.

And she felt compelled then, by something, to reach out and put her hand on his forearm. "How is the bite wound?"

He stopped walking and looked at her. "It's fine. I have been injured much more severely than that."

"But you were injured protecting me. And I am very sorry. I'm sorry that I ran."

"I *did* yell at you."

"Yes, you did," she said. "But I didn't have a plan. I had seen that vulnerable spot in the wall and I thought that I might exploit it to my own ends if I needed to. And then I… I didn't give you a chance. You did tell me not to go there, and I did."

"It's true."

"Why did you want to keep me away from there?"

"Because it is where I stay. It is mine. And I don't allow anyone there."

"Because…"

"Because there is nothing in there but old artifacts and memories. And none of it is worth showing to another person."

"I'm sorry."

"And I did not wish to encounter you until I was ready. I told you, I have not seen another person face-to-face for ten years. I knew that I needed to do it. I knew that. And now I have seen you and the priest. These are all *necessities*."

"Yes, because you must see people at the launch. And it's important to you, isn't it?"

"I have been perfecting this technology for ten years. People will be able to adapt it to their own homes. To their own needs. I am working on a system that can be intuitive enough for someone who uses sign language. For someone who needs an adaptive home. For someone who just wants convenience, certainly, but… I know and understand what can happen in life, to change the course of things for you. There are many ways that technology can improve the quality of life for anyone."

"It has for you. It has allowed you to keep contact with the outside world in some ways, but keep separate from it."

"Perhaps."

"I think it has," she said. "And you're going to be telling investors about this?"

"Yes. And potential buyers. Big clients, who will buy these systems for resorts and large companies. For housing developments. I do not want the system to be prohibitively expensive, rather what I want is for people who have a need to be able to access it. And for those who perhaps want something that is simply frills, then that will be more reasonably priced. But, I feel that it is not so much to ask for those who want frills to pay more."

"You do have a bit of altruism and you."

"Nothing that was not forced upon me. I would never have given a thought to have somebody else live. I clawed my way up from the gutter. That has given me less compassion in most situations. Let me assure you. Because I lived a life where it was all about survival of the fittest. So those who cannot keep up fall behind, and that is the natural order of things. It was not until I had to face my own mortality, my own frailties, that I had to perhaps acknowledge that people are trying a lot harder than I give them credit for. And that perhaps it is not so bad to offer a hand up."

"It has changed you."

"Obviously." He looked at her, and the gaze was pointed. She wanted to roll her eyes at him. She didn't. "Yes.

I understand what you mean. You mean physically. That isn't what I mean." She paused a moment. "Can I see the north tower now?"

"Why would you want to see that?"

"Because I have seen you," she said. "And I am your wife now."

These words felt every bit as much like vows as the ones they'd spoken in the church.

He laughed, low and hard, and doused her certainty. "You are not my wife in any real sense of the word."

"I am your wife in the *most* real sense of the word."

They'd said vows in a church and signed papers. It was real.

"You know, back when this village thrived. We had something called handfast marriages. And they were not real until they were consummated."

A riot of heat assaulted her. And she imagined him wrapping his arm around her waist and drawing her toward his chest. She imagined that kiss that he had declined to give her. She imagined…

She drew slightly closer to him. Then she reached out and plucked the flower out of the buttonhole. She held it close, and twirled it in a circle. "I see. And so without consummation it is not real to you?"

"No. It is not. I believe the Catholic Church would agree with me."

"And yet it must be real enough to deter my father's men, or Mattias from ever coming after me."

"Yes. But they do not have to know whether or not the marriage was consummated."

"Consummated. That's a very cold and clinical way of putting it."

Yet she did not feel cold.

"Do not spin fantasies. The act itself is cold and clinical."

She frowned. "I would hope not. I intend to have a life after this. And so I will find out one way or the other."

"Good for you." He didn't sound like he meant that.

She wanted more of him and she wasn't going to get it here. This conversation was making him cruel, and she didn't know why, but she felt…tender.

"Show me the tower?"

"There is nothing for you to see." But he didn't say no. And when he began to walk into the castle, she went after him, and then she saw that he was leading them toward the north tower. She wondered if this was his way of apologizing.

She trailed after him, up the stairs, and back to that place, which was still upended from the tantrum he had thrown the day before.

"Oh, all of your things…" She moved to the collection, which was the only thing still righted.

"They don't matter."

What he meant was he could easily replace them. She knew that.

The collection though… That long bar under glass. Because this was not a room for anyone to see.

"Is this the collection I'm part of?"

"Yes," he said, hard and offering no explanation.

"Why do you really collect things?"

He looked…embarrassed, almost. He looked away. "A habit. One I didn't indulge in all the years after Apollo and I made success but something about this… I used to pick up whatever I found. I had no money, and one never knew what one might need. If you could find something for free, you kept it. And you held on to it."

Her heart squeezed tight. "You started your whole career that way."

He nodded. "When you are poor, simple objects can

change your life. I suppose out here, bankrupt of all the trappings of the life I once I had, I slid back into that mindset."

He had thought he might need her, and so he'd kept her.

He hadn't even been wrong. It made her want to laugh. And cry.

"It's a rather Spartan room," she said.

"I live a fairly Spartan life. It is simple. And I don't mind that."

"Are you not lonely here?"

He looked at her, his face hard. "Loneliness happens when you let yourself want something. I want nothing. I wake up every day, and I follow the direction my mind needs to go. I need to create things. To invent them. If there are problems, my brain wishes to solve them, and I do that using technology. It is my only real drive. The business stuff… That was never me. That has always been Apollo. I simply want… I need to fix things. And that is all. Personally, as a human being, I require very little. I'm not driven by the need for material wealth. The pleasures of the flesh no longer appeal to me the way they once did. Even then… What I wanted was control. What I wanted was to spend the years taking back what I felt had been taken from me. Empty, useless pursuits."

So, he didn't feel *nothing* about prostituting himself. He had felt very deeply about it for a time.

She chose not to say anything more about that either. More good sense on her part.

"We…"

"We shall leave tomorrow."

"Oh." She felt disappointed by that, and she couldn't even say why. Perhaps because he was refusing to acknowledge that they were married.

*Perhaps because you want him?*

That little voice inside her felt nearly *dangerous*.

She needed to leave him, and all of this, behind, once he helped her. She needed to find out who she was and find her family. She couldn't afford to be so…beset by him.

And yet she was.

"What?" he asked, and she knew embarrassment over the fact he'd witnessed her inner turmoil.

"It is our wedding day. And it will be our wedding night and…"

"You will have dinner as you always do. I will take dinner as I do. Do not spin stories about me. How could you, anyway? Do you not see?"

The problem was she did see. Perhaps deeper than he wanted her to. And she did not find him repulsive. Rather she found him compelling. Rather she wanted to draw nearer to him.

"I'm not spinning stories. I'm just getting to know you. Thank you. For the necklace. Have courage and take heart."

"I didn't even know what it said. I simply found a necklace with the goddess Athena on it, it seemed appropriate."

He was lying. She did not know why he was lying.

"It's a good thing you never get lonely. Because I think most people here would. How nice it must be to want nothing."

He looked at her, his expression remote. "It is the only thing I know."

She left, her steps echoing on the flagstone floor. Husband and wife. Husband and wife. She heard it every time she took one step, then another.

But it was not real. None of it was real.

She had been fooled before, into believing she was a daughter when she was simply a convenience.

She couldn't let attraction, gold necklaces and the lies of her own heart blind her to the fact this was no different.

Not a wife.

A convenience.

She had to do her best to remember that.

# CHAPTER NINE

WHAT SURPRISED ATHENA the most was the manner in which they traveled. And she didn't think that it should surprise her. It wasn't as if Cameron was going to get on a commercial plane. But for some reason, it seemed odd that this man who went nowhere, procured a private jet to take them to Paris.

It was luxurious, not unlike the private plane she had flown on for the very first time with her family only a couple of weeks ago.

It occurred to her then, that she was about to be out in the real world for the first time ever.

And that she had no idea if her family was looking for her.

As the plane descended, her anxiety began to mount.

"Are there news stories about me being missing?"

He looked at her. "There must not be. Apollo would've said."

She nodded. "That speaks volumes to the fact that my father does not know how to put out such information. I really must *not* exist to the outside world."

"All the more reason this is important."

He had tied his long hair back away from his face, and it gave her an even better view of his eyes. She was struck again by how beautiful they were.

When he had spoken his vows to her…she had grown…
Lost in them. In him.

And when they had been dancing…he'd asked her…

She felt a flush of embarrassment.

She was not stupid. She was twenty-eight years old, she might never have had an opportunity to be held by a man, but she did understand desire.

She'd been too shocked, too ashamed to admit it.

That being held by him, that the feel of his large, warm hands on her curves, the scent of him, the way that he was so solid, like a wall of granite, had begun to create a stirring sensation between her thighs.

And he was hers now. Her husband.

Her husband…

Not real.

And yet her attraction to him was. So didn't that matter?

She had to remember that she had jumped out of a moving car to start a new life, and while she knew this… Cameron, was not her final destination, did that mean she couldn't want him?

Did it mean she couldn't have him?

The door to the plane opened, and out there on the tarmac was a limousine.

Suddenly, she was frozen. Because here she was, on the precipice of something much bigger than she was.

"I don't have a passport," she said.

She'd only just had a name change. There was no way he'd gotten her the papers she needed yet. It was one thing to have no documents in a country church with a priest who was likely on Cameron's payroll. But here?

He laughed. "Everything is taken care of. You've no need to worry."

"We won't be… Traveling through immigration? My father made sure that I knew that I couldn't get far without him because I was not in possession of my own documents."

"As I said. It is handled. Do you think billionaires wait in lines to have their paperwork pored over? Of course we don't. And neither will you."

"How does that work?"

"I declared you."

She wrinkled her nose as they walked off the plane and got into the limousine. "Declared me? Like... Like I am an *apple*?"

"Yes."

She huffed. "That's vaguely demeaning."

"Little runaway beggars who technically don't exist in the system should perhaps not be choosers."

"Basically men who have not even spoken to another person face-to-face in ten years should perhaps not think so highly of themselves."

He laughed. "Oh, I don't think highly of myself, little goddess, but I certainly know what I'm about."

"And that is?"

"Getting exactly what I came for."

And then it was difficult for her to banter with him because she was so focused on the scenery around them. The majesty of the buildings, the architecture. She felt something in her spirit move. She had been affected by the Highlands this way, by nature. Not things built by men.

But this artistry, this triumph of humanity called out to her.

In the same way that a mountain did, or a flower.

People didn't have to make things beautiful. They only had to make them functional. But they made art instead, simply because they could.

"What do you think?" he asked, his voice sounding rusty.

"I am an awe. This is more beautiful than any book ever suggested that it could be. This is…"

"Yes, it is."

She watched him closely, for some sign that he was having an emotional reaction. It was impossible to say. He was remote. The only indication that he was moved was the tightness of his jaw, the way that it tugged on the scar tissue on his cheek.

"Where are we going?"

"Apollo has assured me that accommodation has been arranged for us."

"Thank you. For taking me to see this. It's… Important to me."

"I know. I told you, there are things on your list that I can give you. A chance to see the world and comfort is one of them."

"You also said there were things you could not give me."

"Romance, Athena. I have not ever had one bit of it in my soul. Even less of it now."

"I don't believe that. A man who wishes to return to Paris before doing anything else must have a bit of romance in him."

"Or he likes a croissant."

She couldn't help herself. She laughed. Because it was true, he did like a croissant. And he made them with the expertise of someone who had been trained in fine French pastry.

She may not have been very many places, but there had always been fine food at her father's compound, so she was educated on the subject.

The food that Cameron made surpassed anything she had had her father's world-renowned chefs make for them.

"All right. Perhaps that's all. But do you not like the art here? The architecture?"

"Of course."

"What is that if not romance?"

"Just an extension of lust, I would think."

That made her heart hit hard against her chest.

"Are you particularly lustful?" she asked, whispering, her lips suddenly feeling full. Obvious. She swallowed and shifted in her seat.

"That is not a road you want to go down."

"It isn't?"

"No. You did not listen to me when I told you how it was, because you don't wish to believe me," he rested his elbow on the window, his chin on his knuckles. "You should, I have seen many things, and done most of them. When you spoke of experiences you wished to have, you said romance. You did not say sex."

She felt edgy, embarrassed. Her heart was thundering and she knew her cheeks were pink, so she determinedly looked out her own window. "Don't they go together?"

He laughed. Hard and bitter, and she did not know why it made her feel hot.

"No, little goddess. They don't. Lust is selfish. It is all about satisfaction. It is all about the fulfillment of a very base, rough need. It can be over in seconds with no fanfare at all. It is not romance. Its neighbor is greed, not love. Make no mistake of that."

She did not know why she was pushing the subject. Except she couldn't get the way she had felt when they danced out of her head. Couldn't get the way she'd felt speaking those vows to him from echoing in her soul.

She felt confused. By all of this. Because she had escaped her father's compound, and had gone from one cage to another, and yet here she was now, in Paris, in the next phase of that. And she did not feel like Cameron's prisoner. She had gotten to know him these past couple of weeks. She did not feel like his prisoner at all.

He was the first man she had met outside the compound, surely, she should know that meant her feelings were skewed.

He was monstrous. His scars were not something that could be called minor, nor could they be considered something easy to overlook.

He was not handsome. He was not beautiful. He had been once. But his looks were gone. Ruined. Twisted.

And yet.

She had heard the term sex appeal before. She understood it now.

He was feral. Strong. Large.

All things that appealed to her. There was a rugged masculinity to his being that ignited the femininity within her.

His hands were rough, and the way they held her could be gentle.

The paradox of it intrigued her.

She knew that her feelings were improbable. She knew that they would lead her into trouble. She knew that it was impossible.

She knew that she should stop pushing him.

Except, while there was the aspect of him being the only man she knew, which in many ways should deter her, there was also the aspect that… She had him as a resource.

She wasn't making up the way her body felt when it was close to his.

It did not need to be forever to be good. She felt certain of that.

And some would argue that it would be a waste of an opportunity…

He was staring at her.

"What?"

"You are a strange creature," he said.

"A side effect, I would think, of spending so much time in my own company."

"You said you had a friend."

She nodded. "Rose. As I said she… Well, she was a maid. My father decided he was going to sell her and… His former son-in-law rescued her. He's not unlike you."

"In what way?"

"He is scarred. From a fire. It killed his wife. It was years ago, it was… The daughter that I replaced."

He nodded slowly. "I see."

"Yes. Well. I guess they felt that they owed him something. Ares has never seemed like a cruel man to me. He's frightening, certainly."

"The god of war," he pointed out.

A smile touched Athena's lips. "Yes. I suppose so. That's funny. I hadn't thought of it."

"So Rose was your friend."

"Yes. But we were both quite sheltered, so neither of us could really teach the other anything. And neither of us really remember life before coming to the compound. Rose had to work. In contrast, I never learned how to do anything. I can't cook. I've never cleaned. I'm… I'm spoiled in many ways."

"And yet you were willing to jump from a moving vehicle and escape the fate you did not care for."

"Yes. I am not as soft as they think I am. It makes me wonder, again. What exactly happened to me in my years before going there. Because there's something…some connection that I might not know about but…"

She shook her head. "It doesn't matter. Not now."

When they arrived at the glorious marble building, the limo pulled smoothly against the curb, and Athena stood in awe. She was used to luxury. But this was an old-world beauty of a different sort that she had never seen.

When they walked into the building, they drew stares. People looked away quickly, but she could see that they were transfixed by Cameron.

Athena began to speak loudly and quickly in French.

Whatever she could think of. Silly things, laughing and doing her best to draw the attention. She looped her arm through Cameron's as they headed toward the elevator. The doors opened, and they got inside, and once they closed, he turned to her. "You speak French?" he asked.

"Oh, yes," she said. "We spoke Russian as a…a family. I speak Greek and English, French, Italian, German… a bit of Japanese."

"Why?"

"Why not? I had little to do, and so I learned when I could. As I said…my mother wanted me to be frivolous, I think. Malleable. She didn't want me to want anything, and yet I did. I wanted more. I suppose that in and of itself is a triumph when you have been trained to not want at all, and are given every luxury to keep you from ever doing so."

It made her feel stronger than she had a moment before.

"And why exactly did you do all that out there?"

"Because you were uncomfortable. And I didn't like it."

It was honest. That was what struck him. Her honesty.

And her desire to do something for him.

He moved away from her, to the far side of the elevator. "Athena," he said. "Do not mistake me for something better than I am. Many people would be deterred by the scars. But you… You see a project. I am not your project. I am not a victim for you to pick up and make whole."

"I consider myself warned."

"I am who I have always been. And that is not the kind of man that you should involve yourself with."

"I consider myself warned," she repeated. "Do not make the mistake that everyone else has. Do not make the same mistake the man who called himself my father made. I am not soft, and I am not foolish. No matter that men have tried to control me all my life I know my own mind.

I know who I am. I chose to do what I did because I care about you. You cannot stop me from caring."

Everything in him went hard. "And that is where you're wrong. I can. With time."

She withdrew, but he sensed that it was not a retreat. Rather, a calculated move. She would be back. At full strength. One thing he knew for certain about Athena. She was formidable.

The goddess of war.

He would do well to remember that.

It was easy to take her as soft. Because she was so beautiful. But perhaps that was what had made the Athena of mythology equally formidable.

The elevator doors opened and revealed the penthouse. Athena didn't look at any of the surrounding furnishings. Rather she went straight for the open windows that faced the incomparable view below of Paris. The Eiffel Tower. The Seine. She put her hands against the glass, her eyes clearly hungry for the site.

And he felt… Hungry for her.

He recalled what she had said in the car, and knew she had been testing him. The question was why?

He knew why he wanted her. What he could not fathom was why she might wish to test out her sensuality with him.

The man he'd been would have taken her up on that. Without question. Without care. He would have taken her admiration of him as his due and demanded that she worship him on her knees singing his praises with her lips. Her tongue. Yes, he would've done all those things. He was not that man now. And perhaps he should rejoice in the change, or see it as some sort of redemptive moment.

But he did not feel redeemed. He felt as dark and lethal as ever. And she…

*She is a goddess of war.*

Yes.

"I wish to go out," she said.

"We were just out."

"I know. I know we were. But could we… I will need a ring."

He had no idea how he had neglected to realize that. She would, of course. Agreeing to show all the world that she belonged to him.

They had not exchanged rings in the ceremony and it had not struck him that it was missing.

It felt a glaring error now.

"And perhaps it wouldn't hurt for us to be seen prior to your big unveiling. There could be rumors," she said.

"I thought that you did not know anything about popular culture."

"The man who called himself my father actively discouraged me from participating in such things, but aren't all teenagers rebellious? In whatever way we can be. Obviously I was hungry for whatever information I could glean. It was difficult living where I did, but there were always ways to find a magazine here and there. One thing I do know is how hungry culture is for gossip."

"You are a funny creature."

"So you said. And I know."

"What *is* your last name, Athena?"

She looked blank then. "McKenzie. Or, it is now. The only one I know. I would have claimed my father's. But that is not real. It is not real. None of it was."

"I will help you. I will help you find the truth of your past."

He paused for a moment. "If that is what you want. You must understand that the answers might not be what you want them to be."

"Spoken like a man with a dark past."

"It is. There is no happy secret behind me. There is

nothing but tragedy, desperation and debauchery. Nothing but pain."

"And yet it made you who you are."

He laughed. "Yes. It did. The man you see before you is little more than a monster. Why do you think what I have been made could be positive in any regard?"

"Because. I see many positive things in you. You're brilliant. You're very strong. And you are an excellent cook."

"I am not."

"Let's go out. We can ease in. How many years has it been since you were in a restaurant?"

"Ten years."

"And I have never been to one. Please. Let us go out in Paris. We're still no one. No one and nothing."

"But with all the resources in the world."

"A boon for us. Let us enjoy it."

She looked at him, and something mischievous lit her dark eyes. "Put on a suit."

"Why?"

"Because I think you look rather… Dashing in a suit."

"And will you dress for me?"

"Yes."

"Then wear red."

# CHAPTER TEN

ATHENA ZIPPED HER dress up with trembling hands. It was skintight and only went to the middle of her thigh. Much more scandalous than anything she had ever worn while living at the compound. It showed the curve of her waist, hips, left nothing to the imagination when it came to her back end. And as far as her breasts went... It molded to them perfectly, her golden curves pushed up and revealed to a near indecent degree.

But he would appreciate it. She had seen the way she looked at him when they had danced. He looked hungry.

*And you wish to encourage him?*

She did. She couldn't explain her connection to Cameron. Except she was beginning to feel that she had not run into that cabin in the woods out of simple desperation. But that perhaps something had guided her there.

He was a man set apart. A man who had not had anyone come into his home for a decade. So why had she happened upon him? That seemed to be the real question.

Maybe she was silly. She could accept that.

But her whole life had been positioned outside the ordinary. Why should she expect to be any less now?

She didn't know how to fix her hair in terribly complicated ways, so she had left it hanging straight and glossy down her back.

She had put on a bit of makeup, which had been part of the trousseau she had demanded.

And beneath the dress… Beneath the dress was underwear as crimson as the dress itself, wispy and see-through.

The idea of him seeing her and not made her pulse race.

She came out of the bedroom, and there he was. Standing in the center of the room, the beautifully lit city of Paris behind him. He looked severe in a dark black suit, his long hair tied back, his beard trimmed a bit more neatly now.

He was… A glorious contrast. Beastly in part, utterly sophisticated on the other hand.

It was those seemingly incompatible things that made her pulse race. That made her feel giddy with excitement.

His face…

She could not find it hideous.

It was compelling. As was he.

It was painful to look at, in the sense that it spoke of the pain that he'd been through.

And yet.

She could not look away from him. Because there was nowhere else she wished to look more. Not even in Paris.

"Shall we go?" he asked.

"Yes. Are you all right?"

He laughed. "You are no more experienced than I and going out into the world, and you ask if I'm okay?"

"I'm less experienced than you. And I think perhaps that makes it easier. I have no preconceived idea about how anyone might treat me. I have no expectations. You lived a whole other life." She stopped herself. "You lived two other lives."

"Come," he said, his voice gruff.

They went down to the street, where the limousine was waiting for them. She wondered… She wondered if he had driven at all since the accident. She chose to wait to ask the question until they got into the car.

"Have you…"

"No." Like he knew what she was going to ask. "I've not had occasion to drive," he said.

"Does the idea bother you?"

"The idea of driving *you* anywhere does."

She nodded.

"You don't know how to drive, do you?" he asked.

She shook her head. "No. That was definitely not part of my upbringing. Nothing that would give me any sort of independence. It was for my own good, of course. Of course no one in the compound had any idea who I was, so how could it be for *me*?"

"I am familiar," he said. "With such things. And also with how you can find pleasure while also remaining unsatisfied."

The words cut deep. She knew he meant when he'd sold himself. Of course he'd found some pleasures, but it hadn't been…

Whatever he said, that was not the true intent of sex, she was certain of it. She felt more when he looked at her than he seemed to have felt about whole paid encounters.

It was a perversion of something meant to be more.

Just as her whole life had been a perversion of family.

Yes, she had felt joy. Connection.

But they were only slivers of what was meant to be.

She understood him. In this, she understood him.

"It is costly," she whispered. "Taking those sorts of small pleasures. Because on the other side of the wall is a whole world. A feast you sacrifice for the crumb before you."

"Sometimes the crumb is all you can see."

"Yes. So too with freedom, I suppose."

"There is a freedom to driving, yes. But then, that freedom can be easily accomplished with enough money as well. As you can see."

"Provided you're the one in control, yes."

"Perhaps that is the problem," he said, and she sensed the change in subject. "The amount of lives I have tried to live. Maybe the problem is a man can only jump to so many. And this last one... It is what I will not be able to find my way out of."

"I don't believe that. I've had three lives too. The one that I can't remember, the one in the compound, and now this one. I need to believe that I can change again, Cameron, otherwise what will happen to me after?"

He looked at her. Long and hard. And she found herself looking back. Unflinching. Unwilling. "You will do just fine, my goddess. You are a woman of exceptional strength, and there is nothing that will compromise that."

"I don't know that I believe it. It would be nice if I could. But I have no evidence to suggest that I will be all right when I'm out and left to my own devices."

"Perhaps you will make mistakes. Perhaps you will sample all the things that have been withheld from you, and you will find yourself drowning in the excesses. I'm familiar with that. But there's something different about you, Athena. It is your warrior heart, I think. It grounds you. I lost myself. Because I never knew who I was. Except angry. I took joy in manipulating others. Because I felt that somehow they were withholding something from me simply by existing. You do not have that same spite in you that I have in me."

"I don't know. The spite is beginning to feel real. I spent a great many years believing that I was simply spoiled. Protected. I spent a great many years not thinking about how many years were passing. And then I had to wake up. It was like a bucket of cold water being dumped on my head. And I find that I am angry. Because here I am, twenty-eight years old with no real idea of how the world works. And no idea at all where I fit in it. I was not a fit for the life at the compound, not really, because it was not for me. And what is? I do not know. Perhaps I will discover my roots, perhaps I have a family, and I will have no place there either. You're assuming that I am measured because that's my nature, but I believe it is simply because it is all I've ever had the opportunity to be. I'm angry. Because the whole world is out there. All of this before me, and it was denied me. And why? I may never have the answer to that."

"You may not. And so what will you do with that? I let it twist me. The people around me were selfish, and so I let myself become equally so."

"Could I be selfish. Just for a while?"

"Of course you can. When we part, you can live for yourself. Take the money that I give you and spend it on clothes. Go to clubs and dance the night away, buy yourself a luxury car. Take as many lovers as you please."

She watched his face when he said that, and was satisfied to see it darken with something unreadable.

"Is that what you think?" she asked. "That I should take many lovers? I thought that you decided I needed romance."

"It is what you said, not me. But it would likely benefit you to seek something other than romance for a time. Something that is simply light and free."

"Did you find those interactions light and free when you had them?"

He laughed. The sound cynical. "No. If you want the honest truth, I've never found sex to be anything more than a weapon. Used against the other person, or used against my own demons."

"And yet you enjoyed it?"

"Physically, it feels good. But I was dark and twisted long before that car accident. And so the dark and twisted always served me. I took great joy in using beautiful women who begged to be with me. Because I was important and handsome and all the things they prized. Because I was no longer poor, where people would just pay for my services, pay to have a handsome man on their arm, or a secret, shameful night in bed. Yes, I took great pleasure in that power shifting. All the women who graced my bed were symbolic of that. A salve for my rage. Except they were human beings. And using them was wrong. And nothing brought that into sharper clarity then Irina dying in my arms simply because she had the bad misfortune of being my lover for that couple of weeks."

She swallowed hard. "It hurts you. The harm you've caused."

"Yes," he said. "And once Irina died, once the accident happened, I let every bit of harm I ever caused hurt *me*. Cut me. Down to the bottom of my soul. Because something had to give. Because something had to shift. Because otherwise it's all... Because otherwise it's all so ugly. It is all so ugly."

She moved her hand to brush against his thigh. The suit pants were luxurious in quality, soft, his thigh hard. And she could feel a large dent in the muscle there, more evidence of trauma from the accident.

"You are not ugly. Just so you're aware."

He gripped her wrist and pulled her close. "Don't lie."

"I'm not. I don't have any reason to lie. You have told me that you want nothing from me physically, why would I..."

He released his hold on her, and her heart began to thunder hard.

"Let us go choose you a ring. I will not touch you, Athena. And you will thank me for it later. I am nothing more than a curse. Make no mistake. If it weren't for my loyalty to Apollo I would never have agreed to any of this."

"I don't believe that. Because I don't believe that you do a damn thing you don't *want* to do. You are pretending that you had no choice and I cannot for the life of me fathom why. Why you need to believe that."

"It will do you no good to try and peer inside the darkness."

"Blah blah blah," she said, feeling irritated. "So terrifying. As if I didn't live with a crime lord for most of my life."

"Do not push me."

"Somebody has to."

They said nothing, and when they arrived at the jewelry store, he took her hand, but she thought that he pulled her a bit roughly from the car. The only way that he could express his irritation. And in kind, she made sure to bump against him a bit harder than necessary as they walked into the store.

"It seems as if it would be after hours."

"Apollo made a call."

"How handy to have a charming billionaire for a friend. Perhaps I like him."

He turned to her, and he did not touch her, but his eyes pinned her to the spot.

Those blue, electric eyes. "You will not."

"You told me I could go out and have however many lovers as I want to."

She was goading him now and she knew it. It thrilled her. Filled her with that same delicious fear she'd felt at the castle. Was it wrong there was a thrill to it?

She didn't care. She didn't.

Her whole life had been somewhat wrong, why could she not have the wrong she wanted?

And the wrong she wanted wasn't Apollo, but she did like making Cameron go fierce.

"*Not* him," he growled.

"Why not?"

"Because if I have to know a man who has seen your

naked body, I will not be held responsible for what I do to him."

He walked into the shop, and left her standing on the sidewalk, the breath pulled from her body. She scurried along behind him quickly.

"Mr. McKenzie," said the elderly man attending to the display counter. "We were told to expect you. We were also told not to allow for any onlookers."

The windows behind them were suddenly covered with black curtains that fell from the ceiling.

"Thank you," said Cameron.

It was funny, to watch him attempt to interact with other people. To watch him make an attempt at politeness.

"And who is this lovely lady?" the older man asked.

"Athena," she said.

"My wife," he said. "We married so quickly we had time to find a priest, but not the rings. We are about to make our debut as a couple, and I wish for her to have something stunning."

"Because of our love, of course," said Athena. She looked at him and smiled.

She wondered if he would smile back.

So rarely did he smile. Once, she'd seen him do it once. He remained stoic.

"Yes," he said flatly. "Because of our love."

He was maddening. And amusing, even though she had a feeling he was not being amusing on purpose.

The older man pulled out a small tray, with a selection of four different rings.

He was very good at his job, Athena could see, because she didn't need the choice of the whole store. No, these four were all perfect in their own way, and she knew she didn't need to see anything else.

But it was one that was shaped like a pear, glittering

and brilliant, with two sapphires on either side, that was the one that truly caught and held her attention.

The sapphires were like his eyes.

"That one," she said.

"Excellent taste, *mademoiselle*," he said.

He gestured toward Cameron. "Put it on her finger."

Cameron took the ring out of the velvet case.

It looked comically small in his giant hands.

He was such a large man, imposing, and she imagined that it was the beauty of his face that had once softened him. And there was nothing to soften him now. Nothing to make him less formidable than he was.

She appreciated that. Not that she would have ever wished the scarring on him, but there was an extreme quality to him now.

Something that she knew most men didn't possess.

He was unique. And terrifying. Marvelous.

And when he slipped the ring on her finger, she lost her breath. It was as if the ring sliding onto her finger was a kiss, another vow. An intimate touch even though it was nothing more than gems and precious metal.

It felt real. Even though she knew it wasn't. Even though she knew nothing could be further from the truth.

It felt real.

She felt like she might be his.

*What's the matter with you? You should want to be your own.*

She knew that. She shouldn't want to go from the ownership of one man to another. She looked up at him, and their eyes met.

It wouldn't be ownership. The kind of claim that Cameron had staked on her was different.

Except he didn't want that claim.

"Perfect," she whispered.

"We'll take it," said Cameron.

"Wonderful. Mr. Agassi said that he would settle the account."

"I'm certain that he did," said Cameron. "But I will not allow it."

"Something to take up with him. I will not defy him."

"And get you to find me?" he asked the man, who was so small he only came up to the middle of Cameron's chest.

"Mr. Agassi spends quite a bit of money here. On mistresses. He is a valued client."

Cameron laughed at that. Bitter.

"Of course."

They walked back out of the store, and he took her hand. "Down here. There's a small café that serves very no-frills food. But of the highest quality. I think that will be a good experience for your first restaurant. Neither of us needs anything overly formal."

She was still processing what had just happened.

She was wearing his ring. They were walking down the Parisian street together. He was holding her hand.

His hands were so rough.

"Why are you so angry?" she asked.

"Right now? Or in general?"

"Well, start with right now and work your way back," she said.

"Apollo is being heavy-handed. I don't need his charity, and he well knows it. I'm frustrated with him because he strong-armed me into the situation anyway."

"Except he didn't," said Athena. "You were ready. You were ready to leave, and perhaps, Apollo knew that and decided to give you the push you needed. Be honest, Cameron, no one could force you to leave if you didn't want to. You never would've danced with me if you hadn't wanted to, and you certainly wouldn't be here," she said, sweeping her arm wide, "if you didn't want to be. You are a stubborn, beastly man, and you certainly won't be told. So why you are hell-bent on acting as if this is all because of your business partner, I don't know."

He looked at her, and for the first time, she thought she might have succeeded in actually shocking him. His eyes went fractionally wider. "Are you… Are you telling me that you think I know why I have done this?"

"No," she said. "I don't know. But I don't think you do either."

"That makes no earthly sense, woman."

"I think it does. You want this." She stepped in front of him, and she put her hand on his chest. She was shocked to find that his heart was raging there. "You want to be away from there. You do… You don't actually want to be alone you…"

He gripped her wrist again, and pulled her hand away. "Stop toying with me as if I am not dangerous."

"What will you do? Will you devour me? Or will you kiss me?"

"Athena…" he growled.

"Cameron…"

"You do not want this," he said, his voice low. "You have been captive all of your life. You need to go and experience the world. You do not need to kiss the first man you meet."

"Why are you afraid to kiss me? Are you afraid you won't stop?"

"You don't want me."

"I do. I do want you. How dare you tell me how I feel."

"You are being a silly girl. Let us go eat."

And she found herself being hauled into the café, where she was seated unceremoniously. She tried to appreciate the fact that they were in a restaurant. That she was experiencing something new and different. That it was like something out of a movie, and such a simple thing, such a normal thing for other people, and yet so different for her.

Because she was still focused on what it had felt like to

touch Cameron's chest. To feel his heart raging beneath her palm.

The din of the restaurant was a foreign sort of thing to her, and she kept checking with Cameron to see if he was affected by it, but it was as if he was protected by a granite wall. But it closed her out too, and she didn't like it.

He ordered their food. Croque monsieur and a croissant with an egg in the middle. Crepes honey and lemon.

There were baguettes, and other glorious breads. And very strong coffee.

He did not ask her preferences, but there was no need. He'd provided everything.

"Thank you," she said, softly.

"Are you angry with me, or are you happy with me? Make up your mind." And it was like the wall had dropped, his annoyance a way in she was happy to take.

"I'm everything," she said. "All at once. I am so gloriously grateful for this experience. That you're the one who found me. And yet you aggravate me."

"Tell me. More about you."

"There's nothing to say," she said. "Do you want to hear how my father barely spoke two words to me? And how I didn't know that could be considered strange? Do you want to hear about how my mother needed me for emotional support at all times, but didn't know how to offer any in return? People think that I am soft and cosseted because I have never had to do any work. Because when it comes to my physical safety and comfort, that was always managed, cared for. What no one realizes, is how I had to fortify myself. And when I look back on that time, it is like a hollow, dark pit. Because it was never for me. I was a shrine to Naya, not a human being. And I can never go back. I can't. I have been more alive, more real in these last weeks than ever before. And I know that I was your prisoner. But it wasn't the same. I was still able to be more myself. I am still now able to be more myself. So yes. I do find you maddening. Utterly." She laughed. "But I also find you compelling. I find you… I want to help you. I want to…"

"You can't. You know the piece of metal that you saw in the north tower."

"Yes," she said, remembering clearly that large, twisted piece, which he had had under glass.

"That was in my leg. My right leg. That I can walk as well as I can is something of a miracle. That it missed my artery is another miracle altogether."

"Cameron…"

"I have been given an inordinate amount of miracles. I have done nothing to deserve them. Not ever."

"Shouldn't you do something to pay them back, then?"

"I don't know what that would be."

"Maybe that's why you're here. Because you're trying to figure that out. Maybe it will start with Apollo. Your friendship. But it can't… You lived. Your life cannot stay so small."

"Most people would never tell me what to do in the manner that you are."

"Most people haven't lived a life like me. I've never had the opportunity to do anything." She sat there for a moment, and suddenly she felt guilty. She was passing judgment on him. Without really being fair. He had felt as trapped in his life as she did in hers.

The accident had been the thing that he felt had taken away his choice. She had no right to act as if he was simply lightly choosing to stay in isolation. He had not thrown away his freedom, it felt every bit as ripped from him as hers had from her.

"I'm sorry. I have been hideously insensitive."

He laughed. He really laughed. And there was a smile that accompanied it. They drew stairs in the café, and she found herself grinning even though she didn't really know what he was laughing at, and she had a feeling the laughter was somewhat unkind.

"Do you think I care if you been unfair to me?"

"I am the only friend that you've made in the last decade."

"You are not my friend, little goddess."

"Yes, I am. We talk every day. We have for weeks. You have shared your food with me. We are now out to dinner together. You bought me a very nice gift."

"If you mean the ring, that was Apollo."

"Fine. But even so, we are friends, you ridiculous beast."

"I do not have friends. Except Apollo."

"Why is that so important to you?"

"You are a little she demon."

"Maybe so." She bit happily into her sandwich, because she could take joy in the fact only she could have provoked him like this. She was certain. She was satisfied that she had gotten a reaction out of him. One that had simply been anger. "But I am right about you. You left the castle so that you could do something. So you should do it."

"And what is it that I want to do?"

"I don't know. But you told me an awful lot about the tragedy of Irina dying so young. You told me a lot about the tragedy of your upbringing. You have billions of dollars. Perhaps there is something in that. Perhaps there is something that you're supposed to do. You do have another life. Another chance. And you have the perspective of a man who has lived… All of your lives. What is it that you think needs to change? What is it that you think you need to bring to the world?"

"And what is it that you need to bring to the world, Athena? Are we now going to compete in philanthropy?"

"Maybe I'm a missing person," she said. "Maybe that's what I need to do. Maybe I need to help find people who are missing. Like me. People who are being locked away, hidden away. Maybe I need to help fix that. So that women like me can't be sold into marriage. So that women like Rose, my dear friend Rose, can't be sold to pay off debts. I will take the money you give me, and that is what I will do."

"I will match it. You don't need to spend all of your money."

"And what need do you see?"

"No child should sleep on the streets," he said.

"Good."

"It is that experience that creates monsters like me. Perhaps I can at the very least stop more of them from being made."

"Maybe that's why you're out. Maybe that's why you're here."

"You are difficult," he said.

"I never said I wasn't. Or rather, I suppose I'm just discovering that. Which is a bit exciting. Because I spent so much of my life being forced into being biddable. And I have never really thought I was. I have always thought that there might be more to me than that."

He looked at her, and she could not figure out exactly what the expression meant.

"A productive day. Your first time at a restaurant, and a glancing bit of insight into what you're meant to be."

"I think you're mocking me, Cameron."

"I would never mock you, little goddess."

"I don't believe that. I believe that you're mocking me because you find my sincerity uncomfortable."

"You know what's uncomfortable. Having eighteen inches of metal stuck in your leg. And no, that isn't the euphemism."

"I wouldn't have thought it was," she said, wrinkling her nose.

"Did you enjoy your meal?"

"I did. Perhaps we can take a walk?"

She smiled at him. And had the feeling that in his world that smile was waging a war. But that was just fine by her. She was the goddess of it, after all. And he insisted upon calling her a little goddess. So she would not let it go. She would not release hold.

She would instead be the conqueror that he had named her.

Even if it began with a walk.

"Looking for romance, Athena?"

The way his accent curled over her name made her stomach tighten.

"You were quite clear on your opinions regarding that subject."

They paid at the café, and then walked outside. It was a warm evening, couples were strolling down the well-lit sidewalk, holding on to each other, gazing at each other lovingly.

Perhaps that was romance. So soft, so easy.

He did not take her arm.

They walked, with a healthy bit of space between them. It was dark now, and they were performing for no one.

She wondered if either of them actually knew how to perform. Or if so many years left to their own devices had made them…

Perhaps they were too much themselves.

Those people that walked together seem to blend into one. To curve around each other.

Perhaps there was an element of training in that. In learning how to bend.

Athena was a bit like a hothouse flower, if she thought about it. She had been left in the corner of the greenhouse, and left to grow on her own. She had never touched the elements. Had never truly been tested, but she had grown rigid, in her way.

Cameron on the other hand was a hearty thistle you might find out in the Highlands. Too remote, too stubbornly wild to be tamed. Too prickly for anyone to draw near.

She could curve herself around him, just maybe, if she could get herself to bend that way. There would be no way to miss all the thorns.

"This is beautiful."

"Yes." His voice was hard then.

"Is this better? Walking in the dark like this?"

He made a musing sound. "I suppose. I did not think I would ever see Paris again."

"What did you like about Paris? The first time you were ever here."

"That I was a man with means of my own. That I was never a whore here. I liked that about it."

He spoke of that time as though it meant nothing. He spoke of selling its body as though it was something that mattered not at all.

She could tell that it did.

And she remembered the way that he had spoken of sex. How it was not romantic. And yet, she saw the way these people walked together. These people who undoubtedly went back to a bed somewhere and made love. It was physical, certainly. But surely connecting to another person like that was also romantic.

And yet, this man, for all of his experience, denied the existence of any romance whatsoever.

As though his body and soul were two completely separate entities, and what his body engaged in, his soul left the room for.

But now he had been sitting alone in his castle all that time. And she wondered. She wondered if it would be the same.

Or if now maybe that he had been so connected to his

thoughts all these years if... If he would find it different now. If those things would align for him.

"You didn't like being up..."

"You can say it. I was a whore. I sold myself."

"You say that to degrade yourself. I don't like it."

"I cannot say anything to degrade myself. I am degraded under my soul. There is no more that can be done."

"And yet you try. Every time you open your mouth. Every time you say things like that. You try."

"Perhaps you should listen."

"I don't see why I should."

"Athena..."

"Tell me. Tell me really, how it started. Tell me."

"No. There is no need to speak of it. We are walking down the streets of Paris, and you wish to speak of my time as a rent boy?"

"I don't know that I wish to, but it keeps coming up, and I feel the way that you use it to try and distance me."

"I shouldn't have to try to distance you. If you recall, I took you prisoner."

"Please. You took me prisoner, and then offered me the world. You took me prisoner, and then offered to take care of me. What I want to understand is why you were so married to the idea that you were the worst person on earth."

"Ask Irina."

"She's dead, so I can't," said Athena. "And before you say that's the point, I will remind you that you are alive. So perhaps you should find a better tribute than sitting around talking about how you're beyond redemption."

"How do you even give attribute to a woman you felt nothing for? When I tell you about my time as a rent boy... When I tell you that I am... Do you really want to know how it started?"

"Yes. You told me you made more money, but you had to discover that at some point."

"All right. There was a woman. Older. I was seventeen. Every bit as tall as I am now. Not as broad, mind you, because we did not have enough food on the streets. I was quite lanky. But I looked older than I was. Apollo was still working his charm, distracting people while I went in and stole their purse. We stole this woman's purse. We ran. Later, she came to the door of our storage unit that we stayed in. She had followed us. Seen us go in.

"She said that she was sorry to see boys taking to the streets to fend for themselves. She said she wouldn't call the police. She asked me to come to her house. She fed me a meal. It was…"

He had a terrifying, detached sort of look on his face. In his voice. "I thought perhaps she was caring for me. For the first time, I thought perhaps someone was caring for me. Just because. And then she asked for sex."

*"What?"*

"Yes. She was an older woman, attractive enough. She was lonely, she said. And I… I was too. I had seen her as a mother figure, feeding me dinner, taking pity on me even though I had stolen from her. But she did not see me as a son. She offered me the entire contents of her wallet plus two hundred more dollars for sex. I said yes. Because I'm not a fool. I said yes because not only was she not calling the police on me, she was offering to pay."

"That's… That's very…"

"It's unsavory is what it is."

"Yes," she said, honestly.

"That's the kind of man I am."

"You were a boy. Was it your first time being with anyone?"

He nodded. "I wasn't concerned with sex. I was concerned with survival. So… You don't judge me, because you feel that I did it out of desperation. For food. For money. That is true. But the worst was the small, needy part of myself that wish to be touched. That wish to be close to another person." His lip curled. "I learned. As I went on. I learned not to think of it that way. You can't. You might feel something good for a moment, but the shame of it afterward, and the pieces of yourself you leave behind… It isn't worth it. So you go somewhere else. And watch her body do all those things. It's much easier that way."

"Oh."

That told her more about him than anything else ever could have. He went somewhere else. It was how he had survived so many things. She wondered if he had ever found a way to come back to himself.

She wondered if he even wanted to.

She had thought that maybe he separated his body and soul on occasion. But she wondered now if it had been something more final than that.

"I'm so terribly sorry for what the world has done to you. And I am sorry… The way that I spoke of my willingness to leave my family, the way that I spoke of being poor, as if it was a Charles Dickens novel, and not something that is harrowing. Attending to your own survival that way. I am sorry."

He had not grown thorns for the sake of it. He needed them. She wondered if there was a part of Cameron that remained untouched, unspoiled by the world. And she felt desperate to reach down and find it.

She felt like it might be essential to her. To testing her own strength and to…being needed for herself.

For perhaps she had been specifically sharpened and honed to attack the demons that lived in him.

Perhaps she was the goddess of a very particular war. One that lived in him.

Perhaps it was not so wrong to hope that she could be what he needed here, just for a while.

"Do you have any idea how many women have wanted

to fix me, Athena? I laughed at them. While I made them mine in bed. I changed them, they never changed me."

"Did you go somewhere else inside with them?"

"I didn't have to. Eventually, I learned to take pleasure in my power. Do you know, it can be quite intoxicating to have a man filled with shame begging for your body, offering you money, saying no one can ever know. They debased themselves for *me*. And later, they kept on doing it. All these rich socialites. Beautiful women. And they would gladly give their bodies to me, and I could afford to give mine in return for free. And I took great pleasure in feeling nothing but their fingertips on my skin, in feeling nothing but pleasure in my body. Discard them, never think of them again. Not even remember their faces. What did it matter? All those rich people who used me, and I got to use them right back. It's heady, the power in that."

He said those things, so cold. And yet, she knew he wasn't cold. This man who enjoyed good food, who was walking with her now.

This man who had offered to save her. Who had asked nothing of her in return. Not really.

"It begs the question," she said slowly. "Why won't you touch me? If it means nothing."

"Because if I am to learn one thing from what happened to Irina, it will be not to inflict myself on another person again."

"You were not a punishment."

"There are those who would beg to differ."

She looked again at all those couples, walking together. Melting against each other.

She had the strangest sense that whatever was happening between herself and Cameron was somehow deeper. For all that it wasn't an easy stroll. For all that they didn't touch. She had never known another person. Not really. She and Rose had known each other as well as they could.

But they did not remember their lives before coming to the compound. Their friendship was often marred by the disparity between them, by the fact that Rose had to work, and Athena was prevented from helping her with any of her duties.

Athena couldn't let Cameron know her as well as she wanted to. Because there was a limit to what she remembered. But she could know him. As much as he would share. And it didn't matter that he was trying to shock her. Trying to get her with those thorns. Keep her from getting too close.

There was intimacy in this. The kind that she had never shared with another living soul, and he didn't shock her. He did not appall her. Instead, she felt honored.

He had hidden away all these years, and she had seen his face first.

And now she had his story.

"There is one thing that you and I can both fully appreciate," she said.

"And what is that?"

"Here we are. Walking. Free. Nobody's telling us what to do, or where to go. We could leave if we wanted, or we could stay forever."

"Little goddess, I fear that you are spinning fairy tales."

"I'm not spinning fairy tales. The truth is, this is the most that I have ever seen. All in one day. I am… Overwhelmed by it. But it isn't just the place. It's everything that you've told me. This is the deepest I have ever been able to know another person."

He stopped moving. "You should take it as a warning, not as a novelty."

"I don't care what I should and shouldn't do. I am not your prisoner. I'm your partner. And I have spent far too many years kowtowing to what others want from me. I spent too many years in the back of the greenhouse, left to my own devices, in the most lavish of settings, but there was no attention paid to my deeper needs. Talking to you… That fulfills something in me."

"You are a romantic, Athena, which speaks volumes to the differences in our upbringing."

"Yes. I would not say that my life has been normal, but it certainly shielded me from a great many things. You were right. As I said. I did not have an appropriate level of respect for what it meant to have the resources that I did. I feel differently now."

His voice suddenly went hard. "Tell me. Tell me when you first realized your life was not normal."

"I was ten. We watched a cartoon. The little girl went to the zoo. She got a balloon. She got an ice cream cone. I asked to go to the zoo, and my mother said no. I threw a tantrum, I begged, I cried. Screamed about going to the zoo. The next day, a bunch of balloons, a tray filled with ice cream cones, and a lemur appeared in the courtyard. Just for me. Just to make me happy. And I knew that it wasn't the same. It was somehow more, but not at all what I had asked for. If I can have a lemur brought to me, then why would it be beyond my parents' reach for me to go to a zoo? It made no sense. And it was always like that. I would ask for something outside the walls, and they would bring it to me. That was why when… I'm ashamed of this."

"Tell me," he said. "I should have some of your shame since you had all of mine."

"When my father first said that he was having me marry Mattias I was excited. I didn't know the man. But I was… Ready. I was ready to leave. I was ready for something new. For… I wanted romance. Yes. But I wanted sex as well. Do you have any idea how difficult it was growing up in a compound surrounded by grim-looking guards. With your hormones raging like that. I had fantasies about them. But if any of them touched me my father would've killed them."

"And why didn't you run away?"

"Did you not just hear the part about the guards? No. It was unspoken. If I ran away they would come for me. I just always had the sense that if that happened, I would break something. And the consequences of it would be unpleasant. Like I said. I began to have a sense that all was not normal when I was about ten. There were just some things that I knew. When I realized what manner of man Mattias was, when I realized this was not the fulfillment of any kind of fantasy, that was when I decided that I had to run. That was when I decided that it had to happen, no matter that it was frightening or unpleasant. It was worth whatever consequence to get away then."

"You had fantasies about the guards?"

"I might not have been allowed free rein to everything, but there was a library. I am quite educated on what occurs between men and women, even if I've never experienced it myself. Yes, there were always strong handsome looking men looming about. And I was a teenage girl. Of course I did."

"But none of them ever touched you?"

"No. Because that's how terrifying my father is."

"A pity."

"You're telling me. I could've passed the time quite nicely."

He laughed, and she felt buoyed by that.

At least he found her amusing. The subject of her childhood seemed to have eased some of the tension surrounding his.

"I was given nearly everything except what I wanted most. Freedom. The very definition of a gilded cage, I know."

"Do you suppose it was better, better than what I had to endure?"

"Yes. Because here I am, escaped now, on the other side

of it, and certainly more innocent that a person my age should be, but also protected, in many ways. I wouldn't have remained so. Because in the end…" She smiled, though there was nothing amusing about it. "I would've been turned into a horror as well. That's the way of it. The world sees people as commodities and when you don't have any power agency of your own, someone is always waiting for the opportunity to sell you."

"I sold myself."

"Only because somebody was a very insistent buyer."

"Well, that is the truth of it."

They looked at each other, it was dark, and his face was mostly hidden in shadow, she imagined hers was as well. She couldn't make out the scars on his face. She couldn't make out his expression, or much of anything at all.

"We go to London tomorrow."

"I will be pleased for that."

"You will like it."

"I will."

She wanted to stretch up on her toes and kiss him. She was nearly dizzy with her need to draw closer to him. But he had been very clear that he didn't wish for that to happen. He said it was to protect her, but she had a feeling…

So much of his past, his trauma was tied to the things that people had taken from him. From his body.

She couldn't walk with him, talk with him, hear the story that he told about that woman he had thought cared for him, and then asked him for sex, and then kissed him.

She would mean for there to be feeling behind it, but she didn't think that he would be able to do more than that. She wouldn't be any different, really. It would feel like she was using him. Like she had offered some sort of emotional balm only to turn it into something base.

She wouldn't do that. They walked on, and her knuckles brushed his. She caught her breath. And then she deliberately wrapped her fingers around his hand, the rough warmth a comfort, a need and a deep pain all at once.

In the darkness, they held each other's hands and walked back to the penthouse.

# CHAPTER ELEVEN

WHEN HE WOKE up the next morning he was in a foul temper. They would be having dinner with Apollo tonight, and the following night would be the product unveiling.

He had no patience for any of it. The first thing he remembered was the way the soft skin of Athena's hand had felt against his own.

He growled, sat up and looked around the bedroom. It wasn't big enough. Not sufficient enough for all the rage that poured through him. He wished to ride Aslan across the moors.

That was the only way to exorcise the demons that hounded him.

This was the *real* reason he had stayed in the middle of nowhere.

Because with Athena next door, the way that he really wanted to cope with the need that was coursing through his veins was to crash through her bedroom door and...

He would not.

The very idea made his stomach curdle.

There were competing, terrible needs inside of him, and he did not care for them at all.

He knew all about the physical release that came with sex. He had honed his own need to be only that. It was why he was so able to ruthlessly and efficiently find release on his own.

Because it meant nothing. Yes, he liked the softness of a woman's body. He had enough experiences to know exactly what he would choose when he was in control over the selection of his partners, and he preferred women. He liked the way they looked. The way that they smelled. The shape of them. It was certainly an added pleasure to have a partner. But he did not need it. He had gotten rid of that need. That yawning, ridiculous need that he'd still had at seventeen. That had made him so naïve and hopeful. That had made him think perhaps…

He had extinguished that. He was not a better man for it, but he was a man who had survived.

He did not wish to introduce Athena to his brand of sex. It was cold. It was transactional. And now… It would be far too rough. At least now. While he was so close to the edge.

And never. The bottom line was never.

He got in the shower, and turned on the cold spray. He gritted his teeth. And then he went to the fridge and took out some eggs and cream.

He got out some flour. There were fresh strawberries in there as well, and he quickly made crepes.

He was just finishing making some very strong coffee in the French press, when Athena appeared.

She was wearing…

Next to nothing.

A silken robe, with a lacy garment underneath. Her black hair was tousled. She looked… Much more appetizing than the breakfast that had been spread out before them.

"Good morning."

She smiled, and her smile looked wicked. "Good morning."

She took a tentative step into the kitchen, and looked up at him again. "I've never seen you in the act of cooking. I hoped to catch you quite often at the palace, but I never did."

"And why do you look sheepish this morning?"

She looked away. "I do not wish to make you uncomfortable."

He laughed. He could not help it. The very idea this little creature could make him uncomfortable.

His laughter, though, seemed to provoke her outrage. "I have a rich fantasy life, Cameron," she said, as her cheeks turned a deep pink. "A woman has to do something while she tries to go to sleep."

"You are a vixen."

"You have pushed me to be."

"It is probably for the best that you were kept under lock and key all those years if you are so easily provoked. You would've been trouble."

She laughed., though it was not an easy sound. "I would've been. Yes. I would've been. Because believe me, those guards would've all been mine."

"Big talk."

"Who's to say my big talk isn't true. None of us can prove it."

He gritted his teeth, pushing back against the idea of Athena fantasizing about him before she went to sleep. She was being deliberately provocative. She had been that way ever since they had arrived.

But then… She'd been testing the waters with him since she had first come to the castle. Going into the tower when he had told her not to. And now pushing him physically after he had told her no.

But he had held her hand last night. And there was no earthly reason for him to do that. It wasn't a sexual gesture at all. It was something more. And he shouldn't have allowed for it to happen. But he had enjoyed the feel of her skin against his far too much.

*So much for your grand declarations that you would never touch her.*

Well. That was never going to work in a literal sense. Not when they had to make their debut as a couple. Not when they would absolutely have to touch in that venue. But he did not have to touch her last night. And he had anyway. It was an indictment against his soul.

What was one more?

"This looks delicious," she said. But her eyes were not on the food.

He had no idea what game she was playing. But then… There was a chemistry between them. A magnetism. That she felt it in spite of everything was perhaps not as unfathomable as he had initially told himself.

The basic human desire to mate was not unique. And was typically not sensible.

And as she had said, she had been cloistered, and kept away from exploring her sexuality.

A pity she would not be doing it with him.

He set the crepes out before her, and put fresh cream and strawberries on the top.

Then he poured her a strong cup of coffee, and watched intently as she took her first bite. She hummed, the sound sensual. And then she took a sip of the coffee, closing her eyes for a moment before looking up in meeting his gaze.

"Thank you. For sharing this with me."

There was something unspoken then. The way she curled her lips up spoke of something intimate.

She was thinking that eating his food was tantamount to sensuality.

She wasn't wrong, unfortunately. Because he felt her enjoyment.

He was giving her something that gave her pleasure, and he could not remain unaffected by that.

She had brought his body to life in a way that he had found untenable from the moment he had first seen her.

General arousal was one thing. The desire for another person was…

Unprecedented.

Even before the accident he had never wanted one person with the ferocity he wanted her.

"It is a very short flight to London."

"I figured. Geography being what it is." She was being salty with him. And was clearly unrepentant about it.

"You need to stop being a brat. I was explaining the itinerary to a woman who has never been anywhere before. Many would find that helpful."

"You were speaking words to fill the space without having to acknowledge the tension between us."

Everything in him went hot and sharp.

"Let's acknowledge it then. I could take you in the bedroom and have you. You would enjoy it. It doesn't matter that it's been years, I know what I'm doing. I could kiss you, bare your beautiful breasts and suck your nipples into my mouth." His own words started to make him hard. Her breath hitched. And he realized he had miscalculated. He had attempted to frighten her. But she was aroused. Yes, this girl was aroused.

"Then what would you do?" she asked, the words a breath.

She was pushing, and he was through coddling her. If she wanted to push, let her see where it went. Let her see who truly held the power here.

Let her see he could unravel her without ever once putting his hands on her, because sex and desire were simple alchemy, and he knew the ingredients and wielded them well.

He growled. "I would put my hand between your legs and see if you were wet for me."

She nodded, the shining curiosity in her eyes stoking his need. Pushing him further. Making him want to push and push. He could feel his sex grow heavy with desire, his heart thundering as he saw, vividly, in his mind the picture he painted with his words.

"And then, I would stroke you. Pushed a finger inside of you while I rub my thumb over your clit. Push one finger inside of you, and then another, give you a taste of what was to come."

"Yes," she said, her eyes going glassy.

He gripped the edge of the counter, and looked across the space at her, his eyes meeting hers directly.

"I would kiss my way down your stomach, between your legs, where my tongue would slide over all that wetness. The taste of you… It would be better than this cream. I would devour you. There is nothing that tastes so good as a woman in need of satisfaction, and I bet that you are the sweetest of them all. I would eat you until you begged for me to stop. Until the pleasure was far too great. I would make you insane with it. Cry out my name."

She was shifting in her chair, her desire clearly building.

And he felt himself slipping.

Losing the intention of this little exercise.

Losing himself in her eyes.

In the way her skin went rosy and her lips parted.

"And then finally, I would take you. It would hurt the first time. But I would thrust into you hard, and take us both over the edge."

She let out a shaking breath, and he could see that she was on the edge of release without even being touched. And this was dangerous, he knew it. This was everything he should have avoided. This was…

It was words. It wasn't bodies. He had had so many words with Athena. And somehow it was different.

"Touch yourself," he gritted out.

She obeyed quickly, pushing her hand between her thighs, over the top of the robe, so she didn't reveal any part of herself. But she pressed her palm expertly against her mound, and let out a short, sharp cry. And then she slumped in her chair.

*"Oh."*

"That's what I would do," he said, turning away from her.

"Well let's do it then," she said, her voice sounding thick.

"No. We have business to attend."

He was affected. Shaken by what had just happened. He was so hard he was in pain. He needed another shower. Not a cold one this time.

"Why would you…? Why would you…?"

"Enough," he said. "To show you. That you are playing with me, and you don't know what you're doing. I can make you come by talking to you. I can make you feel all kinds of things, but I would not feel any of them in return. Be grateful that I refuse you the thing that you ask for. Be grateful, you stupid girl."

And then he turned, and left her sitting there, but he was not unaffected.

Not at all.

# CHAPTER TWELVE

SHE FELT SHAMEFACED, on the flight to England.

She almost couldn't even enjoy the sights of Big Ben and Westminster Abbey, the London Eye, Buckingham Palace.

Almost.

He had not shamed her past the point of all enjoyment.

But she couldn't... She could not believe that she had *done* that. That she had let him spin a story that had created such a deep arousal in her that she had responded without ever...

And she supposed, that was the point of it. The lesson. Proof that she was much more naïve than she cared to admit. Much more naïve than she thought.

Yes. She supposed that was the point. He had effectively used his experience against her.

But she was not going to weep. No. She was too strong for that.

He might think that he had gotten the upper hand. But he...

He had felt something. She was sure of it. He hadn't planned that. It had just... Happened. She was nearly almost entirely certain.

She needed to believe that. Because otherwise... Otherwise, he was in much greater control of all this than she was.

*Does that surprise you? You don't know anything about men. You don't know anything about life.*

That wasn't true. She knew about life. She knew about what she wanted. She knew that he... That he called to her.

She could talk about the hands of guards at the compound all she wanted, and she enjoyed it, because she could see that it put him on his back foot. But none of them would have ever been able to bring her to orgasm simply by speaking.

She had *touched* herself in front of him.

Through her clothes, but the fact remained that she had done so.

She felt scalded by that.

And yet...

It had certainly been one of the more adventurous things she had ever done.

In some ways, she was proud of herself.

Because she felt as if it could only have ever been them. She was a replacement for nothing, in fact he was actively trying to resist this, which made her feel like it could only be here creating this need, and bringing him to the edge.

They arrived at the London penthouse, equally glorious to the one in Paris, with a fantastic view of the Shard.

She knew that she should be soaking in the iconic nature of the view, but the only thing that felt iconic to her was Cameron.

She felt slightly nervous at the idea of meeting Apollo tonight.

Apollo was Cameron's only friend.

Except for her. She would not allow him to diminish the connection between them. They were friends.

Friends who had... Who had had a very charged sexual encounter this morning.

There was chemistry between them. She was clear on that.

He was the one who seemed to take issue with it.

It was tied up in him, in his own baggage, she knew that. But that didn't make it any easier to try and sort through it all.

She hadn't asked for this. She had wanted freedom. She had gone and gotten herself tangled up in possibly the most damaged man on the planet.

But he was a good man. She was sure of that.

That was… There was that at least.

But it didn't help her now. Didn't help with all of her attention.

She busied herself, getting ready for their dinner tonight.

She put on a blue dress, sleek and like midnight.

She rather enjoyed seeing her body in such provocative clothing.

She enjoyed it even more when she stepped outside and stood face-to-face with Cameron, who clearly enjoyed it as well.

"Excellent," he said. "I see you readied yourself."

"I did consider wearing a burlap sack. But I wanted to make a good impression on your friend."

"Good."

She looked at the tension in his jaw. "Are you nervous to see him?"

He turned to her, his blue eyes sharp. "I am not nervous. I do not get nervous."

She laughed. "You're a liar. You are nervous. Of course you are. You've been hidden away in a castle for the last decade. All of this is extremely new to you."

"None of it is new to me. There are no mysteries yet remaining in humanity for me, lass. People are selfish, greedy, filthy creatures. And stepping away from them for ten years will have done nothing to change that. They are also shallow and vein. I will no longer challenge their vanity, but I will engender discomfort. That's because of the shallowness. You can't win everything, I suppose."

She tried to read him. Tried to look deeper. The shock of his blue eyes, of the need she felt when she was near him made it nearly impossible. "But it won't be like that with your friend."

"Difficult to say."

"Is it only Apollo tonight?"

"Yes. He felt that it would be best."

"I agree. It is nice to know that your friends know you so well."

He growled, and she suppressed a smile.

"You don't like that. You don't like having it pointed out to you that you have friends."

"You are not my friend."

"I am. Who else have you spent this much time speaking to?"

"Of the things we have talked about? No one," he said, his voice suddenly honed to a fine blade.

She searched his face.

He was accustomed to using sex as a weapon. And of course, this was no different. The fact that he had talked to her, and not touched her even once, the fact that he had kept his distance, the fact that he had not taken his own release, all of that was part of it. Him taking control. Because he was afraid. He was afraid that she would test his control.

He didn't like it. More than that, he loathed it. She had the power to challenge him. Whether or not he wanted to admit that. He wanted to pretend that he was immune. To everything. But he wasn't.

And she was… She was learning something. How to knit herself into another person's life. How to develop a relationship. And yes, she supposed in many ways theirs was built on forced proximity in the same way her relationship with Rose had been. But it felt different also. She didn't have to befriend him. He hadn't had to talk to her. They were a means to an end for one another, and yet for some reason, in spite of all that, they had gotten to know each other. It felt real. And it felt like it mattered.

They rode in the limousine to a large manor house outside of the city.

"Does he live here?" she asked, breathing out and in.

"Yes. Sometimes. Apollo goes wherever he wishes."

"It's amazing."

"He will preen if you show him that sort of appreciation when you meet him. He loves to impress."

"Well, I am suitably impressed."

And she could see that statement put Cameron in a dark mood. She would be lying if she said she didn't appreciate that. That she had roused jealousy in him.

For that was what it was. She was impressed with his friend's house, and he didn't like it.

They walked to the front door, which was opened for them ceremoniously.

She held on to Cameron's arm as they were ushered into a grand foyer that was every bit as grand as the exterior had been.

Robin's-egg blue wallpaper and gold details created a clean, stunning site. But it was the restored gold chandelier hanging from the ceiling that truly stole the show.

"This is *glorious*," she said.

And then, a tall, dark-haired man in a suit walked in. His jawline was sharp, clean-shaven. His brown eyes were nearly black, his skin golden brown. He had broad shoulders and large hands. He was truly one of the most beautiful men she had ever seen.

It was an easy sort of beauty.

It reminded her of the easy romance that she had seen while they were walking in Paris.

Cameron did not have an easy beauty.

But it compelled her.

He compelled her.

She wasn't sure what it said about her that she didn't want easy. That as beautiful as she could see Apollo was, he did not appeal to her in that same way.

Goddess of war…

Perhaps that was it. Perhaps she was destined to be at war. Perhaps it was what she craved.

She knew for certain that she didn't want soft. She knew for certain that she didn't want to bend easily, nor did she want anyone to easily bend around her.

All those things became clear when she gazed upon the glorious visage of Apollo.

Because many women would have fallen to their knees then. Melted down at his feet.

And she felt absolutely no inclination toward it.

"You must be Athena," Apollo said, grinning widely. "How nice to meet a fellow Greek."

He spoke to her in Greek. She spoke back in Greek.

"I do not know that I'm Greek, though I have learned Greek."

He frowned. "Athena? Your name is certainly Greek. And you speak it as if you have spoken it from the cradle."

"I…"

She was stunned then because…of course. Her family had been Russian, and she was Athena, which she'd thought was a bit of an extravagance, but perhaps it wasn't.

She'd felt as if Greek was a language she'd learned, yet much like English she didn't remember learning it.

Maybe she had always known.

"Sadly for you both, I speak Greek. Because of you," Cameron said, directing that at Apollo and redirecting Athena's musings.

"One of my many sins." His gaze raked dispassionately over Cameron.

"It is good to see you."

"Is it?"

"Yes," Apollo said, and Athena was almost certain that she heard his voice get rough with emotion, even if it was only a slight change.

"You're both ridiculous," said Athena. "You love each other. You might as well show it."

"That's a very strong word," said Apollo. "But we spent a great many years needing each other, that much is certain."

"It is good to see you," said Cameron, his voice desperately flat, which Athena knew meant that he was fighting back emotion of some kind.

"*Men*. Honestly. Is it so terrible to admit that you're friends? And that you have hated your separation?"

"I have not hated our separation," said Apollo. "With Cameron gone I have much less competition for women."

"Are you so simple?" asked Athena.

"Yes. I am." But there was a dark light behind his eyes that told her he was not. And anyone who mistook him for being simply a beautiful face would find themselves at a disadvantage indeed.

She looked back at Cameron. "Are you going to say anything emotionally literate?"

Cameron looked bland. Which was no mean feat. "I've no plans to."

She let out an exasperated sigh. "I suppose we best go in and have dinner. Since we are not going to have the emotional reunion I was hoping for."

"Are you invested in an emotional reunion?" Apollo asked.

"I am invested in Cameron's emotions."

She could feel Cameron's gaze on her. Fierce, and questioning. He didn't understand why she would freely admit that. But why would she be ashamed? She cared for him.

She wasn't embarrassed by that. She was… She was happy about it.

Here she had spent all these years shut away, and now she was friends with him. She was… She wanted him.

She wasn't ashamed at that. She was glad of it.

"Are you? I confess, I was not sure in what manner Cameron managed to convince you to present yourself as his wife."

"He is not presenting me as his wife. I *am* his wife."

Apollo looked between the two of them. "Indeed. How interesting."

She looked at Cameron and treated him to a sunny smile. "He's very noble, actually. He saved me. I owe him a great debt."

Cameron growled. "I did not save you. I took you prisoner."

She patted his hand. "I think we both know that isn't true." She grinned at Apollo.

"You got soft in your time rusticating."

"I am *not* soft," said Cameron.

"You certainly don't look it."

"No," Cameron agreed, his lip curling.

"Let's not get into that." Athena sat down next to him. "Let's just have dinner."

"She is quite something," said Apollo.

"She is *irritating*," said Cameron.

For some reason the exchange cheered Athena immensely.

"You look much more ready for tomorrow night than I anticipated. If she has accomplished that, she has certainly done more than I've ever managed to do it all those years of phone conversations. I applaud her."

"Thank you," she said to Apollo. "It is nice to be appreciated. Cameron appreciates me, he just can't admit it."

That earned her another sharp gaze, but she was enjoying herself far too much to be chastened.

She had been embarrassed earlier. About her response to him.

But she felt... Free of that now. Did it matter she cared for him? If she wanted him. There were other things holding him back, things that had nothing to do with whether or not he wanted her.

It was the same reason he could not cry with joy and give his friend a hug because he had seen him for the first time in ten years.

He was a prisoner to his feelings.

She didn't need to take that personally. And she did not need to be a prisoner of hers simply because he was.

She didn't have to be a prisoner anymore at all.

She heard footsteps, and looked up. Standing in the doorway was a very young-looking woman with wide, luminous eyes. She smiled, and her blue eyes sparkled.

"You didn't tell me that we had guests, Apollo."

"I thought that you would be studying."

"I was. But then I got hungry. Very mean not to tell me."

Athena was confused for a moment about what relationship he might have to this... This girl.

But then she stepped into the room, and met Athena's gaze. "Hello. I am Hannah. Apollo is my guardian."

"Oh," said Athena.

Cameron, for his part, looked questioningly at his friend.

"I don't usually live here," she said. "But I am on holiday from school."

"Yes, and she has a final exam yet to take before she is fully on break."

When Apollo addressed her, she blushed, her cheeks turning a deep rose. "Yes. I do. So... I can't stay for dinner but..."

"You can stay," he said.

She smiled happily, and took a seat next to him.

Athena, for her part, was grateful for the company, even though the girl was quite a few years younger than her. She had actually been to university, so... She knew more about the world than Athena did.

After dinner, the men got up and retired to the study to discuss business. And that left Athena alone with Hannah.

"He's terrifying," she said, clearly speaking of Cameron.

Athena went rigid. "He isn't."

"I didn't mean because... You know, they just both have that... That manner about them. Apollo would terrify me if I didn't know him. He's been very good to me since my parents died."

"I'm sorry," said Athena.

Hannah forced a smile. "It's okay. I mean... It isn't. But they were never very much around when I was younger anyway. I was away at school all through the year, and then even when I was home they were often gone. Off on adventures. When I was sixteen they... They were killed in an accident. They were on a canoeing trip and their boat capsized. It was terrible. But my father was good friends with Apollo, and he... Anyway, Apollo is the manager of my trust. And my guardian. Until I am twenty-five."

Looking at her, Athena guessed that was a few years away.

"And how old are you now?"

"Nineteen." She smiled very prettily, in that way nineteen-year-olds could.

"He gives you freedom?" Athena asked.

"Oh, yes. I'm very grateful to him."

But there was something hollow in the way that she said that.

"And you and Cameron are... You're his wife?"

She nodded. "Yes."

She felt sort of guilty, but she didn't know how far their ruse needed to go.

"It must be quite something. To have all that focus on you."

There was a wistfulness in Hannah's tone that made Athena feel sorry for her.

Then she wondered… If she was any different than this girl. Who wanted a man so far out of her reach he might as well have been on another planet.

*No, you know it isn't real. The desire might be, but you know you will have to move on after. You might be Greek. You might have a family. McKenzie is just a name he gave you, but it isn't your name. You have to find your name. Remember that.*

# CHAPTER THIRTEEN

"ALL THE TIMES we talked and you managed not to tell me that you have a ward."

"It wasn't relevant to any of our business."

"I see."

He stared at his friend hard.

"Don't judge me," Apollo said. "Athena is clearly under your thumb. And you know exactly which way I mean that."

"I haven't touched her. Not the way that you mean."

He hadn't. Even now, he hadn't.

"But you *want* to," Apollo said.

"She's beautiful. Who wouldn't want to?"

Apollo poured himself a measure of scotch, then turned to look at Cameron. "Why the sudden pretense that you're a man of honor?"

"I might ask you the same." He looked hard at Apollo. He only *suspected*, he wasn't *certain*, but when his friend looked away, it confirmed it.

He had a forbidden attraction to his ward. A woman who was substantially younger than him, and under his protection.

"Touché." He knocked back his scotch, his breath hissing through his teeth. "I have done very few things in my life that are worthy of being called honorable. Looking after Hannah is one of the few. I owed her father. He was… He was a friend."

"Friends I don't know about."

"You disappeared for a decade. You don't get to be childish about the fact that I had other friends. It is my job to take care of her, and I will."

And he didn't have to ask Apollo why that meant he could never put his hands on her. Because it was the same reason he wouldn't touch Athena.

They were damaged. Women who had even the slightest air of innocence about them were not for them.

Not in the slightest.

They'd cauterized their souls long ago to keep from bleeding out, and they were bonded over this, but he very much doubted they could truly bond to anyone else. Even their relationship was not…

They were not emotionally literate, as Athena herself had said.

"And you really do intend to let her go once this is all over?"

"Yes," Cameron confirmed. "I have promised her freedom. And my protection."

"Perhaps there is hope for both of us then. Perhaps we can at least play men of honor when we need to."

"I do not give myself so much credit."

Apollo paused. "Do you know anything about where she came from."

"She was the adopted child of a crime lord. Russian."

Apollo looked thoughtful. "That is very interesting. I had an interaction recently with a man called Castor Xenakis and he was recently reunited with his sister. She's married, and free now, has been for a year. But she worked as a maid for a crime lord. Russian, I believe."

The words resonated inside of him.

"Athena told me that her only friend at the compound was a maid, and they were Russian."

Apollo arched a brow. "Interesting. Don't you think? For what it's worth, I believe she is Greek, or at least of a family who is, she speaks the language too well."

"Do I not speak it well?"

"No," Apollo said, simply.

"And where is Castor Xenakis now and how do I get in touch with him?"

"He will be there tomorrow. Perhaps it would do you well to meet him. And Athena as well."

"I do not wish to expose Athena to any sort of danger. If there is even a chance that anyone there will—"

"No. Castor is on a mission to end that man. Whatever he intended for Athena, Castor will help keep her safe if anything. And he may have an idea of who her family is."

"You think she has a family?"

"Well, if the maid did, why wouldn't Athena?"

It was true. If the maid had a family, why wouldn't Athena?

All of this was very interesting. Very interesting indeed.

"Tomorrow," said Apollo. "You can ask Castor yourself."

# CHAPTER FOURTEEN

FOR THE PRODUCT launch itself she decided to wear gold.

The dress that she wore was nearly like armor, gold leaves made of metal fashioned into a bodice that clung to her curves. The skirt was a shiny material that shimmered like liquid when she moved. She had tied her hair back tightly, and applied her makeup in a dramatic fashion, her eyes smoky and seductive. If she said so herself.

She took a breath before walking out of the room, and put on her necklace.

*Have courage. Take heart.*

She pictured what it had been like when she'd done the same in Paris. When she'd seen him standing there in his suit.

It made her smile. That this wasn't the first time. That they were them. And this was something they did.

She walked into the living area, but he wasn't there.

She turned a circle. "Cameron."

He did not answer.

"Cameron!"

He didn't answer.

So she walked right for the door of his bedroom, and without knocking, she opened it.

He had been standing bent over the desk, gripping the edge. Wearing nothing but a pair of dark trousers, his torso bare.

He stood, straightening, his dark hair loose around his shoulders, his blue eyes intense.

His body…

He had scars. His body had not been spared them. But his muscles were… Glorious.

Her mouth dried.

He was perfection.

The scars only enhanced it.

He was like a thing honed from rock. A mountain.

He was power and glory. And while he made her mouth dry, he made that place between her thighs wet.

She barely held back the gasp of pleasure that rose in her throat, but the sound was enough to shake him from his thoughts.

"What?" he asked. It was a growl more than a question, but she was used to that with him.

"We have to go," she said.

She took a step toward him, and he took a step back.

He had the look of a predator, assessing the situation. Knowing that there were only two options. To flee or to inflict lethal damage.

"I am just finishing getting ready."

His jacket and shirt were on the back of his chair, a tie draped over the top of them. He had upended a chair, she could see. He was…not well.

"Can you admit to me that you're having difficulty with this?"

"It is… I did this many times before. Before the accident. Before I looked… I did this many times before. Many of the people in the room will be people who knew me then. It is… I cannot stand pity. I cannot."

"Why not?"

"Because I'm a *man*. I am not a broken *thing*."

"But surely you have experienced pity before to hate it so much?"

He laughed, hard and cynical. "Yes. I have. Well spotted."

"Why is it so bad?" she asked, her tone a near whisper.

"When they pity you they take advantage of you. When you let yourself be pitied, you begin to feel sorry for yourself. And when you begin to feel sorry for yourself, you embrace that needy, horrid thing inside of you that demands you let them touch you. I do not need pity."

"You're afraid of it. Because that woman…"

"*Enough.* You don't know me. Nobody does."

"*I* know you. I do. You can say that I don't, you can try to be angry about it. You can push back at me all you wish, but I do know you, Cameron. She shamed you. You wanted affection and she used that against you. And you are afraid of having that happen to you again. It is logical. Reasonable. There is nothing wrong with you that you wish to avoid being hurt like that again. But you do have control now. You are not that boy. You have Apollo. And you have me. We won't let you down."

"I don't need anyone."

"And it would be so bad if you did?"

"Yes," he said, his tone caustic. Bitter.

"Cameron," she said softly. "Why is it so bad to have people who care."

"Because it means nothing. In the end it means nothing. People will choose their personal addictions every time over connection and it will never, ever last. And then what are you left with? Nothing."

And he stood there, looking at the white shirt sitting on the chair.

Everything in her felt jagged, broken. And suddenly the necklace around her neck burned.

She walked over to the chair, and lifted the shirt up. "Come on," she said.

He didn't move. But she did. She walked up to him and unbuttoned the cuff of the shirt, maneuvering it slowly over his hand, and up his shoulder. The touch felt erotic, and yet she hadn't meant it to be, but there was an intimacy to this she hadn't counted on. "I have no problem getting you ready to go myself."

"What the hell are you doing?" He was affected, or he wouldn't be angry.

"I'll dress you if I need to."

"I'm not a *child* or an *invalid*," he said, but allowing her to shrug the shirt up over his other arm too, and draw it into place. She looked up at him, so close. She could smell his skin again. She loved the way he smelled. She began to button the shirt. And that made her smile even broader.

"What?"

"I have to say, I've had quite a few thoughts about the buttons of your shirt these last few days. But I never imagined doing them *up*."

He put his hand over hers, and stilled her movements. "You play a dangerous game."

"You keep telling me that. And yet, I find myself consequence-free. I imagine you want to tuck it in yourself."

He did so, and she took his jacket off the back of the chair as well, putting it into place. She left the jacket open, let the top two buttons on his shirt undone.

"You don't need a tie. For the shirt or for your hair. Leave it like this. You keep thinking that you have to step up to the podium and be the man you were before. But you're not. You're the man you are now. Look at you." She moved out of the way so that he could see himself in the mirror, and he lowered his head.

"Look at yourself," she repeated.

He lifted his head slowly, and she could see the moment his eyes met his own there.

Then she moved to him, and she reached up and unhooked her necklace.

"You're strong, Cameron McKenzie. You do not need

to be the Cameron McKenzie you were before. I cannot be the Athena I was before I was taken to my family. I don't even remember who I was. I can only be the Athena I am now." She turned him toward her, and put her hands on his chest. She could feel his heart raging there. "I am the Athena that I decide to be. Your warrior goddess. Thank you. For giving that to me." She put her hand over his, then slipped it from where he clung to the vanity, and turned his hand palm up.

Then she pressed the necklace into his hand.

*Have Courage. Take Heart.*

He looked into her eyes, deep. She felt it like a touch.

Like his words earlier, but different. Sexual yes, but more than that.

Deeper.

This, she thought, was like making love. She knew another person might never understand.

But Cameron had had sex with strangers. All physical, no feeling. What he did not have was someone to piece him together when he was broken. To touch him, just to touch him, and not to get anything back.

To listen to him. Understand him.

He took the necklace, and slipped it into his pocket, then put his hand over hers and held it there, hard. Firm. "You are strong," he said. "Do not let anyone make you feel different."

"So are you."

When he lowered his hand, he kept hold of hers.

"Shall we go then? You have a product to launch."

"Yes," he said, his voice rough. "I do."

# CHAPTER FIFTEEN

HE COULD NOT explain what had happened in the room. He could not explain the weakness that had overtaken him when he had been frozen, barely able to bring himself to put the shirt and suit jacket on. He could not explain why he had allowed Athena to do it for him.

Yet somehow, when she did it, it was as if she was putting armor in place for him. As though they were going into battle together.

And now they were standing outside the venue, all lit up with banners hanging down the side, promising the largest product launch in the company's history.

He could explain what he had created effortlessly. Could explain to everyone in the room why they wanted it. And yet...

Was it fear that he felt now?

There had been a time in his life when fear had been a constant companion. He had purposed in himself to never feel it again.

Maybe that was a foolish thing.

When he had nearly died in that car accident, he had felt fear. When he had watched the life drain from Irina, he had felt fear.

Perhaps he had never left it behind. Perhaps, like when he was a boy on the street, it had simply become part of him, and he had not noticed it anymore. Had not been able to call it for what it was.

But with Athena by his side, he felt stronger.

*Have Courage. Take Heart.*

He had got that for her and then...

Somehow it had been right for him.

He had lost his sense of why he had wanted her there in the first place. It had been about public opinion at first. But that wasn't the case now. Now he recognized that he wanted her there because of himself.

Because he actually... He wanted to do this. He wanted to show that he was capable.

To show that he didn't need pity. They walked up the stairs slowly, and when they entered the crowded ballroom, there was a hush that fell over the crowd.

It was to be expected. And that, he thought, was a better reason than any not to delay the announcement until later. So with Athena on his arm, he walked straight to the center of the room, and right toward the podium.

He stood in front of the microphone, and he could see Apollo standing down there in the front of the crowd, looking at him questioningly.

"I know this was not the scheduled time for the speech." he said. "But let us not pretend that I'm not the elephant in the room, so to speak. I have not been in the public eye these last ten years. And I know there were rumors about why. You can see that they were true. The accident that I was in ten years ago, that made headlines around the world, and left supermodel Irina Sharapova dead, disfigured me. During that time, I went away to heal. During that time, I put my mind to good use, and I have spent all that time making this new smart home system. It is leagues beyond anything that we have ever done before. Leagues beyond anything anyone has ever done before. From facial recognition, to remote access, nonverbal cues and accessibility features, it is the most sophisticated system for any home. I was able to turn an entire medieval castle into a high-tech wonder. We will do a demonstration of the features later on tonight, but I felt that you should know that I believe strongly enough in the product that I've shown my face for the first time in ten years."

"And who is the woman?" The question came from one of the reporters at the front of the room.

"This is Athena McKenzie. My wife. So I guess you could say I have not only worked on product development these last ten years.

"No further questions about my personal life," he said. "The focus of this is the new smart home system, and nothing more."

He gripped her hand tightly, and led her down the stairs.

And then, he took her out to the dance floor. "It is time to put our rehearsals to good use, don't you think?"

"I…"

He brought her into his arms, and the feeling of her pressed against him was more potent now. Now that he had seen her eyes go cloudy with pleasure. Now that he had watched her find her release.

Now that she had dressed him. Now that she had heard his darkest secrets.

She would go on to live brilliantly. She would go on to be the woman that she wanted to be. She would find her family. He would see to that.

But for now, they would dance.

This was all he would allow himself. The only intimacy.

No matter how he wanted her.

Precisely because he wanted her, that was why. That was why he couldn't have her.

Athena's heart was still pounding. Her hands rested on his neck. She wanted to kiss him. How was it they hadn't kissed? It seemed wrong.

It seemed as if she would've had to kiss him a hundred

times. She was his wife. Tonight she had buttoned his shirt for him. Put his jacket in place. She had been his support the way that a wife ought to be.

But they had never kissed.

Her lips burned with the need of it. And yet her soul was ignited by the knowledge that she had him in ways no one else ever had.

*You are not remembering to let it be only desire...*

How could she?

There was no *only* desire.

Not with him.

Not with them.

She was lit up with the knowledge of him in a way she was certain only lovers could be.

They went through the evening, dancing, dinner. Everyone wanted to talk to Cameron. And Cameron was... incredible.

Finally, hours later, they had a moment to breathe.

"Cameron..."

"Cameron," said Apollo's voice from behind them. Athena turned, and they stopped dancing. There was a man, a sinfully gorgeous man, standing next to Apollo, and on his arm, was an equally beautiful woman.

"This is Castor Xenakis, and his wife Glory. I told you that Castor recently found his sister."

"Yes," said Castor. "My sister Ismena—Rose, as you know her, was just rescued from the compound of a crime lord."

And Athena's world went sideways.

"What?" Athena asked, or she thought she did.

Maybe she just screamed it. Inside her own head.

"With Ares's help, that's Rose's husband, I've collected some information that might be of use to you." Castor was still talking. Athena's ears were buzzing.

"I..."

"I think I have information on where to find your family. There was a news story. It was part of my search. I spent years looking for human trafficking victims. There was a missing girl called Athena. Taken from a beach. She and her twin brother were kidnapped. They were held for three months."

"No… A twin brother?" She felt like she was breaking apart. Like something inside of her was being shattered.

"Please don't tell her all of this here," said Cameron, putting his arm around her waist. "If there's somewhere where you can speak privately…"

"I apologize. Do you not remember any of this?"

Athena shook her head. "I don't."

"Let's go," he said. "To the garden in the back."

Cameron held tightly to her as they were propelled out of the venue. Once they were outside, Castor reached into his jacket and took out a file. "It's all here."

And suddenly, something in her mind broke wide open. "Constantine Kamaras. My brother is Constantine. He was my twin. And there was… A baby."

"I… There are some things in that file you will want to look at. Some things that you will need to know. Cameron, may I speak with you for a second?"

Castor took Cameron aside while Athena sat there, trying to catch her breath. He came back a moment later. "We don't have to stay," he said.

"Yes, we do," she said. "It's… It's for you it's…"

"Tomorrow. We will go back to America tomorrow. We will arrange to meet your family. I have already talked to Apollo about speaking to them."

"We can't just… I don't know…"

She was fighting memories, and also reaching for them. She could remember forcing a boy to sit and watch a cartoon with her about ponies…

*This is stupid, Athena. But you will do stupid things for me!*

She'd grinned at him. Just like she did to Cameron now when she suggested something silly and he reacted darkly.

Perhaps she'd started training to handle Cameron even back them.

She saw more fragments in her mind.

A woman, beautiful and glamorous. Her mother?

A handsome man in a suit, graying. And an older man who was completely gray. A father and grandfather?

Then there was a baby…

"My mother and father?"

"Living," he said.

"My baby brother…"

"Let us speak more about this after."

"But…"

"Athena, this was too much to ask you to think about here. Let us speak more after."

She made it through the rest of the evening feeling numb.

Cameron's presentation was amazing, but she could hardly grasp the details. She had a family.

She had a family. So had Rose, the entire time.

Had it been the man who'd adopted her who had kidnapped her? She didn't think so.

She didn't think so.

She didn't know why, only that…there was some darkness. A gap…

They got into the limo after, and she looked over at Cameron. "Will you tell me? Will you tell me everything?" For some reason the most desperate thing was about the baby in her memory.

"I am very sorry to tell you this, but your younger brother passed. A year ago."

Something in her broke. The little dark-haired boy went

from pudgy baby to wicked toddler. He'd been maybe two or three the last time she'd seen him.

And she would never see him again.

"*No*," she said. "That isn't fair. Isn't fair that I would miss him like this I..."

"I know. Your twin is married. He is the father of twins himself."

She felt awash in emotion. Pain. She had a twin brother. He was a father. That made her not only a sister, a twin, but an aunt as well. And the youngest brother...

She tried to remember him.

She remembered playing on the beach with the dark-haired boy. Her age. Dark eyes. She remembered feeling connected to him. Deeply connected. As if he was another part of her.

As if she could sense what he was thinking. Feeling.

"I remember. I remember Constantine. My twin he..."

There was a bedroom. And everything in it was butterflies. She could remember jumping on the bed with him. Laughing, reaching for the little paper butterflies that hung from the bed.

"I have a family. I wonder if my mother and father still..."

"According to this file, they live still."

"I need to go to them. I need..."

"Of course you do. Of course you need to go to them. Right away."

"Cameron, you will come with me."

"I will take you to America. I will take you as far as that."

She looked up at him, her heart suddenly torn. This was what she'd wanted, come to her sooner than she could have imagined. And Cameron...who had not left Scotland or his castle other than this past week, for a decade was willing to fly to America for her as if it was no more than a ride across the moors on Aslan.

"We should call them first… Will we…"

"I'll have Apollo contact them. We will make sure that they are ready for your arrival."

"Thank you. How can I ever thank you. You made me a real person tonight, and now you're giving me back my family."

"I guess now you know. You are Athena Kamaras."

Athena who remembered nothing of who she was, that Athena would have loved that without condition, would have lived for this. It was not the family that made her ache now. It was the name. She had been Athena McKenzie.

She had been so certain she would not cling to that, and yet now she felt she was.

And Cameron was so quick to want that undone. It hurt, and it shouldn't.

Kamaras.

She was a Kamaras. She had a family. A place.

Where she was the desired daughter. Not a replacement. Not a doll.

It was all she had ever wanted.

She blinked to keep tears from falling. "Yes. Yes. Now I know."

# CHAPTER SIXTEEN

ATHENA WAS VERY quiet the entire plane ride to the United States. Her family lived in Massachusetts, out in the country. He had done his due diligence on them, to make sure that they were the sort of people she should be brought to.

And he… His time with her would now be at an end. He would take her to her family, and he would leave her there. It was perhaps the most selfless thing he had ever done. Because everything inside of him wished to hold on to her. To crush her against his body and claim her for his own. To make her his in every possible way.

Yes, everything in him longed to do that. Absolutely everything.

But he could not. Because he might be a beast on the outside, but he had learned to care for someone other than himself. What he wanted was Athena's happiness. And he could never give that to her.

"I remembered something else," she said softly.

"What is that?"

"I remembered the day we were taken. It was terrifying. Constantine fought. He fought everyone. He tried to save me. They separated us. I was put in a small room, and given tea. Given cookies to eat. I was lonely, and I was afraid of what was happening to Constantine. And then… They told me my brother died. They told me that Constantine was dead. And then they took me into a small room, and everything after that is blank. I think it was the trauma of hearing that my twin had died. I think it is what stole my memories. They told me… They told me he was dead. And…"

Even now he could see that it hurt her to talk about this. Even knowing her brother was not dead. He could see the little girl she'd been, the fear, the terror. She wanted to comfort him.

"He is not. He lives."

"My younger brother. He is dead."

"Unfortunately. He died in a car accident. Your return to your family will undoubtedly bring them great joy. It will heal some of the wounds. Can you imagine. Your parents must feel as if they lost two children. And now you've returned to them."

"That is quite a lot of pressure."

"I don't have a family to return to. I don't say that to try and make you feel only good things, because of course this will be tinged with all manner of bittersweet joy and pain. Only that it is a miracle to have this. I want you to look forward. Not back."

She nodded slowly. "Of course."

He sat down next to her. And she closed the distance between them by putting her hand on his. He did not pull away.

The plane landed on a private airfield, and his car took them to the edge of the property. Right up to the gates. They parted for them, opening wide. Just as the clouds gave way, and the rain began to fall.

And he felt like something had given way inside of him as well.

*This is why you can never let anyone too close.*

This was why.

He had never wished to care, not again. He had never wished to want, not again.

He had worked too hard to harden himself.

Far too hard to let it all be undone now.

She got out of the car, and stood there for a moment, looking up at the house. "I remember this place," she whispered.

"And what are your memories?" He needed to know that she would be safe here. He needed to know that she wanted to be here.

"I was happy. My mother… My mother loved me. My father…"

"Good. Then it is time for me to let you go."

She turned to him, slowly. There was no sound around them except for the rain, and he hated it.

"You're not coming in with me?" she asked.

He shook his head. "This is something you need to do on your own. You do not need me, Athena. I was a man who was small enough to take you captive, because I could not go out into the world, and so I tried to keep you with me. I did that with a stag. I did that with Aslan. But you are not an animal. You are a woman. And you are not mine to tame and to keep. I should have you wild, Athena. You are the goddess of war. And you are strong." He reached his hand out, and pressed the necklace he had bought her into her palm. "Thank you for giving me the use of this. But I will send it to you now."

"No… Cameron…"

The rain slid over her face, like tears, and it took him a moment to realize that there were tears there as well. Mingled with the raindrops.

Her sadness at leaving him was real.

She should not be sad. She was going back to her family. She was leaving him. She was finally getting the freedom that she wanted.

"Go," he said. "Go and do not think of me again."

"But I will. I will every day. Cameron… You cannot possibly… You cannot."

"Go, Athena."

She turned to look at the house one more time, and took two steps away from him. And he felt that piece of himself that had given way exit his body and begin to move away with her.

He knew he would never get it back.

He did not want it back.

And suddenly she stopped. She turned toward him, and she ran. Her body hit his with the force of a soldier on the attack. She wrapped her arms around his neck, stretched up on her toes, and she kissed him. Deep and hard.

She parted her lips, her tongue tangling with his. And he was powerless. Powerless in the face of this glorious tactical maneuver. This conquering.

He held her.

And he kissed her. Like he was starving. Like he would never be filled again. Like there was nothing except this moment. Except them.

Like his face wasn't ruined.

Like his soul wasn't ruined.

Like he didn't have to give her away to set her free. He clung to her. And she to him.

His skin was damp and slick, the kiss even more so.

But hot with it. Needy. Greedy.

Ten years of deprivation. And yet, he knew he had never kissed another person like this.

Kissing was not something he had indulged himself in.

It was not part of paying for sex.

And it was not part of control.

There was no control in this at all.

He had given sex away with no thought at all. For many, many years. He did indulge in all manner of depravity. And yet this was somehow new. This was like an entirely different experience. When Athena took his hand, he felt like a virgin. When Athena had pulled his dress shirt onto him, buttoned it for him, it had felt more erotic than anything he had ever experienced.

And when she kissed him, she branded his soul.

He was jaded and hardened, scarred and he had no defenses against this. This was unlike anything. She was unlike anything.

And that was why he had to release her.

He stepped away.

His heart was raging, his body begging for him to take her. Begging for him to put her back in the car and lay her across the back seat and have his way with her.

But he would not. Because the man that he was, that man would have done so. That man would've taken this moment meant for her, and he would've made it his own. That man would have kept her under lock and key simply to satisfy his own needs. He would not do that. Not to her. Because she would not be another casualty of his casual lust. Of his need for control. Of his utterly bankrupt soul.

She would not be his victim.

Because Athena was too glorious to be anyone's victim.

She would walk on. Free of him.

And she would soar.

He knew that she would. Because she had been glory and strength personified from the moment he had first seen her, even curled up in the bottom of that hovel. Even that had spoken of her strength.

"Go," he said, cupping her chin with his thumb and forefinger, brushing away the water droplets on her lips. "You have found the life that you were meant to live. You have found your freedom. Take great joy in it."

And then it was he who turned away from her.

He got in the back seat of the car, for he could no longer drive. He told his driver to take him away from there.

And he knew then that he was as much a prisoner now as he had ever been. He still couldn't drive. He still couldn't have her. He was still scarred.

And he would go back to the castle. One successful launch event did not heal wounds as deep as his own. There was only one thing in his life that he could feel remotely proud of.

He had set her free.

If he could not have changed. If he could not have healing. If he could never himself be whole, then he would have that.

It would have to be enough.

# CHAPTER SEVENTEEN

ATHENA WAS SHAKING, from the inside out by the time she walked up to the door. She heard Cameron's car pull away, and something broke within her. She was about to meet her family. And she was elated to have come this far. Filled with joy at finding them, and yet... She would be leaving Cameron behind. And that felt devastating. That felt like a blow she was not certain she could recover from.

*Look at everything you have lived through. This will not crush you.*

But she had to kiss him. And it was...

She closed her eyes for just a moment, and relived that. The glorious crush of his mouth against hers. His heat and his strength. Her desire to be closer, closer still, the realization that she would never be able to be close enough.

She had been such a childish thing when she had first met him. Her notions of romance had been so soft.

Cameron had ruined her. He had ruined those dreams. Because she had tasted something much sharper and clearer than she had ever been able to manufacture in the mists of her mind. He had shown her that she was a warrior. And soft and simple would never do.

*Good your life is soft and simple. Here you are. On the verge of meeting your family. Either the fulfillment of their dreams or the reopening of a wound.*

She took a breath and squared her shoulders, and knocked.

The door opened. And she was face-to-face with a woman, two inches shorter than herself, black hair pulled back into a bun. She was beautiful. "It's you," the woman said. "Athena. Athena." And she started to cry. She reached out and wrapped her arms around Athena, and Athena new.

"Mom."

She was ushered inside, where her father was. And she suddenly just knew who they were. And she felt it. It was a reunion, as her memories came flooding back to her. They were not strangers. She was not meeting her family. She was being reunited with them.

"I can't believe this," her father said, kissing her head. "After all these years."

"Yes. I'm here."

And then she looked up, and saw at the bottom of the grand staircase, a man. Tall and dark, his intensity bright and clear. There was a woman with red hair standing next to him, holding him tight.

"Do you remember me?" he asked, his voice rough.

"Of course, Constantine." Athena smiled, and for some reason she remembered the silliest thing. "Do you remember, we used to watch that cartoon about ponies."

And he didn't speak. He took a step forward and folded her into his arms. And for the first time she felt the completeness that she had forgotten ever existed within her.

"We have a lot of catching up to do," he said, his voice rough.

They sat together for hours. And when her parents went to bed, and Morgan gave Constantine a kiss and went upstairs, it left just her and Constantine.

"Tomorrow you'll meet the children," he said. "When I found out Morgan was having twins I..."

"Twins. That's wonderful."

"It did not feel wonderful. I felt as if I had let you down, Athena. I thought you were dead. All these years."

"They told me you were dead. And I think it broke me. I didn't remember. I didn't remember my family. I didn't remember where I came from."

"Apollo told us that you had been adopted. By a different family than the one who kidnapped us."

She nodded. "Yes. I couldn't remember anything before I came to them. I understand now it was because of what happened to us when we were with the kidnapper. When he told me that you were dead."

"I remembered. All these years, I remembered. They tortured me by telling me they were hurting you."

"I'm sorry. No harm ever came to me. I was kept safe. Kept away from the world. I didn't know who I was. And when the man that I called Father decided to sell me off in marriage I escaped."

"When was this?"

"A month ago. I escaped and I found a castle. As fantastical as it sounds."

"Nothing sounds too far-fetched after my experience with losing you and finding you again. I heard Castor Xenakis saved you."

"Cameron McKenzie saved me."

"Cameron McKenzie? The tech genius? The one that disappeared from society ten years ago and reappeared with… With his wife."

"Yes."

"I did see something about all of that, but I hadn't looked closely because immediately after I received a phone call from Apollo telling me that you were alive. He said nothing of Cameron, and these last twenty-four hours has been a blur of us coming to terms with this… This unexpected miracle."

"I married him. To help him reenter society. He married me to keep me safe. He knew that if I was his wife my father would not simply be able to find me again and... He isn't my father. That man that I just sat with here for hours is my father."

"You were told about Alex?"

"Yes. I am very sorry to hear that."

"Me too. He was a difficult child. A selfish man. But he would've changed. Given enough time. I will never think it was fair that he lost the ability to try."

"You met and married Morgan around that time."

He laughed. "Morgan was... She was Alex's fiancée. It's a long story."

"We have all the time in the world."

It was only later the next morning that Athena got the text from Apollo. She did not know how he had gotten her information.

"I wanted to give you Cameron's information. So you can reach him. This is the access to his intercom system. So that you can speak to him at the castle."

He gave her instructions to download an app, and a code to enter to talk to him.

Her mouth went dry.

She knew that Cameron had meant to leave her here.

But he was her husband. And she did not wish to leave him.

She had what she'd set out to get. A place. And she felt like she had one here, truly. The Kamaras family had already shown her more love in this short space of time than the people she'd known as her family ever had.

But she still wanted.

She still wanted *him*.

She had told herself over and over it wasn't real, and yet she knew now that it was. Because when put back into the life she'd been stolen from, she still wanted him.

Still felt married to him.

She entered the information quickly, and she thanked Apollo, who didn't respond. And then she opened the app, and pressed the button.

"I'm fine, not that you asked."

Hearing his voice made her heart leap.

"It is evening here. And how did you get this information?"

"I think you can guess."

"Be with your family, Athena."

"I *am* with my family. And don't speak to me if you don't wish, but I'm going to share with you."

And she did. She told him about her family. About Constantine, about his wife. All the stories that she heard about her brother Alex.

She talked to Cameron every day.

He did not all always talk back, but she decided she didn't need him to.

She was not willing to break her connection with Cameron.

She was home for Christmas, and still she spoke to Cameron every day. She got to know her niece and nephew, her sister-in-law, who was a lovely woman with a brilliant smile.

She reconnected with Rose—Ismena. She went and visited her and Ares at his villa in Greece. And then went with her family after that on a vacation on Constantine's private island.

She saw the world. She could dress how she liked. She went shopping with Morgan, she played with her niece and nephew. She ran barefoot through the field behind her parents house simply because she could.

She slept in her old bedroom. Her family offered to let her stay at their home forever. But they also told her she could buy her own place.

She bought a townhouse in Beacon Hill, and had it decorated exactly how she wanted. She was an heiress, and had all the resources to do whatever she wished. She lived in the city. She got up every morning and walked. Wherever she wished. However far she wished. She kept in touch with Castor and his wife, and they talked about the issue of trafficking, and how she might contribute to helping women who were brought out of situations that were similar to hers, but much uglier.

And she talked to Cameron.

But he became more and more silent. And she could imagine him, sitting there in the north tower. Doing nothing but listening.

She watched the news for any sign that he had come out again. But it was as if he had vanished.

That one appearance, and then no more.

She on the other hand had become a sensational news story. Her return to her family had resulted in her adoptive father's arrest. And not just his, but many, many other men who were connected to him. Including Mattias.

It was like she and Rose had started an avalanche. One that she was very grateful for.

Her father had a security detail on her, and they were of course all good-looking men. She thought of what she had said to Cameron. How she had crushes on the security detail at her kidnapper's compound.

Though they were not the ones who had kidnapped her on the beach, they had held her all those years, and she had begun thinking of them that way. Yes, in spite of the fact that she had all the freedom in the world, and those men around her, she felt not even the slightest bit of interest. She could think only of Cameron.

"I need to go back," she said to Constantine, one night when he and Morgan were visiting her at her townhouse.

"To McKenzie?"

"Yes. Because no matter what, I'm Athena McKenzie."

"You are not. You are ours."

She shook her head. "I'm my own, Constantine. Or have you not realize that yet. And my heart is with Cameron. I love him."

"You know, Stockholm syndrome…" Morgan began.

"I do not have Stockholm syndrome. I could do whatever I want, I could go wherever I want. I could have whatever man I want, and I only want him. I have experienced the freedom the world has to offer. And I love being with you. All of you. I will never abandon you. But if I didn't love him, then my life would be complete right this moment, and it isn't."

Morgan's face was filled with understanding. "I do understand that. You may not have seen it, but your brother is an absolute beast himself. And I loved him anyway. I couldn't escape that, no matter how much I wanted to."

"I don't even want to," said Athena. "I want to be with him."

"Make use of my private jet," said Constantine. "It will get you there the fastest."

# CHAPTER EIGHTEEN

HE KNEW WHEN she arrived at the castle. All of his sensors went off. He had thought it strange that she had not spoken to him in twenty-four hours. And now, he knew why. She was here.

And he was… Certainly not fit for company. He knew she had noticed that he had stopped speaking to her and now she was here.

"Open the door to me, Cameron," she shouted from outside the gate.

And he did. Because he was weak.

And then he opened the doors to her as well, because he was weak. And then he was down the stairs, and waiting in the antechamber, because he was weak.

And when she came into the chamber, it was he who crossed the space. It was he who pulled her into his arms. And it was he who lowered his head and conquered her mouth. Claimed it.

He had tried to be a good man. An honorable man. He had tried not to do this. To leave her be. And yet she had not left him.

How was he supposed to forget her when she did not let him.

How was he supposed to forget her when she kept on talking to him. His goddess. How was he supposed to let her go. And now he was not. He was clinging to her tightly. Now, he was feasting upon her lips, holding her against his body, relishing in the feel of her breasts crushed against him.

She was so soft.

So strong and so perfect.

She was everything. Everything he wanted. Everything he needed.

This wasn't about whether or not he'd been with a woman in ten years. Because Athena was nothing like those other encounters. His need for her was nothing like that previous, physical need. There was no amount of self-gratification that could erase his desire for her. Because it was not the same. His need for her was everything he feared.

That well of need that he had only ever let out once before. That had been crushed and destroyed and turned against him.

And yet it was also somehow something totally unique, even sharper. Even more dangerous.

And he did not possess the will to release her. Not for his sake. Not for hers. Instead, he carried her up the stairs. To the north tower, the place that he had told her she could never go.

He carried her there and into his bedchamber.

It was Spartan. Nothing really but the bed.

And he laid her down across the bed, standing away from her and slowly removing his clothing.

He did not feel fear over letting her see his scars.

Athena had seen his every scar already. The real ones. The deep ones. The darkest ones that were in the recesses of his very soul.

Athena knew him. For better and for very much worse. She was his wife.

And it was not supposed to mean anything, and yet it meant everything. Just as she did. She watched him, her eyes sharp as he removed all of his clothing.

And then he joined her down on the bed, moving his

hands over her curves. She was wearing a coat, which he stripped quickly from her body, and he looked into her eyes as he pushed his hand beneath her skirt, closing his eyes briefly, letting his breath hiss through his teeth as his fingertips moved along her smooth skin.

She was a gift. One he had not earned. And one he surely did not deserve. One he would not turn away from. For he did not have the strength left in him. Not anymore. It was not just ten years of being alone. It was a lifetime.

And he had kept all of this, all of this need, all of this desire, locked away.

And now it was flooding from him. Hemorrhaging. And he could do nothing to stop it.

He pushed his hand between her thighs, slipped his fingertips beneath the waistband of her panties, and found her wet for him. And it was as if it was the only time it had ever happened in all the history of all of mankind. That this was for him. His.

It was what he wanted. For her to be his and only his. For this moment to be the only moment. For this breath to be the only breath. This breath where his mingled with hers and their hearts beat as one.

Where he could feel the evidence of her desire coaching his hand, and it never had the chance to turn into anything else.

It never had the chance to sour. To become a disappointment.

It never had the chance to be what it would inevitably be.

Him breaking her.

*Is that really what you're afraid of?*

He pushed that thought aside, and he let himself feel.

For the first time in ten years. For the first time since he was a boy.

For the first time since he had hoped that someone was

showing the smallest bit of care for his safety, for his well-being, but who only wanted to use him.

There had never been any control.

And surrendering it was the last thing he would ever do. Except now, he was doing just that. Now, he was surrendering.

To this. To her.

He pushed a finger inside of her and watched her face contort with need. Desire.

She arched her hips against him. When he had let her go, he had tried to do it without ever putting his hands on her. She had kissed him. She had branded them both. She had undone all of his good intentions. This was her fault.

She had come back to him. This was her fault.

The consequences…

He had tried to spare her.

He had tried to spare her him, but she simply wasn't allowing it.

And what was to be done?

He was at his end.

He had been a man cursed these last ten years. Concealed away in stone.

He had hardly been a man at all.

And now here he was with her.

Keeping one hand between her legs, pleasuring her there, he reached his other hand around behind her back and undid the zipper on her dress, moving his hand from between her thighs only to divest her of the garment.

He took off her panties. Her bra. And he looked upon the glory that was Athena.

She was golden, glorious. Her round, firm breasts had tight dusky nipples hardened into points, and they called for his touch. For his tongue.

The dark thatch of curls between her thighs made his body ache with the need to sink inside of her.

Just the sight of those glorious curves, of her womanly glory.

She was everything.

And he needed her. More than anything. More than his next breath.

He kissed down her body, sucking one nipple deep into his mouth. She gasped, crying out as she arched against him, and he gripped her hips, pressing his hardness down against her softness there and letting her feel just what she did to him. Her hands were all over him. Moving down his back, over his chest. All over his scars. But she did not stop and single them out. Did not stop and touch them.

She did not act as if they were an independent piece, something separate to him.

She touched all of him. As if every bit was Cameron.

And every bit was whole.

Only Athena could have done this. Only Athena could have waged this war and won.

She moved her hand down between them and wrapped her fingers around his shaft, squeezing him tight, slowly licking her lips as she made eye contact with him, before wiggling out from beneath him and pushing him onto his back.

"This is my fantasy. I have been thinking about this for very long time. Remember, all those long years I was kept away in a compound."

"Yes, and you have not been there for a while. You've been free."

"That's right," she said, rubbing her palm up and down his hardness. "I have been able to do whatever I wanted. Be whoever I wanted. I have seen the world. I have tasted freedom. And here I am. Because I wanted no other man, Cameron. And I touched no other man. I need you to know that. I need you to understand."

"Athena…"

But she lowered her head and slicked her tongue from

the base of him to the tip, before taking him into her mouth and swallowing any of his objections along with him. His breathing was ragged, his control at its end. He moved his fingers through her hair, caressed her face as she licked him, sucked him, and shattered all that remained of his control.

"Not like this," he growled. He moved her away from him, and then turned her onto her back, kissing down her stomach, and then curving his arms around her thighs, clasping his fingers over her stomach and holding her fast as he dragged her to his mouth and began to eat the sweet center of her.

He licked her, deep. Pushing his tongue into her honeyed depths as he extracted every scream of pleasure from her that he could.

If he was going to ruin her. If he was going to ruin them both, then it would be thorough and complete. Because he was a monster who left nothing unharmed. Who left no recognizable pieces in his wake. He burned everything to ash. And it would be the same with her. The same with them. And he would relish the journey. Hell was the destination. And so getting there had to be everything.

And yet this was not like sex as he knew it. It was something more.

It was their walk on the Seine. It was the moment when he'd talked her to orgasm in the kitchen. It was when she'd put his clothes on him and given him her necklace. It was a kiss in the rain and vows in a chapel.

It was seeing her huddled in the hut and knowing, *knowing*, that she had to be his.

It was every part of him and every part of her, mingling together. The broken and the beautiful. The monstrous and the divine.

Power and glory and all the things he'd always feared.

And everything he needed to go on breathing.

She was shaking, crying out, she shattered over and over

again, her fingers woven through his hair, tugging hard, her heels digging down into the mattress.

And when he was satisfied that she had reached her peak enough times, he moved up and captured her lips. He had not kissed her enough.

It would never be enough. There would never be enough.

And that in and of itself was the most sobering, horrendous realization of them all.

There would never be enough of this. He was doomed. And he would not turn back even knowing that.

She wrapped her arms around his neck, and looked into his eyes as he positioned himself at her slick center. He pushed inside of her slowly, and she never looked away. She was so tight. And he was lost.

"Cameron," she said, as he filled her completely.

And he began to move. And this was different. Completely different. Being inside of her was not like being inside of any other woman. The pleasure that he found here was not like any other pleasure. This was not a race to release. This was not about control. He was not solidifying his power, he was surrendering it. To her.

And with every arch of her hips against his she gave it back, but it was made something more. Just as he was.

He wanted it to go on forever, but he knew it could not. And he could feel her pleasure building within her, and then when she cried out his name, her internal muscles pulsing around him, he gave up his own.

His growl reverberated off the walls as he poured himself inside of her. As every last vestige of control dissolved.

As the goddess of war made him hers.

And when he came back to himself, to them, she was clinging to him, gazing up at him.

"Cameron," she whispered. "I love you."

# CHAPTER NINETEEN

SHE FELT HIS withdrawal emotionally before he physically left her.

She had known that that might be a mistake. That saying it might be a problem. She had known.

But she had also known that she was here to take all.

To conquer all.

And there was only one thing that did that. And that was love.

It was not strength or might or power. It was not manipulation. It was only love. And she had that for him. It radiated through all of her. Through everything she was.

And even in his fear, she was strong.

She stood up, naked and completely unashamed. Stood before him proud.

"Don't run from this now."

"No, Athena. This cannot be born. This is why I did not want to touch you. This is why…"

"Yes. I know. Because you don't want me to get too close to you. Because you don't want anyone to get to close you, that is why you left me on the doorstep of my family home. That is why you didn't stay with me. It is why you didn't touch me before. Because you knew that if you did you would have no protection left."

"I kept away from you to protect you. You and your hungry virgin's eyes. How do you feel now?"

"Strong. But I already did. I knew what I wanted before I arrived at this castle. I want you, Cameron. I'm Athena McKenzie. I know who I am. I know that I got a family name when I found Constantine, but you are the family I choose. Don't you see? I went out and I saw the world. I could have had anyone. But I didn't. Because what I wanted was here. I am an heiress. I bought a house. I furnished it with all things that I loved. I saw myself living a life that I created. A life without you.

"And it was not enough. It was not enough because it was not you. I am not a prisoner. And I know what is out there. I have been to beaches and cities. I have had a glorious family Christmas. And in and amongst all of that, I felt sadness. Because I missed you. Because I want you. I kept on living out there so that you couldn't tell me I didn't understand. I talked to you every day over the intercom because I chose to. Not because I was a prisoner. I'm not. I am the goddess of war, and I will fight for you. I will fight for us. And if you resent that, then you must take your own self to task. Have courage. Take heart. You told me to find my strength. And I have. Do not join the chorus of men who have tried to tell me what I am. What I shall become. I have already proven that I am stronger than those around me have ever been willing to give me credit for. You were the one person who saw it, Cameron. Don't sell me short now."

"It is… It is impossible," he said. "It is me."

The words were broken. Ragged. "I am a monster," he continued. "And there is no fairy-tale ending waiting for us. You saw the headlines, beauty and the beast. But you cannot kiss me and make this better. Here we are, I have your virgin blood on my sheets, and I am still a monster."

"And I am Athena, goddess of war, Cameron, and I was made to fight this battle. I thought my journey was to find my place with other people, but I had to find myself, so I could make the space I needed. And I have done it. And now I know who I am. I know what I want. I want you, and you can't tell me I don't. Do not make me into an object for your trauma to hold on to, that is how you turn a person into your personal plaything, a piece of a collection and steal all their humanity. That is what I was for my mother, and I will not be that for you."

"I am scarred…"

"Your scars are the mark of who you are, not a monster. A man who survived."

"I am nothing more than a broken boy. It's all I have ever been. Wanting love sent me down a path I could not come back from. It is a twisted sort of thing to sell your body, and to learn to wall your soul away so that nothing can touch you. And at the same time to want… To want desperately for even one encounter to do something to ease the loneliness inside of you. I came here to face the loneliness. To accept it. Because I've never been very good at it.

"Stolen moments, fleeting bits of closeness where someone else might put their hands on me and I might feel like I'm not the only person in this world. I cannot separate that need from how sordid it all is. I cannot…"

"You know that what happened between us was not sordid."

"And what will happen when you are done with me? What then?"

"Have I ever given you reason to not trust me? I have crossed the world to be here with you. It's what you fear is inside of you. You fight an enemy in your own self. Do not turn me into your foe, Cameron McKenzie. I was your gift. If you believe in anything, believe in that fate that brought me here. Because I do. It brought me to you. It brought me to my family. It rescued me."

"You rescued yourself. The minute you threw yourself out of that motorcade."

"Fine then. I rescued myself. Trust me to carry on knowing exactly how to rescue us both." And she realized then that she had it wrong. Just that one thing.

"Actually, I can only rescue you just so much, can't I? You must take those next steps yourself. You are at the crossroads, and you must find a way to decide. To step into the light. The only person who can break the curse is you. Because I can kiss you and love you, and believe that you are the man I know you are. A man worthy of those things, but unless you believe it, I cannot fix it."

"Athena…"

"Do you love me?"

And he looked like he might shatter.

He wished she had not asked that.

It was the splinter in the glass that set the whole pain fracturing.

*Do you love me?*

He could lie. He had lied so many times in his life about so many things. To himself, to everyone else.

*Do you love me?*

"Yes," he said, the word raw. It was destroying him. From the inside out. She was destroying him. He would gladly jump back into that car, and that twisted heap of metal, before facing this. But he had not been given a choice. It was killing him. Because there was nowhere to hide. There was no way to protect himself.

He had told himself, he had told her, that he needed nothing. That he did not care, that he did not love. Yes, he had told her that. And he had believed it. But here he was, confronted with the truth.

He had, all these years, wanted love more than he had ever wanted anyone other thing in all the world. He was broken with his need of it, and it was that which scared him above all else.

He'd had to close himself down to survive. And perhaps the thing that angered him most about his own part in Irina's death was that he had not even given himself a chance to care for her. Because it was there. That ability.

It was only he refused to share it because he was small and mean and terrified, like the boy he had been out on the streets.

The boy who'd had to learn how to sell his body without selling his soul.

*But you can have your soul back now. And you can give it to her. That's what you want.*

It was true. It was what he wanted more than anything.

And in the end of all things, if he did not do this, what did his life matter?

If he could love Athena, and she could love him in return, and he had survived that accident, and he had survived that childhood, and he had survived selling himself, over and over again, only to find the reality of intimacy and love and sex now, at thirty-eight years old, then if he turned it away, what was the point of surviving at all.

"I love you," he said again.

But it wasn't easy, and the words didn't get any easier. He pulled her to him, her naked body against his, and he kissed her. Desperately. Deeply. All over. "I love you. I love you, dammit, Athena, and it hurts."

"That's okay," she said, pushing his hair out of his face. "I don't want an easy love. And I came to that conclusion all the way back when we were walking along the river in Paris. I watched all those people with their soft gazes, the way that they held each other, and I knew that for us it could never be that. I had an idea of romance. But this… This is real. Jagged and sometimes painful, but it's worth fighting for. You and I… We are survivors. We are miraculous. But nobody ever said the miraculous was easy. In fact I think living miraculous is a very hard thing to do.

And who else should be able to but us? Who else to try this wonderful, improbable love, except us?"

"I love you," he said again. "I want you. I want this."

"We can have it. Because I love you too. And this is where I choose to be. It's where I want to be. With you."

"Beauty and the beast indeed."

"No. The goddess of war and the beast. We both set about conquering each other. And I feel we did a pretty good job. And that we will keep on doing so. For the rest of our lives."

"Well that might really be how we live happily ever after," he said.

"Yes, Cameron. I believe it will be."

# EPILOGUE

HE AND ATHENA had made good on the promises they'd given each other. Athena's work helping trafficking victims, and his own helping children on the streets wove easily around each other, and their foundation—which provided education in technology and the chance at a new life, had helped save nearly five hundred children from life on the street or in captivity.

They were working hard to make sure that there weren't children who felt discarded, abandoned or forgotten.

Cameron went from being a boy that nobody cared for, to a disfigured man living in isolation, to a husband, a brother-in-law, and honorary son, and a father in the space of less than a year. He could never have imagined such a thing.

As he sat in the expansive living area of the family estate in Massachusetts, and looked around at this newfound family, as he cradled his infant son in his arms, he knew one thing for certain. His own imagination had been terribly lacking. And it certainly never would have manufactured such a life of love for him. Simply because it had been too afraid.

But now he knew better. Now he knew that what lay ahead had the potential to be so much better than what was behind them. Now he knew that there was more to life than what he could see.

Now he knew Athena. He knew a goddess walking around on earth.

And so everything was possible.

With love, all things indeed, were possible.

\* \* \* \* \*

# COMING SOON!

We really hope you enjoyed reading this book.
If you're looking for more romance, be sure to
head to the shops when new books are
available on

# Thursday 16ᵗʰ
# February

To see which titles are coming soon, please visit
**millsandboon.co.uk/nextmonth**

# MILLS & BOON®

## Coming next month

## THE HOUSEKEEPER'S INVITATION TO ITALY
### Cathy Williams

"I'm not following you. Where is he going to move to? London? Leonard has always told me how much he hates London."

"Not that he's actually been there more than a handful of times," Alessio returned drily. "But no. London wasn't what I had in mind."

"Then where?"

"I have a place at Lake Garda in northern Italy. It's close enough to get there on my private jet in a matter of hours so the trip shouldn't be too taxing for him."

"Oh, right. Okay."

"If we plan on leaving in roughly a week's time, it will give me sufficient time to get the ball rolling with the company so that I can install some of my own people to tie up all the loose ends. I'll also have enough time for my PA to source the best crew available to get this job done here and of course, there will have to be time spent packing away anything valuable that needs to be protected. I suggest several of the more robust rooms in the West Wing would be suitable for that."

"Wait, hang on just a minute! We…?"

*Continue reading*
THE HOUSEKEEPER'S INVITATION TO ITALY
Cathy Williams

*Available next month*
www.millsandboon.co.uk

# MILLS & BOON

## THE HEART OF ROMANCE

## A ROMANCE FOR EVERY READER

### MODERN

Prepare to be swept off your feet by sophisticated, sexy and seductive heroes, in some of the world's most glamourous and romantic locations, where power and passion collide.

### HISTORICAL

Escape with historical heroes from time gone by. Whether your passion is for wicked Regency Rakes, muscled Vikings or rugged Highlanders, awaken the romance of the past.

### MEDICAL

Set your pulse racing with dedicated, delectable doctors in the high-pressure world of medicine, where emotions run high and passion, comfort and love are the best medicine.

### True Love

Celebrate true love with tender stories of heartfelt romance, from the rush of falling in love to the joy a new baby can bring, and a focus on the emotional heart of a relationship.

### Desire

Indulge in secrets and scandal, intense drama and plenty of sizzling hot action with powerful and passionate heroes who have it all: wealth, status, good looks…everything but the right woman.

### HEROES

Experience all the excitement of a gripping thriller, with an intense romance at its heart. Resourceful, true-to-life women and strong, fearless men face danger and desire - a killer combination!

To see which titles are coming soon, please visit

## millsandboon.co.uk/nextmonth

# LET'S TALK

## Romance

For exclusive extracts, competitions
and special offers, find us online:

**f** facebook.com/millsandboon

**y** @MillsandBoon

**◎** @MillsandBoonUK

**Get in touch on 01413 063232**

For all the latest titles coming soon, visit
**millsandboon.co.uk/nextmonth**

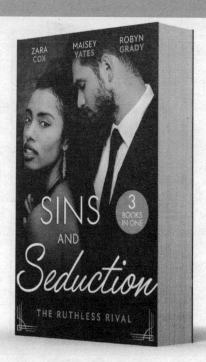